GELLAN PARKER AND THE BLACK OWL

A. L. WICKS

Library of Congress Control Number: 2020949372

ILLUSTRATIONS BY ANA GRIGORIU-VOICU

Ebook: 978-1-955867-03-0
Paperback: 978-1-955867-00-9
Hardback (jacketed): 978-955867-01-6
Audiobook: 978-1-7348740-3-7
First trade paperback printing: November 2021

PUBLISHED BY PLOPPLETOP PUBLISHING LLC
CHICO, CA
www.ploppletop.com
contactus@ploppletop.com

For Violatte K. Sanders, for being the first person to see that this book could become what I wanted it to be.

We know what we are, but know not what we may be.

— William Shakespeare

CONTENTS

CHAPTER ONE

TRIPPED UP

Gellan skidded sideways through the back door of his uncle's sweet shop, just managing to catch the edge of an enormous mixing bowl before he tumbled into it. He looked as though he'd been shoved through by the blast of wind and rain that followed him.

Uncle Ivan, who had been half-concealed as he bent over a second, larger mixing bowl, raised his chin just above the rim and peered at Gellan through glasses that had slid to the end of his long nose. His mustache twitched, and he gave a short sniff as he shoved his glasses back up, before disappearing into the depths of the bowl once more. Gellan slammed the door shut behind him with his foot and dropped his shoulder bag to the floor.

"I knew you wouldn't make it," said Uncle Ivan, his voice echoing inside the cavernous bowl. "If you'd checked the—"

"I *did*," said Gellan, squelching his way toward the oversized sink in the corner, attempting to unzip his sodden jacket. "I thought I had enough time."

"Still need some practice, then," Uncle Ivan grunted as he wrestled an enormous lump of speckled dough out of the cauldron. "It's not just clouds, you know," he wheezed, heaving the mass onto a nearby counter. It landed with a heavy thump. "An' it can come from all directions. It was pulling too hard from the west." He picked up a heavy rolling pin and waved it toward Gellan. "Need somethin' to keep you busy for the afternoon?"

Gellan looked up quickly, one arm still stuck inside a sopping sleeve. "No, I was actually... I mean, Jordan asked me to come over," he said, attempting to sound disappointed. "For homework," he added, wringing out his jacket over the sink.

"Best change first," Uncle Ivan said, turning to the counter. He began thumping the rolling pin back and forth with quick movements across the dough. "Don't want you missin' school for gettin' a cold."

"I never get sick," Gellan said, edging his way back to the door, "and it's only—"

"All the same," Uncle Ivan interrupted, without looking around. "Anyway, your shirt's inside out, so..." He firmly jabbed a thumb behind him.

Gellan glanced down, and then groaned. He grabbed his shoulder bag and slumped his way up the circular staircase to the second-floor apartment. After emptying the contents of his school bag onto his desk, he hung it to dry on one of the posts at the foot of his bed. As he pulled at his shoelaces, he caught sight of his reflection in a drooping mirror on the wall and found that the three pencils he had lost during math class were sticking out of his thick, curly red hair. He sighed and plucked them out, dropping them with a clatter amongst his binder and books.

From the moment he'd woken that morning, he had known it was going to be an upside-down sort of day. When he opened his eyes and found he'd somehow gone spelunking under his bed, stuck between the stalactites of his bedsprings and the stalagmites of his laundry, strange things had been bound to follow, however desperately he tried to prevent them.

For a moment, he had considered skiving off school. But that surely would have meant a day of being up to his elbows in either cookie dough or dish suds. So off he'd gone, hoping any oddities wouldn't be too noticeable.

His hopes were soon dashed when a small black bird landed directly on his head in the middle of first-period PE class. It refused to be shooed away until it had plucked several hairs from his head, which must have made such a pleasing addition to its nest that it kept coming back for more. He'd ended up with detention from Coach Hayworth ("Whether birds like your red hair or not, your baseball mitt goes on your *hand* and not your head, Parker"), and decided he'd better stop in at Bernard's Barbershop soon.

In second period, the blue ink in his pen refused to come out as anything other than bright orange. Then at lunch, his watch alarm had gone off for no reason and wouldn't stop until it was at the bottom of the marsh behind the school.

His next-door friend, Jordan, had laughed about it all their whole way home, and Gellan had arrived home feeling stormy. He knew he would never be able to settle down to boring, unsurprising things like chores and homework for the rest of the day, so he had raced off down the road to the ocean cliffs—only to be forced to turn back by the arrival of a downpour.

He sighed again as he changed into dry clothes (taking care that his shirt was right side out this time), then sat down at his desk to rewrite his orange-inked essay. He would simply have to wait out this topsy-turvy Tuesday...

Unfortunately, Wednesday started out nearly as bad.

He was walking to school with the rest of the neighborhood kids when he tripped on... nothing. The others were so used to Gellan tripping that none of them even paused to look back at him as he hopped on one foot for a moment, swinging his arms wildly to regain his balance. When he was finally properly upright again, he promptly ran smack into something else that was not there. He knew, then, that he was once again destined (or doomed) to end up in some kind of trouble by the end of the day.

This happened more frequently than he liked to admit—though occasionally it was not his fault. Sometimes, he couldn't help feeling it was entirely his mother's doing. After all, she surely had tempted fate by naming him after the great explorer, Magellan.

From the moment he could scoot (which was remarkably early), he had begun worming his way under furniture. His mother had quickly learned to block the exposed gap underneath beds when she grew tired of retrieving a wailing Magellan, over and over.

Anything remotely low enough and big enough to fit him and his over-padded diaper had been fair game (including the inside of Halloween jack-o'-lanterns). He had tumbled in and out of cupboards (they were always mostly empty—he never knew why). He'd gotten stuck in the toilet on multiple occasions, trying to figure out where the water came from and where it went.

And then his mother's cat, Pixie, taught him to climb.

His knack for finding hand and footholds was so incredible that his mother started placing trinkets at the top of cupboards and closets. Not to keep them out of his reach, but to keep him occupied long enough once he got up there that she would hopefully discover him before he tried to climb down himself. Getting down was more precarious, and though cats might always land on their feet, toddler Magellan usually didn't manage to.

When his mother died a few years later, Gellan had to move in next door with his uncle and aunt, Ivan and Misera Parker. His aunt had never liked him much—and her dog, Frenchie, absolutely detested the cat. But that was where he and the cat still were, seven years later, when he turned thirteen years old.

Gellan himself hadn't changed much in those seven years. His uncle had once told him that he'd given up trying to keep track of Gellan a long time ago—he simply said a little prayer every morning that Gellan would manage to get back home every day, no matter where he wandered off to. Gellan had taken that as permission to wander and explore as much as he wished, so long as he got back home alive. Which, so far, he'd managed to do.

With a range that increased every year, he now often found himself some distance down the coast, usually high up on the cliffs above the ocean, just as the sun was setting. After a frantic scramble along the beach at the base of the cliffs and a top-speed bike ride back to town down the winding coast road, he frequently got home later than he was supposed to.

He would rush to make dinner while simultaneously running through his other chores. Then he would throw himself down at his desk and calmly pretend that nothing interesting had happened that day when Uncle Ivan poked his head through the bedroom door.

Uncle Ivan played his part in the charade by pretending to believe that Gellan had been doing his homework the whole time, though he usually acknowledged Gellan's success in surviving another day with at least a grunt. If he was feeling particularly talkative, Gellan might get a "Well, yer still alive, I guess" and a jerk of the head toward the kitchen.

And as long as Gellan got his chores done, his aunt never acknowledged his existence at all.

Once in a while, though, Gellan would get back so late that even Aunt Misera would be very worried. The distress of finding the dinner table cold and empty would inevitably send her straight to the couch. She somehow managed to loll across the entire couch in a lethargic state of half-starvation, endlessly wailing about her dreadful situation. Soon even Frenchie, who was half deaf by this point, would heave himself out of his fat-miniature-poodle depression in the overstuffed chair to get away from her ear-piercing shrieks. Gellan usually toppled over him as he burst through the back door right at that moment, nearly colliding with Uncle Ivan, who popped up through the circular staircase just then.

But these situations never ended entirely badly. Aunt Misera had enough strength to receive a heaping dinner tray in her room; Uncle Ivan was able to work long into the evening, getting some extra baking done for his sweet shop; and Gellan had the benefit of finding a rather long list of extra chores taped to his bedroom door, which left him with plenty of things to occupy him for several days. Still, Gellan quickly learned that life was much easier when Aunt Misera got her dinner when she expected it.

Over time, he had also learned how to lessen the likelihood of ending up in trouble, despite his name.

On *this* particular Wednesday, however, Gellan had just managed to get both feet firmly back on the ground after tripping on nothing and started down the dirt path once more when he felt something hit him straight across his forehead. He was used to running into spiderwebs—that seemed to come with the territory of being called Magellan—but whatever this was, it felt *much* thicker and heavier. He grabbed at his forehead, but the thing slipped past him. He turned to see what it was, and... as usual, there was nothing there.

Mystified, he inched his way back, waving one arm high in the air until his hand made contact with something. He grasped it tightly, squinting in the deep shade between the tall trees.

"What's the holdup, Gellan?!" Jordan hollered from several yards away.

"Dunno!" Gellan called back. Three young boys passing him on their way to school winced and covered their ears, then scurried away. "C'mere, would you?"

Jordan watched Gellan with a mixture of amusement and bewilderment as he walked back.

"Right here," Gellan said, stepping aside and pointing. "Wave your hand right here."

Jordan hesitated, then batted at the air with his hand. "Um, what exactly—?" he asked as he made bigger and bigger movements. A couple of neighborhood girls passed them on the path, giggling behind their hands.

"Can't you feel anything?" Gellan asked. He shoved his hair back from his forehead and tried to ignore the girls. Jordan, on the other hand, began jumping and flapping about on purpose, the laughter of another set of girls goading him on to even greater heights of pantomime. His overloaded backpack began swinging from side to side each time he jumped. Before Gellan could say anything, Jordan gave a comical yelp as he was swung around by the momentum, landing like a turtle on its back amid the undergrowth.

"Nope," Jordan answered belatedly, attempting to overbalance his uneven shell but finding himself stuck. "Must've been a spider web." After another minute, he gave up and accepted the hand Gellan was offering him.

Gellan grunted as he struggled to pull Jordan to his feet. "Geez, Jordan, your backpack weighs more than you!"

"That's not hard to do," Jordan said, attempting to shrug. "Anyway... *school*. Let's *go*." He walked off, brushing leaves off his pants and combing sticks out of his hair as he went.

Gellan turned and batted at the air once more, just for good measure. He was startled when his hand bumped against the same unseeable something. It was thick and rough, like the ropes he purchased from the hardware store. He pulled on it gently at first; there was a rustling sound high above him. He grasped it firmly and gave it a hard yank. A snap and a loud screech came a split second before he felt a splat on the back of his shoulder.

Reaching a hand around, he felt something wet and sticky. He groaned when he saw the white and gray substance covering his fingers. A bird high above him let out a series of raucous squawks as he ducked underneath a nearby tree, brushing his hand off on the moss and ferns covering the ground. He grabbed a few fronds to scrub off the back of his shoulder as best he could.

"*Honestly,* Gellan!" Jordan bellowed from far ahead. "*C'mon!* You'll be late!"

Gellan stood up too quickly and bumped his head on something, but in the gloom, he wasn't sure what it was. He stumbled out from underneath the tree, rubbing his head and hoping against hope that he wouldn't have any more mishaps that day.

With a last glance back, he finally hurried after the others.

Meanwhile, a few hundred miles north, someone else had just bumped *his* head after dropping something under his desk. To young eyes he undoubtedly looked old, with his wild, salt-and-pepper, shoulder-length hair and pure white goatee. The creases at his deeply turquoise eyes also gave some indication of his age, though nothing could possibly tell the full truth.

Rubbing the back of his head, he absentmindedly set a jumbled pile of papers on a topsy-turvy stack of books. He sat back and stared off into space for several minutes before his eyes slowly returned their focus to the desk in front of him, hidden beneath a heaping assortment of paper and ink. Heaving a great sigh, he shoved his chair back and stood up. He turned to examine the books on the shelves behind his desk, pulling out one after another and flipping through each of them briefly before rejecting each of them in turn, dropping a few onto his chair and replacing others on the shelf. With a wave of his hand, the bookshelves suddenly displayed an entirely different assortment of books, and he ran a hand across the new set of old spines.

He spotted a rather large volume quite high up and worked it out of its place. He turned, book in hand, only to find that he had nowhere to set it down, and now he had no place to sit either. So he simply stood and held the book across one arm while turning pages with the other hand, muttering to himself as he did.

"From below? ...There's no indication of any particular—possibly a mistranslation... perhaps The List... no, I checked... one would... hmmm, would that best translate to 'to discover?' Or perhaps 'to place?' What else could it—"

He paused unexpectedly, and after a moment he bellowed out "Cline!" without looking up from his book. There was a thud just outside the door.

"Well, now, *really,* Faulkner," she said as she bustled through the door. "There's no need to shout."

"I know," he said mildly and turned another page, continuing his perusal without any further mutterings.

"You've had barely *one* day back in your office," Cline said, clucking her tongue as she looked around. "I don't know how anyone could possibly manage to—"

Faulkner cleared his throat far more loudly than was necessary and Cline pursed her lips, huffed for a moment, then set about cleaning and tidying. She checked the spines of books and put them back on shelves that came and went, sorted papers into various piles, and rolled up large, poster-sized papers filled with maps and other drawings, placing them neatly in upright bins under the expansive windows.

Once she had managed to clear his chair, Faulkner sat down. When part of his desk could be seen again, he set the heavy book on it.

"Anything interesting?" she asked as she shoved a curious-looking object resembling a giant timepiece into a corner cupboard.

"No."

"Nothing at all?"

"No."

She pursed her lips again and cleared away some cobwebs by an old wall torch with a wave of her hand.

It took her quite a long time, but eventually she had finished the work down to the very last paper. She looked half-tempted to pull the book out of Faulkner's hands and put it away, but she resisted and left the room.

It was some time later, as the light in the room was beginning to dim, that Faulkner heard footsteps thudding up the stone spiral staircase leading to his tower office. A moment later, a much younger man rushed through the arched doorway.

"Faulkner, have you seen—?! No, apparently you haven't, or you surely..." He stopped, as Faulkner still hadn't moved.

"What is it, Roman?" Faulkner asked, looking up at last. He seemed to come out of a reverie at the expression on Roman's face and immediately jumped up. "What? What is it?"

"Look—come—over here!" said Roman, moving toward the windows and motioning Faulkner over. "The sea—I've never seen anything like this before!"

Faulkner hastened to the windows, where an impressive view of the sea spread far below him. His mouth dropped open as he took in the spectacle. "What in the gammet blanders?!"

He watched for a moment longer, then turned and swept from the room.

At that very moment, Gellan was swinging his right leg up to hook his foot onto a small rocky outcrop, halfway up the side of a cliff. He gave a great jump with his left leg, throwing his weight toward his right, and rolled over onto the shallow ledge. He was immediately up again, reaching for the next familiar handhold as the splashing sounds continued below him.

He glanced over his shoulder for a moment, his cheek pressed against the cliff. The sea was churning and frothing with the extraordinary movement of fish and other sea life. He could see innumerable creatures emerging from the water, hovering for a moment, and then splashing down again. The spray they were casting up was being blown straight toward him, making his clothes damp and frigid in the February air.

He turned his gaze straight down to the shoreline, looked north and south one last time to make sure there was no one to observe him, then turned back to the cliff.

He found his foothold and tested his grip with a couple of one-footed hops. Then, fully bending his knee, he sprang upward and grabbed at a rock he had climbed to many times. His hand found the thick rope he had placed there a couple of years before, and he hauled himself up and over the wide, smooth, solid stone that marked the entrance of a small cave. It slanted immediately downward into the side of the cliff, making it impossible to see the cave from almost any angle.

After Gellan had discovered the cave—by goating about, as his uncle called it—he had tested the cave's discoverability from many angles, before gleefully concluding that the cave was invisible from anywhere humans might normally be (and most places where they weren't).

It was only about the size of a small living room, and the ceiling was almost low enough at the front to make him feel he needed to stoop, before the slant opened things up more toward the back. He followed the rope deeper into the cave to where it was tied around a large, rough stone, the only protrusion anywhere in this unimpressive hobbit hole.

He shivered and rubbed his arms, then grasped at the strap of his shoulder bag, which was hanging heavily against his chest. He pulled the bag around and lifted the flap, staring at an odd wooden box. It was shut tightly and bound by three leather straps, one of which ran lengthwise along the whole box beneath two cross-straps.

The circumstance of this box coming into his possession was unusual, even for Gellan.

Earlier that day, as soon as school had let out, he had biked down the winding road to the ocean. He had parked his bike behind Old Jack's shed, as usual, before working his way along the shoreline at the base of the cliffs. It was low tide, and he poked into some familiar areas as he wandered further and further south.

All of this was perfectly normal.

Then, as he had neared Cramer's Cove, something had wrapped itself around his leg like the tentacles of an octopus, immediately cutting short his momentum. He had fallen straight forward, just missing some rocks and thankfully ending up with nothing worse than a face full of sand.

He had awkwardly attempted to shift himself around, his shoulder bag hitting him in the head and sand making its way uncomfortably up his shirt. He finally managed to work himself into a sitting position, knees bent, and look toward his ankle—but there was nothing there.

Until that morning, he would have considered this to be highly unusual, but with a feeling of déjà vu, he reached out and closed his fingers around what was unmistakably a coarse, thin rope.

He worked his fingers around the rope, and managed to find one end of it. After several minutes, he was able to disentangle it from his ankle. Still holding the rope, and forgetting to worry about what might be at the other end of it, he began moving hand-over-hand along it. It led him up onto a very large rock and down into the water of the shallow tidepool formed in its bashed-out center.

His hand reached the end, bumping something else he couldn't see. His fingers found the edges of the elongated, narrow box, which was surprisingly smooth compared to the craggy rock that had half-swallowed it.

With a tight grasp on the box, and settling his feet firmly, he had pulled hard... and suddenly, the wooden box and the rope that encircled it materialized in front of his eyes.

With a shout of astonishment, he threw himself backwards, just managing to catch himself before he tumbled off the side of the rock. When he scrambled back to the spot, in the clear water he could see a wooden box a bit longer than his hand and only a couple of inches wide. He tried to wrench it out but it barely shifted, having been wedged in by shells and other growths that had formed around it.

He found a rough, fist-sized rock and set to work, pounding and chipping away the obstructions, trying not to soak himself in the process. After several minutes, he grasped the box once more and, after a mighty pull, it came free with a muffled grinding sound.

He had paused there for a moment, standing next to the tide pool, turning the box over and over, looking for a seam that would indicate the location of a lid, but he could see none. He had begun to pick at one of the leather straps with his fingernail, but at that moment he had sensed movement around him.

He turned and saw that little sea creatures in the tide pool were fluttering about, behaving in a way he'd never seen before. He leaned over to get a better look, watching open-mouthed as the sculpins raced around while the anemones bobbed and waved.

Then one little sculpin suddenly broke the surface of the pool. It seemed to act as the starting blast of some unknown event and, like an expanding reverse wave, Gellan watched the sea come to life. Within seconds, the sound had become deafening as hundreds of fluttering and jumping creatures added their own noise to the roar of the waves.

He had stood and watched for several moments, dumbfounded, his arms hanging loosely at his side, the box grasped in one hand. Then, realizing that the sun was already low on the horizon, he had shoved the wooden box and the rope into his shoulder bag and run along the shore at the base of the cliff toward his cave.

Now he was really beginning to feel the cold seep through his damp jeans as he knelt on the floor of that cave, high above the ocean. He pulled his flashlight out of his bag, finally able to examine the box closely.

It was growing dark, but in the gleam of the light, he found a miniscule, perfectly straight line along one side of the wooden box, just above one of the cross-straps. If he could unpick the tight, thick stitching on the lengthwise strap first, he might be able to wedge open that crack without having to unpick the two cross-straps.

He settled his flashlight on the large stone and arranged his position so the light would shine just where he needed it to. Pulling out his penknife, he worked it underneath one of the stitches, but it had been strengthened by seawater and wouldn't budge.

Switching tactics, he gripped the penknife near its tip, between his thumb and forefinger, holding it like a pencil. He worked at one of the stitches, scraping at the fibers bit by bit. At the moment it finally broke, there was an unexpectedly loud snapping sound.

Gellan worked his knife under each stitch, pulling it through the leather with much labor. With nighttime descending, it was growing colder and he was now shivering uncontrollably. His hands had become stiff and he was having to tighten all his muscles to keep some sort of control as he worked at each stitch.

After nearly forty minutes, the last stitch pulled free and the strap gave way and fell back, making the hairline crack in the wood more visible.

Gellan worked his penknife into the crack, wheedling it back and forth along the seam, wedging it open. In the small indents his knife made, he could see a hard, yellow substance.

At last, the top third of the face of the box broke away and slid upward. With a triumphant "Yes!" Gellan held the box up to the light, anxious to see inside it. He was immediately struck by the fact that the contents were entirely dry.

He turned the box back and forth in the light and saw an object held fast in a thick cushion. It looked like a candle, though it was clearly made of some type of metal; its thin handle was bright and untarnished, with stiff decorative strands of something winding up and down it. The same strands also wound over and around a bulbous end that reminded him of the giant decorative lightbulbs he saw in the lighthouses along the rocky coastline—except that this miniature one appeared to be made of some kind of large crystal or rough-cut diamond rather than glass.

He reached into the box, but the moment his fingers made contact with a metal strand, a very bright light filled the cave. He gasped, reflexively shoving the box off his lap and lunging backward, his heart pounding. The light went out after a couple of seconds, but it had been so bright that an odd fog hung in front of his vision, and it was an unusually long time before his eyes were able to fully adjust back to the dim light of his flashlight.

He craned his neck to look at the object in the toppled box, half expecting it to explode. When he was quite sure it wasn't going to do that, he slowly reached for the box—and a foghorn sounded from outside, causing him to jump and his heart to race once more. He knew he really couldn't linger here any longer, or Aunt Misera would be the least of his worries. The tide was coming in and it would soon make the stretch of beach just below the cave narrow and treacherous, especially with no moon to help light his way tonight.

He found the top piece of the box and slid it back into place, then paused for a moment. He wasn't sure what to do with the box. He really didn't want to leave it here, but neither did he want to take it home. After a brief moment of consideration, he concluded that the cave was the better option.

Near the back of the cave, where the rock dipped further down, there was a small crevice. It wasn't nearly big enough to properly hide the box, but he shoved it in sideways as far as it would go. He cut off a small section of the rope and shoved it in his pocket so he could examine it more closely later, then settled the rest of the rope in a coil beside the box. He looked around briefly, but he already knew there were almost no small stones and practically no loose dirt in the cave —nothing he could use to cover them.

He nodded grimly to himself at a sudden idea, then took a deep breath and ripped off his wet jacket and shirt. He disentangled them and pulled his jacket back on as quickly as he could. He tucked the dark shirt around the box before stepping back and shining his flashlight at it. In the darkness, the black shirt and the box beneath it seemed to disappear into the rock.

Gellan gave a nod of satisfaction, threw his flashlight and penknife into his shoulder bag, and ran to the edge of the cave. With a last glance toward the box as he slid backward over the edge, he began the familiar descent much more slowly than usual, because it was now too dark to see.

CHAPTER TWO

THE FIRST IS EASIER

G ellan reached the bottom of the cliff at last and began to run as quickly and carefully as he could on the narrow strip of sand. The flashlight in his hand was his only light and he had to watch his footing; this stretch of coast was rocky and dangerous.

After about twenty minutes, he reached the familiar gap in the cliff where stone steps had been carved to hide the movements of smugglers in centuries past. He clicked his flashlight off and thundered up all sixty-nine of them, moving swiftly past Old Jack's cottage, sitting near the edge of the cliff and overlooking the ocean.

The light was on and he could see people inside. He heard the door open and he hastened quickly into the shadows of a patch of tall cedars. He paused and listened hard, trying to quiet his breathing. He caught words like "never before" and "tidal wave coming?" and "very odd."

He watched a threesome climb into a car and trundle off, then he turned and made his way to the back of the shed. He fumbled behind it until his arm made contact with the handlebars of his bike. A minute later he was careening down the winding road, calculating that with the force of the wind blowing in behind him, he should be home in thirteen and a half minutes. With only a few feet of road lit up by his flashlight, he knew he was going recklessly fast. But he also knew what was probably already in store for him from Aunt Misera.

The small town of Ferndale came into sight at last, and less than a minute later he was rounding the final turn. He looked anxiously to the end of the block, where a gray Italianate storefront stood on the corner, with a sign that said *Sweet Pickings* over the large display window. As he sped around to the back, he was astonished to see that only the back porch light was on. He didn't have time to wonder where his aunt and uncle could be, however, as he maneuvered deftly between the small standalone garage and the large garbage can that sat next to it, both legs on one side of the bike, ready to jump off. He skidded to a stop in the narrow alley on the far side of the garage and threw his bike up against a giant old oak tree. Its girth took up nearly the whole corner between the garage and the two tall fences that formed the alley.

Gellan pounded up the back steps to the second floor, pulled out his key, and let himself in, shivering as the warm air washed over him.

Before he did anything else, he went into his room and quickly changed into warm, dry clothes, balling up his damp ones and shoving them under his bed. He felt exhausted, but he knew he couldn't stop yet. After setting some water in a pot on the stove, he pulled on a sweatshirt and headed back down the outside stairs. He barreled through the gate on the near side of the garage into the chicken yard, setting the chickens in a flutter on their roosting bar.

Out of habit, he glanced over at the garden, where the tiny house he used to live in with his mother had once stood. The memories of the past always seemed a little bit closer under the cool stillness of night, and he pulled his hoodie closer around his neck, turning his back to the garden.

He counted the chickens to make sure they were all there, then filled up their feed and water, ignoring their pointed glares and annoyed clucking.

Back inside, he was glad to see that the water had reached a full boil. He knew he had to stop his shivering before his aunt and uncle came home, so before dumping the pasta into the pot, he dipped a mug in and pulled out some of the water. He topped it off with water from the tap until it was just cool enough to drink, then gulped it down while he threw pasta into the pot with his free hand.

He put some spaghetti sauce into a slowly-warming pot and slices of bread in the toaster, then sprinted down to the shop to sweep and check the locks. Then back upstairs to set the table and lay out the dinner before finally throwing himself down at his bedroom desk, wondering where his aunt and uncle could possibly be.

Only a few seconds later, he heard a familiar rumble as a car turned the corner and pulled into the garage. The click of a lock and *'fwish'* of a door told him that Uncle Ivan and Aunt Misera had come in through the back. He heard Aunt Misera walk down the hall to check on Frenchie, and Uncle Ivan poked his head into Gellan's room.

"We already ate," he said. "I guess you must've been back pretty late?"

Gellan's heart sank. "Uh, well, I—"

Uncle Ivan grunted. "Smells good, anyway," he said. "I'm sure we could do with a bit more." He turned and left.

Gellan sighed and sat back in his chair for a moment. Eventually he got up and moved into the kitchen to begin serving up. Aunt Misera entered a moment later, followed by a waddling Frenchie and Uncle Ivan, who grabbed the salt and pepper on his way to the table.

"A proper dinner at last," said Aunt Misera to the air above Gellan's head. "You wouldn't be*lieve* how little I've had to eat all day." She kicked off her shoes and flopped into the chair, watching Gellan butter a slice of bread for her. Gellan made sure the butter went right to the edges, the way she liked it, before putting it on her plate and sliding it over to her.

"We were out at Old Jack's place," Uncle Ivan said to Gellan. "He called me down in my shop, just as I was closin' things up, and he told me somethin' interestin' was going on in the ocean and he wanted me to come see it."

"Really?" Gellan asked, trying to look interested. "What was it?" He hoped he sounded convincingly curious.

"Honestly, it was just a bunch of fish splashing about," Aunt Misera said to Uncle Ivan. "You'd think he'd never seen a fish jump out of water before. The things that amuse people in this town..."

Uncle Ivan stared at her for a moment, but didn't say anything. He unintentionally made eye contact with Gellan, then immediately turned his face to his plate and began to eat.

Aunt Misera suddenly took a deep, shuddering sigh. "I don't think I have the energy to sit here, Ivan," she said in a choked voice. "I'm absolutely worn out."

"Of course, Missy," Ivan said, putting his fork down and pulling a tray out of the cupboard. He refilled her plate and set it on the tray, then followed Aunt Misera to the bedroom.

"So when did you actually get back?" Uncle Ivan asked quietly a few minutes later, as he sat back down at the table with Gellan.

"A while ago," Gellan said. "I got all the evening chores done."

Uncle Ivan grunted and stared at Gellan for a bit longer than usual. Gellan pretended not to notice, looking down at his plate and taking a bite of spaghetti.

He ate as quickly as he could, dropped his dishes in the sink, then ducked out of the room, saying, "I'll do the dishes in a bit."

Late that night, a high-pitched whistling sound was coming from somewhere in the wind as Gellan looked down on a frolicking ocean. Inky froth in the skies above him, turbulent purple waves beneath him. He could almost feel the air flying across his face, his hair whipping in the wind.

It took several minutes for him to realize that his dream and the sound were intertwining from two different levels of consciousness. As the dream faded, his senses sharpened around the sound.

A minute later, fully awake, he realized a torrent of wind was lashing the building, and the whistling sound became clearer. He climbed out of bed and examined the old wooden window frame; it had swollen with the moisture in the damp ocean air and couldn't quite close properly anymore. He'd been meaning to fix it for ages, but he hadn't gotten around to it, and now the gap between the window and the sill provided the perfect conditions for the wind to whistle through. It was reaching such a pitch that he was worried it would wake Aunt Misera.

He grabbed a sock and attempted to stuff it in the gap—only to stop mid-shove, startled by a pair of round, glinting eyes blinking slowly at him just on the other side of the window pane. He fell backward, his heart pounding. A moment later, his eyes managed to distinguish the full shape of a little black owl sitting in the branches of the maple tree that grew at the corner of the building.

As he stepped back to the window, the owl tilted its head and blinked at him. Gellan stuck his face right up to the glass and the owl moved closer, hopping along a branch that led up to the window. A moment later it shook its head and scrunched up its neck as a particularly strong gust of wind ruffled its feathers.

"Where'd you come from?" Gellan asked quietly. The owl shifted from one foot to the other, blinking its large eyes. "Is that supposed to mean something?" The owl pulled its neck back in as another gust of wind rolled past.

It seemed awfully tame. But surely no one would be outside with a pet owl in such a storm, and at such a time of night. He checked up and down the street just to be sure, but he could see no one. Perhaps the owl had been blown off course in a migration and didn't know where it was.

As it continued to blink at him, Gellan glanced back at his bedroom door, then reached up to undo the latch on his window. The moment the latch clicked open, the owl turned and spread its wings, quickly soaring away on the strength of the wind.

Gellan relatched the window, a strange feeling washing over him. The owl had seemed to bring a sense of... something or somewhere else. But that was nonsense. Perhaps it was just the storm, heaving through the air, that gave him the odd sensation.

He shook himself and grabbed a piece of paper. He drew a quick sketch of the little owl before his observations faded from memory. In the dim light of the streetlamp, it had appeared to be entirely black except for a small band of white just above the feet and tiny speckles of white around its large black eyes. Its beak and feet had been an oddly bright, yellow-orange color.

He put down his pencil, shoved the sock more tightly into the crack, and then climbed into bed, pulling the covers up to his chin. The peculiar feeling lingered over him as he drifted back off to sleep, the apartment rocking slightly, like a ship being tossed in the waves of a raging sea.

The events of the day before seemed almost dreamlike in Gellan's mind when he woke up the next morning. He glanced out of the window as he dressed, looking for the little owl, but it was nowhere to be seen. The wind had settled down to a whispering zephyr, and for a moment, he wondered if he'd imagined it all. Then he saw the paper with the drawing and his notes, so he knew at least the owl must be real.

He went into the kitchen and found Aunt Misera sitting in front of the small television, drinking her morning cup of chamomile tea while she watched the news. The presenter, who was wearing a navy-blue blazer and had perfectly coiffed hair, was interviewing a rather puffed-up sort of man.

Gellan busied himself with slicing bread, filling the toaster, and getting out some jam and butter. He was adding a second batch of bread to the toaster when he caught a few words that made him freeze.

"...Odd ocean events are a little harder to trace than land events,"

Mr. 'Puffer' was saying. "With an earthquake, for example, measurements from several solid land points can tell us the *precise* time and place it began."

Gellan kept buttering and jamming his toast, his back to his aunt, but he did it much more quietly now so he wouldn't miss a word of the interview.

Mr. 'Coiffed' jumped in eagerly. "Well, that's an interesting comparison, isn't it? I mean, with people talking about it on social media with the hashtag 'Poseidon's *Quake*'? It seems to have really—"

"Let's not perpetuate the use of that *terribly* unscientific term," Mr. Puffer interrupted, crossing his arms over his chest. "I know I shouldn't expect the public to use accurate descriptions *all* the time, even for something as *obviously* important as this. But to suggest that a mythical *thing*—like Poseidon—had something to do with this, well then—" He threw up his hands and looked away, clearly annoyed with public ignorance.

Mr. Coiffed cleared his throat. "Well, back to the science, then," he said in a pleasant tone, obviously attempting to mollify his very important guest.

Gellan picked up his plate, trying to keep the tower of toast from toppling, and tentatively sat down in a chair behind his aunt where he would have a decent view of the television, listening closely while he worked steadily through his breakfast.

Mr. Puffer took a deep breath. "As I was saying, this case isn't as easy as an actual earthquake. But based on what we've pieced together so far, we've narrowed the starting point down to a *sixty-seven-mile-long* section of coast in northern California." He sounded extremely pleased with himself as a picture appeared on the screen behind him, showing the area of coast marked in red.

A piece of toast in front of Gellan's gaping mouth dripped jam onto the table when he saw Ferndale clearly labeled within that section.

"My goodness, they're making a lot of fuss about fish," he heard Aunt Misera mutter. "If they'd all been whales, now *that'd* be something worth talking about." She sipped her tea with an air of superiority and dropped a crust to Frenchie.

"Sixty-seven miles?" Mr. Coiffed asked. "That seems like quite a large span." He caught the look on Mr. Puffer's face at the same moment Gellan caught the jam dripping off his toast. He immediately stuffed the last bit into his mouth. "But when one considers the *full* extent of the western coastline, of course... Well, um, is it possible that a satellite caught images that would help identify the trigger point?"

"That's a very good question," Mr. Puffer replied. "It's possible, but only if a satellite happened to be going over that area *and* was taking images right at that moment."

"Were there any?"

"Not that we've found. Yet. Please remember that it hasn't even been a full twenty-four hours since it happened. In any case, we've assembled a large team of scientists to work on this for some time to come, so I'm sure we'll be able to come up with lots of answers."

"Will the results justify the cost, d'you think?" Mr. Coiffed asked.

"If you consider that a recurrence of this event could delay ships"—Mr. Puffer jabbed the air with a finger—"which would throw *ports* and deliveries off-*schedule*"—a second finger—"and all that could potentially stall the *entire* economy...!" A third finger, as Mr. Puffer swelled larger than ever. "Well, that would be a *huge* cost to us all—so of course it's worth it!"

Mr. Coiffed leaned forward, intrigued. "I had not heard of any reports of ships being delayed," he said. "Where exactly—"

"Reports are still pending," said Mr. Puffer. "I'm just saying that I'm sure we all agree that the cost of avoiding potential economic disaster is worth every penny." He emphasized the last two words with more jabs at the air.

Mr. Coiffed looked at him blankly for a moment, then blinked and glanced down at his notes. "Erm, let's switch gears just a little bit," he said, making a funny backwards-pedaling motion with his hands, "and talk about the possibility of a reoccurrence. Perhaps you can give us your theory about what may have caused it?"

"Well," said Mr. Puffer, slowly and importantly, "we have a few ideas, but since *everything* has a scientific explanation, all we have to do is keep collecting data and put it all together. Eventually we'll have enough information to understand it, and then to predict it. It's the first time in recorded history that the events of last night have ever been described, and science can't possibly foresee something that has never happened before, you know."

"Mm-hmm," said Mr. Coiffed, nodding, a perfect smile plastered on his face. "Well, thank you for taking the time to..."

Gellan grabbed his plate and headed to a small desk in the living room that was squished into a tiny gap between all the tall bookcases filled with Uncle Ivan's innumerable books. He sat down and opened up the laptop, leaving his plate abandoned off to one side.

He was just typing "posiden's quake california" into the search engine when his uncle walked in through the front door that led down to the street. Uncle Ivan stopped in the doorway; when Gellan looked up, they greeted each other with raised eyebrows.

Gellan spoke first. "Were you already down in the shop?"

"Since when is anything more important to you than finishing your breakfast?" Uncle Ivan stepped through and closed the door. "What are you looking up?"

"Nothing important," Gellan said, closing the browser window. He shut the laptop and hurried back to his room, taking his plate with him.

───────────

That evening, after spending his whole afternoon on the list of chores that had appeared on his bedroom door after school, Gellan found himself sitting alone at the dinner table with Aunt Misera. This unpleasant experience happened occasionally when Uncle Ivan worked longer than usual in his shop. Aunt Misera didn't say a word as she shared her potatoes and sour cream with Frenchie, who was obviously enjoying his dinner more than Gellan was.

Gellan hardly tasted anything, swallowing it all as fast as he could, before retreating outside. As he walked down the back steps, a gusty breeze took aim at his cap and he could smell rain in the air.

He walked through the gate into the back yard and found that the chickens were all settling down to roost in the open-air run again.

"You silly birds," he said as he tried to shoo them into the shelter of their coop, but they refused to budge. He shook his head at them, then walked over to the kitchen garden, stepping over the waist-high driftwood fence he'd built to divide it from the chicken yard.

His uncle had given him free rein in this garden. A quarter of it was dedicated entirely to peas—he loved peas of all kinds, and he especially loved cooking with the flat, sweet, sugar-podded ones. The rest of the garden was filled with a hodgepodge of plants, from lettuce and carrots to sage and peppermint.

He made his way around the horseshoe path, pulling a weed here and there and checking for slugs. Rain began to sprinkle down and he shivered, shoving his hands deep into his pockets. His right hand bumped against the piece of the rope he'd cut off in the cave, and he pulled it out of his pocket, examining it for the umpteenth time that day. If only he could find someone who could tell him when it had been made or what it was made of, then maybe—

A strange noise behind him made him look over his shoulder, but there was nothing there except the chickens. A gust of wind had probably pushed the garbage can a bit, causing it to scrape against the cement on the other side of the fence. He plucked at some of the threads of the rope and rubbed them between his fingers. He had never heard of any rope fibers that could become invisible, and no matter how thoroughly he searched online or in the library, he still hadn't come up with anything to explain it.

There was another noise behind him, louder this time. He turned and focused his gaze on the bit of fence that ran from the garage to the oak tree. Suddenly, a light appeared there, momentarily visible in the cracks. Then a shadow loomed up against the fence, indistinguishable in shape.

Gellan lifted his foot and then paused, realizing that crunching noise of the pebbly path would quickly give him away. He looked around for a moment, his right foot hanging in the air, then threw his leg into the soft soil of one of the garden beds in a giant step. His foot landed quietly, but now he was stuck with his legs sprawled so wide that he was unable to go either forward or backward.

He heard a strange 'thock' sound and tried to watch the fence without losing his balance, his arms outstretched in a remarkable yoga pose. There was another swish of the light, and then footsteps.

Gellan leaned over and placed his hands carefully and quietly on the path; then he picked up his left foot and threw that leg behind him toward the garden bed. He felt a little ridiculous as he slowly walked himself backwards with his hands until he was able to regain a standing position.

Picking his way quickly through rows of turnips, he watched the haze of light through the cracks in the fence grow dimmer as he tried not to get high-centered on the driftwood fence. Then, abandoning all caution, he ran across the chicken yard as, with a last scraping sound, the light disappeared. Gellan collided with the fence, smooshing his face against one peephole after another, but saw nothing.

He kicked the fence in frustration, then sighed and leaned his forehead against it. With another thought, he ran around to the back steps and burst through the back door at the top. Thankfully, neither Uncle Ivan nor Aunt Misera were in the kitchen. He peered out of the kitchen window, hoping he'd have a good view of the oak corner, but he knew perfectly well that the garage and the canopy of the oak tree completely blocked it from every possible angle.

Next he ran into his room and grabbed his flashlight out of his shoulder bag, pausing for a brief moment to glance out of his bedroom window, though the vantage point from there was predictably no better.

He managed to escape back outside, noticed only by Pixie, and made his way quietly down the steps. He crept across the front of the garage and peered around the corner. His bike was still there—along with a complete absence of anything out of the ordinary.

After several fruitless minutes during which he only found a couple of spiders amongst some fallen acorns, he headed back inside, feeling extremely miffed. The kitchen light was on now, and Uncle Ivan was washing dishes at the sink.

"What was so interesting behind the garage?" Uncle Ivan asked as Gellan shut the door behind him.

"Nothing," Gellan said. He set his flashlight on the table and took off his jacket.

Without a word, Uncle Ivan stepped away from the sink and dried off his hands as Gellan took up his position to finish the job. Gellan continued to watch the garage intently as he washed, hoping to see someone (or something) emerge from behind it.

But nothing more at all happened that night until he was awakened by a tapping sound on his window.

As he came to, he realized it was interspersed with a funny chirrupy-hooting sound. He rolled over and saw two familiar, large black eyes looking straight in at him through his window.

He got up and walked over to it. "I didn't expect you back," he said, grinning as the owl shifted its feet and chirruped at him. "I don't have any food for you. You're an owl—you're supposed to catch your own food."

The owl turned its head to one side and chirruped again.

Gellan looked over his shoulder at his bedroom door to make sure it was shut, then reached up and slowly unlatched the window, keeping eye contact with the owl. Rather than flying away again, the little owl inched forward on the branch.

With a bit of maneuvering, Gellan quietly removed the screen and shoved it underneath his bed. The little owl picked up something in its beak that Gellan hadn't noticed sitting on his windowsill, then hopped through the open window and dropped the object onto Gellan's desk.

"What's this?"

Gellan reached forward and picked up a single forget-me-not flower—the kind that grew wild on the edges of the woodlands. He'd often picked a few himself, near the cemetery, to lay on his mother's grave. He stared at the small flower for a moment, then looked back at the owl.

"Uh, thank you," he said.

The owl watched intently as Gellan placed the flower between the pages of his notebook and pressed it down tightly. Then it fluttered to the top of his desk lamp and began preening, apparently in no hurry to go.

Taking care that Pixie couldn't get into his room, Gellan snuck into the living room with his flashlight. It took him several minutes to locate the book he wanted: *Owls of North America*. Once he was back in his room with the door firmly shut, he began flipping through the pages one at a time, searching by the light of the streetlamp. As he canvassed the book, the little owl stopped preening and watched him turn page after page, its head tilted curiously to one side.

"Nothing," Gellan said as he reached the back cover. "Not a single owl that looks anything like you." The owl clicked its beak. "So, are you from America or not?" Gellan tentatively reached out a hand and ran a finger along its chest. The feathers felt soft and smooth, and the owl closed its eyes for a moment. Then, without warning, it suddenly spread its wings and took off noiselessly through the open window, soon becoming indistinguishable from the darkness.

Gellan arrived home from school a little later than usual the next day. It had taken him a long time to get back to sleep, and he'd been so tired at school that he had fallen asleep during math and had to stay after to redo the lesson.

He tried to make his way behind the shop without being seen—he was hoping to head straight down to the cliffs.

"Gellan, I hope you're not planning on going anywhere!" Uncle Ivan called out the back door of his shop as Gellan reached for his bike.

Gellan shoved his bike back into its place a little harder than was necessary, then sighed and walked out of the alleyway.

"I need your help in the shop for a while," Uncle Ivan said when Gellan came into view, before turning and letting the door swing shut behind him.

Gellan followed slowly. He hadn't been back to the cave in two days and he wanted to check on the wooden box, partially just to make sure it was actually there and hadn't been a figment of his imagination all along. Instead, he stepped into the back of the shop, the smell of sugar, chocolate and fruity concoctions hitting his nose in an unpleasant way. The dehumidifier hummed in the corner, keeping the whole shop dry so the confections didn't melt down into sugary, shapeless puddles.

Gellan dropped his bag near the back door.

"How was school?" Uncle Ivan called to him from the front shop area, a book on tulips sitting open on the counter next to him.

"Fine." Gellan didn't feel like talking. The whole school day, the only thing anybody had seemed to talk about was the ocean and fish and fairytales about sea monsters, and he certainly wasn't going to bring that up.

"The shelves all need to be wiped down," said Uncle Ivan, adjusting his apron, which was covered with brightly colored rainbows and unicorns.

The shop was crammed with shelves and tables, jars and decorative crates, all filled with unusual candies, pastries, homemade marshmallows, fruit-shaped marzipans, and other confections, along with several loaves of specialty breads. Uncle Ivan made a lot of goods himself, but he also imported several of the confections and candies from around the world.

Gellan hated the idea of being stuck in the shop, moving endless numbers of jars and platters, but he knew he really didn't have a choice, so he sighed and got a small bucket of water. He dug through the apron closet until he found a plain green one, and pulled it on. Then he grabbed several rags, sticking them in the pockets and all along the sash of the apron.

As he walked back into the front of the shop, Uncle Ivan handed him an iPod and a pair of earbuds. "Here," he said to Gellan, "you might as well make the best use of your time and listen to an audio-book while you work. I put *Robinson Crusoe* on it for you. I think you'll like it."

Gellan gladly took the iPod and shoved it in his back pocket, then stuck an earbud in his right ear.

Uncle Ivan had barely begun entering numbers into different columns on the computer at the end of the counter when a young family entered the shop. Gellan saw Uncle Ivan's face lift, and watched as the little boy and girl responded to his bright eyes and exaggerated expressions. A few minutes later they skipped out of the shop, each carrying their own small bag of chewies, their father following behind with a heavy brown paper bag.

A few moments later a young couple entered the shop hand in hand. This time Uncle Ivan made himself available for answering questions, but his grumpy, downturned expression stayed put.

Gellan used to think that Uncle Ivan was always cross. But as he'd gotten older, he had realized that Uncle Ivan simply had one of those faces whose normal, relaxed expression looked rather dour. The only time that changed a little was when his eyebrows pulled the rest of his face up, which usually happened when children were frolicking through his colorful shop. Gellan remembered Uncle Ivan sometimes looking at him that way when he had been younger.

Over the course of a couple of hours, many customers came and went, including Lars Jenson, who came in just after five o'clock. He burst through the door and immediately began wimbling on about needing something quickly for his wife for their anniversary. Uncle Ivan silently cut him off when he pulled out a large, perfectly packaged basket of sweets and confections topped with a large pink-and-white bow.

Gellan had to cover his mouth to suppress a laugh when Lars got stuck halfway out the door, juggling the large basket alongside his briefcase. Uncle Ivan's mustache twitched at Lars' predicament, but his face otherwise showed no hint of amusement.

"Lucky he remembered before he got home," Gellan said, still grinning.

"It's not luck," said Uncle Ivan. "I sent him a message. He always forgets his anniversary, so I make sure I'm the one that reminds him." He buried his nose in the computer screen again, peering at the dollars and cents on his spreadsheet.

A few minutes later, he got up and turned on a TV just through the doorway in the back; the news floated by, the volume turned down low. Gellan could see the screen as he washed the glass panel on the front of the counter display.

The presenter went on from one piece of news to another: two California beaches had been closed because of a sewage spill, a discussion on goat milk, airplanes being grounded in the Midwest because of unexpected storms, and a shoe that somehow solved every single foot problem known to humankind.

Then there was a shift to a different area of the studio and a political reporter began to share his opinion of the events of the day in Washington, DC. Gellan didn't know one senator from another and he never could understand what they were all arguing about, especially since it seemed to change every week.

The noisy back-and-forth issuing from the TV faded into the background along with *Robinson Crusoe*, as Gellan drifted away into his own thoughts about the events he'd experienced in the past couple of days. The colored stripes and bright sprinkles in front of him blurred as he saw instead the smooth wooden box and the jagged red line on the map, the dark churning sea and the blinding white light, the coarse rope and the sleek black owl...

Uncle Ivan chose that moment to cough loudly, causing Gellan to lurch and slosh his arm straight into the bucket of water up to his elbow. He looked up with a scowl as he squeezed the dirty water out of his shirt sleeve, and saw that Uncle Ivan was still engrossed with entering numbers into his computer.

Gellan glanced back at the TV. There hadn't been any improvement—a man he didn't know was giving a speech about something to do with... the sea? He grimaced and rolled his eyes. He hoped everyone would soon forget all about it and realize it had all been a big nothing. Strange things had happened to him before, and most of the time there was a perfectly logical explanation.

The man was tall and regal-looking, in a typically dapper politician's suit, and he used exceptionally well-trained gestures. However, the reactions of the people around him—both those sitting on the platform and a few visible in the crowd—caught Gellan's attention. Some were shifting uncomfortably; others were covering their mouths with their hands. But there was one older man sitting just at the edge of the camera's view who was staring up at the senator, a grave expression on his face.

"...far too much emphasis on something that is of no import," said the politician, pressing his thumb on the podium to emphasize several words. "Some may try to use this situation to their advantage, but it is more likely to create disadvantage and distrust between the communities of this nation, including those that..."

"You've done enough for today," Uncle Ivan said suddenly, coming out of his spreadsheet serenity.

Gellan didn't wait to be told twice. He barely gave a thought to the deepened furrow in Uncle Ivan's brow as he ripped off his apron, dropped it in the laundry bin along with the heap of rags, and chucked the hairnet into the garbage can. He left the iPod on the desk in the back and bolted out of the back door.

There he skidded to a stop and sighed at the dimming sky, knowing it was too late to go down to the cliffs. He'd have to wait for another day.

***

Faulkner was sitting in his chair, his right ankle resting on his left knee, staring at the wall in front of his desk. His chair turned from side to side in a perfect rhythm—from behind, one might think it was a giant metronome moving on its own, except that it would occasionally pause and a hand would sweep out in an unusual gesture which, it wouldn't take long to notice, corresponded with the addition, deletion, or change of the chalk marks on the blackboard wall in front of him.

There was an extensive amount of writing (which was rather difficult to decipher because of its uneven scrawl), three sections of maps, various numbers and calculations, what looked like three family trees only partially filled in, and a single, large circle with a question mark in and several names written to one side of it.

There was a knock at the door, and Roman entered before receiving any reply.

"Sir," Roman said to the chair, "candle room in five minutes."

"Thank you," Faulkner said, sticking one hand out in a nodding gesture.

Pigeon:
Security code—confidential information.
—Montague

The note had just arrived as Faulkner entered the candle room. After reading it, he sent back a quick reply.

Montague:
12, 11, 00. Proceed.
—Pigeon

Faulkner drummed his fingers on the tiny table in the closet-sized room where he sat. There were several rows of candles, each one different from the next, sitting on numerous wooden shelves lining the walls. In the middle of the tiny table there were three unlit candles—a tall blue one, a thicker-but-shorter green one, and what should have been a pure white one swirled with gold, though it was so caked in dust it was almost entirely gray. He was staring intently at these three candles.

A few moments later, a flame appeared out of the green candle with a soft hiss. The flame turned a similar green color, and a paper unfurled itself out of it and flew upward. Faulkner reached out and grabbed it in midair.

Request for you to send someone to protect Henry Gilding. I believe he's made an egregious error—though it may have been intentional.
—Montague

Faulkner paused for a long moment, tapping the end of the wooden pen on the table. It was made of a particularly hard wood, and it made a pingy sound. Then he shifted his grip on the pen, dipped the tip in the inkwell, and wrote:

Is that necessary? Our manpower is a bit strained at the moment. I'm not sure I can spare anyone.
—Pigeon

Unfortunately, yes. I cannot protect him, but you might be able to.
—Montague

Faulkner paused again. He had a sense that Montague was right, though he had no idea why.

I'll see what I can do. Most of our scouts are gathering information along the west coast at the moment and our troops are managing a situation on Heklah Island.
But I'll try to find someone. Can you give me any further details?
—Pigeon

Please forward any information your scouts may find. I have a particular reason for needing it.
Many thanks. His most recent statements seemed to expose too much.
Regarding the Gildings, Cremstoll, and all of us.
—Montague

I heard what he said. It may just be utter nonsense. Besides, practically the whole family are wynklers now and he's much less important than he thinks.
—Pigeon

Whether you think it is nonsense or not won't change the fact that others may choose to take action. The Gilding family must not be compromised— whether or not they are all wynklers now is beside the point. You know as well as I do that they are integral to the history and protection of Gilsthorne and Cremstoll. We can't risk that kind of exposure.
—Montague

Faulkner sent off a short reply—but nothing came in return. He quickly scribbled another note that didn't so much ask as plead. A tiny poof of dust was sent up as the flame sucked it away. A moment later his curiosity was no more satisfied than before, and he knew the conversation was over.

Possibly. Nothing certain. I will inform you when I choose to do so. The first is easier than the last.
—Montague

CHAPTER THREE
DRINA

Faulkner sat back for a moment, the cogs of his mind spinning furiously, trying to see if he could add any new pieces to the puzzle. Though he knew it was likely fruitless, he stacked all the notes from "Montague" in front of him on the table, placed his hand on top of the notes, and tapped his hand with his wand... then heaved a sigh. Nothing.

Of course, it didn't help that he had no idea who Montague was. The transfer charm worked best if you knew the person who had done the writing. Still, as guarded as Montague was, he would surely have protected all his notes from such a simple spell. Most witches and wizards did it as a matter of course.

"Henry Gilding?" he muttered to himself, his right foot tapping restlessly. "Arrogant, self-absorbed, wynkler politician! Of course the family is important—in general. Sort of... But with the direct line being so muddled—there are so many of them at the moment they're practically a dime a dozen!" He scoffed.

Then his foot stopped. Henry Gilding.

Faulkner knew he was only *mostly* a wynkler... which did make him different than the rest of the Gildings... and if Montague thought he could be important...

But who could he ask? He scanned the shelves of candles and his eyes landed on a straight, tall copper candle. Uncas Wylde? That was probably just as hopeless—the historian was as elusive as his name. However, he *was* the only person who had full access to the Hall of Records in Philadelphia, though he never seemed to have the time (or desire) to help. Faulkner tapped his chin, considering for a moment more. With no other avenue to pursue at the moment anyway, he scribbled out a short note.

It was a long shot, but he was sure that all he needed was one key, one missing link that would connect all the dots. Then he would know what had to be done.

Faulkner pulled the copper candle off the shelf and, still holding it, sent off his note. It would likely be at least two or three weeks, and possibly two or three months, before he could expect a reply. He set the candle on the table and left the room, locking it behind him with a wave of his hand. He watched until the edges of the door had melted into the wall, making it indistinguishable in the long hallway, before walking away.

As his legs carried him down corridors and up stairs, he grimaced at a succession of thoughts, shaking his head again and again and rubbing his forehead. His brain felt like a hive of angry bees, unable to get rid of the bear of ignorance.

In his distraction, he paused at a gap in the wall and punched a number into the old phone that sat there.

"Yes, sir?" said Roman cheerfully when he picked up.

"I need to speak with Historian Wylde as soon as possible," Faulkner said. "Can you think of any way to make that possible without President Humphrey getting wind of it, aside from the candle?"

"That would be especially difficult to do right now," said Roman. "I would think that, because of Poseidon's Quake and its proximity to us, they're probably watching the whole west coast closely at the moment."

There was a pause of several seconds. It wasn't that Faulkner distrusted President Humphrey; they got along well enough and had always had a cordial and informative relationship. It was just that he would prefer to avoid President Humphrey's notice at the moment until he knew more himself. None of their limited phone connections beyond Cremstoll were fully secure. He could never be sure of having total privacy on any of them, and this was something he simply did not want to 'let out' until he knew what was in the bag.

No, he told himself, it was better to let the general population of Cremstoll rest in blissful ignorance as long as they could. And anyway, he wasn't entirely sure his suspicions were correct.

"I'll just have to wait for a reply through the candle connection," Faulkner sighed. "I think it's my best chance at the moment."

"Right-o, sir," said Roman.

"Would you be able to meet with me for a few minutes before the end of the day?"

There was a chuckle on the other end of the line. "Well, I'm having dinner with my family at the moment, but I can pop down there around eight for a bit after I help my wife get the kids in bed, if you really need me."

Dinner? Faulkner looked out the windows as he climbed the last couple of steps to his office, realizing for the first time that it was entirely dark outside. No wonder it was so quiet in the building. He looked at his watch and realized that eight o'clock was closer than he had thought.

"Oh, I didn't realize... Never mind, it's not that urgent. I'll see you tomorrow. Oh wait, wait! Roman?"

"Yes, sir?"

"Get a hold of Jocundoff. Tell him I need to see him as soon as possible too."

There was a pause, and then Roman said, "Will do." The phone clicked.

Faulkner made it back to his office, where he paced around and around, occasionally adding notes to the blackboard in scrabbled handwriting with a flick of his hand.

"No, no, no!" he said suddenly, and with a great sweep of his hand, a giant line ran across the full length of the board. "Something is everywhere, so everything is *somewhere*! I just have to find it."

He threw himself down at his desk and pulled a large open book toward himself, drumming his fingers as he searched, though he practically knew it by heart at this point.

After a few minutes he was back on his feet, head down, shuffling through the corridors, going nowhere in particular. He found himself once again walking along the basement corridor next to a familiar stretch of wall, automatically holding out his right hand and dragging it along the wall for a few inches until it hit something. With a firm grip on the doorknob, he used his wand to open the door and stepped through into the candle room once more.

He saw, to his amazement, that a note was sitting on the table next to Uncas Wylde's candle. He leaned over it in disbelief.

12, 11, 00. Proceed.
–U.W.

He couldn't believe his luck! Knowing he wouldn't be able to hold Wylde's attention for long, and hoping that he hadn't already missed his chance, he immediately scribbled out a note making several requests. He knew that if he asked for one thing, Wylde would undoubtedly decline. But if he asked for several things, he just might get an answer to one or two of them.

The few minutes he had to wait seemed to stretch on, but at last, another note with a MajMinster letterhead unfurled from the flame.

Since nearly the whole Gilding family has been wynklers for several generations, we are not likely to have much information related to any single one of them. However, there may be something in the Gilding family archives. I think I should be able to at least answer your first question, though I don't have time to answer them all.
As for the so-called Poseidon's Quake, I have already been searching in the

archives for any mention of it, but I have found nothing at all. There is no mention of it ever happening before, if that's what you're asking.
—U.W.

Perhaps if he pressed a little... Faulkner sent off another note.

Of course it's important. But your perspective is different from mine.
—U.W.

I'm sure you can see as well as I can the fragile situation of Cremstoll. All I need is a bit of your time to gather some information that might help me.
—Pigeon

Perhaps. I am aware of the situation of Cremstoll, and I think that you may be misinterpreting things. I doubt any of us can say for sure.
—U.W.

Faulkner thumped the table in anger.

The Dark Days haven't happened for almost four hundred years! I'm sure you know the history as well as I do, and if it's anything to go by, this is a critical time for Cremstoll.
If you have access to any pertinent information, all I ask is that you allow me to make use of it.
Or perhaps your priorities have changed.

Seething and frustrated, Faulkner sent the note without even signing it.

Sometimes the cost of doing something is too high. And sometimes we can't change the course of things anyway.
You seem to fear that the worst of times approaches. I think, perhaps, it could be the best of times. It may be wise to sit back and watch things unfold for a while longer. We'll know soon enough.
I will send information to you as I am able, and choose, to do so.

–U.W.

Faulkner put the candle back on the shelf and left the room. "The best of times? Or the worst of times?" he muttered to himself, then sighed. "Perhaps it will be both."

As he approached the staircase to his office, he saw James Jocundoff leaning against one of the large windows overlooking the sea.

"Excellent," Faulkner said, ushering Jocundoff up the stairs. "We'll make this quick."

"They're called red bean mochi and they're from Japan," Uncle Ivan mumbled, reading off the label on the package, his mustache galumphing along for the ride.

It was a Thursday afternoon and Gellan and Jordan were sitting at a corner table in the sweet shop with an assortment of foreign candies and confections in packages spread across the sideboard, and evaluation forms in front of them. Uncle Ivan often used the two boys to taste-test new sweets he was considering stocking in his shop.

"Ith tewy..." said Jordan.

"And thuper fluffy..." Gellan added.

"But it has pretty much no flavor at all," concluded Jordan, as he finally managed to swallow. He shoved the other half aside. "Blegh."

Gellan nodded in agreement, his mouth still uncomfortably full of sweet cotton.

His uncle pointed to the forms on the table in front of them and they circled a few things before handing them to Uncle Ivan, who stapled them to the red bean mochi package. Both boys took large gulps of water as Uncle Ivan slapped down new forms in front of them. He ripped open another package and handed them each a small ball.

Gellan sighed before putting it in his mouth. He liked the confections in his uncle's shop, especially when he got a brand new one and not one that had sat for a few days. But there were times when it all lost its appeal—like when he wasn't quite sure what he was sticking in his mouth.

Gellan and Jordan sucked and chewed silently for a moment, and then Jordan gagged and actually spat it out into a napkin. Gellan just managed to swallow his, but his mouth was left with an unpleasant mix of spicy and tangy flavors. Uncle Ivan watched them without a twitch of expression.

"What," Gellan gasped after a long drink of water, "was that?"

Uncle Ivan looked at the package. "Hajmola from India."

"Uh-uh. Nope. Definitely not that one," Jordan said, shaking his head. "Your shop is called Sweet Pickings, Mr. Parker, and that one was *not* sweet."

Uncle Ivan pointed at the forms and they obediently filled them out.

After about ten more rounds of sweets and forms, both boys made it outside with an uncomfortable feeling in their stomachs and a few coins in each of their pockets.

"I don't think your uncle pays us enough," said Jordan, who was sucking on a lemon drop and examining a half dollar coin. They wandered aimlessly down the wooded path that led them toward the school grounds.

Gellan reached into his own pocket and closed his fingers around an old copper coin that hadn't come from his uncle. It had appeared on his windowsill that morning, along with a seashell which had a carving on it that looked unmistakeably like the object in the wooden box.

The little black owl had been leaving him gifts every day—ocean-smoothed stones, a scrap of paper, a bit of rope—but none of them had seemed to have any meaning until this morning. It had been difficult for Gellan to pay attention at school the whole day, his mind taken up with worry about the wooden box and the object in it. He hadn't made it back to the cliffs since the day he had found them, nearly two weeks ago; something had seemed determined to hinder him every day. But nothing was in his way today, and he only had to wait a couple more hours for low tide.

Gellan absentmindedly took out the lanyard holding his house key and started swinging it around and around, offering grunty-nothings in reply to Jordan's chatter—until he suddenly found himself flat on his face on the damp path.

"Good grief, Gellan." Jordan rolled his eyes and walked on.

Gellan brushed himself off as best he could, quite sure he had a muddy smear somewhere around his nose, then glanced down at his shoelaces, just to be sure.

He got up and had started walking after Jordan when he realized he had dropped his key. As he swung back around to look for it, his foot caught on something and he fell again. This time Jordan didn't even look around, though Gellan heard him groan.

"No—Jordan, wait," Gellan called. He got on his hands and knees and swung his hand back and forth near the spot where he'd tripped.

Jordan turned, an eyebrow raised, but when he saw Gellan's hand appear to collide with something, his mouth dropped open.

"What in the world?!" he exclaimed, jogging back.

"It must be what I tripped on," said Gellan. The thing was cold and hard, with a strong, rough hook on the end of it. "Here... feel right here." He pointed to the empty air just above the path.

Jordan crouched down and moved his hand forward, but after a moment he looked confused as his arm continued to sweep through the thin air.

"There's nothing there," he said indignantly, pushing himself back.

Gellan reached for the spot again. "Yes there is," he said. "Right here." He grabbed Jordan's fingers and guided them to the spot, tapping his fingers on the hard object.

"Whoa!" Jordan said. "What *is* that? Why can't we see it?" He pulled on it, attempting to twist it free from the ground.

"I don't know," said Gellan, letting go of it.

Jordan's hand immediately flew up and he fell back.

"Ouch!" he shouted as he landed hard. "What'd you do that for?!"

"I didn't do anything!" said Gellan. "I just... let go of it."

Jordan reached for it again. "Well, it's gone now. Whatever it was."

"What?!" Gellan reached for it and found it easily. "No it's not. It's right here." And then an odd thought occurred to him. "Wait a second—Jordan, here, take hold of it, all right?"

"Why?"

"I just want to try something. Can you feel it there?"

Jordan nodded.

"Okay, I'm going to let go. You just hang on to it, okay?"

A moment later, when Gellan let go, Jordan almost lost his balance again.

"That's *weird*," Jordan said. "So... I can only feel it when you're already touching it?"

"I dunno," Gellan said. "I guess so."

They stood up slowly, staring down at the path. Jordan swung his foot around, then shrugged and looked at Gellan. Gellan took his turn, and the hook immediately caught the edge of his pants. After steadying himself, he looked around at the arrangement of trees to fix the spot in his mind.

"Wait a minute!" With a sudden realization, he walked back and forth, waving his hand in the air, attempting to find the same spot of a couple of weeks before, until it bumped the invisible rope once more. He tugged on it and heard the branches bristling above him again.

"Want to try this one?" Gellan asked.

Jordan gave him a funny look.

"No, really, it's just some kind of rope or something..."

Jordan shrugged, then hopped and jumped while waving his hand about once more. His eyes widened as his fingers grazed the end of the rope. He jumped again and managed to grab it, this time hanging on tight as the rope bounded and recoiled again and again, making him look like he was ringing an invisible bell. Gellan had to jump a little each time to keep his grip on it.

"Better let go before I do," Gellan said after a minute.

"Just let go and see what happens," Jordan said gamely.

Gellan shrugged and released his grip, and a moment later Jordan was sprawled across the ground.

"That's just the weirdest thing," he said, rubbing his hindquarters. Gellan saw his expression change a little as he stood up. He seemed unnerved as he looked from Gellan back to the ground, then to the air above them. "Are you sure you're normal?"

"Uh, yeah," said Gellan, crossing his arms in front of him. "I'm as normal as you are."

"Or maybe you're as *odd* as I am," Jordan replied with a grin. But when he looked down, the smile disappeared again and he took a step back. "I guess that—well, at least now we know why you trip so much. I always thought it was because you were just clumsy."

"I'm pretty sure that most of the time it *is* because I'm clumsy," said Gellan, shaking his head.

"We'd better go," said Jordan, taking a few steps further away. "This place is giving me the willies. If we stay here much longer, a troll will probably pop out of the ground and grab us or something."

Gellan nodded and looked around for his house key. He found it half-trodden into the dirt. Picking it up, he wiped it off on his jeans as he jogged after Jordan.

"I'll be here for a few days," she was telling Mr. Price, the postmaster, when Gellan walked into the post office half an hour later. She was holding up an ID card. "If any mail comes for me, you are required to hold it here."

Gellan kept an ear trained on the front counter as he checked his aunt and uncle's postbox. He didn't recognize the girl, and in a small town like this, a newcomer was something of interest to everybody.

She was a bit shorter than him with coarse, straw-straight hair hanging long down her back. Her eyebrows were rather thicker than usual, and she had an odd, squished sort of nose.

"Are you traveling on your own?" Mr. Price asked. "You don't look old enough."

"I hope not everyone in this town is too nosy," she said coldly. "As you can see from my ID card, I am an adult."

"Very well," said Mr. Price, slapping a paper down on the counter in front of her. "Fill out this form, please."

Gellan moved toward the counter, pretending to look at the postcards in the revolving rack, and Mr. Price glanced at him knowingly. The corner of his mouth twitched as Gellan strained his eyes sideways. He was just able to make out what she'd written in the "first name" box—*Andrina.* She finished filling it out before he could read any more and whipped the paper toward Mr. Price. Then, taking care to give Gellan a glare, she left the post office.

Mr. Price turned his back to the counter and filed the paper in a cubby on the wall. He let out a sound like a horse blowing as he turned back around.

"Well now, Gellan," he said with a glance toward the door. "How can I help you?"

"I just need to mail a package," Gellan said, "for my aunt." He set his handful of mail on the counter so he could pull the package out of his shoulder bag and hand it over to Mr. Price, who put it on the scale. While the shipping cost was calculated, Mr. Price glanced at the top letter on the pile.

"The Smithsonian Museum Conservation Institute," he read out. "What in the world did you get a letter from them for?"

"Dunno," Gellan said, and he shrugged, but he didn't look at Mr. Price.

He paid for the shipping from a small clutch of cash, then headed back outside and down the main street, keeping an eye out for the strange girl as he made his way home. But he didn't see her at all, and anyway, he was anxious to get somewhere he could read his letter.

He handed Uncle Ivan all the important mail and the change, then went upstairs and dropped a single large, purple envelope on the small table next to the sofa for Aunt Misera, before hurrying to his room and ripping open his letter.

The Smithsonian

46

Museum Conservation Institute
Washington, DC 20560

Mr. Gellan Parker
P.O. Box 844
Ferndale, California 95977

Dear Mr. Parker,

Thank you for your interest in having your historical object identified and properly managed. However, we regret to inform you that the object was either lost or mishandled during shipment, and was not present in the box we received. We hope you are able to locate the missing object, but we cannot take responsibility for its disappearance.

If you happen to have a picture of the object or you are able to provide a detailed description, we would be pleased to help you identify, date, and learn to care for your historical object.

Yours sincerely,

Lawrence Hillman
Director

Gellan smacked his forehead. Of course they didn't think it was in the box! They probably couldn't see *or* feel it—and now he'd lost a section of the mysterious rope for no reason. Though it was amusing to imagine the confusion of someone opening his seemingly empty package, it didn't get him any closer to identifying the rope. Or the strange flashlight.

He grabbed his shoulder bag and stuffed the letter into it, and a few minutes later he was on his bike, the brisk wind blowing away some of the overcrowded thoughts in his head. An hour after he had left the post office, he was pulling himself over the ledge into the cave. He shone his flashlight at the back wall—and his heart nearly stopped. The box wasn't there.

His heart pounding, he ran to the back and swept his light back and forth. When this revealed nothing, he ran his hand along the wall where he knew the box should have been. His hand collided with it at the same time that its shadow suddenly gave it away in the glare of his flashlight. He shook his head, tempted to scold the box for its nonsensical habit of disappearing any time he wasn't touching it.

He pulled off the black shirt and was just about to pick up the box when a loud gust of wind rushed past the cave. He flipped around, but didn't see anything unusual. His first thought was that there might be an approaching helicopter, but he hadn't heard an engine.

He ran to the edge of the cave and leaned out. Almost directly beneath him now, running along the shoreline, was the girl from the post office. But it was what happened next that made him stare.

The girl ran for a few seconds, then jumped and gave a great sweep of her arm. The next moment, she seemed to be sitting on moving air as though she were riding along in a comfortable armchair.

She flew further up the coast, shrinking into the distance, before Gellan came to his senses. He tossed the black shirt back over the box, grabbed his bag, and quickly scuttled backward over the cliff edge.

By the time his feet were back on the ground, she was so far ahead of him that he could only see her by her movement here and there amongst the rocks, though she seemed to be back on her feet, walking along like a normal person. He began to run, trying to keep her in his view while taking care with his footing.

When he finally reached Cramer's Cove, he scooted around a large rock and stopped, expecting to see her only a few yards away—but the cove was empty.

Then he heard a noise behind him and he spun around. She was standing there, pointing a short stick at him in a defensive position.

"How long have you been following me?" she asked.

He stood still, his mouth hanging open.

"How long have you been following me?" she demanded. "What did you see?"

He shook himself a little and then, deciding the truth was best, said, "I only—I saw you jump and float along, like you were... sitting on the moving air... or something," he said. "I wanted to know how you did it."

She stared at him for a moment, and he noticed that one of her eyes floated slightly off to one side. Then, her expression softening only slightly, she dropped her arm to her side.

"I've always been able to do it. Since I was a child," she said.

"Can you teach *me* how to do it?" he asked.

She paused, looking him up and down for a moment.

"No," she said.

"Why?"

She didn't answer.

"How old are you?" he asked.

"Looks like everyone in this town *is* too nosy," she said. She brushed past him, continuing north around Cramer's Cove.

Gellan turned and followed. It was still a good distance back to town, and unless she could magically transport herself, he figured he'd have plenty of time for more questions, whether she liked it or not.

She was walking fast, but since he was taller than her, he didn't have any problem keeping up. They were just about to round the edge of the north end of the cove when they heard the sound of a motor coming from behind them.

A funny expression crossed the girl's face, and she immediately threw herself behind some large rocks. Gellan watched with curiosity and amusement as she scrunched herself in.

"You—get in here!" she snapped at him.

"Why?"

"Just—please?"

Gellan shrugged his shoulders and ducked behind the rock, then leaned over, trying to see through some gaps as they waited for the boat to come into view.

"It's probably just one of the fishermen, you know," Gellan said.

"Fishing boats go out to sea and back," she said, shaking her head. "Patrol boats go up and down the coast."

Gellan didn't entirely agree, but he didn't argue the point.

"What do you have to worry about from patrol boats anyway?" he asked. "Surely it wouldn't matter if they saw us just walking along the shore."

She didn't answer him, and a moment later the boat came into view. Gellan was surprised by how new it looked, especially compared to the boats he was used to seeing in the port at Bayview. He could see two men on deck and one in the pilot house.

"It's unmarked," the girl noted.

Gellan glanced at her, then looked back at the boat. It was nearly out of sight, but he realized she was right—there were no markings on it at all. A shiver ran down his spine.

"Who do you think they are?" he asked.

"More like what do I think they're doing," she said, as the boat completely disappeared from their view.

"Fine," he said, shrugging. "What do you think they're doing?"

"I think they're trying to find evidence of what started Poseidon's Quake," she said.

"Poseidon's Quake?!"

"Haven't you heard of it? It's been everywhere in the news."

"Yeah, I heard about it," he said in a flat tone. "I was hoping people would stop talking about it soon. I don't see why it's such a big deal."

The girl stared at him with narrowed eyes for a moment, then shook her head and strained to peer through the gaps in the rocks as she looked up and down the beach. After only a few minutes, Gellan's legs began to grow stiff from being scrunched, and a bruise was surely forming on his right hip thanks to a protruding rock. But for some reason, he felt like he shouldn't move until she said so—so he stayed put.

She waited what felt like an eternity before motioning for him to get out, and he clumsily shoved himself to his feet, his legs tingling. They continued north, back toward Smuggler's Staircase.

"My name is Gellan," Gellan said after a long time.

"What?" she asked, looking straight ahead.

"I said my name is Gellan."

"Oh." She didn't say anything more, though she quickened her stride without looking at him.

Gellan took a deep breath. "What's your name?" he asked.

She paused, then said, "Drina."

"I don't think I've ever heard that name before."

"No, I don't expect you have," she said. "It's probably not common around here. It's an Italian name."

"Are you Italian?" he asked.

"Part."

"How long will you be in Ferndale?"

"I don't know."

"What are you here for?"

She didn't answer. He sighed. He wasn't used to being the talkative one. He'd always found that people *liked* to talk about themselves, so he only had to ask a question or two of almost anyone before they were off and running.

Just before sunset, they finally reached the top of the cliff. Gellan aimed for Old Jack's shed, but Drina simply started down the road back to town. Gellan climbed onto his bike and peddled over to her, balancing carefully as he slowed to a crawl alongside her.

"Are you going to *walk* back to town?" he asked.

"Maybe."

"How did you get here?"

"Here, meaning...?"

"Ferndale."

"I took the train."

"What train?" No passenger trains came anywhere near Ferndale.

"And I used other methods."

"Well, you can ride on the back of my bike, if you'd like," he said. "It's got foot pegs."

She kept walking.

"And the wind is coming in behind us, so it wouldn't take us too long to get back to town," he added.

She stopped and looked over at his bike. He got off, giving her a chance to look it over. After a moment of consideration, she said, "All right."

Gellan straddled the bike and held it steady as Drina climbed on. She grabbed his shoulders in a rather unnecessarily vice-like grip, but he didn't say anything and immediately set off.

With the wind in their ears, neither of them said anything the whole way back to town. Gellan was just slowing as he turned onto the dirt path that cut across to Main Street when she spoke.

"Did you grow up your whole life here?"

"Yeah!" he shouted, the wind still a little too loud for normal conversation.

Suddenly she pointed, her arm stretched out in front of him. "What's that?!"

CHAPTER FOUR
ACCIDENTAL MAGIC

Gellan stopped his bike, trying to see what Drina was pointing at. "What d'you—?"

She jumped off and walked forward a few more paces, looking straight up into the canopy of the trees. "How long has *that* been there?"

"What?" he asked again.

"Can't you see it?" she asked. Gellan shook his head, and she appeared to be very surprised. "So it's been concealed somehow? Probably from the wynklers," she said. "But then, *you* should still be able to see it."

"Me?" he asked. "Why?"

"Well, I mean... you saw me wind riding," she pointed out.

"So?"

She rolled her eyes at him, the first expression he'd experienced from her that seemed familiar and normal. "Most people don't see that kind of stuff, Gellan."

He cleared his throat. "Erm, what stuff?"

"Magic things. Enchanted things," she said.

Gellan's eyebrows flew upward. "Magic?!" he asked. "As in real *magic* magic? Like spells and fairies and... like in the hobbit books?"

"Uh-huh," she said absently, looking straight up, then around, as though something else might appear.

Gellan looked around too, and then realized...

"Wait a minute," he said. He got off his bike and dropped it, then reached out his hand and waved it around as he neared the familiar spot. His hand made contact with the rope he and Jordan had felt earlier.

"So you can feel it," Drina said. "You just can't see it?"

"*You* can *see* it?!"

"Of course," she said. "You'll probably start seeing more things too, if you can already feel them."

"What kind of things?" Gellan asked.

"The stuff left behind. You know, the remnants, the wisps, the marks."

Though Gellan still didn't fully know what she was talking about, part of him seemed to understand what she meant, and a shiver ran down his spine. "How do I do it?" he asked.

"I... don't know. You just expect it, I guess." She shrugged.

"Expect it?"

"Yeah," she said. "You know it's there. Just expect your eyes to see it."

Gellan looked toward his hand, hanging in the air. For a fleeting moment, he thought he *could* see something there—then it was gone.

"What is it, exactly?" he asked, stepping back and pointing up into the trees.

"I don't know," she said. "It looks like a rope ladder. But one side seems to be caught high up in a branch, so it's tilted. That's why only one side of it is within your reach. And there's a small building up there," she added, pointing. "It looks like it could be an old watchtower or something."

"How come I can feel the... the magic things, when I can't see them?" he asked.

"Well, most people can't feel *or* see them."

"No, I mean—why are my eyes, uh..." he searched for the right word, "...deficient, when my hands are not?"

Drina stopped and turned to look straight at him. "That's an odd question," she said. She seemed thoughtful for a moment, then shrugged. "I don't know. Anyway, it's cold and it's getting late, and I'm hungry, so let's go. How much further is it to town?"

"Oh, just around the bend," he said. "I can take you to wherever you're staying."

"I'm just at the red motel at the end of Main Street," she said as he picked up his bike.

"Well..." He paused for a moment. He had never asked a friend over for dinner before—Jordan had always joined them for dinner without Gellan needing to ask him—and he wasn't quite sure how to do it. But he wanted to have time to ask her more questions. He coughed, his voice catching in his throat. "Would you like to come over for dinner tonight?"

She hesitated, then shook her head. "No. But... thanks."

When Gellan stopped in front of the motel, Drina jumped off and thanked him, then walked away without another word. Gellan arrived home a couple of minutes later, his thoughts reeling. He was pretty sure he wouldn't sleep much that night, even if the little owl didn't wake him up again.

Gellan would have been very interested to know that he was the subject of a letter Drina wrote later that evening. She was in her hotel room when a note flew up from a candle on a small side table.

Dragonfly:
Submit your daily report. Include location and safety information.
–Aeneas

I am safe and well. I arrived in Ferndale, California this morning. I am staying in a small motel in the town for the next couple of days while I scout out the coastal area north and south of here.

There's a boy here that can feel, and sometimes see, magical occurrences. From what I could learn, he has always lived here so it's probably impossible that he's had any training. I only know that his first name is Gellan. Perhaps he should be checked for on The List. He seems old enough to be at Gilsthorne. Was he missed?

Also, there's an odd watchtower here that looks like some of the old huts on Cromllech Island, except that it's high in the trees. It appears to have had some kind of concealment charm used on it, and it looks extremely old. Nothing else yet.

—Dragonfly

No reply came for several minutes. Drina carefully twisted her hair and pinned it in a loose bun on the top of her head, then finished getting ready for bed. She pulled out a book from her bag, set the candle on the nightstand, and climbed under the covers. At last there was a hissing noise, and a paper flew up. She leaned over and picked it up.

You are instructed to obtain more permanent lodging for five or six days—perhaps the hotel you're staying at will allow you to take the room for that long.

Find out everything you can from the locals about Poseidon's Quake, and find out more about the boy. Also, take a picture of the watchtower and send it to us (from the ground—please don't try to climb up there).

Are you keeping up with your homework? Please don't forget to submit your assignments. You'll be receiving a new list tomorrow morning.

—Aeneas

Drina acknowledged the instructions, then immediately turned out the light. There was work to be done tomorrow.

By 7:43 am the next morning, Drina had discovered Gellan's first and last names, the names of his aunt, uncle and mother, where he lived, and what his uncle did for a living. But no one seemed to know who his father was.

"I guess Jane Parker never told anyone," the receptionist at the motel said with a shrug. She was a middle-aged woman named Ingrid with a lovely southern drawl.

"Jane Parker? So she was... Gellan's uncle's sister, perhaps?" Drina asked.

"Now, I don't rightly know," Ingrid said after a long, thoughtful pause. "Could be her husband was Ivan's brother and she kept that last name even after she came here."

"But you don't know for sure?"

Drina was holding a large bowl of oatmeal, courtesy of the hotel breakfast lounge. She was perched on a stool near the desk, where Ingrid was typing away at her computer while she answered Drina's questions.

"No," Ingrid said. "I doubt anyone does. Jane Parker hardly said a word to anyone when she was alive, and she sure don't say anything now, God rest her."

"And Ivan Parker hasn't mentioned it either?"

"Not that I know of," said Ingrid. "I don't think I've ever heard Ivan say a word to anybody, 'less he has to. He never smiles either. He's a funny sort of man. Wears those funny aprons covered with hearts or flowers or smiley faces, but has a face like a sour old donkey. They say he has secrets—he doesn't tell anybody anythin' about his past. They say his wife doesn't even know where he's from or who her mother-in-law is. No one knows why, but there's lots of guesses. Half the time, folks 'round here go into his sweet shop to look at him and wonder about him as much as to buy some of the bread or sweets he sells. There's enough stories floatin' around about him to fill a book— not that it's the boy Gellan's fault, mind," she added, reaching out a hand toward Drina to emphasize the last point.

"Oh, of course not," said Drina. "Erm... how long ago did Jane Parker die?"

"My goodness, it probably hasn't even been ten years," Ingrid said. "Gellan was just a little 'un then."

A hotel guest stopped just long enough to hand his keycard over the counter, and Drina took the opportunity to help herself to another spoonful of oatmeal.

"You can go see her grave, if you're wanting to," Ingrid continued. "I think it's in the graveyard just up from Ivan's sweet shop. Lots of people go there, you know. It's a beautiful cemetery."

Drina's spoon stopped halfway to her mouth and she stared at Ingrid, who gave her a flash of a smile in between her typing. What in the world did Ingrid mean, "lots of people go there"?

"What sort of boy is Gellan?" Drina asked after a long pause.

"Oh, I don't know him so well, personally," Ingrid said. "But everyone knows the Parkers could never keep track of that boy. He just wanders wherever he feels like going. There probably isn't a corner in Ferndale that Gellan doesn't know about."

"Really?" asked Drina, letting the word dangle in the air.

Ingrid took the bait. "Oh yes," she said. "Heaven's sake, one time George Mason found him on the roof of his shop when Gellan was only seven or eight years old. There he was, just sitting there, leaning against the ledge and watching everyone on the street below! George asked him how he got up there—it's three stories up, you know—and Gellan just said he'd climbed! George still hasn't figured out how the boy managed it."

It was getting busier now, and Ingrid didn't have any more time for talking; Drina managed to hold her attention only long enough to secure the room for a full week.

It didn't take Drina long to find a bike rental shop, where she rented a lime-green cruiser. With this new mode of transportation, the first thing she did was to return to the mysterious watchtower to take a picture to send to Roman, before heading to the post office to give Mr. Price her new address and ask if there was any mail for her.

"Strangely enough, there is," he said, handing her a letter. It was addressed to her room at the motel, and she knew it must be written on Hagudash paper.

She thanked him and asked for directions to the Chamber of Commerce, where she grabbed a map of the town. As she biked up and down the streets, she made little notes on the map. She'd never really had a chance to travel for fun, and the sights in Ferndale made her feel like a tourist for the first time in her life. She saw hedges and trees clipped into funny shapes, quaint old houses and shops painted in Victorian style, picturesque scenery created by old-time family farms, and a perfect little park, where she managed to do some homework.

At lunch, she found an old-fashioned sandwich and ice cream shop where people were gathering to talk. She listened to the town gossip while she enjoyed a rootbeer float and a freshly cut ham sandwich.

In the late afternoon, she pedaled down Berding Street toward the cemetery while she snacked on a bag of popcorn in the front basket of her bike. She stopped in front of the heavy metal gates, jumped off the bike, and walked it up the short drive, staring. She'd never seen such a beautiful cemetery before. It was sloped up a hill backed by spruce trees and rhododendrons, and the stonework throughout made it seem more like a garden.

She parked her bike, then shoved the bag of popcorn into her backpack so the gulls couldn't pilfer it, before setting to work wandering up and down each row, looking for graves bearing the name 'Jane'.

There was a Jane Morris (1872–1918) and a Jane Willaims (died Jan. 8, 1764 aged 76 yrs & 9 mos.). She wondered how much of a discount the stonemason had given to the family for spelling 'Williams' wrong.

She was wandering further and further up the hill with no luck on finding 'Jane Parker' when she heard a shout. Looking down the hill, she saw Gellan running up through the maze of paths toward her.

He raised his hand and waved. She waved back stiffly, then turned away and continued her task.

"What're you looking for?" he called to her as he jogged the last few paces.

"How did you know where I was?"

"I saw you bike past while I was doing my chores."

"Hmph. How was school?"

"I'm sure it was good. What're you looking for?"

She looked at him. "What does that mean? Don't you like school?"

He shrugged. "Well enough. What're you looking for?"

"You might want to try being more persistent," she said, rolling her eyes.

Gellan didn't ask again, but he continued to wait, his hands stuck in his pockets; she could feel him staring at her as she moved along the path.

She looked back at him for a long moment, then said, "I'm looking for your mother's grave."

"What?! Why?"

She didn't say anything.

"Well, you won't find it here," he said, crossing his arms in front of his chest.

"Care to lead me to it?"

"No."

"Then I'll just keep looking," she said.

"Fine," Gellan said. "But can you answer some questions for me while you look?"

"Maybe," she said.

"What's your name?"

"You know my name."

"What's your *whole* name?"

She swung around. "What's it to you?"

"Why do you expect *your* questions to be answered if you're not willing to answer *mine*?"

She threw up her hands in frustration. "You know what I think? I think it's a good thing we won't be around each other for much longer!"

He shrugged. "Yeah, probably. What's your name?"

She shook her head and rubbed her forehead. "Fine. It's Andrina

Sarah Morello." She continued walking along, but she wasn't really paying attention to the names on the stones anymore. "Now it's your turn. What's your full name?"

He paused a moment, but apparently decided that fair was fair. "Magellan Dominic Parker."

"Magellan?"

"Yeah. After the explorer."

"Oh. Interesting," she said. "I don't think anybody in town knows your first name is actually Magellan. And how did it become Gellan, and not Jellan?"

"Dunno. My uncle, probably. How old are you?"

"I can't tell you that."

"By orders or preference?"

She shot him a look. "You're quicker than I thought."

He just stared at her.

"Okay, fine. By preference," she said, "since you're not an authority figure. But probably by orders if they knew you were asking."

"Well, then, you *can* tell me."

"How's that?" she asked.

"Because you know I won't tell anyone else. Especially not an authority figure."

"And how would I know that?"

"Because I don't tell anyone anything," he said. "At least not until I absolutely have to."

She turned her back on him and walked away. "I think you're asking too many questions."

"Yeah?"

"Yeah."

"Well, from what Ingrid and Mr. Mason told me, you're asking an awful lot of questions yourself."

She spun around again. "What are you? The town know-it-all?!"

"What are *you*?" he shot back. "A nosy journalist?!"

Drina stiffened, but she didn't give in. "How old are *you*, then?"

"Older than you."

"And how would you know that?" she demanded.

"I don't," he admitted. "But I'm taller than you. And there are girls in my grade who are taller than you. I don't believe you're eighteen."

"Fine," she said. "I'm not eighteen."

"Younger or older?"

"Since that's apparently the main thing you want to know, then FINE—I'm younger than eighteen," she said. "And that's *all* I'm telling you."

He grinned, clearly hugely satisfied.

"But under the government of the jurisdiction where I come from," she said smugly, "I don't have to be eighteen to be considered an adult."

"What?!" he exclaimed. "What d'you mean?"

"Where I come from, the age of majority, or the age at which a person is legally considered an adult, is seventeen," she recited. "*Or, if a person younger than seventeen years of age has demonstrated the ability to make decisions and carry out assignments or there is an exigent circumstance for considering a person to be of age, that person can be given adult status for limited duties and situations.*" She nodded triumphantly and walked on.

There was a pause for several seconds before Gellan called after her, "And which of those three are you?"

Drina turned, grimacing as she shook her head. "Really, Gellan? Does your curiosity know no bounds?" She turned away from him again.

Unfortunately, he was clearly not going to give up yet. He scooted past her and stood against the rock retaining wall of the next terrace, watching her.

"Does it really matter so much?" she asked finally, glancing up at him as she moved closer.

"Yes."

"Why?"

"Because I want to know how you get to do what you're doing."

"Why?"

"Because I want to do things like that too."

"What is it exactly that you think I do?"

"You're some kind of journalist, or... or a scout."

She looked up sharply, and his face broke into a triumphant grin.

"You are, aren't you? I knew it!" he said. "I watched you all day today from the top of the old jeweler's building."

"You were supposed to be in school," she said indignantly.

"I know," he said. "But I wanted to know where you came from and why you're here. So how old are you? Where did you come from? Why are you here? And how did you learn to do the stuff that you can do?"

"You mean the magic?"

"Yeah," he said, "the *magic*." He grinned.

"Lots of people can do it," she told him.

Gellan's face fell. "Lots? As in most?"

"Kind of. Lots of people are born with at least a little bit of it, but for the vast majority of people, it fades quickly. It really only stays strong in a small proportion, but there are still lots of us that can do magic. Pretty much everyone where I come from can."

"Oh." He looked at the ground and scuffed his foot, shoving his hands into his pockets.

She looked over at him. "What's wrong?"

"I dunno," he said. "I just kind of thought it made me different—in a good way—for once. You know, being able to see the magic." He sighed, his shoulders slumped.

She watched him for a moment. "Why does that matter so much?"

He shrugged, and jerked his head in a funny way. There was another pause as Drina watched him carefully.

"Well, maybe if—" She made a sudden pivot, trying to catch him off guard. "What more do you know about Poseidon's Quake?" she asked.

The only noticeable movement was a sideways twitch in his jaw.

"Are you hiding something?" she probed.

"How could I be?" he said after a minute. "It's been all over the news."

"I think you know exactly what I mean," she said. She waited, but he obviously had no intention of letting her silence goad him into saying anything. "Tell me some part of it that you haven't told anyone else, and I'll tell you how old I am," she said.

He looked up. "Who has to tell first?" he said eagerly, before his face fell as he realized his mistake.

"You," she said, and grinned. "You *do* know more, don't you?"

He stood thinking for a minute, staring down the steep hill and out over the Ferndale valley. A fine mist from the sea was blowing over it. A moment later, he turned to look at her squarely, crossing his arms over his chest. "Fine. But if you don't keep your word, I'll not tell you a thing more. Ever."

"Fair enough," she said.

He gave a sharp nod, adjusted the strap on his shoulder bag, and strolled off purposefully down the hill. She stood there momentarily, confused, then decided she'd better just follow.

Just inside the cemetery gate, Gellan grabbed his bicycle and took off, with Drina only a pace behind him.

The truth was that he had no intention of telling her anything of significance, but he knew he had to make it *seem* like he did. His mind raced the whole way down Lost Beach Road toward the coast, desperately thinking of some important-sounding nothing he could tell her in exchange for the information he wanted, but he was coming up blank.

He parked his bike behind Old Jack's shed, set off down the Smuggler's Staircase, then headed south along the base of the rocky cliffs. He walked for several minutes before stopping—he didn't want to go much further, or he'd be too near Cramer's Cove.

He cleared his throat and looked around. "I was near here when a wave of jumping fish came rushing by," he said. "Then after that, the whole ocean was full of jumping fish and there were birds everywhere." She stared at him. "I was soaked through just from the spray," he added for good measure.

She looked up and down the coast. "From which direction did the wave come?"

"Erm... I'm not sure," he said.

She looked sideways at him. "You won't tell me, you mean."

He kept his face still. He didn't want her to read any answers in it. "Your turn," he said.

"From which direction?!" she snapped back.

He kicked the ground. "I don't know!"

He stomped off, kicking a few pebbles into the ocean as he went. He'd had just about enough of her. Why couldn't she act like a *normal* person?

He stopped some distance away and looked back at her. She had a stick out and was waving it around in small gestures, peering past it like she was shining a flashlight into the nooks and crannies of a shadowy old house—only it was broad daylight and she was pantomiming into thin air. He couldn't imagine what in the world she was doing—

Then a thought occurred to him and he did a double-take.

"Drina, what is that thing?" he asked.

She ignored him.

"Drina, what *is* that?!" he repeated as he jogged over to her.

"Is that the question you want answered in exchange for the non-existent information you gave me?"

He thought for a moment. "Yes."

"It's my wand," she said, distracted as she peered past him.

"A wand? As in a magic wand?!" he asked.

She nodded, still poking her way along the beach.

"Would it work for me?" he asked eagerly.

"Not likely," she said.

He stuffed his hands into his pockets and turned away. She twiddled her wand in her hand for a moment, watching him. She looked around carefully, and then, to his astonishment, she held the wand out.

"All right, then," she said, "since there's no one around, I guess we could give it a try. I'll teach you a simple spell. Just hold it down to your side for a second."

His eyes widened, and he carefully reached out and took it. "Which end do I hold on to?" he asked, testing out both.

"The end I handed to you. The thicker end."

He oriented the wand in the correct direction, then carefully hung his arm at his side, holding the wand gingerly as though it would break.

"Okay, this is just a spell that gives off a bit of a spark," Drina said. "And remember, it might not even work at all. I think you might have a bit of magic in you because you can feel certain things, but it might not be enough to actually... well, I guess we'll see."

Gellan nodded eagerly.

"You say 'ill-loo-min-ARE-ay,'" she said, "and you give it a small swing, kind of like you're throwing a frisbee straight up."

"Illuminare," he practiced, his arm still at his side. "Illuminare. Illuminare." Several orange-yellow sparks shot out of the end of the wand, and Gellan jumped back with a yell.

Drina looked surprised. "Um, that's a... good sign." She sounded uncertain. "Well... now bring it around, like this, and swing it up and out."

Gellan mimicked her movement a couple of times. He just *had* to get it right and show her he could do it. He took a deep breath, positioned himself, and with more gusto than he intended, said, "Illuminare!" as he flung his arm in a large, sweeping gesture.

A huge gush of sparks shot out of the wand and flew high into the sky, bending out over the ocean. Even in the daylight it seemed very bright. Gellan and Drina both stood rooted to the spot, watching it until it slowly flickered and died far out to sea.

Gellan glanced at Drina. She had her hands over her mouth; she looked bewildered and slightly frightened. She dropped her hands and looked over at him.

"I didn't think—or I never would have—"

From far off they heard the sound of a motor in high rev, and

Drina gasped. "Oh no!" She grabbed the wand out of Gellan's hand and began to run. "Come on!"

Gellan didn't understand why she suddenly seemed so afraid. "What?" he shouted as he jogged after her, adjusting the strap of his shoulder bag.

"Gellan, come ON!" She looked back at him, and the expression on her face spurred him forward.

She rounded the corner to Cramer's Cove where they'd hidden before and shoved herself behind the rocks. He jumped in behind her, and she grabbed his jacket and pulled him in tighter. A boat came into view seconds later, heading south. It seemed to be the same unmarked boat they'd seen the day before.

"Who are they?" Gellan whispered, his heart pounding in spite of his insistence to himself that there really was nothing to worry about.

"I don't know," she said, "but we simply must *not* be seen here. Or anywhere near here. Not after your—oh gosh, I can't believe this— what are they going to say?"

"Who are you—?"

"No questions," she hissed. "If I'd known—"

The boat vanished from sight, but Drina refused to let Gellan move for several minutes. Then, just as she was saying, "Okay, I think maybe—" she stopped and grabbed Gellan's jacket to keep him from moving. The sound of another boat was approaching from the south. They watched as it came into view, going much more slowly, followed by the first boat they'd seen.

When the two boats had finally disappeared, Drina turned and looked at Gellan.

"Gellan," she whispered, "I think we could be in serious trouble."

"Trouble as in detention kind of trouble?" he asked.

She shook her head. "No. I think we could be in danger. There are certain people who are desperate to find the starting point of Poseidon's Quake, and—and whatever may have set it off. They may think that your flare—well, it might just make them think—anyway, we've got to get away from here. Do you know of someplace we can go?"

"Can't we just go back to town?" Gellan asked.

Drina paused for a moment, then shook her head again. "I doubt it. If they have someone patrolling the coast like that, they've probably got someone monitoring the roads by now too. If they see us heading away from the beach—no, I don't think we'd better try. We need a place where we can hole up for a bit without being so cramped like we are here. We could be stuck for a few hours."

Gellan was quiet. He knew just the place, but he didn't want to take Drina there. The box was hidden there, and he was quite sure she'd be able to see it. But he couldn't ignore the gut instinct telling him she was right—they needed to get away from here.

"All right," he said finally. He looked at his watch. "The sun will set in about fifty minutes, and it'll be fully dark about forty minutes after that. Do we have that much time?"

"I don't know," she said. She cleared her throat nervously. "No, I don't think so."

"Well, let's get as close as we can before nightfall. It'll at least get us away from here," he decided. "We need to head further south anyway, and there are lots of rocks along the way, so we can hide as often as we need to."

"Where are we going?"

"To the cave where I was yesterday, when I saw you go by," he said.

"I didn't see a cave anywhere along there."

"I know," he said with a goofy grin.

Drina gave him a tentative smile. "All right, then," she said. "Check carefully, and then we'll make a run for it. If you hear or see anything at all, don't hesitate a second to hide behind the rocks again. Thank goodness they're plentiful along here."

He nodded in agreement and, after checking up and down the coast, began shifting himself out. Once they were free of the cramped space, they both craned their necks in every direction, including straight up, but they didn't see anyone.

"All right," Drina said. "Go, go!"

Gellan turned and started running as fast as he could along the beach, his legs feeling prickly and uncomfortable. As they pounded across the sand, he noticed that Drina managed to keep pace with him, even as he sped up.

It was a good four minutes before they heard another sound. Gellan dove behind a large rock, and Drina followed. They both pulled their hoods over their heads and waited silently until whatever was causing it came into view.

This time it was a large, black helicopter, and it was flying very low. Through gaps between the boulders, they could see three or four people inside it. One side door was open, and a man was scanning the beach with a pair of binoculars, one leg hanging out.

Gellan drew in a sharp breath and pulled his hands into the sleeves of his jacket. "Wow, they really are serious about all of this, aren't they?"

"Gellan," Drina whispered, "we're going to have to be very, very careful."

"If they've got helicopters, I don't think even the cave will be hidden from them," he said, his heart sinking.

"Don't worry about that," said Drina. "I can definitely protect us there, as long as we can beat them to it."

"Should we just stay here?"

"We could be stuck for hours. And besides..." She was quiet for a minute. "No, I definitely think we should try to make it to the cave. Then we'll only have one opening to guard against. Presumably."

"Okay, we're not far now," said Gellan. "But it takes three or four minutes to climb to it. And I don't know if you—"

Drina chewed her lip. "We'll have to risk it. Once we get there, I don't think they'll be able to find us. It's our best chance now."

The helicopter was nearly out of view. As soon as it disappeared, Gellan extricated himself as quickly as he could and ran full out down the beach. After another three minutes, they were at the base of a familiar cliff.

"This is it!" he said.

They heard another engine and ducked behind some rocks. The sound was deep and bellowing, coming from further out to sea. After a moment, Drina seemed to realize something; she pushed herself out.

"Gellan, I think we've run out of time. It's up there?" she asked, pointing.

"Yeah!" Gellan shouted.

"Then climb! Fast!"

CHAPTER FIVE
THE CAVE

Gellan grabbed at the rocks and Drina followed right behind him, mimicking his hand and footholds. Gellan had never felt afraid when climbing the cliffs before, but this time he did. He also had never climbed so fast.

A great bellowing blast hit them, and at that moment, as Gellan reached for Drina's hand to guide her to the next handhold, he felt a great wave of fear wash over him. Suddenly, feeling like he was whirling, he found himself kneeling on the floor of the cave just inside the opening with Drina at his side. Not sure what had just happened, and trying to keep away the nausea of fear, Gellan grabbed the rope and pulled it into the cave, and they immediately moved backward into the darkness.

Shaking slightly, Drina pulled out her wand. She took a deep breath and then said "Visia obstructinum," swinging her wand around in front of her in a broad, clockwise movement, as though she was tracing the edges of the cave entrance.

Gellan saw a slight haze appear across the whole entrance of the cave. Drina dropped her arm and sat down slowly, her legs shaking. It was silent for several seconds, except for the sound of their ragged breathing.

"Are you all right?" Gellan finally asked.

"I'm fine," Drina said, her forehead on her knees. "You?"

"Fine. What is that thing?" he asked.

"It's called an obstructos," she said without looking up. "It's like a one-way window—we can see out of it, but they can't see in. It works against everyone, including witches and wizards."

"But they'll still see a big black opening where the cave is, won't they?" Gellan asked.

She shook her head. "No. From the outside it'll look like whatever it's touching. So in this case, it'll look like the rocks of the cliff, making it indistinguishable from the rest of the cliff face."

"Oh, cool!" Gellan said. It was silent for a moment, and then he gasped. "Drina, look!"

She looked up, and inhaled sharply just as another booming blast sounded around them from an enormous ship that was just coming into view. A large helicopter was landing on its deck at the same time another one was lifting off. The second helicopter rose up, blocking the setting sun from their view for a moment, and then zoomed toward the shore. Gellan watched as it drew closer and closer. It seemed to be angling straight for them.

"Uh, Drina," he said nervously, "are you *sure* they can't see us?"

"Positive," Drina said. But she slid backwards a few more inches into the darker shadow of the cave.

A short distance from the shoreline, the helicopter turned south. Gellan let out a long breath, and Drina passed a hand over her face.

"Now that we're safe," she said after a minute, "we need to start thinking about phase two."

"Meaning?"

"Our bikes are parked behind that shed," she said. "They could find those and connect them to us, especially since mine is a rented bike. And what if your uncle or aunt reports you missing when you don't turn up at home? Or someone notices I haven't been to my room at the motel? We need to get in contact with people and get some things taken care of."

"Uh, how exactly are we going to do that?" Gellan asked.

"I'll show you," she told him. She held up her wand and said, "Leuf." The tip of her wand lit up, filling the cave with light. "Here, hold this," she added, handing the wand to Gellan.

He held it gingerly, glancing toward the back of the cave where the box was still hidden in partial shadow. He hoped Drina wouldn't notice it until he could find a way to hide it better.

She shrugged off her backpack and opened a small zipper on the top. She reached in and pulled out a candle, set it on the stone floor in front of her, then took out a pen and some paper. The paper had an official-looking letterhead in the top right corner, bearing her name:

Andrina Sarah Morello
Cremstoll Scout

She tapped the note and the letterhead disappeared; then she scribbled out a quick note, her hand still shaking slightly.

Aeneas:
Urgent. Confidential.
—Dragonfly

She held the paper over the candle. Gellan wondered what in the blazes she was doing—and then gasped as a flame reached up and sucked the paper into it. A small puff of smoke slowly unfurled.

"What in the world was that?!" he exclaimed.

She looked at him. "It's a communication candle," she explained. "It's connected to Roman Roberts—he's the one I report to. It goes from my candle through to his."

"Oh, right," said Gellan. "Totally normal. A candle sucks a piece of paper in and ejects it miles away out of another candle."

She blinked at him. "Well, yeah. It's a pretty simple thing, really.

But—I guess I forget how odd it seemed to *me* when I first saw them work. So yeah, they're kind of strange."

"Why do you sign it as Dragonfly if your name is on the letterhead?"

"I'm an... I'm not a... Scouts all have code names, and fully qualified scouts wouldn't use the letterhead."

"Then why do you use it?"

"I'm not saying anything more about it right now. I need to focus."

Before a reply even came, she began writing another note, explaining their situation. Gellan watched a helicopter swoop by, followed by a boat on the water below. He was beginning to appreciate the first-rate view they had of the spectacle unfolding in front of them.

After only a couple of minutes, the candle hissed and a paper unfurled out of the momentary flame.

Dragonfly:
12, 2. Proceed.
—Aeneas

Gellan read over Drina's shoulder as she finished writing.

Aeneas:
I am with the boy, Gellan Parker, in a cave about two miles south of Lost Beach Road, adjacent to the town of Ferndale, California. I do not believe we are in immediate danger, having secured ourselves in the cave. However, a magical flare was accidentally sent up about forty-five minutes ago, and a couple of patrol boats immediately started canvasing the area, along with a couple of large, black helicopters. All are unmarked, so I don't know who they are.
A few minutes ago, shortly after we made it to the cave, a large frigate came into view from the southeast.
I need further orders and instructions. I don't dare leave this cave until we are sure it is safe.

I also believe it is imperative that certain things are taken care of to remove suspicion about either Gellan or myself. Our bikes are behind a shed near a house at the top of the cliffs, and Gellan's uncle needs to be informed that he is safe. His name is Ivan Parker and he should be at his sweet shop, "Sweet Pickings." Also, I had secured a room at the Red Motel for a week, and if someone notices that I haven't turned up it may arouse suspicion, so my records there need to be erased.
–Dragonfly

"Thanks for leaving out the fact that I was the one that sent off the flare," Gellan said.

"It's superfluous to the situation now," she said as she sent the message.

Another note arrived after only a couple of minutes.

Are you sure you're safe and well-hidden? Do you have your scout pack with you? Is it fully stocked?
We are sending someone immediately to remove your bikes and make contact with Gellan's uncle. Do NOT leave the cave.
–Aeneas

Yes. Yes. And yes.
Understood.
–Dragonfly

"How long do you think we'll be here?" Gellan asked.

"I don't know," said Drina, sending the last message.

"But you say your pack is fully stocked. Stocked for what?"

"Survival," she said. "Scouts are required to keep everything that might be required to survive any situation with us at all times. I tend to overpack, but in this case, it means we'll be fine. Even comfortable, thank goodness."

"Overpack?" Gellan glanced in disbelief at the scrawny backpack.

A sly look crossed Drina's face. "Didn't you ever watch *Mary Poppins* as a kid?"

"Yeah..." Gellan said slowly.

"Well, *she* had a carpet bag. *I* have a backpack. That's pretty much the only difference."

"Can I see?"

"Not yet," she said. "There's no point in unpacking things until we know more."

The sun dipped below the horizon, and they watched as two rowboats landed on the beach some distance north of them. About a dozen people immediately disembarked and began scouring the beach with flashlights. Each carried a second tool in their other hand —some were holding what looked like the prodding sticks Gellan had seen fishermen use; others carried a hammer or a trowel.

About ten minutes later, the candle spouted another note.

Dragonfly:
You are required to stay where you are until further notice. It will be at least several hours until we can rescue you. Two senior scouts have arrived in Ferndale. Your bikes have been found and removed, and your records have been erased at the Red Motel. They are now heading to Gellan's uncle's shop to inform him of the situation and advise him on what we feel is best. We obviously cannot give orders to Gellan, but we would ask him to write to us and let us know if he would please agree to stay where he is. We believe it is imperative for his safety, and yours.
–Aeneas

Drina nodded grimly as she read the message. "Well, I guess we're stuck here, at least for the night. I hope they get things sorted out with your uncle soon, or he might raise the alarm."

"Oh, he won't worry about me for at least two or three hours yet," Gellan said. "I made a crockpot dinner and did all the chores I could before I followed you to the cemetery. So he'll just think I'm intending to get back late."

"Oh, thank goodness," she said, looking relieved. "That buys us more time. In the meantime, *do* you agree to stay here until we have more information?"

Gellan looked out of the cave. Three more rowboats had landed, and the beach was swarming with people.

"Yeah," he said. "I really don't see any other good option."

"Then here," she said, handing him a piece of paper. As he took it, he saw with a start that the official letterhead had changed. It now read:

Gellan Parker
Citizen of Ferndale

"Nice," he said. "I suppose that's totally normal too?"

"It's Hagudash paper," said Drina. "It updates itself when it detects new information."

"Interesting," said Gellan. He swapped her lit wand, which he was still holding aloft, for the pen she was offering him, and wrote:

Yes, I'll stay put in the cave until we get more information. But please let me know when someone is able to meet with my uncle, and what he says. Make sure they tell him I'm all right and I'm safe.

"How should I sign it? You're using a code name."

Drina thought for a moment. "Roman will know it's you because of the letterhead, so maybe you'd better not sign it at all."

Gellan nodded, then watched curiously as the note was sucked out of his hand.

"Well, that's that," said Drina. "And since we're going to be here for a while..." She shoved her wand back at Gellan and hauled her backpack closer, reached in, and began pulling things out in quick succession. Two canteens of water, two tents, several pillows, a large lamp, a couple of sleeping bags, something that looked quite like a camping toilet...

Gellan's mouth hung open as she continued to pull out items—a couple of pans, some utensils, some textbooks, a puzzle...

"Uh, what's the puzzle for?" he asked.

"That's for you," she said. "You might need something to do to keep yourself busy if we're in here for too long. Unless you don't think you'll go crazy stuck in a space the size of a kitchen?"

"Oh, right. Thanks. What about you?"

"I've got homework I can work on," she said, pointing to the textbooks. "I got a new list of assignments this morning."

"Homework? For what?"

She looked at him like he was daft. "*School.* What else?"

"What school do you go to?"

She shook her head, and he knew she didn't want to answer.

"Is that everything you've got in there?"

"Of course not," she said, arranging the lamp off to one side. She took her wand from Gellan to tap the lamp, and a warm glow filled the cave. She handed the wand absentmindedly back to him as she reached for more things to organize. "This is only the stuff that we need so far. Scouts always carry enough supplies for three or four people. But as there's just the two of us—anyway, we'll have plenty. Oh"—she realized Gellan was still holding the lit wand—"we don't need that light anymore. The spell to turn it off is *duwn.*"

"Um, considering what happened when I—" Gellan began, uncertainly.

"That was a doing spell," she said. "This is an undoing one, so you should be fine." Still, he noticed that she didn't look away until he'd successfully turned the light off without causing a catastrophe.

She took her wand from him and shoved one of the small tents into his hands. "Here, set this up for yourself."

He began pulling out the rods and fitting them together, and it was a moment before he realized that she was just standing there, watching him.

"What?" he asked.

She didn't reply, but grinned and then pointed her wand at the bag that held her tent.

"Convenio," she said, and the tent sprang out of the bag and into place.

It was very small—barely big enough to fit a single person with a pillow and a sleeping bag.

"How about you do that for my tent?" he asked.

She tapped her chin thoughtfully and Gellan thought she was going to say no, but then she pointed her wand at the rods in his hand and said, "Convenio." The rods jumped out of his hand, and a moment later his tent was fully assembled.

"Thanks," he said. He nudged the tent with his toe, then grabbed the top rod with his hand and gave it a little shake.

"It's perfectly sound," said Drina, rolling her eyes.

"I know," he said. "I only—I was just making sure."

She turned her attention to something else, and on the pretext of arranging his tent 'just so,' Gellan dragged it toward the back of the cave until it sat right in front of the wooden box that was covered with his black shirt.

He enjoyed a very short moment of satisfaction before he heard Drina say, "So was it you that hid that thing in this cave? Is that why you didn't want to bring me here?"

He froze, then slowly looked around at her. She glanced over at him as she arranged her sleeping bag in her tent on the other side of the cave.

"Now I know for certain that you *do* know more than you're saying," she said, turning to face him.

Gellan tried to arrange his face into a look of innocence, but knowing he was failing miserably, he turned and busied himself with grabbing the other sleeping bag and rolling it out in his tent.

A rumble of thunder echoed out at sea, and the wind picked up as they set up camp for the night. They both paused in their work and looked outside when large drops of rain began to fall. Gellan watched in amazement as they trailed down the cave entrance like drops on a windshield.

"Wow!" he said, walking forward and reaching tentatively toward the obstructos. He waited for Drina to stop him, but she didn't. His hand went through a cold object until he felt raindrops. He withdrew his hand and watched the drops sliding and merging with one another—the effect was mesmerizing.

"Wow," he said again. "I have *got* to learn how to do some of the things you do."

"Just don't stick your hand through it in the broad daylight," said Drina. "They'd be able to see it."

"Could they come through it, if they knew it was there?" he asked.

"Magical people could," Drina said. "So let's just hope that there are only non-magical people out there. But really, I doubt anyone would be climbing the cliffs the way you do."

"Can they hear us talking through it?" he asked.

"Not unless it's a very loud sound that would vibrate through it," she said. "But since it's essentially rock on the other side, it'd have to be very, very loud."

It was quite dark now, and as Gellan took in the view once more, he could just see a helicopter landing on the frigate as the downpour of rain increased.

"I'm glad we don't have to worry about getting wet," he said. "I don't mind being cold, really. Not for one night anyway. But I hate being wet."

He glanced over at Drina. She was near the front of the cave, arranging food, plates, and utensils on a little side cupboard she'd just pulled from her backpack.

"Not used to camping much?" he asked. "I hope you didn't forget a sink so we can wash the dishes."

She didn't reply and he assumed she was rolling her eyes at him again, but a moment later, he smacked his forehead as she pulled a small sink out of her backpack and arranged it next to the cupboard.

"Do you know how to cook?" she asked him.

"Yeah," he said, "I do."

"Really?" She seemed genuinely surprised.

"My uncle started teaching me as soon as I was old enough to lift a spoon," he said, shrugging.

"I'm not great at cooking," she admitted. "I'll keep things tidy and do dishes if you do the cooking."

"Deal," he said. "I'll get something going right now—I'm starving. So, what've we got?"

He held back a chuckle as he scanned the options. She had several boxes of pasta and a couple of jars of pasta sauce, a bag of rice, some fruit and vegetables, potatoes, pancake mix, jam, peanut butter, cartons of juice, cooking oil, and a loaf of bread.

"Well, they certainly make sure you don't go hungry, whoever your people are," he said, rolling up his sleeves. "Any preferences?"

"Nope," she said.

As he looked through the supplies, trying to decide what to make, he suddenly felt how strange all of this was. He was about to cook a homemade meal in a cave high above the ocean where they were stuck because he'd accidentally done some magic—which he hadn't even known he *could* do until about two hours ago. The events of the last couple of days seemed absolutely implausible, yet here he was.

He cleared his throat as though that would also clear his mind, then picked up a pan and drizzled some oil into it. He set it on the odd stove Drina pointed to and looked it over, trying to work out how to turn it on. Drina reached over with her wand and tapped it, muttering something indistinguishable, and it immediately glowed red.

"Uh, thanks," he said, watching it for a few seconds.

"Just tell me if you need it to be hotter," she said, turning back to what she was doing.

"Drina, could I ask you—?" he began as he grabbed an onion and set to work chopping it.

"Ask me what?" she returned when he didn't finish his sentence.

"It's just—yesterday, when I saw you flying. How do you do that? Is it easy to learn to do?"

"It's not flying," she said. "That's different. Where I come from we call it wind riding, but out east I know they have a different name for it. I think they call it breezing or something like that."

"Is it hard to learn to do?"

"Not the basics of it. But it *is* hard to keep it going for more than a few seconds," she said. "I'm still not very good at it. When you saw me go past, I was practicing. It would make traveling a bit easier for me if I could do it better."

"And most people don't see those kinds of things?"

"They could see me jump and when I land, but not in between. Not when I'm actually wind riding. But most people don't *really* look, and they tend to see what they *think* should happen anyway."

"That seems kind of dumb."

"Even witches and wizards do it too—sometimes in reverse ways. It's nobody's fault, really; our brains can only process so much. Distraction is a powerful weapon. So is disbelief."

She rummaged in her bag for a moment and pulled out a pair of binoculars. She used them to look up and down the coast, and then out to sea.

Gellan glanced up at her as he minced some garlic cloves. "Anything?"

"No," she said. "I guess they've stopped patrolling for the night. Probably because of the rain more than the darkness."

She dragged the toilet to the back of one corner of the cave, then pulled a curtain from her backpack, which she attached to the cave wall around the toilet with a tap of her wand at each corner, saying, "Adhero."

She was just checking the edges of the curtain to ensure full coverage when the candle, which was still sitting in the middle of the cave, ejected a note. Being the nearest, Gellan grabbed it and read it out loud.

Gellan's uncle has been notified. The senior scouts were able to give him Gellan's handwritten note, which helped a lot.

Gellan paused, wondering how *that* conversation had gone. "*Mr. Parker, we'd just like to inform you that your nephew, Gellan, is stuck in a cave high up on the cliffs. But don't worry, we got this note from him through a candle.*" If only he could've seen Uncle Ivan's reaction.

He continued reading:

One of the senior scouts has been able to observe the activities in the area and believes that it is primarily a contingent of the National Guard of the

U.S. Government. We don't know for sure yet if you'd be in danger if you were discovered in the area, but we feel certain you did the right thing by finding a place to hide until we know more.
Send further information immediately, even if you think it is trivial. Any small detail may be important.
–Aeneas

Drina pulled out a piece of paper to write a reply.

"How did the senior scouts get to Ferndale so quickly?" Gellan asked as he poured water over some dehydrated meat.

"There are several of us heading up and down the coast at the moment," she said. "When I notified them of our situation, they probably sent out messages immediately to all the other scouts, asking for their locations, and the two that were closest to us were sent to help us."

"But they still might've been miles away," said Gellan. "I mean, how did they actually get to Ferndale itself so quickly? And then down to the cliffs to get our bikes? And then how did they get our bikes away without being noticed?"

"They appeared there, took the bikes, and left."

"Uh... how—?"

"You disappear from one place and reappear in another."

"You can do that?"

"*I* can't," said Drina. "Not yet, anyway. It's tricky, and dangerous if you get it wrong, but it's by far the quickest way to travel in situations like this. But Roman said he sent two senior scouts, so they are likely able to do it just fine. Anyway, be quiet for a second, would you? I need to write a reply."

After she sent it off, Drina sat thinking for several minutes. Gellan saw a funny look cross her face as she stared out of the obstructos.

"What?" he asked. "What's wrong?"

"Is that... *thing*... important?" Drina asked.

Gellan hesitated. He didn't know what to say.

"Technically it's my duty to inform them about things that are important," she said, looking over at him.

He opened his mouth to speak, but she held up a hand.

"But unless you say anything specific to me, I have no *real* reason to think it's important. And I've learned enough to know that there are very specific laws that govern the ownership and responsibility of magical objects."

Gellan's curiosity teeter-tottered with his natural reserve inside his head. Now that he knew magic existed, that thing *did* seem to be a magical object, and she was the only other person he knew who could see it and possibly tell him what it was. But... could she be trusted? He wasn't sure yet.

"How do you know it's definitely a magical object?" he asked.

"Because of the blue light," she said.

He started and looked back toward the box as he scraped the pan to keep the onion and garlic from burning. "*Is* there a blue light?"

It was her turn to look surprised. "You can't see it? How on earth did you—" Then she shook her head. "Never mind, don't tell me. I don't want to know." But she seemed very perplexed.

"Who are those people we're writing to?" Gellan asked as he chopped some potatoes. "Why would they send you so far out on your own?"

"It's partially because these are extenuating circumstances, and partially because that's just how things are where I'm from."

"And where is that, exactly?" he asked.

She hesitated for a moment before answering. "It's... called Cremstoll."

"Is that top secret information?"

"No, it's just—we don't usually talk about it with other people, but it's probably fine for me to tell you that. And anyway, nobody else would believe you if you tried to tell other people about it, and you wouldn't be able to find it on regular maps."

"Why?"

"Just because. I'm not explaining it right now." She worked a table and two chairs out of her backpack and set them off to one side right at the front of the cave, then placed the candle in the middle of the table.

"What's it like there? In Cremstoll."

"It's an odd place," she said. "But... it's wonderful too."

"Well, *that's* enlightening," he said sarcastically, but she didn't offer any more information. "Did you grow up there?"

"No."

"When did you go there? Did you have to find it?"

Silence.

He sighed and watched her untie the rope from the rock at the back of the cave. She used her wand to shift the rock more to the center of the cave. Then she pointed her wand at it and said, "*Ferveate calore.*"

Heat immediately began to emanate from the rock, quickly filling the whole cave.

"*You* might not mind being cold," Drina said, "but I do. I don't like being wet *or* cold."

"Is that thing safe?" Gellan asked.

Drina looked at him. "How would it not be safe?"

"What if it gets too hot? Could it—I dunno—set our tents on fire or something?"

"Of course not," Drina said, rolling her eyes. "It's called a fire-stone..." She trailed off, then chuckled and said, "Oh. But no, even though it's called a *firestone*, it doesn't actually make fire. It's more like a... like a..." She crinkled her face and tilted her head to one side. "I forget the word—oh yeah, it's like a *radiator*. Anyway, it's perfectly safe. We use them all the time at Gilsthorne."

"Gilsthorne?"

"Oh!" She put her hand to her mouth. "Well, I guess it probably doesn't matter anymore if you know. Gilsthorne is the school I go to. In Cremstoll."

"Why would it potentially matter if someone knows?"

"Well, it's not exactly something we broadcast: Hello, world, there's a school for young witches and wizards to learn how to control their magic and do different things with it. Yeah, normal people would just *love* that."

Gellan stared at her for a moment. "You're serious? It's really a place? That's really what you do there?"

She shrugged. "Yeah. Along with math and other stuff, of course —but no more questions," she said quickly as he opened his mouth. "I've had enough of them today."

He hunched his shoulders and turned back to his work. A few minutes later, he was putting a steaming pan of meat and potato hash on the table. They both sat down and he filled their bowls, then foraged through the cupboard until he found the bread.

"Butter?" he asked.

She shook her head. "No, sorry," she said, her mouth already full.

He joined her at the table and began to eat, trying not to stare as she wolfed down the first bowlful, then helped herself to second and third servings.

She finally noticed him watching her and shrugged. "I mostly just eat sandwiches when I'm out on my own," she said. "I told you I didn't know how to cook very well, and it's so nice to have a hot, home-cooked kind of meal again." She motioned toward the rain pelting on the obstructos and grinned. "I just didn't expect my next one to be in a cliff high above the ocean."

CHAPTER SIX

ESCAPE

ellan woke early the next morning. Only a hint of light was detectable through the canopy of his tent. He sat up and rubbed his eyes. He'd slept more soundly than he usually did. The sleeping bag was wonderfully soft and comfortable, and the cave was filled with that kind of warmth that surrounds you and gently seeps into your body.

He unzipped his tent and looked over at Drina's tent, which was still shut tightly. He got up, walked over to the obstructos, and looked outside. He could see fuzzy shapes amidst the thin morning fog, one of which was surely the large frigate still anchored some distance offshore. He squinted toward it—both helicopters appeared to be gone.

He leaned as close as he could to the obstructos, trying to see up and down the shoreline. He still couldn't see the helicopters anywhere, but he was surprised to see several groups of people already spread out along the beach. It looked like one person was even climbing the face of the cliff about a hundred feet north of the cave.

Some figures were wearing the same beige camouflage uniforms many had worn the night before. But several others had joined them, and most of these were in dark gray uniforms with masks covering the lower half of their faces. The rest were in civilian clothes, some with white lab coats over their clothing.

Gellan grabbed the top of Drina's tent and shook it. "Drina, I think you should wake up and see this," he said in a hushed voice.

She immediately unzipped her tent and got up, trying to wipe the sleep from her eyes. She shook her head in amazement as Gellan pointed out his observations.

"Gee whiz," she said, bemused. "You don't do anything by halves, do you? No, sir. You've got to send up a flare bigger than any I've ever seen and bring half the National Guard here, haven't you... I don't know what in the world is going on," she went on after a moment, "but they must want to find something pretty bad."

She saw Gellan glance toward the back of the cave.

"Is it that thing?" she asked. "Is that what they're looking for?"

"I don't know," he said honestly. "I don't even know what it can do." He pointed to the people in the gray uniforms. "Are they part of the National Guard too?"

"I don't think so," Drina said. "I have no idea who they are. But..."

She trailed off, and Gellan looked over at her. "What?"

"I just... I had no idea how much this all would... I just wonder if you'll need to get away from here for a while. Maybe go to Cremstoll with us, or something."

"Go to *Cremstoll*?" The possibility seemed both wonderful and horrible. "What would I do there?"

"Go to school, make friends, have adventures, get in trouble," Drina said. "You know, all the stuff you do here."

"Very funny," said Gellan. "But where would I stay?"

"Gilsthorne School has dorms."

"Oh." Gellan sighed. He didn't know what he wanted to happen anymore.

"I thought you'd be happy about that idea."

"I am. Sort of. I'm just not sure..."

88

Drina looked at him for a moment, but she didn't pursue it any further. They continued to watch the scene below as one man barked orders, his mask contorting with his face and his chest expanding like a bellows, a double stripe of black running diagonally across his chest.

"Who d'you think *he* is?" Gellan asked.

"Dunno," said Drina. "He probably thinks he's the boss or something. I mean, see that guy there?" She pointed to a man in a camouflage uniform. "I thought he was in charge last night, but now that these new guys have shown up... I think I'd better tell Roman about those—those gray guard people. I think they may be a different group altogether."

She scratched out a quick note and sent it, then joined Gellan back at the obstructos.

"I'm starting to think you're probably safer here than you would have been even at home," she said after a while. "The whole town knows that you roam these beaches more than anyone else. Especially now that those gray guard people have shown up—I wonder if they would've taken you for questioning, just on a whim, to see what information they might be able to get from you."

Gellan hadn't considered that. Surely they wouldn't have... would they? A shiver ran down his spine.

"I'm going to make breakfast," he said, turning away.

While he flipped pancakes, a note from Roman arrived. He repeated that they were not to move or show themselves in any way. He told them that the two senior scouts in Ferndale had reported that the town was inundated by troops in dark gray uniforms and that they were working to figure out who they all were.

Then Drina paused as she read the note, and Gellan looked up.

"What?" he asked.

"Nothing," she said, setting the note aside.

"I know that's not all," he said. "Either you read it to me, or I'll read it."

"They just—it's says that they..." She stopped again. He looked at her pointedly and she returned his gaze sadly. "They raided your uncle's shop. And the apartment. Apparently there was some... some damage done. But it does say your uncle and aunt are unharmed," she added quickly.

"What?!" He ran over to her and grabbed at the note, reading the last couple of paragraphs. Anger surged up his throat. His uncle had never hurt anyone. Why in the world would they have done this? It wasn't Uncle Ivan's fault—he had nothing to do with any of this!

He tossed the paper aside. Drina picked it up and stowed it in the folder where she was keeping all the notes.

"I'm so sorry," she said. "But I have to admit, I'm glad you weren't there when they came looking for... you, or whatever else it was that they were looking for."

He shrugged. He didn't want to talk about it. Part of him wished he *had* been there; maybe then they would've left his uncle's shop alone.

He was just setting the finished pancakes on the table when a shadow fell over his face.

"Drina!" he said in an urgent whisper.

She whirled around, and he pointed to a pair of black boots leaning against the top of the obstructos.

"It looks like one of them is rappelling down the side of the cliff," she said.

"Will it hold?" he asked nervously.

"I think so," said Drina. "It should. I'm pretty good at the obstructos spell. And he hasn't slipped through it, so he's not a wizard..."

It was the oddest thing, watching someone slowly jump their way down what appeared to be thin air. The man was nearly eye-level with them when Drina said, "Oh!" and hastily pulled out her wand.

"Drina, wait! What're you doing?!" Gellan hissed.

"Don't worry," she said. "I'm just going to take a picture of his uniform so I can send it to Roman. It might be useful in helping to identify them."

She pointed her wand at the man and said, "Sollus imago." A blue light shot out, swirled up and down, and then reentered her wand—

all within a split second. She pulled out a piece of the letterhead paper, pointed her wand at it and said, "Scripto imago." The blue light reappeared, this time carrying the image of the man, and planted itself onto the paper.

Drina wrote a quick note describing how she had gotten the image and sent it off to Roman. Then they watched the man continue his descent until he reached the bottom.

"Thank goodness," Drina said, passing one hand across her face. "Well, let's eat. I'm hungry."

"It's a good thing smells can't go through that thing," said Gellan as he popped open the syrup, "or he might've known we were here."

They spent the rest of the day keeping themselves busy with watching the people on the shore, sending notes to Roman, reading his responses out loud to each other, and trying not to get on each other's nerves. Neither of them seemed able to settle down to anything, though Drina had her school books spread across the table and Gellan tried to work on a puzzle of a strange red bird. It didn't help his already-agitated state that the puzzle pieces kept shimmering with fire as he was holding them, making him drop them with a start, though he was never actually burned.

"It's a picture of a firebird," Drina said, when he snorted in frustration. "What d'you expect?"

Gellan couldn't tell if she was joking or in earnest. When it happened again, he gave up on the puzzle and decided to make an afternoon snack for them both. Drina had brought plenty of food, and he thought it might as well be used.

The afternoon wore on slowly. Gellan noticed Drina had a habit of picking at her fingernails while she was thinking, and she was quick to point out that he cleared his throat a lot.

It was late in the day when a long note came, informing them that Lydia Driscoll, one of the senior scouts, had visited Uncle Ivan's sweet shop and repaired some of the worst damage. Lydia hadn't dared repair it all, in case the troops came calling again; it might have raised suspicion.

She had had a lengthy discussion with Uncle Ivan, who had eventually agreed to a plan proposed by the scouts, just as Drina had surmised—to have Gellan taken to Cremstoll until the whole thing settled down, with the stipulation that they arrange a way for Uncle Ivan to see Gellan before they left.

"...and it says that further details on our rescue will be forthcoming," Drina finished reading aloud.

She looked up at Gellan, seeming surprised at the look on his face.

"What?" she asked.

"I'm being *sent* to Cremstoll, whether I like it or not," he said. "How do I know I can trust you people any more than I can trust the ones out there?"

At first, Drina looked stung. Then her face became angry, before settling into a frown. At last she gave a small sigh.

"You're right," she said. "You *don't* have any reason to trust Roman or me or anyone else from Cremstoll. But those people out there"—she pointed toward the people demolishing the beach with shovels and pickaxes—"definitely have some kind of agenda, and I *know* you'd be in danger if you stayed here. But"—she shrugged—"just like any other place, you will find some good and even great people in Cremstoll. You'll also find some horrible and awful people. And then there are a lot of people that are in between."

She paused, rereading the note, apparently thinking.

"And I know I probably don't have to say this," she suddenly said, "but if I were you, I certainly wouldn't mention *that* thing"—she pointed to the back of the cave—"to anyone."

"Yeah. I've been wondering what to do about that," said Gellan. "I don't dare leave it here. And I don't know how I could possibly take it with me to Cremstoll." He shook his head in frustration.

"Is that what has you so worried?" she asked.

"That's part of it."

"Well, let me think on it," she said. "I'm sure we can come up with something."

After they'd eaten dinner, Gellan watched as the sky grew darker and the sun went down. He had never been stuck in such a small space for such a long time. His arms and legs felt irritable with restlessness, and it was all he could do to not snap at Drina.

It appeared that he hadn't succeeded because Drina decided to go to bed early, shutting herself in her tent with a book and the light of her wand, leaving Gellan sitting alone near the front of the cave.

He watched the moon shine variably on the ocean through shifting cracks in the clouds. He could hear occasional shouts and yells from the people outside, but he hardly cared what was going on out there anymore.

He wished more than anything that things could go back to normal, the way they had been before he'd found that horrible wooden box. He had the fleeting thought that if he found a way to destroy it, all of this nonsense might stop. But he knew he didn't have the courage to do that; in the back of his mind, he felt it was the best proof he had that he was special, like Drina, and he didn't want to destroy that feeling. He also had a small thought that the box, and the object in it, had reached out specifically to him, and that made him responsible for it.

No, that was silly. But then again—why else would the rope have entangled him?

Was he sure it *had* actually wrapped itself around his ankle? Maybe he had gotten himself caught in it somehow. And why would it have happened now, and not before? He had roamed these beaches for years. Maybe it had just picked the next person that had walked by, and maybe he was supposed to give it to someone else...

"Right," he said to himself. "Exactly who else did you have in mind?"

No, there was something that told him Drina was right. That thing was his responsibility now, whether he liked it or not.

A familiar chirrupy hoot interrupted Gellan's thoughts, and he saw a small black shape shifting its feet on a narrow ledge of rock off to one side of the cave mouth. The little owl was a welcome sight. The big black eyes turned to face him, and he was quite sure it could actually see him.

He reached out, slowly moving his hand through the obstructos, and it stood there, blinking slowly as he stroked its chest. A moment later it was gone, off to find itself some food. He sighed and sat back, longing to be able to fly away from this situation himself.

After a very long time, he climbed into his tent and zipped it shut, hoping they would find a way to escape the cave the next day.

First thing the next morning, Drina handed Gellan a note she'd written.

In order for me to return to Cremstoll with Gellan, I am requesting a full discharge from this scouting mission.
–Dragonfly

"There," she said. "What do you think?"

"Why would you want to be discharged from the mission?" he asked.

"It's the only way I can think of to solve the problem of that thing," Drina said. "And anyway, my time is almost up. I was only supposed to be gone for a maximum of three weeks."

"I'm not following," Gellan said, looking at her blankly. "How does you being discharged from this mission solve the problem of what to do with that thing?"

"As a scout for Cremstoll, I am under a strict obligation to obey and fulfill orders of any mission I am commissioned to do. One of those orders is to tell them everything I learn that I know or believe is relevant to the mission I was sent on. And that thing," she said, pointing, "may be relevant. I don't know yet. But once I'm discharged from this mission, you can tell me more and we can figure out what to do, *without* me being under obligation to tell them about it."

"So you don't trust them either?" Gellan asked.

"It's not that I don't trust them..." Drina hesitated. "I just don't want to be *obligated* to tell them about it. That's why I need to be discharged."

"Couldn't you just not tell them about it without being discharged?" Gellan asked. "It isn't really a—"

She shook her head. "No, definitely not. Using magic is a responsibility, Gellan. Magic has effects on you that are stronger than the effects of actions committed without magic. I am under a magical contract to fulfill all my duties as a scout. Breaking a contract, failing in one's obligations, being dishonest, or anything else like that, has effects on everyone, whether they're magical or not. But for those of us who *do* use magic, the effect is stronger."

"What kind of effect?"

"Well, it's like—" She stopped, thinking for a moment. "You'll see people in Cremstoll whose physical features themselves have degenerated. It's like you can see a grayness, a... a shadow beneath their skin." She shivered. "It really is awful. That's why I have to be strictly honest in everything I do. And you will too, especially if you *do* choose to use magic. So just keep that in mind."

She held the note up to the candle and Gellan watched it disappear.

It took a long time for Roman to write back, but finally a note unfurled itself from the candle.

Dragonfly:
Your request is approved. You are immediately released from your obligations related to this mission, and you are only required to perform the necessary duties to help effect the rescue of yourself and Gellan. We are still working out details. I'll send you further information as soon as I can.
—Aeneas

Drina nodded in sad satisfaction as she read the note aloud.

"Well," she said, "that's that."

"So now what?" asked Gellan. "Why haven't they gotten us out of here yet? You'd think that people who can do magic—"

"I don't know," she said. "I was wondering that too, to be honest. Maybe it's a trickier situation than they thought. But they could also be..." She was lost in thought for a moment before she shook herself back. "Anyway, it gives us time to figure out what we're going to do. About that thing."

Gellan had been trying to come up with something all morning; he still hadn't decided how much he wanted to tell Drina. She was watching him as if she could see the debate going on behind his eyes.

She coughed, then said, "I'm fourteen."

"You're fourteen what?" Gellan asked, not really listening.

"I'm fourteen years old," she said.

"You're *fourteen*?!"

"Yeah, I turned fourteen a few weeks ago. In December."

"How in the world do you get to be a scout when you're just fourteen?!"

"That's how they do it where I'm from. And anyway, this *is* a bit unusual. They don't usually send us off on such long missions. But given the circumstances... and I guess they really think there's something important about—"

"Why are you all of a sudden telling me this? I've been asking you for three days!"

"Because now I can."

"Oh. Meaning I can tell you things now too." He crossed his arms in front of his chest.

"Only if you choose to. You know I won't press."

"But *you* want me to."

"To be honest, I don't think you have many other options," she said with a very practical air. "I don't think anyone in the rescue party should know about that thing, no matter who they send. We definitely shouldn't leave it here. And I don't think you can manage to conceal it on your own without me. But I need to know some basics about it before I figure out how to do that."

"Conceal it?"

"It emits a faint blue glow. Other witches and wizards, like me, will be able to see that immediately," she said. "I need to figure out if there's a way for us to hide it and conceal that light, at least long enough to get it to a safe place in Cremstoll."

"*I* can't see a blue glow. Are you sure anyone else will?"

"Definitely," Drina said. "I don't know how strong the magic is that's causing that. But the people I work for are highly trained in magic. So, either by training or natural ability, they would surely see it. I mean, I'm not *that* great a witch myself, and I saw it immediately."

Gellan considered all this, pacing back and forth in front of the obstructos for several minutes. At last, he heaved a great sigh and made his decision. He walked to the back of the cave, pulled off the black shirt, and brought the wooden box back to the table where Drina was sitting.

"I found it the day that Poseidon's Quake happened," he said. "In fact, I... I think it might have been what set it off."

Drina drew in a breath. "What?! Why do you think that?"

"Well, when I pulled it out of the water—it was submerged in a tidepool in a large rock—the fish in the tidepool started going crazy. And then one of them jumped, and the next thing I knew, the whole ocean behind me seemed to be filled with jumping fish."

"Oh my gosh," she said, covering her mouth. "You really *did* set off Poseidon's Quake. I'm really, really glad you didn't tell me that before now!"

"I'm just *guessing* I did," he said. "Or this thing did, anyway. But I have no idea what it is. I brought it straight here to the cave. It had these leather straps on it, and I managed to get one of them off, and then this piece slides up."

He slid up the piece of wood, exposing the object inside.

"What in the world is *that*?!" she whispered.

"I don't know," said Gellan. "I was hoping you could tell me. But don't touch it. It lights up when you touch it."

"It lights up?"

"Yeah. I just barely touched it and it made a light that was so bright that—"

"Put the lid back on it, would you?" Drina said. She looked uneasy.

He slid the lid back into place. "So *now* what do you think we should do?" he asked.

"I don't know." She was rubbing her forehead, as though massaging her brain physically would squeeze an answer out of it. "There's a spell that—no, I don't think that would do it... But even if —perhaps if we—but is that safe enough?"

"There was a rope attached to the box," said Gellan. "I tried sending a piece of that to the Smithsonian Institute to have the fibers identified and dated, but they said there was nothing in the box. They weren't able to see it. *I* couldn't see the rope either, until it wrapped itself around my leg and tripped me."

"It *wrapped* itself around your *leg*?" she repeated, shock spreading further across her face.

Gellan nodded.

"And you sent a piece of the rope to the Smithsonian Institute?! Oh no! I only hope no one puts two and two together, or recognizes your name or something—"

She was wringing her hands and pacing back and forth now.

"If we could just get it there, somehow, then—but wait! If it wrapped itself around your leg, that seems to indicate—" She stopped, spun around, grabbed her backpack, and started rummaging in it. "I've got one of those 'hidden pocket' bags," she said, pulling out a pair of socks and tossing them aside. "The bag, and everything in it, should be concealed when you're wearing it."

"Really?" asked Gellan. "That sounds promising."

"It's just a basic one," said Drina, dropping a dish towel on the ground and sticking her arm back into her backpack. "I don't know if it'll be enough, but it might work. If we could just get it to Cremstoll safely, then we'd have time to think of something else more permanent. The thing is, the bag only conceals things that are in your full and honorable possession." A scarf made its appearance. "That's the other potential problem—I'm not entirely sure that thing *is* in your full and honorable possession, but I would hazard a guess that it *is*—and anyway, the hidden pocket will tell us one way or another."

"And if it is in my, uh... full and honorable possession... will the bag hide the light from other people too?"

"I don't know. But it's worth a try," she said. "Here it is."

She pulled out a silky, emerald-colored bag with a long drawstring.

"I'm giving this to you, so it's yours now," she said.

"No, really, you don't—"

"I'm sorry, but I have to," she said. "The bag has to be yours if this is going to work. That way, when it contains *your* objects and *you* are wearing it, everything in it should be invisible and undetectable by everyone else. Do you agree to accept this bag?"

He nodded, taking it reluctantly from her outstretched hand.

"Like I said," she went on, as she put the other items back in the backpack, "it's just a basic one, but let's try it."

Gellan picked up the wooden box. "Should I put it in by itself or with the box?" he asked.

Drina considered a moment. "I think you'd better put it in with the box. We can't leave the box here, and I don't think we should destroy it. By destroying it, you might 'inform' the object"—she made quotes with her fingers in the air—"that you don't want it or that you reject your possession of it, since the box appears to be made specifically for that thing. It'll be a bit bulkier for you, but I think we'd better take the whole thing."

Gellan shoved the box into the bag and pulled the drawstrings tight before looping it over his neck. Nothing seemed to happen, but when he looked up at Drina, she looked positively gleeful.

"It's gone, Gellan!" she said. "It worked! The bag, the box, the light —it's all gone!"

"Wait, really?" he asked. He looked down at the bag. It all felt rather anticlimactic somehow, but he certainly wasn't going to complain about that after all the overexcitement they'd had. "It'll flop around if I don't—maybe I'll try—hang on—"

He stuck it inside his shirt. Then, unsatisfied, he walked behind the curtain, took off his shirt, put one arm through the loop of the drawstring, and arranged it so it sat just behind his right arm, before putting his shirt back on.

He stepped out from behind the curtain and turned, holding out his arms. "What do you think?"

"It's great!" she said, with a thumbs-up and an eye-crinkling smile.

———

It was growing dark outside once more when a note flew up from the candle. They raced for it; Drina got to it first and snatched it away from Gellan's reaching hand. She smirked in triumph, then read it aloud.

We are sending Professor Jameson Wilkes to retrieve you—

"Oh my gosh, they're sending Professor Wilkes?!"

"Who's he?" Gellan asked.

"He's a teacher up at the school for some of the older classes, and he also does some work under Lieutenant Governor Sedargren. He's a very accomplished wizard—probably one of the best in Cremstoll. But as an underage scout, I'm under Governor Faulkner. So if they're sending Professor Wilkes—" She stopped mid-sentence.

"Then what? What doe you think it means?"

Drina shook her head. "I don't know."

She continued reading.

Based on what the Senior Scouts have discovered, the Gray Guard, whoever they are, is planning on blowing up sections of the cliff tomorrow morning. Apparently they've decided that whatever they think set off Poseidon's Quake is better off being destroyed rather than being in anyone else's posses-sion. We haven't yet figured out what exactly they're looking for, but we have to focus on getting the two of you out of there at this point. We must effect an escape tonight.

Drina, as soon as you can after it's fully dark, remove the obstructos and embed your signall in the rock just above the cave. Be sure to pack every-thing and don't leave any trace of your stay there.

Wilkes will retrieve you from the cave with a pocket bubble and take you to where a sky pod will remove you from the area. Gellan will be taken to see his uncle briefly and then you'll both be brought to Cremstoll.

We would like you to leave behind the stellamore that you should be carrying with you. Plant it somewhere in the cave where it can be found, but try to make it look like it wasn't planted there.

When Wilkes arrives, make SURE you BOTH enter the pocket bubble immediately.

–Aeneas

Gellan was left with more questions than answers, but Drina seemed to comprehend it all because as soon as she finished reading the note aloud she threw it onto the table and began grabbing things and forcing them into the backpack.

"They're mad. This is crazy. How in the world did we end up in such a crazy, ridiculous—"

She continued her tirade as Gellan picked up the note and began rereading it. He couldn't make any more sense of it than he had the first time around.

Drina finally paused for a moment and straightened up. "You could help, you know," she said.

"Right. Sorry." Gellan stowed the note in the folder with the others, then started moving things next to her so she could easily reach them and put them in the backpack.

"What's a pocket bubble?" he asked after a few minutes.

"I've only been in one once," Drina said. She grimaced. "It's not the funnest thing in the world, but basically, it's like a miniature room that someone carries in their pocket. You can jump into it and be carried for a short time. I expect they were trying to figure out a different way to do it so they didn't have to actually send a person into the area. But I guess they didn't manage to—" She paused. "Even though *we* know you've got enough magic, *they* don't, and I kind of don't feel like telling them that. Yet. So, I guess the pocket bubble is the best option we've got," she concluded with a shrug.

"Is there any way they *could* get us out of here without actually sending someone?" Gellan asked.

"Well, there are a handful of ways. But most require magic beyond what I can do, and none are really feasible or less risky. We'd better hurry."

It took them ten more minutes to pack everything except for the lamp. They walked back and forth, double and triple-checking to make sure they hadn't missed anything.

"Are you sure that's everything?" Drina asked. "No litter or anything?"

"I think so," Gellan said, "unless you've dropped a bobby pin somewhere. My aunt uses those and I'm always finding them in the oddest places around the house."

"I don't generally use bobby pins," said Drina. "I have to use bigger clips with my hair."

"Then I think we've probably got everything," he said.

"All right," said Drina. "Now we just have to plant the stellamore."

"What *is* a stellamore?" Gellan asked.

For answer, Drina stuck both of her arms deep into her backpack and carefully pulled out an object about the size of a fist, wrapped in leather. "*This* is a stellamore," she said, carefully pulling back the flaps of leather before setting the whole thing in his hands. It was heavy for its size, and he could feel a slight buzz through the leather. "Just be careful not to touch it, or you'll get a small shock."

It was an odd, crystal-like object that looked like a large, uncut diamond, but the surface appeared to be slightly rough, like a fine sandpaper. He turned it this way and that, watching sparks of different colors issue back and forth inside it.

"What in the world—?"

"It's just a tool, really," Drina said. "In the hands of witches and wizards it can be used for several different purposes, but for anybody else, it'll just be a funny stone with an electrical charge that eventually dissipates and dies out."

"And exactly *why* are we supposed to leave it here?" Gellan asked.

"Well, presumably they're hoping the wynklers will find it and think that this is what they're looking for," she replied, pulling out her wand and moving the firestone back to where it had originally been. "And come to think of it, because it has those sparks inside it, it's perfect. They might even think it's what caused the flare."

"Win-klers?" Gellan asked.

"Non-magic people," Drina said. She reversed the heat spell on the firestone, and the temperature in the cave dropped noticeably. "Let's plant the stellamore back here, by this rock."

Gellan handed it to her, and she carefully used the leather wrap to shift it where she wanted it to sit. Then, using her wand, she blew dust from the floor of the cave to lightly coat the stellamore, making it look like it had been there for years.

"Why do you call them wynklers?" Gellan asked.

"It's what they've been called for hundreds of years," she said as she shoved the leather wrap into the backpack. "There's a handful of different stories about it. The one I've heard most often—let's see—I think the 'wyn' part comes from the letter 'w' because you can't tell magic people from non-magic people just by looking at them, just like you can't tell the two halves of a 'w' apart." She formed a 'w' shape with her two thumbs and forefingers to demonstrate. "So back when Cremstoll was first founded, the non-magic people living there were called the wyns.

"And then, several decades later when Cremstoll was more protected and hidden by spells and stuff, the wynklers, or wyns, weren't supposed to be able to find it anymore. But every now and then, a few non-magical people *did* find it—no one is quite sure how. And the funny thing is that they were almost always from... uh, hang on..." She tapped her wand thoughtfully against her forehead, her eyes overbalancing her head to the right. "It's that place that's north in Europe, but it's not a country? It's a group of countries—you know —like Norway and... and..."

She looked at Gellan for help, but all he offered was a shrug.

"Well, anyway, pretty much all the non-magic people who lived in

Cremstoll at that point were from Norway and countries like that, and so the 'kler' part was added, because it comes from their language or something. And that's how they became known as the 'wyn-klers.' Now we just use that term for all non-magic people."

"Am I a wynkler?" Gellan asked.

"Are you kidding?!" Drina shook her head at him. "You're definitely a wizard—you'd *have* to be to produce a flare like you did."

Gellan turned away so Drina wouldn't see him grin. He had been wondering if he could call himself a wizard or not—it seemed a very presumptuous thing to do—but now she had done it for him.

Drina turned off the lamp and shoved it into her backpack, leaving the cave dark as well as cold. Still, Gellan felt a bit sorry to be leaving it.

"All right, I think that's it," she said as she stuffed the candle into a pocket on the inside of her coat. From another pocket, she pulled out a small egg-like object. She tapped it with her wand and said, "Leuf."

Nothing happened.

"What's that?" Gellan asked.

"It's my signall," said Drina. "Only those with magic can see the light."

"*Is* there a light?" Gellan asked.

Drina held it up. "Can't you see it?" she asked.

"No," Gellan said, his heart sinking. "I can't."

"Really? You're a funny one."

"So much for being a wizard," he said.

"You're still a wizard," Drina said. "It's just—I guess your magical talents are in other things."

"So that's what you're going to use to let Professor Wilkes know where we're at?" Gellan asked, motioning toward the signall.

"Yeah," she said. "But at the moment, there's still a lot of them out there, *and* the moon is nearly full. I don't dare take down the obstructos."

They both stood and watched the shadowy outlines of dozens of people in the bright moonlight. Nearly every person had a flashlight, making the beach look like an upside-down sky, especially with the reflection of the moon hanging in the ocean just past the breakers.

"We'll have to wait," Gellan said. "We have until morning. I doubt they'll work all night. And it's cloudy here more often than not, especially at this time of year. I bet the moon will be covered soon."

They spent the next couple of hours watching, waiting, doing jumping jacks and other exercises to keep warm, and trying not to fall asleep. It wasn't until past midnight that they could no longer see anyone on the beach—either by moonlight or by the tell-tale beams of flashlights. They watched and waited for several more minutes, just to be sure.

Eventually, Drina carefully pulled out her wand. She glanced up and down the shoreline one more time, then waved her wand in a counterclockwise direction as she whispered something. The obstructos disappeared.

"Gellan," she whispered, holding out the signall to him, "I need you to hold it up to the rock. I'm not quite tall enough to reach."

Gellan jumped forward and grabbed it from her hand, holding it squarely in the center of the rock above the cave.

Drina put the tip of her wand up to the small gap between the rock and the signall and whispered, "Adhero."

Gellan slowly let it go, making sure it was good and stuck. Then they retreated into the cave, their backs to the side wall. Drina kept leaning out for a moment to glance nervously up and down the shore. At one point, a familiar little hoot resounded and a small rush of wings fluttered past.

About ten minutes later, they heard a whooshing sound and a large gust of wind swirled past the cave. Drina's hand closed on Gellan's wrist in a vicelike grip; her hands were very cold.

A moment later, a large black man was rising up on the wind and planting his feet on the ledge of rock at the opening of the cave. Without a word, the wind still swirling around him, he held out a glowing glass orb about the size of a tennis ball. Drina dragged Gellan forward as she squeezed her eyes shut tightly, and he felt himself being sucked into the pocket bubble.

CHAPTER SEVEN
CREMSTOLL

A moment later, Gellan felt like he was hiding in a very small glass cupboard.

He tried to say something, but his lips wouldn't move. He saw Wilkes snatch the signall off the rock, though the image was distorted. Then they began to rise higher and higher toward the top of the cliff, and Wilkes put the pocket bubble in his coat pocket so that all Gellan could see was the inside lining.

The next few minutes felt very long to Gellan; he had never really been prone to motion-sickness, but this was an entirely new experience. They rose and fell at intervals, though much more gently than Gellan would have expected if Wilkes had been running, so he could only assume they were still wind riding. Drina's fingers seemed to be unable to release their tight grip on his wrist, and he was beginning to lose feeling in his hand.

Then, all of a sudden, the motion stopped. Gellan heard a "chink" sound on the surface of the pocket bubble, and Drina pulled him with her as she pushed herself out into the fresh night air.

Gellan coughed and took a deep breath, then looked around. It was too dark for him to recognize his surroundings. He was about to speak when an enormous hand was placed over his mouth. Glancing up, he could just make out Wilkes shaking his head at him.

Wilkes grabbed Gellan's coat at the nape of the neck and bodily moved him forward through the trees while Gellan desperately, though unnecessarily, attempted to keep his feet underneath him. Drina was already several paces ahead of them.

Gellan couldn't figure out what she was aiming for, but a moment later he could just barely make out a large, strange object under the canopy of the trees. As they came closer, he found that it looked something like a sleek, aerodynamic, metal-and-glass carriage, though it seemed to have misplaced its wheels.

Drina ran toward it, pulled open the doors, and jumped inside. As Wilkes (and Gellan) reached the carriage, something moved on top of it. Gellan just managed to get a glimpse of a very large creature with a rider sitting astride it before he found himself being thrust through the open door. The way this was all playing out was not making him any less nervous about agreeing to go to Cremstoll, and he wondered if it was too late to back out of it.

Before he could, however, Gellan found himself squashed into the corner on the same bench as Wilkes while the doors swung shut. The carriage immediately began to lift off the ground, the only sound coming from the whoosh of very large wings pulling against the air.

Gellan braced himself as they careened across the sky; he could alternately see stars above and the shadows of the trees below as the carriage swung around. A few minutes later, he saw the lights of Ferndale at an angle below them. Then they were swinging back and forth like a slowing pendulum as they were gently lowered into the trees some distance from the cemetery.

Gellan felt the bottom of the carriage hit the ground, and the large creature settled onto the roof with hardly a sound. None of them moved for several seconds, and the stillness became so quiet that Gellan thought he could hear the crinkle of the mist of his breath unfurling.

Then Wilkes took out his wand and held it straight up in front of him. Holding the bottom quite still, he rotated the top of the wand in a small circle. Gellan's eyes widened as four ghostly-blue shapes appeared. He recognized himself huddled next to two other shapes that were obviously Drina and Wilkes, beneath the shape of whoever was guiding the sky pod.

The shapes faded and Wilkes let out a heavy breath.

"There's no one nearby," he said very quietly.

It was the first time someone had spoken since they'd left the cave, but it was the deepness of Wilkes' voice that made Gellan start.

They sat and waited. Gellan started shivering, and he noticed that Drina was also shaking from the cold.

After a few minutes, they heard a soft tap on the roof. Wilkes quickly held up his wand and repeated the same spell. This time, two more shapes appeared on the side closest to the town. Wilkes slowly eased the door open and stuck his head out. After a minute, he turned to Gellan.

"It's Lydia, with your uncle," he said. "Come on."

He opened the door of the carriage and stepped out, lighting the tip of his wand. Gellan could just barely see his uncle, who seemed to be managing the back end of his old trunk and attempting to keep up with a woman who was leading the way toward them at a fast pace, carrying the front end of it.

As soon as they were within whisper-distance, the woman hissed at Wilkes, "Turn it down!"

The light on the tip of Wilkes' wand was immediately reduced so low that Gellan could barely see anything at all. The woman pulled the trunk (and Uncle Ivan) over to the carriage and shoved it inside. Then she marched Uncle Ivan back to Gellan.

Gellan didn't like any of this. He knew the woman was probably just doing her job, but his uncle had had enough to deal with over the last few days. He again considered refusing to go to Cremstoll, but... he really wanted to be able to do what Drina could do. So he gritted his teeth and settled for glaring at the woman—which of course she couldn't see in the darkness.

Uncle Ivan stood in front of Gellan for several moments, neither of them saying anything. Then Uncle Ivan cleared his throat, stuck his hand into his pocket, pulled out a pen and a pad of paper, and handed them to Gellan.

"These are so you can write to me," he said quietly, still somewhat breathless. "This lady here"—he jerked his thumb at her—"is going to do some kind of connection thing with candles."

"Right," she said, stepping forward and withdrawing two plain gray candles from her pocket. She arranged them so that Gellan and his uncle each had their fists around both candles—right fists on top and left fists on the bottom.

Then, waving her wand in a circular motion over the loop of their arms, she said, still in a whisper, "Velox loqueris." In the residual light from the spell, Gellan saw that the candle in his right hand remained a muddy gray, while the left one had turned a deep green.

"Let your right hands go," Lydia instructed. "The candle you are left with is your connection to the other person."

"Apparently we can send notes to each other through these things," Uncle Ivan said, looking at the gray candle.

"I think you know how to use it by now?" Lydia asked Gellan.

He nodded in reply. "Do you know how long I'll be gone?" he asked, sticking the green candle into his shoulder bag.

"Dunno," said Uncle Ivan. "I guess until all this funny business passes. These people think you'll be safer there than here for a while." He shot a look at the woman, as though he was having the same reservations as Gellan.

"He will be," Wilkes said. Gellan glanced up at him. There was something reassuring about his voice, and Gellan gave his uncle a half smile.

Uncle Ivan's mustache twitched, then he stuck his hand into his other pocket and pulled out two small pastry boxes. "For you and the girl," he said, handing them to Gellan. "I hope she likes them."

Gellan felt like he would've liked something else, perhaps a good-bye hug from his uncle, but he didn't know how to ask for one. So he just reached out and took the two boxes.

"Thanks," he said, looking down. "Uncle Ivan, I'm sorry about all this. I'm sorry that they damaged your shop and the apartment and— is Aunt Misera okay? Are you all right?"

"Never mind, never mind," Uncle Ivan said gruffly, sweeping one arm back and forth. "This Lydia here said she would fix it all in a few days, so no harm done. And don't worry about me or your aunt—we're fine."

Gellan let out a large breath. He had been worrying about how in the world his uncle would be able to fix the damage *and* run the sweetshop without him there. But if Lydia took care of it all, he knew Uncle Ivan would get on fine.

"Now, listen," his uncle continued, "if I don't hear from you for more than three days in a row, I'll find this Crummyshell place and bring you straight back. Understand? So make sure you write every day or two. Unless, of course, you *do* want me to come get you." He shot another look at Wilkes and Lydia.

Gellan swallowed hard, then nodded. "I will."

"Time to be going," Wilkes said. "Mr. Parker, Lydia will escort you back. Just go about your business as usual over the next few days, and try to make sure lots of people see you working in your shop and just doing what you normally do. If anyone asks where Gellan has gone, give them as little information as possible."

Uncle Ivan reached out and patted Gellan on the shoulder, paused for a moment more, then turned to follow Lydia back toward Ferndale. Gellan heard a loud sniff from him as Wilkes swept a huge arm around him and guided him back to the carriage.

Gellan hesitated as he climbed in, turning to watch his uncle plodding away until he became indistinguishable in the darkness. Then he was in the sky pod once more, sitting on the same bench as Drina, since his trunk was taking up the spot next to Wilkes.

As soon as the doors were shut, they felt themselves rising once more. The lights of Ferndale came into view as they cleared the tree line.

They flew over the town, heading north, and Gellan watched familiar shops and roads and houses disappear behind them. He saw several dark shapes skulking around the edges of town and wandering through the alleyways, but none of them seemed to pause and look up at the strange spectacle in the sky.

After a few minutes, Gellan settled back into his corner, feeling very tired now that most of the worry had gone. He felt Drina tap his arm and looked around at her. She was holding out a pillow, which he took gratefully. Then he remembered the little boxes his uncle had given him; he picked one up off the bench next to him and handed it over to Drina.

"Here. My uncle said this was for you. It's probably some of the puff pastries he makes for his sweet shop," Gellan said.

"Really?!" She took the box from Gellan and held it to her nose.

Gellan smiled as she carefully opened it and examined the contents with delight.

"Will you tell your uncle thank you for me in your first letter?" she asked.

"Sure," he said.

Gellan realized that Wilkes was looking at them, and he held out the other box to him. Wilkes waved it away graciously, but Gellan insisted.

"I've had so many of them, sir," he said. "I don't like them so much anymore."

Wilkes smiled at him and accepted it. "Thank you," he said, his deep voice resounding in the small space.

"How long will it take to get there?" Gellan asked as Wilkes opened the box.

"About four hours," said Wilkes, putting an entire chocolate puff pastry in his mouth. He enjoyed it for a moment before continuing. "We should arrive shortly before sunrise. Try to get a little rest, if you can. I'm sure tomorrow will be a long, busy day for you."

Gellan bunched the pillow behind him as best he could and tried to find a comfortable way to recline, but the wooden box seemed to poke him no matter which way he sat. When he finally managed to find a decent position, it didn't take long for the gentle rocking of the carriage and the steady whooshing of air to lull him into a light doze.

He slowly drifted off to sleep, his dreams as full as his thoughts had been.

Gellan woke some time later, his neck kinked and his legs stiff. He glanced over at Drina—she had the pillow on her lap and was bent over it, fast asleep. Rubbing his neck, he looked out of his window. The moon was close to setting on the western horizon, and its light was spread out in a long path across the ocean. He craned his neck to look out of the other window; he could see the coastline some distance off.

Wilkes spoke quietly. "We're more than halfway there now. Our macrodon is making good time."

Gellan looked up at him—the professor's large eyes seemed luminous in the darkness. "Macrodon?" he asked.

"It's the creature that's carrying us," said Wilkes. "You'll see him when we land."

"Who's the person riding him?" Gellan asked.

"Her name is Jillian Clark," Wilkes said. "She's one of the most skilled trainers we've ever had. She requested to be the one to come."

"Why?"

Wilkes shrugged. "We're all a bit curious about the incidents along the California coast."

"Why?"

Wilkes blinked at him. "Why not? Aren't you?"

"Oh, yeah, I am," Gellan said, and looked back out of the window. "I just feel sorry for her. She's probably freezing out there."

"Not at all," said Wilkes. "She's in a thermal suit—plus I'm sure she's done a spell so I'm sure she's totally fine."

Gellan was very glad to hear that. He shifted into a different position and tried to sleep for a while longer, but he had butterflies in his stomach and his mind was racing. At last he felt Wilkes nudge him hard, and he sat back up. The sky was just turning gray, the sun still several minutes away from rising.

Wilkes pointed out of the window. "Cremstoll," he said.

Gellan carefully stood up, bracing his hands against either side of window, and looked out. They were over open ocean now, and the coast was no longer visible. To the north, he could just see a cluster of islands, though they were still hazy because of the distance.

"Is it those?" he asked, pointing to the islands. He wished the sun would rise and bake away the fog.

Wilkes nodded. As Gellan strained his eyes to see them more clearly, he shifted and accidentally bumped Drina. She stirred and lifted her head. When she saw Gellan looking out of the window, she suddenly seemed very wide awake.

"Are we there?" she asked eagerly.

Wilkes nodded at her, and she jumped up next to Gellan. Together, they watched as Cremstoll expanded in their view.

"Just wait till you see!" Drina said with excitement.

"Are all those islands part of Cremstoll?" Gellan asked.

"Yes," Drina said. "There are thirteen large islands altogether in the main Cremstoll archipelago. There are two more over there." She pointed west toward the other window, then moved to look out of it. "Yes, you can just see them."

Gellan scooted over to the other side and strained his eyes. They passed through a particularly foggy area, and when they came out the other side, Gellan was able to make out the shapes of some of the islands much more clearly. He could see one some distance away, and a large, pale, lagoon-like area next to it, but he couldn't see a second island.

"Oh look," Drina said from the other side of the carriage, "there's Lingot Island. I've been there, to help collect windflowers and hoblot plants from the caves there."

Gellan joined her and looked where she was pointing. "Do people live there?"

"No, it's too rocky and steep for people to live on. Most of the islands are. Out of the thirteen big islands, people only live on five of them."

"Maybe too steep for most people..." Gellan murmured to

himself. Though Drina pretended not to have heard him, he saw her grin.

Gellan could clearly see all thirteen islands, though some were bunched so closely together and surrounded by dozens of tiny islets like winged seeds scattered beneath a maple tree that it was difficult to make out where one ended and another began, unless they were directly over it.

"What are those?" Gellan asked, pointing toward tall stone towers dotting the outermost islands.

"Those are the watch towers," Drina said. "Back when Cremstoll was founded, the area wasn't nearly as safe a place as it is now. They were used for defense by linking up when Cremstoll was threatened, but they haven't needed to be used for a long time."

As they swooped over the edge of another island, Gellan noticed several trees toppled over. "What happened there?"

"That's from the windstorm we had three months ago," Drina replied. "Didn't you experience any of it in Ferndale?"

"Oh," said Gellan, recalling the storm. "Yeah, a bit. I didn't realize it was so bad up north."

All the islands were very green, with an occasional cluster of buildings forming villages and towns in the ones that were obviously inhabited. But as they flew closer, he could just barely see one island, quite far off, which was almost entirely covered by buildings.

They were passing close to one of the inner islands now, and Gellan saw that it seemed much larger than most of the others; he couldn't see to the other side of it. It was very rocky and mountainous, and there was a single deep canyon near the west side, as though a gash had been cut straight through into the interior.

Gellan thought for a moment it must be one of the uninhabited islands—until they cleared the ring of mountains and hills that edged the island. He saw that the interior was much more level except for a large, extremely vertical hill that could nearly pass for a mountain itself, right in the middle of the rolling plain, with a lake and a forest spreading out to the east of it. The lake narrowed to a river on the far eastern side, which began wending its way through the ring of mountains to the ocean.

"Look! You can just see the towers of Gilsthorne Building," Drina said. "They're on Gilsthorne Hill—there—in the middle of the island!"

Gellan could see a ridge running straight from the outer mountains nearly to the center one, with a large bridge filling the final gap. A road stretched out along the ridge, ending at high walls of stone that climbed around and up to the structure on top of the hill, where Drina was pointing.

"That's not just a building," Gellan said as they flew close enough for him to see it more clearly. "That's practically a castle!"

"No, it's just the towers, up on top. It's all centuries old, and it's got the most amazing gardens!"

"Is it the government building?" he asked.

Drina shook her head. "Of course not!" she said. "The government doesn't need *that* much space. Not to manage Cremstoll. It's the school, remember?"

"Oh, right, you said the school was called Gilsthorne," Gellan said. Then he did a double-take. "Wait, *that's* the *school*?!"

"Of course. The story goes that a long time ago Old Man Gilding, the man who began building Gilsthorne, believed that education was *the* most important thing. So it became law that every year, the people of Cremstoll had to add at least seven stones to the structure —one for every island we lived on—to help the people remember that the foundation of a good society is for every generation to be given a good and proper education. It's kind of a funny ceremony."

Gellan expected they'd turn toward the hill and land somewhere in the large courtyard in front of the towers, but a moment later, they began angling off in a different direction. Gellan turned to Wilkes with a confused expression.

"Isn't that where we're going?" he asked, pointing. "I thought I was being taken to the school."

"They want us to stop on Providence Island first," Wilkes said. "That's the northeast island, where the government offices are."

"Why?" Gellan asked, the butterflies in his stomach threatening to fly up his throat.

"I expect they want to ask us all some questions," Wilkes said, "to see if there are any other details they might need to know."

Gellan looked over at Drina, and she widened her eyes and shook her head. He closed his mouth and turned back to the window, watching Providence Island as they drew nearer. Though it was covered in buildings, most of them were whitewashed with red-shingled roofs and trimmed occasionally with deep blue or green. It looked like a quintessential old seaside city.

There was a very large wharf that almost entirely enclosed a harbor on the east side of the island. Gellan could see a couple of early risers walking along it, looking up at the sky pod with curiosity. The wharf stretched right up to where it bumped against the side of a steep hill on the northeast corner of the island. On the flattened top of this hill was a large open square, ringed by several elaborate stone structures. One was a stately gray Georgian edifice, with evenly spaced windows and a steep roof. A short distance away from it was a perfectly round building, surrounded by pillars and looking a little too much like a giant mausoleum. Gellan shivered and tightened the strap on his shoulder bag.

As they drew closer, he could see the most impressive building was the one that stood at the north end of the square. It was an expansive Baroque-style structure made almost entirely of white stone, and they seemed to be headed straight for it.

Wilkes saw him looking at it and pointed. "That's the capitol building," he said. "I expect that's where we'll be going."

Drina grabbed the pillows they'd been using and stuffed them in her backpack. Gellan sat back down, the box in the hidden pocket digging into his side as he braced himself for the moment of impact. The ground came nearer and nearer, and just as they bumped gently down, the sun peeked over the horizon. The white stone building lit up in front of them, every stone sparkling as the sunlight glinted off thousands of tiny crystals in the rock.

Gellan heard a gentle thud on top of the carriage as the weight of the animal above them settled onto the roof. Wilkes opened the doors just as a giant wing whooshed by. Tucking Gellan's trunk under one of his arms, Wilkes set off across the square, Drina following close behind him.

Gellan stepped out and turned to look up at the—what had Wilkes called it?—macrodon? It was sitting contentedly on top of the carriage while the rider, Jillian, removed its harnesses. Gellan let out a sound of amazement.

Jillian looked down at Gellan. "He's beautiful, isn't he?" she said as she lowered the saddle to the ground by its straps. "This is Torlin. He's our strongest male, but he's usually very gentle."

Torlin looked something like a giant black weasel with enormous bat-like wings. He had a large patch of silvery hair on his throat. Gellan reached up and touched Torlin's tail, which was hanging down the side of the carriage. The fur was soft and sleek.

Torlin switched his tail a couple of times, but not in an agitated way, and Gellan could've sworn he saw the macrodon look back at him with amusement.

While Gellan watched Jillian continue to undo the thick, heavy straps, a light rushing sound next to his ear made him flinch, and he saw a small, black shape with outstretched wings soar in a long arch up to the roof of the gray Georgian building. When it landed, it called down to him with its familiar chirrupy hoot. Gellan's heart lifted a bit; his little friend had followed him to Cremstoll.

"Where do you keep him?" he asked Jillian, pointing up at Torlin as she climbed down the ladder on the front of carriage.

"I don't," Jillian replied, jumping off the last rung. "He lives on one of the outer islands with the other macrodons. They mostly eat fish from the ocean, but sometimes they'll eat rabbits and other rodents, and they graze on grasses or fresh leaves."

"How often do you use him?"

"Not often." She walked over to Gellan, a heap of harnesses over her shoulder. She was tall, with rich brown skin and wavy black hair. "Are you interested in magical creatures?"

"I dunno," said Gellan. "He's the first one I've seen. I think."

Gellan suddenly felt another, larger rush of air hit him, and he ducked his head. Torlin had unfurled his wings; with a graceful sweep, he rose into the sky and flew off. Gellan watched him go for a moment, then suddenly realized that Wilkes was bellowing his name across the square.

"Bye," Gellan said hastily to Jillian as he began walking away. "And thanks for..." He didn't quite know what to say.

Jillian nodded and walked off, and Gellan turned and jogged over to where Drina and Wilkes were standing. There were two normal-sized adults and one very short one in their greeting party. Gellan did a double-take, quite sure he might be looking at a fantastical dwarf for the first time in his life, like the ones he'd read about in fairytales —only he didn't quite look like Gellan had imagined. He tried not to stare at the dwarf, who was rocking back and forth on his feet, though it would have been perfectly fair, since that was exactly what the dwarf was doing to him. The dwarf's eyes were an extraordinarily light blue color, and he didn't seem to need to blink very often. Despite looking very young, his hair was a rich, bright, silvery color, and his skin was so pale it had a blueish-gray tone to it.

"Gellan," said Wilkes, motioning toward a dark-haired woman with olive skin (Gellan looked up and tried to focus on the humans in front of him), "this is Madame Guillèn, the governor of Cremstoll." She nodded at Gellan and he nodded back. "This"—Wilkes motioned to the younger man with light brown hair—"is Roman Roberts—"

"I'm the one that you've been writing to all this time," interjected Roman, holding out his hand with a broad smile. Gellan took his hand and shook it briefly. Roman's eyes seemed kind and cheerful, but Gellan had learned that you couldn't always trust appearances.

"—and this is Worley, one of the pipkins from the school," finished Wilkes.

"Hi," said Gellan, feeling awkward and mistrustful, and not quite sure he'd heard Wilkes correctly.

"I'll take Master Gellan's trunk," said Worley, in a croaky little voice that made Gellan jump. Wilkes nodded at him and placed the trunk on the little cart next to Worley, who immediately set off with it.

"And if the rest of you will follow me," said Madame Guillèn, turning and heading for the glittering white building. As they trooped after her, Gellan noticed that Roman hung back a bit and took up a position as the caboose of the party. Gellan glanced over his shoulder at him, but Roman seemed determined not to acknowledge that Gellan had noticed what he was doing.

They walked through the large entrance doors, across a spacious atrium, and up a very large double-spiral staircase that made Gellan feel like he was inside a conch shell, until they reached the seventh floor, then down a long corridor edged by windows. Gellan looked out toward the sea as they marched along. It was bright and sparkling in the morning sun. He could see a couple of small boats heading out of the harbor through the gap in the wharf.

The group gathered in front of two large, ornate wooden doors. Madame Guillèn didn't pause for a second, and the doors opened for her as she marched in.

"Ah, he must be here," said a voice inside. "Excellent."

Drina, noticing that Gellan was hanging back a bit and that Roman had stepped forward with the rest of the adults, sidled over behind him. Pausing for just the smallest moment as she walked forward, she whispered, "Remember, you have no obligation to say anything," and then continued walking into the room.

Around a very large oval table were several nameplates, one in front of each chair. Gellan was surprised to see one that said "Gellan Parker" to his left, right next to Madame Guillèn, who sat at the head of the table.

Gellan pulled the chair out and sat down, slumping to one side to avoid the corners of the wooden box. He shifted his shoulder bag to that side, even though he knew the lump of the box shouldn't be visible to anyone.

Wilkes sat to his right in front of a nameplate reading "Vanquor Ebenezer Jameson Wilkes," and Drina had been seated on the other side, directly across from Gellan. There was a bushy-haired man to her left with a nameplate declaring that his name was "Vice Governor Abelard Faulkner," and a handsome, dark-haired, youngish man to the left of Faulkner, whose name appeared to be "Lieutenant Governor Benedict A. Sedargren."

Roman shut the doors as they all sat down, then took a seat on the other side of Wilkes.

"First, Faulkner, is there any information yet on how exactly the flare got reported to the U.S. Federal Government?" Madame Guillèn asked. "Do we know who saw it?"

"No," he replied. "We don't know who it was or why they considered it important enough to report." Before she could draw a breath to ask another question, he added, "I think we may also want to consider the possibility that it was seen by more than those who are themselves witches and wizards, which may explain how it got reported so quickly."

"I would think that was impossible," she said. "A magic emittance from a wand is never seen by wynklers."

"I wouldn't say never. It has happened, though I don't know how or why in this case," Faulkner said. "A local fisherman took a picture of the flare and the picture ended up in the wynkler newspapers. So we have to assume it *was* visible to wynklers."

Madame Guillèn pursed her lips and nodded, considering Faulkner's words, before turning to the next thing on her agenda. Gellan kept his eyes down, hoping not to be noticed.

"Your report please, Wilkes," Madame Guillèn said.

Wilkes told her how he and Jillian Clark had arrived in Ferndale just before midnight on Saturday night. They had met up with Lydia Driscoll and Caleb Marble, the two senior scouts. Together, the four of them had arranged the meeting spots. Then, under the cover of darkness, he had made his way up and down the coastline until he had spotted Drina's signall. He stated that after checking for anyone around, the only two forms he could see were Drina and Gellan, high up in the cave, so he felt quite certain that he had successfully retrieved the two of them from the cave without detection.

Sedargren nodded and folded his arms as he leaned back, seemingly very pleased by the report. Gellan's eyes were drawn to Sedargren's hands; his entire pinky and the tip of the ring finger on his left hand looked black and purple. Whatever had caused the injury must have been a pretty painful accident. After a minute or two, Sedargren noticed Gellan staring. His expression changed, and he unfolded his arms and dropped them beneath the table.

Madame Guillèn was continuing with her inquiries and directives. "Roman, I want you to watch for reports on the wynkler news to make sure the stellamore is found and to see what they say about it. In fact, any further news at all about that region, I want a report on it."

"Yes, ma'am," said Roman, glancing at a pen that was scribbling away on the paper in front of him.

"Drina, do you have anything further to report?" Madame Guillèn asked, turning to her.

"No, ma'am," said Drina. "I expect you've been given copies of all my notes?"

"Yes, of course. Are there any other details you can think of? Anything we ought to know?"

Drina sat and thought for a few moments, her eyes moving around as though she were scanning the inside of her brain. "No, I don't think so," she replied.

"You will let us know if you think of anything else, won't you?" said Madame Guillèn. Then she turned to Gellan. "Now then, Mr. Gellan Parker."

Gellan jumped and looked up at the stern woman. "Yes, ma'am?"

"Is there anything you'd like to report?"

He cleared his throat. "Yes, ma'am."

CHAPTER EIGHT

THE COB

Out of the corner of his eye, Gellan saw Drina's eyes widen.

"It was me that set off the flare," he said. "I don't think Drina thought I could do it, and... I didn't know that I could either. She was just letting me try out her wand—anyway, it wasn't her fault."

It was silent for several seconds, and then all Madame Guillèn said was, "Indeed?"

"I *knew* there was something else going on," Faulkner said. "Drina's not the kind to do something like that, accident or otherwise."

"Yes, well," Madame Guillèn said, turning to Faulkner, "you'll remember that a scout is supposed to be in full control of his or her wand at all times. There will still need to be an inquiry, especially given the mess it created."

The color drained from Drina's face, and Faulkner frowned.

"But it did help us out a bit, you know," the vice governer pointed out. "In the end."

"Um, how's that?" Gellan asked.

Madame Guillèn shot a look at Faulkner before answering.

"Well... we wondered if there was... something of particular interest along that section of coast that may have set off Poseidon's Quake." She sounded as though she were choosing her words very carefully. "Thanks to your flare, the Gray Guard people have practically torn the place apart, and they haven't found anything. Except the stellam-ore, presumably."

"Oh," Gellan said. "But then, what do you think *did* set it off? Poseidon's Quake, I mean. What were you looking for?"

"That's still undetermined," Madame Guillèn said.

"Do you think Poseidon's Quake had something *magical* about it?" Gellan pressed.

Madame Guillèn gave a little cough. "The nature of the event would lead us to presume that there is... *some* part of it, at least, that is related to magic, yes," she said.

"But still," Gellan said, "do you really think it's *that* important?"

She looked at him, one eyebrow raised. "Don't you?" she retorted.

Gellan shook his head. "I doubt it. It probably doesn't mean anything at all. It seems like a whole lot of fuss over nothing, if you ask me. Strange things happen in the ocean all the time."

It was apparent that Madame Guillèn did not like that answer one bit. She stared at him, and for a moment Gellan thought she might be about to shout at him. Instead she pursed her lips and turned away. She asked a few more questions and gave a few more orders, mostly to Sedargren and Roman, but the meeting broke up soon after that.

When Gellan next dared to look at Drina, he was surprised to see she had a small smile on her face and an amused look in her eyes. The man called Faulkner leaned over and spoke to her. She looked up at him and shrugged her shoulders. He gave a little nod, and then got up and walked around the table, holding his hand out to Gellan.

"Mr. Parker, I'm Abelard Faulkner," he said. "I'm the vice governor under Madame Guillèn."

Gellan shook his hand. It was rough and thick.

"Before a student is officially enrolled in Gilsthorne, they typi-cally have to go through a series of tests to ensure they are eligible," Faulkner explained as he walked both Drina and Gellan out of the room and down the corridor. "So even though what apparently brought you here was a display of rather more magic than we're used to seeing in untrained wizards, we'll have to wait until you've been officially evaluated before we get you fitted up with all of your magical books and other school supplies. However, since it appears you're going to have to attend the school, for the next little while at least, whether you pass the evaluation or not, you'll need a school uniform and a few other basic things for the non-magic classes."

Gellan nodded, then had a sudden realization.

"Sir, I have no money with me," he said. "I've always just gone to the public school in my town. My uncle didn't send any..." He didn't want to finish the sentence. He looked down, his face flushing.

"I know that," Faulkner said. "Lydia made arrangements with him. He'll be sending what he can to cover costs, but in any case, we use different money. Whatever he sends is going to have to go through the exchange, which usually takes a day or two. In the meantime, there's a fund for covering unexpected expenses when things like this come up."

"Does that happen very often?" Gellan asked as they descended the large double-spiral staircase.

"Well, no," said Faulkner. "But it's there, and it's for instances like this. We'll stay in touch with your uncle and see what we can do. Just out of curiosity, have you always lived with your uncle and aunt? Are neither of your parents alive?"

Gellan looked at Drina. She gave him a side smile and shrugged. He took that to mean, "*You* decide what to say."

"Well... my mother died when I was six," he said. "Before that, she told me that my father was still alive, but that I... that I would probably never meet him."

Faulkner looked surprised. "He's still alive?"

"Well, he was alive seven years ago. I don't know if he is now."

"But you've never met him?"

"No."

"How is your uncle related to you? Is he your father's brother or your mother's brother?"

"I actually... don't know, sir," Gellan said. He suddenly realized just how little he knew about his own family. His face went red again.

"And you have no other relatives?"

"I know my uncle's mother is alive," Gellan said. "I suppose that would make her my grandmother... one way or another. But I don't know who she is or where she is."

"That's very..." Faulkner put his head down and stroked his chin. He seemed bothered by something, but said nothing further as they walked out of the building. Drina and Gellan looked at each other as they followed him, not sure where they were going.

Suddenly, Faulkner stopped. "Oh, uh, sorry. This way," he said, doing a full about-face and heading straight back into the capitol building. He seemed to disappear into his thoughts once more as he walked in front of them, his eyes staring blankly at the ground. He turned down a small hallway at the back of the building. Gellan looked over at Drina, who shrugged.

"Here we are," said Faulkner, looking up at last as he opened the door to a small office. They stepped in and saw a young man in his twenties, just taking off his coat.

"Oh good," said Faulkner. "Orin, I need to put you in charge of these two today."

"Sir?" said Orin, one arm still hanging inside his coat.

"Gellan just arrived here in Cremstoll, and he'll be starting at the school tomorrow," said Faulkner. "I need you to take him to The Cob and help him get the things he'll need, and also show him around a bit. Anything else you were going to do can wait a day."

"Yes, sir," said Orin as he pulled his coat back on. "Anything in particular that I need to be sure to do?"

"He'll need some of the basics for the rest of the school year," Faulkner said. He pulled a piece of paper out of his back pocket, then wrote a short note, signed it, folded it and sealed it—all with his wand—before handing it to Orin. "Give this to Cline. She can give you the money necessary out of the school fund. She'll also be able to give you a list of exactly what he'll need for now."

Orin took the paper and nodded.

"Get him fitted up with a couple of school uniforms and a single set of robes," Faulkner continued. "And make sure they get a good breakfast and lunch. Then have them back here by six-thirty so I can take them up to the school in time for dinner—he'll need to be placed this evening."

"Yes, sir," said Orin again, putting on his cap and grabbing his umbrella. Then he motioned for Drina and Gellan to follow him. "This way."

They went back up the spiral staircase to the top floor, then down a large corridor that was flanked by the same large windows that had been on the seventh floor. At the end of the corridor, off to the side of a large stone staircase that also spiraled upward, was a small office. It was brightly lit, and an older, fussy-looking woman was sitting at the desk in front of a nameplate that read "Edith Cline, Clerk".

"I've got an order from Faulkner to take this boy to get some school supplies," Orin said to her as they approached, handing over the piece of paper. "He gave me this."

Edith Cline broke the seal and read it quickly, then scooted her chair back from her desk. She tapped a wall to their left with a wand, and a heavy metal door materialized.

"Stay here," she said sternly as she disappeared behind the door. There was a scraping sound, then a few chinks and plunks, and she reappeared.

"Here," she said, handing a small satchel to Orin. "This should be plenty." It clinked as Orin took it from her and put it in his pocket. "And remember," she added sternly, "it's tracked."

"Of course," said Orin. "Not to worry, I'll manage it well."

"And?" Cline said in a raised tone.

"And I'll return the excess to you," Orin said. "Now I just need the list of what he'll—"

Cline shoved a piece of paper at him before he could finish.

"Right, thanks," he said, taking the paper and stepping back a little. He turned around. "All right, you two. Let's get you some breakfast."

As they left the building and crossed the square, Gellan asked, "What did Faulkner mean by taking me to The Cob?"

Orin threw out an arm just before they began descending the steps that led down from the square, causing Gellan to lurch to a stop.

"You can see it from here," Orin said. "See how the streets fan out from the government square?" Gellan nodded, and Orin dropped his arm and began trotting down the steps. "We call it The Cobweb, or just 'The Cob,' because if you look at it from above, the government square is in the northeast corner of the island, and all the roads lead out away from it, like a cobweb that's stuck in the corner of a door," he explained. "So the government square is 'The Corner,' and all that"—he motioned in front of them—"is 'The Cob.' It's where most of the shops are."

At the base of the hill they walked beneath a large triumphal arch that denoted the entrance to The Cob, and as Gellan walked through it, he felt like he was stepping into another world. From far above, the small city had all looked decently congruous. From street-level, however, the view was entirely different, and Gellan's neck turned back and forth as he tried to take in the strangest conglomeration of buildings and shops he had ever seen.

They passed a tiny one-and-a-half story shop with handmade musical instruments hanging in its windows. It looked oddly narrower in the middle, as though it was being squeezed between the two tall shops on either side, one of which inexplicably had vines growing out of its roof and down the face of the building.

The further they walked, the stranger things seemed to get. There was an odd, wobbly tower shop with telescopes and binoculars as well as other peculiar, mirror-like objects in the window display; a stone hut with a giant wooden flower sign out front; two tall mirror-image off-kilter buildings—one stuffed to the rafters with decorative pots and gardening tools (the sign read *Potter's*), and the other filled with plants, seeds, and wind chimes (this one read *Plants*).

Gellan's senses were inundated as they moved deeper into The Cob. His nose detected several things at once: a very strong floral scent mixed up with the smells of fish and spices, smoke and cheese, all backed by the smells of the sea.

The familiar sound of the waves joined the cacophony of other sounds—some familiar and some strange. Gurgles (from below), swishes (from above), as well as squawks and clatters and clinks (from just about everywhere else). Gellan soon felt swallowed up in the clamor of people crowding the sidewalks, some of whom were in normal clothes while others wore very odd ones. Adding to the over-stuffed feeling of the street was a myriad of plants—trees and bushes, flowers and vines, and even herbs and vegetables, which seemed to be growing in every available square inch that wasn't needed for walking or living space.

There was a little eatery called *Winkle Dee's* that appeared to hail from Shakespearean England with its timber structure and a chimney sticking straight up at the front of the building, giving it a unibrow appearance. The next building over was a stone-fronted building with a single large, round hobbit-like window and a sign over it that said *The Snicker See*. Growing between these two buildings was an enormous tree that towered over both, under which a plethora of forest-floor plants such as ferns and hostas covered the ground.

Down the road, where it began to curve around slightly, Gellan could see a round building that looked like a red-topped circus tent. On the sign, beneath a picture of a cup and saucer, were the words *The Wabbit Hole*.

Gellan and Drina followed Orin as he ducked into a little shop called *Tuffo's*, and soon had a large stack of crêpes with various toppings in front of them. Gellan was famished. He ate crêpe after crêpe—one topped with salted caramel, several filled with sweetened cream cheese and fruit, and a savory one filled with eggs and ham. They were all delicious.

"We should be able to get all of your non-magical books at *The Quigrapher*," Orin said as Gellan finished the last crêpe. "It's the largest bookshop in town. I'll take you to the *Dibbin and Bob* to get you a couple of uniforms and a set of robes." He scanned the list. "Other than that, there aren't any other specific supplies that you'll need until you've been evaluated and placed."

"So no wand yet?" asked Drina. "We already know he can do magic."

Gellan perked up.

"A child may be observed to do strange things, but that doesn't mean he is a wizard," said Orin. "Not until after he has passed an *official* evaluation."

Drina looked away, chewing on her lip. Gellan sighed and stabbed a stray blueberry. "If I pass my evaluation, will I be able to come back to school next year if I want to?" he asked.

Orin shrugged. "Presumably. *If* you pass."

Gellan swallowed. "Is it hard to pass?"

Drina nudged him with her elbow. "Don't worry about it," she said. "I'm sure you'll be fine."

"But... just say I don't. Are there other schools in the country that teach magic? Maybe I could try again at one of those."

"Yes," said Orin. "There's one somewhere by the Great Lakes—I think it's in Minnesota. And there's another one on an island off the coast of New Jersey. They're both smaller than Gilsthorne, though."

"When do kids normally start coming to Gilsthorne?" Gellan asked.

"The September after they turn twelve," Orin said. "It's just not a good idea to be teaching magic to kids younger than that."

"So I could've technically come at the beginning of this school year?" Gellan asked. "What if I'm not the only one who was missed?"

"Well, there *may* be cases like that," said Orin, looking extremely dubious. "But I doubt it, to be honest. The List records the birth of every witch or wizard in the country, when they're named. Which is why it's a bit odd that you're not on there, if you're sure you can do magic."

"Are you absolutely certain he's not on there?" asked Drina.

Orin nodded as he stood up and stretched before putting on his coat. "I happened to be with Roman a few days ago when your note came about looking for Gellan's name on The List. We checked, and

Gellan definitely wasn't anywhere on there. That's why I think his magic isn't strong enough, so... I wouldn't get my hopes up if I were you. Are you two done eating?"

Drina and Gellan both nodded and pulled on their coats.

"D'you think he's right?" Gellan asked glumly as they followed Orin out of the shop.

"Don't be silly," Drina said. "Of course not." She lowered her voice. "But I don't mind him thinking that, to be honest. It'll keep people from being suspicious about you."

"So you think I just got missed, somehow?" Gellan asked, walking as closely to Drina as he could on the crowded sidewalk. "Otherwise I would've been told about Gilsthorne sooner?"

"Yes, of course," said Drina. "You would've gotten a letter, like I did. And after that fl—" She caught herself. "And after what happened, I have no idea how your name was kept off The List."

"Do you think someone made it happen?"

"I doubt it," Drina said. "But I guess it's possible. I thought The List was infallible, so I don't know how else..." She shrugged.

As they turned down a narrow, cobbled road that was even more crowded, Gellan suddenly heard a high, squeaky voice that stood out above the rest of the commotion. He stopped and turned, trying to see behind him as he was pummeled on all sides from passers-by.

A moment later, he was able to make out the squeak more clearly. "Master Gellan! Master Gellan!" the voice was calling. "Master Gellan, wait!"

Gellan could see a little bob of silvery hair weaving through the crowd, and a tiny pipkin pushed his way between the knees of a portly woman, who was thrown off-balance by the large crate of writhing plants she was carrying. A man in the crowd used his wand to steady the woman before she toppled onto him as the little pipkin skipped aside to avoid a snatching vine hanging down from a building. It was clearly a female pipkin; her eyelashes were much longer than Worley's and her chin was narrower. She paused a moment to catch her breath, then heaved a small bag up on top of her head and said, "Here, Master Gellan. This is for you. Master Faulkner asked me to bring it to you."

"Um, thank you," Gellan said as he took it from her. "What is it?"

"Pipkins don't look into what's not theirs," she said, clearly offended. "We know what's not ours, and we know what is." Then, before Gellan could reply, she turned around and dashed away, deftly skittering from one open spot to the next as the crowd shifted and moved along.

"Don't open it yet," said Drina, pulling Gellan toward Orin, who was waving at them. "Let's catch up to Orin first, or I think we'll be taking him to Imple's Infirmary to treat a stroke."

"What kept you?" demanded Orin as they rejoined him. "Where'd you get that?" he added, seeing the bag in Gellan's hand.

Drina explained, and Orin said, "Well, I guess you'd better open it if it's from Faulkner."

Gellan undid the leather tie, looked into the bag... and gasped. It was filled with several large and small coppery coins, a few silvery coins in different sizes, and two small gold coins with square holes in their middles.

"What? What is it?" Drina grabbed the edge of the bag and pulled it over so she could see inside. Her mouth dropped open. "Faulkner wouldn't just give you all that, would he?"

Gellan held the bag out; Orin seemed stunned as he examined the contents. Then a look of anger clouded his eyes. "It would be highly unusual if he had." He grabbed the note hanging from the side of the bag. As he read, his eyebrows relaxed, though only slightly. "Well, it looks like it's in order," he said, tossing the note aside.

Drina picked it up, and together she and Gellan read:

Gellan,
Your uncle was able to get things taken care of much more quickly than we anticipated. These are the funds he sent along for you this morning. You can use them to buy your school things. I would still advise you to use them carefully, or they'll run out faster than you'd expect.
Sincerely,

Vice Governor Abelard Faulkner

"That's good news, right?" Drina said, her face brightening as she finished the note.

"Yeah, I guess so," said Gellan. "How do I know how to use them? I'm not used to these kinds of coins."

"I had to get used to it too," Drina said. "But if you just remember that each brass farthing," she pointed at a penny-sized coin, "is worth about a small loaf of bread. And it's four brass farthings to a copper penny." She pointed at another coin that looked remarkably similar. "Then it's seven copper pennies to a silver jack, and nineteen silver jacks to a gold ducat. And then, of course, your half-pennies are worth about *half* of a copper penny, which is the same as *two* of the brass farthings, which end up being eight to one of the oval groats. These ones," she said, pointing to a silvery coin that had a slight oval shape. "I still have to do quick math in my head, sometimes, but it's not too hard to remember." She trailed off as Orin started chuckling at the look on Gellan's face.

"Um... right," Gellan said, as he shoved the pouch into his shoulder bag. "I'll just... keep that in mind." It added a considerable weight, and he had to shift the shoulder strap to the other side as they set off once more.

After another ten minutes, they crossed a wide cobblestoned road to what was probably the most interesting building Gellan had yet seen in The Cob. It looked a bit like a cathedral, but it was built entirely of whitewashed brick instead of stone. The numerous arched windows and the multiple steep roofs made the whole thing look architecturally coherent... and somehow, very out of place.

They pushed through the heavy crystal and wood doors, and an enormous space seemed to expand in every direction as they entered, making the building look even bigger on the inside than it had on the outside. Gellan found the middle spot of the cavernous atrium and spun on his heel while looking straight up into what would have been the bell tower if it had been a church. Some of the light that came in had been split by the prismatic shapes in the windows, and it filtered down in rainbow hues upon each of the seven stories of shelves crammed with books of every shape and size. There were people on every level of the bookstore—searching for books, reading on giant poufs, or climbing up and down the multiple staircases.

Orin walked up to the counter to speak to the man on duty and hand him the short list of books for Gellan. The man took the list, skimmed it quickly, and nodded, then grabbed a basket and walked over to Gellan. His nametag read 'Philo Reid,' and though he straightened his half-moon spectacles as he peered down at Gellan, he left them perched on the end of his nose.

"If you'll just follow me..." he said, handing the basket to Gellan before turning and leading the three of them up a flight of steps, past several shelves of books, and through a narrow doorway into another section of the building.

Mr. Reid pulled a book off one shelf, looked it over, and compared it with the list. "*History of the American Continent, 1400s-1700s*, by Hesther Hastings," he said, reading the title aloud. He shoved the book at Gellan, who dropped it into the basket as he followed Mr. Reid down a long stretch between towering shelves.

Halfway down, Mr. Reid waved a wand and another book came floating down toward them from several feet up. After comparing it to the list, he handed it to Gellan, who glanced at the title: *Life Science— Magical and Nonmagical Creatures*. He flipped through a few pages and sighed, then held the book out for Drina to see.

"This is almost the same book we used at my school in Ferndale," he said.

"*Almost*," she emphasized. "Anyway, true science is super important, whether you use magic or not. Besides, there's some magic you can't do without understanding science."

Gellan caught up with Mr. Reid just in time to be handed another book—*Charmed Grammar*. This time Gellan groaned out load.

"Honestly, Gellan," Drina said, coming up behind him, "I would've thought that—"

"I know, I know," he said. "It's just not what I expected."

"Then you have absurd expectations." She was getting huffy,

which he'd already experienced a couple of times when they'd been stuck in the cave. He decided it was time to stop talking.

The last book on the list was for math. He didn't mind math, really; he thought numbers were interesting—how they fit together in precise and predictable ways. He liked that you couldn't twist numbers around; they were what they were. But though the book was called *Math Magic*, he didn't see how there could be anything very *magical* about numbers.

Before they went back downstairs to pay for the books, Drina turned to Orin. "Do you mind if I go look for a particular book while we're here?"

"No, go ahead," he said. "Let's browse here for a while. I'm supposed to keep you two occupied until six-thirty."

Gellan followed Drina up two flights of steps to a section labeled 'New Releases.' She didn't seem to know quite where she was going.

"What book are you looking for?" Gellan asked.

"It's the first book in a new series that was supposed to come out a couple of weeks ago, while I was traveling down the coast," said Drina.

"Who's the author?"

"It's a new novelist. I wonder if—no, it's not going—somewhere..." She thumbed down a line of books. "Here it is!" she exclaimed, pulling out a book. She looked at it for a moment with happy anticipation, then stuck it under her arm.

They trooped back down the stairs and found Orin, his nose deep in the politics section. They left him to himself, and for the next couple of hours they meandered through the book cathedral, looking through the astonishing variety of books. It felt very strange to Gellan to see familiar books (he found some of the exact same cookbooks his uncle had used to teach him how to bake and cook) sitting next to books containing recipes for magical concoctions. It wasn't necessarily the conjunction of such varying recipes that was so odd to him. It was the fact that one book was perfectly normal and quiet, while the other one had a picture of a woman on the cover that shook her ladle at him furiously, screeching, "You ignoble little—"

when he had the audacity to return the book to the shelf after perusing it.

As a large clock chimed somewhere deep in the cathedral, Drina, Gellan, and Orin congregated back on the first floor of the shop. Orin took Gellan into an area filled with wooden pens and feathers—

("They're *quills*," said Drina.

"Anyway, they wear out too quickly. You'll want normal dip pens," Orin said, pointing.

Drina picked out a few and put them in Gellan's basket.)

—and some ink—

("Why on earth would anyone put the ink inside a pen? How can a pen write properly if the ink is on the inside instead of the outside?" Orin muttered to himself after Gellan tried to explain what 'pen' meant to him in Ferndale. He picked out two bottles of ink and shoved them at Gellan. Drina took them and carefully placed them in the basket.)

—and some paper.

("At least I know what *this* stuff is," Gellan said.

"No, wait," said Drina, pushing his hand away from the paper he was reaching for. "You don't want *that* kind of paper, or the teachers might think you're trying to cheat."

"Could you just get me some normal paper?" Gellan asked with a sigh.)

When he finally had everything he needed, Gellan held out his heavy basket and the bag of coins to Drina. "Could you do it for me?" he asked. "Just this once?"

"All right, just this once," Drina said. "But you have to learn sometime—"

"Just this once," he repeated, handing the bag of coins over to her.

After leaving *The Quigrapher*, they headed down a cross street to a large shop overflowing with clothing and fabric.

Within minutes, Gellan was standing on a round turntable, trying to keep his balance as it rotated back and forth. A young woman called Faye examined the hems of the gray tweed, second-hand pants he was wearing, her short, spiky brown hair making her look like an oversized version of her pin-cushion as she directed pins into the hems with each tap of her wand.

Gellan got a feeling of dread in his stomach as Faye next picked out a matching necktie and bowtie, a couple of collar shirts, a gray tweed vest to match the pants, and a cap. She pointed him back into the dressing room, her measuring tape coiling itself around her wrist and spare pins flying back into the pin-cushion.

As Gellan put each item on, he became even more certain that there was no way he'd be able to pay attention in his classes feeling so pinched. He heaved a sigh before reluctantly stepping out of the dressing room, spreading his arms so Faye could evaluate his appearance.

She soon had him back up on the turntable, fussing over sleeve lengths and half-sizes up. Gellan wondered if the box hiding just behind his right arm was throwing her off balance, or if she was always this fussy about fittings. Back to the dressing room to try on the next-size-up shirt—back out onto the turntable, getting prodded and pinned...

Drina grinned at Gellan's very apparent discomfort. "What's the matter, Gellan?" she asked in mock surprise. "Not used to collars and ties much?"

"No," he said with a pronounced frown, crossing his arms. Faye snapped her fingers at him, and he dropped his arms to his sides.

Last of all, Faye pulled out two cloaks. A large, black, formal-looking one, slightly faded, with a set of interchangeable cuffs, some-what worn. And a much thicker, gray tweed cloak.

When she was satisfied at last, Faye sent him to change back into his regular clothes, and they left with a small shopping bag containing the ties, cuffs, and cap. The other items would be sent up to Gilsthorne after the hems had been finished.

Noticing that his two charges seemed tired, Orin let Drina and Gellan sit on a bench in one of the many public gardens while he went off to find some lunch. Gellan was just leaning back on the bench, trying to snatch some sleep for a few moments, glad to be relieved from the weight of his shopping bags, when Drina nudged him.

"Gellan, look... do you know him?" she whispered. Gellan opened his eyes and looked where she was motioning. A man was sweeping outside a shop on the opposite side of the street.

"No, why?"

"It looked like he was staring at you a moment ago."

"Drina, I know about five people total here. He's probably just—"

But then, out of the corner of his eye, Gellan saw someone leaning over the roof of a building across the street. His eyes flicked up, and for a split second, he made eye contact with a little old man in a funny green hat just before he disappeared.

Gellan looked over at Drina and saw that she had seen the man on the building too. Then he noticed that the man who had been sweeping had disappeared.

"D'you think it's—you know—the thing I'm carrying?" Gellan asked in a low voice.

"I have no idea how it could be," Drina said. "It's completely hidden. *I* know you've got it, but even I can't tell you're carrying it." She shrugged and looked around again, nervously chewing her lip.

After that, neither Gellan nor Drina could fully relax, even as they enjoyed the sandwiches Orin returned with. They filled their afternoon with some window shopping, browsed through *The Snicker See*, got lost amidst the shelves and shelves of odd ingredients in *Amicus Apothecary*, and threw bits of their lunch leftovers to the seagulls from the pier, all with continual glances over their shoulders and exchanges of worried looks.

As the afternoon wore on, Drina and Orin answered Gellan's occasional audible question. He learned that nilla nog was something you could either eat hot, drink cold, or spread on toast. He discovered the reason his wynkler watch no longer worked, and they stopped at a little shop so he could get himself one that would work properly in Cremstoll:

"There's loads of magic interfering here," Orin explained. "We've built a few things so that we can communicate with people in other parts of the country when necessary. But mostly, we don't really care because we don't need them anyway. Magical objects work anywhere."

And he quickly learned not to brush up against any unknown plant, or he was liable to be squirted at, dusted with perfume (ranging from pleasant to horribly odoriferous), or pelted with seeds and spines.

Around six o'clock, Orin led them down a little side street, saying, "Since we only have a little bit of time left, let's go to the shop where my girlfriend works. She'll be getting off soon anyway."

Before they could answer, he pushed through the door of a small boutique and was soon engaged in talking to the pretty shop assistant as she organized a rack of umbrellas. Drina and Gellan amused themselves by snickering at some of the odd little hats, cloaks and other outerwear on display.

After a while, Drina checked her watch. "Orin," she called over to him, "we'd better go. We're supposed to meet up with Faulkner in just a few minutes."

"I'll be quick," they heard the girl say, and Gellan noticed for the first time that she spoke with an accent.

She disappeared into the back and returned a moment later with her coat on, then linked her arm through Orin's after locking the door behind them all.

"Sorry for not introducing you before," said Orin as they walked up the street toward The Corner. "This is Elodie Ivshin. We knew each other when we were at school. This is Gellan, and Drina. Faulkner asked me to keep them busy for the day."

Elodie smiled at them both, but didn't say anything. Gellan thought she seemed a bit shy.

"Where are you from?" Gellan asked her.

"From France," Elodie replied. "My parents came here when I was a girl, but I still sound part French, I guess?"

"No, your English is very good," Drina said, and she glared at Gellan—who wasn't quite sure what he had done to deserve that.

Orin led them up to The Corner, across the square, and up the now-familiar double-spiral staircase back toward Cline's office.

"Good," was all Cline said when they arrived, before pointing at a couple of chairs by her office wall for Gellan and Drina. They sat, and she held out her hand to Orin. He handed her the bag of coins she had given him that morning.

Orin turned and gave Gellan and Drina a small salute in jest, then winked and waved good-bye as he and Elodie walked away.

Gellan wandered over to the large windows and looked out at the sea, the lights of the small city twinkling on the water as the color of the sky began to change with the setting sun. He heard a noise behind him and turned in time to see Faulkner sliding down the staircase cross-legged, the stone steps having shifted to form a smooth surface. He stuck out his legs at just the right moment and landed on his feet with a deftness Gellan would have thought impossible for someone his age, before trotting over to them as Cline clucked her disapproval.

"Had a good day?" he asked, ignoring Cline. They both nodded. Faulkner threw a large black cloak around his shoulders. "Well, then, let's get you two up to the school. This should be enlightening."

CHAPTER NINE
GILSTHORNE

They followed Faulkner out of the building and down toward the wharf. It was a short distance to the docks, where a set of small, unusual boats were gently rocking in the water. They looked sleek and new, similar to the glass and steel carriage they'd ridden in last night.

Gellan followed Drina and Faulkner inside and sat down on a bench. His shoulders were aching, and the wooden box was digging into his back. Drina looked over at him, and he knew she could tell what he was thinking when she gave him a sympathetic smile.

"What's this thing called?" Gellan asked.

"It's a sea pod," said Faulkner, sitting at ease on the opposite bench, his left ankle on his right knee. "Drina, why don't you do the honors?"

Drina pulled out her wand and tapped it on the side of the boat, saying, "Gilsthorne Island, please."

The sea pod immediately began to pull away from the docks and Gellan watched in amazement as it guided itself around the southern end of Providence Island, on a direct path to Gilsthorne Island.

Under the darkening sky, Gellan could see a very rocky beach backed by steep, low mountains that, in some places, rose straight up out of the sea. These were covered in thick patches of evergreen trees, whose steep, upright growth made the mountains themselves seem taller than they were.

A few minutes later, Gellan climbed out of the sea pod behind Drina and Faulkner and into one of several unusual carriages lined up in a parking area. This time Faulkner took out his own wand, tapped it on one of the walls, and said, "Gilsthorne Building." The carriage immediately began bumping its way up a winding road.

"Sky pod, sea pod... let me guess... land pod?"

"Well, yes, actually," said Drina.

Faulkner chuckled and pulled his hands out from behind his head in an open-armed shrug. "Why make it complicated?"

After about twenty minutes of winding along the ascending road through the outer ring of hills and mountains, Gilsthorne Hill finally came into view as the ribbon of road straightened out like a red carpet stretched across the ridge. They raced along it, farmland whizzing by on the west side, far below them, and a river rumbling through thick trees on the east side.

Drina pointed to a large cluster of lights to the northwest. "That's Gilsthorne Village."

With Gilsthorne Hill growing in their view, Gellan could see there was a spring gushing from the east side of the hill, the water running turbulently down a rocky path, adding to the large lake Gellan had seen from the air. The lake was silvery and smooth, reaching into dozens of nooks in the valley.

As they trundled across a bridge connecting the ridge to Gilsthorne Hill, Gellan couldn't help the goosebumps that rose on his arms. The towers were lit up on top of the hill, and there were lights at intervals in the defense walls and towers, wrapping all the way down it. Set against the inky sky, it was an impressive sight.

The carriage slowed and came to a gentle stop. Faulkner got out first, followed by Drina and a slightly confused Gellan.

"Aren't we going to the towers?" Gellan asked.

"Of course not," said Drina. "The Great Hall is on the bottom floor of Gilsthorne Building."

"But the building is high up there," Gellan said, pointing to the obvious structure up on top.

"There are a few classrooms up in the towers and a couple of meeting halls, along with a few dorms," she said. "But this part of the hill is the main section of Gilsthorne Building."

"Wait—the school is inside the *hill*?!" he asked.

"Of course! That's what I already told you," Drina said. "It's been carved out in large sections inside the hill."

They passed through a tall wooden gate and into a very large courtyard. There was a fountain off to one side in the form of an enormous, serpent-like dragon, the water spouting from its mouth and the tip of its tail. Even in the darkness, the eyes gleamed and sparkled, giving Gellan an eerie feeling as he walked beneath an arch of water. He tripped on a loose cobblestone, caught himself clumsily, then hastened toward the hill.

He could see Faulkner standing next to a pair of giant wooden doors set directly into the rock, but Gellan's attention was caught by an enormous clock, lit up from behind, high above the doors. It had been worked into the natural undulations of the rock, creating a wobbly edge. The hands of the clock looked large enough for a full-grown man to stretch out on, and they were pointing to—

"I thought it was about seven o'clock," Gellan said to Drina, pointing up. "Not eleven-something."

"It is," said Drina. "That clock hasn't worked in ages."

"Come along or we'll be late," said Faulkner, motioning Gellan forward as he pushed open the large wooden doors. "And nothing starts off quite on the right foot if you're late to it. As it is, we haven't had a student start in the middle of a school year in ages," he added, ushering Gellan through the doors and into a large entrance hall.

"Is that a problem?" Gellan asked.

"Not exactly," said Faulkner as the doors swung shut behind them. "Just unusual."

A few yards further into the entrance hall, there were two stone staircases—one going left and the other right—and another pair of enormous wooden doors just beyond them.

"The Great Hall?" Gellan asked, pointing at the doors. Drina nodded.

"Wait here, both of you," Faulkner instructed, before disappearing around the side of the left staircase.

While they waited, Gellan ran his hand over one of the staircase banisters, imagining how much time it must have taken to chisel it all out of solid rock. He followed their path upward with his eyes, to what he could see of the second level. His neck tilted further and further back as pillars of integral rock continued to draw his gaze upwards, and he began to realize just how expansive Gilsthorne Building must be.

"Does it fill the *whole* hill?" he asked Drina.

"No," she said. "Everything beneath us is solid—I think—but from here up, maybe a third of it is tunneled out? We don't want it to collapse down on us or anything. And when you've got lots of kids practicing magic for the first time, solid rock is probably the best. You certainly wouldn't want to be in a wooden shack or something."

"How in the world do they keep it warm during the winter?" Gellan asked.

"There are plenty of fireplaces," said Drina, pointing at an ornate stone fireplace, several logs crackling away on the hearth. "Besides, you can always use a firestone in your dormitory if you get cold."

"Oh, right. Then why don't they just use firestones everywhere? Why bother with fireplaces at all?"

"There's just nothing like a lovely fire," said Drina, smiling as she held her hands out to warm them.

Gellan wandered past oversized chairs and study tables toward the fireplace, and warmed his own hands as he watched the smoke rise up through the serpentine chimney. Drina settled on a pouf some distance away as they waited for Faulkner to return.

In the glow of the flames, Gellan could see a couple of charts on the walls. One was a diagram of plant parts and the other mapped the patterns of the ocean currents. Opposite these were two full-length paintings of a dignified old man and a plump, cheerful-looking woman, both of whom had been painted sleeping in chairs in a library. Gellan noticed an odd object in the far corner and pointed to it.

"What's that?" he asked Drina.

She shrugged, and then a stuffy voice to Gellan's left made him jump.

"That is a rather sophisticated sundial, though of course it's useless in here. It sits there purely for decoration, meant to stimulate the minds of students to ever-greater heights."

Gellan swung around, and saw the man in the painting sniff at him. "Do you have any other questions, young man?"

"What are—" Gellan cleared his throat. "Uh, *who* are you?"

"Professor Maric Gillespie, at your service," he said, removing his hat and replacing it again. "I am here to answer questions during your study time in this room. And just so you know, I am particularly knowledgeable about math and architecture."

"Oh," said Gellan. "Uh, thanks."

"The teachers don't have time to monitor all the study halls," Drina said. "So the people in the portraits do it. Almost all of the portraits in the study halls are people who were—uh, are—professors." She looked confused for a moment, not sure how to express it. "In any case, they can be very helpful."

"Oh," said Gellan. "And do the mice and rats help sew clothes for the students?"

"*No*," said Drina, catching his twinge of sarcasm and throwing it back at him, "but students have been known to use them to send secret messages to each other at night. Some students have their own pet mice or rats for that very reason—but I personally don't think having to take care of a mouse or rat is worth it."

"So you can have pets here?"

"If you get it approved."

"Any pet?"

"Well, probably not *any* pet. I'm sure they'd veto a hippogriff or something." She rolled her eyes at him.

"D'you think they'd approve a macrodon for a pet?" he asked with a grin. "It'd be so cool to fly anywhere I want to!"

"Try a broomstick. You don't have to feed it."

"Broomstick? Witches and wizards really actually use broomsticks to fly?"

"Uh, *yes*—" said Drina. "What else did you think they were for?"

"How about sweeping?"

"It's much easier to just blow away the dust or vanish it away with a charm. *So* much better than sweeping with a broom," Drina replied. She turned her back to Gellan. "I wonder why Faulkner is taking such a long time."

"He's probably trying to find out where they put my trunk. Maybe they lost it somewhere."

"The pipkins would never lose anything," Drina said. "It's probably in one of the teachers' offices or something, just until you're placed."

"Placed?"

"Into a dormitory, and in a spot in the Great Hall. They do it when everyone is together. That's why Faulkner wanted to bring you here for dinnertime," said Drina.

Just then, Faulkner came around the side of the staircase toward them. "All right, you two. Follow me," he said, beckoning them over.

Faulkner led them back the way he'd come—around behind the staircase and down a long hallway. Gellan saw another pipkin rocking on his feet in happy anticipation, a little cart standing empty next to him.

"You can give your things to Midgley," Faulkner instructed. "He'll put them in your new dormitory for you."

Gellan gratefully unloaded his parcels and shoulder bag into the little cart and watched Midgley trundle off. Faulkner turned and opened a side door to the Great Hall, and Gellan's stomach turned over as the dinnertime noise of dozens of people resounded through the corridor. He reluctantly followed Drina through the door, and Faulkner stepped in behind them.

Gellan found himself in a cavernous room with a large tree

growing directly out of the stone floor in the center of the hall. There were lots of round tables set in a spiral around the hall, with the tree at the center point.

Most of the light in the hall came from lanterns hanging thickly from the lowest branches of the tree, though these were still several feet above the students' heads. More lanterns speckled all the way up the height of the tree. Gellan craned his neck back as he followed its trunk upward with his eyes, but he still couldn't see the ceiling. More light was provided by candles nestled in candlesticks built directly into the tables.

There were three long tables where the teachers sat. These were raised on short platforms and ran along three sides of the room. The walls behind them undulated along, and there were tiny ribbons of gold and silver woven through the dark stone, which glinted in the light of the lanterns.

Behind the narrowest wall, opposite the large entrance doors, were two large windows through which Gellan could see the night sky.

The most interesting feature, though, was an enormous map that had been painted on the back of the entrance doors. Gellan could see staircases and doorways, hallways and vast rooms, and he realized it must be a map of the school itself.

Drina was standing off to one side, right against the wall, so Gellan slunk over next to her, trying to look inconspicuous. Faulkner shut the door and then stood expectantly beside them. A wizard in the center of the teacher table in front of the windows got up and cleared his throat.

"Quiet, please... If you'll allow me... Thank you." His voice rang through the hall, and the noise quickly died away.

Drina leaned over. "Professor Fisk," she said, nodding toward the man. "He's headmaster of the school."

"It is quite unusual," Professor Fisk said, "for a student to arrive in the middle of the year. But we have the pleasant opportunity now to add one more to our ranks. As you all know," he continued, "each time a student is placed it may cause some shifting about."

There was a murmur through the hall.

"If this means that you happen to be moved a bit," he continued, "remember that it is an *opportunity* and *not* a tragedy." With that, he sat down and looked over at Faulkner.

Faulkner waved for Gellan to follow him past one of the teachers' tables to a corner next to the large entrance doors, where a small table stood. Gellan tried not to look at the sea of students to his left as he walked. A few were watching intently. Most were still eating, showing little interest in their new schoolmate. He focused on the map, and now that he was closer to it, he could see it had hundreds of names on it—many more than the number of students or teachers here. On the table was a box of gray candles, a basket full of small slips of paper, a pen, and a candlestick.

"Take one of those slips of papers and write your name on it," Faulkner instructed Gellan.

After a moment of hesitation, Gellan simply wrote "Gellan Parker."

"Good," said Faulkner. "Now, choose a candle from the box, put it in the candlestick, and send the slip of paper into it."

Gellan obeyed, picking up the candlestick as he held the slip of paper up to the candle, and the paper disappeared with a small poof of smoke.

After a brief moment, there was a sudden rush of wind and Gellan looked over at the crowd of students. The hundreds of candles that had been stuck in candlesticks a moment before suddenly wrenched themselves free and began rushing around the hall. Students were gasping and shrieking, ducking beneath the tables and chairs, or using books or plates to cover their heads. Some of the round wooden tables seemed to be expanding and others shrinking, which added creaking and groaning sounds to the melee.

Gellan threw himself backward against the map on the wall as his candle pulled free of the candlestick and joined the fray. He looked up at Faulkner and was surprised to see a large smile on his face—he, at least, appeared to be thoroughly enjoying himself as he watched the chaos. Drina, on the other hand, who was still standing by the door they'd come in, was covering her mouth in astonishment.

As quickly as it had started, the candles all settled themselves into new candlesticks, and the commotion shuddered to a standstill. A deafening silence followed. The only movement was a handful of papers, which had been thrown up in alarm by overzealous students doing homework at dinner and were now floating to the ground.

"Well!" said Professor Fisk in a booming voice after a long moment, "that was extremely entertaining! Grab your plates, one and all, and follow your candles!"

Even greater pandemonium now ensued. Students who had been shoved to the ground by expanding tables picked themselves up. People began calling out and waving to each other when they found candles with familiar names on them; students were constantly bumping into each other, and no fewer than eleven plates crashed to the floor. Two or three girls were even weeping as they tried to make their way, bleary-eyed, through the jumbled mass.

Order slowly resumed, and one by one, each student sat down. Some appeared quite cheerful and others extremely disgruntled. The largest table now had eleven students sitting around it, and the smallest had only three. Gellan realized that Drina had joined the crowd and was now sitting at a table quite near the tree, filling a clean plate in front of her.

Faulkner finally held up his hand, and quiet filled the hall.

"Where is Mr. Parker's candle?" he asked.

Everyone looked to their left and right, and then a boy with extremely thick black hair right in the middle of the hall raised his hand.

"Here, sir," he said, pointing at an empty chair next to the tree.

Gellan was still frozen with his back against the map. Faulkner turned and looked at him, then jerked his head toward the tables. Gellan unstuck himself and made his way stiffly through the maze of tables and chairs. He slid into his chair and looked down—though he did notice that his candle was still a painfully dull gray color, despite everyone else's candles being one of the colors of the rainbow.

Professor Fisk's voice echoed across the hall once more, calling for attention. Gellan looked up and saw that several of the teachers were conversing in small bunches, pointing at the map. Some of them left the hall looking annoyed.

"Well, seeing as how it'll take some time for the staff to move your things to your new dormitories," Professor Fisk said, "I think we'd better stick around for some dessert."

The boy sitting next to Gellan grabbed a clean plate and began loading it up with food—potatoes, rolls, and a thick cut of ham. There wasn't much left in front of them as it was, and a few moments later the food and the platters disappeared, with dishes of desserts appearing in their stead.

The boy shoved the plate over to Gellan. "Here. Most of the desserts are pretty sugary, so I don't think you'd want to fill up on them, or you'd be sick."

Gellan sat up straight and looked at the boy for the first time. His thick black hair was combed to one side, and beneath that was a set of brown eyes and sparkling white teeth.

"Er—thanks," said Gellan. "I didn't know the food would disappear like that." He gratefully grabbed a roll and, without any butter around, simply dipped it in the gravy that the boy had slopped onto the mashed potatoes, and began to eat.

He looked around a little bit as he ate and was startled to realize that his gray candle had his name written on it in his own handwriting.

"How'd it get—?" he asked, pointing to his candle.

"That's what you wrote on the paper, isn't it?" the boy asked. "That's your collocandle now."

"My what?"

"Your collocandle—your placement candle," said the boy, "for while you're here at Gilsthorne. We all have one. But... I've never seen anyone with a gray one." He shrugged and tilted his head, looking closely at Gellan's candle, trying to make out the letters. "Geller Porker?" he asked.

"Gellan Parker," Gellan corrected.

"Nice to meet you," said the boy. "I'm Roger Sumner. Where're you from?" he asked, as he served himself a piece of chocolate custard pie topped by a thick white meringue.

"I'm from California," Gellan replied. "How about you?"

"All over," said Roger. "I was born in Australia, and we lived there for a while, and then Canada, and then Philadelphia. That's in Pennsylvania." He took a large bite; it was a few seconds before he could continue. "My family moved here a few years ago, because my parents wanted me and my sisters to go to Gilsthorne, of course. How come you're starting in the middle of the year?"

"Things just... worked out that way, I guess," said Gellan. He stirred the gravy into his mashed potatoes and took a big bite, then looked around the hall. He pointed up at the tree and turned to Roger. "Isn't this basically a giant cave?" he asked.

"Well... yeah, I guess so," said Roger, thinking. "I've never heard anyone describe it like that before, though."

"Then how does the tree grow?" Gellan asked.

"No idea," said Roger. And he didn't seem to care to have an idea as he stuffed another piece of chocolate pie into his mouth.

After finishing his mashed potatoes, Gellan pulled a pie tin closer to take the last piece. He turned to Roger as he eased it onto his plate.

"What do the colors of the candles mean?"

"They show the group that you belong to," said Roger. He had turned around on his chair, his arms folded across the back of it; he looked bored, and with nothing else to do, he seemed happy to answer Gellan's questions. "Usually we're grouped with the people who are most like us—at least in the Great Hall. In the dorms it's more of a mixed group—sometimes people who are too much alike don't get along very well."

"What are the groups?"

"See the tapestries on the wall over there?" Gellan saw him pointing to small pictures on fabric, above the center teachers' table. "The reds are the dragons, the oranges are the hippogriffs, the yellows are the fairies." He spun around and started at the end of the opposite side. "The greens are the luths, the blues are the firebirds, and the purples are the satyrs."

"Dragons and firebirds and satyrs? Those aren't real. Are they?"

"Ummm, pretty sure. All except the satyr," Roger said. "I'm not sure about that one... but then again, they're supposed to be pretty elusive, at least according to legend. So maybe there are *some* out there? I dunno."

"So what does being in a particular group mean?"

"Well, it's... I dunno, it's supposed to help us somehow," Roger said. "And it's important during the Fifth Year Friest, which is held every five years... I think. And there's a common room for each group, in case people want to use it. But considering that there are dozens of common rooms throughout the castle for each section of dorms, sometimes the group common rooms get used and sometimes they don't."

"What about me? How come I have a gray candle? Does it take a while for the color to show up?"

"No, it usually goes one color straight away," said Roger.

"Great," said Gellan, sighing.

"Don't worry about it," said Roger. "It probably just means you can join whichever group you want."

"Or none of them."

Roger shrugged, unconcerned.

"How come when I put the paper into the candle it moved everyone else's candles?" Gellan asked, reaching for a chocolate chip cookie.

"Whenever anyone puts their paper in, it always shifts people a bit," said Roger. "We all do it at the beginning of every school year, and it's usually set for the whole year. The giant map up there is called the Magix—no, Magnim—well, I can't remember the first word, but we just shorten it to 'the Mag Map,' which basically just means 'the map on a large board.'"

"What does it do? The Mag Map, I mean," asked Gellan.

"Well, it basically sorts us all—you know, like people's personalities, their likes and dislikes, their age, that sort of stuff. And it decides who is most compatible with who, and it organizes everyone the best way possible. That way, we get put into dormitories with other boys that we're most likely to get along with. With this many kids, I guess it's best to do what you can to keep issues at a minimum." He paused, looking around. "But—I've never seen it do anything quite like that before."

"Like what?"

"Shift pretty much *everybody* because of one person," Roger said. "I mean—look! Everything is just—" He spread his arms, inviting Gellan to look around, not quite sure how to finish his sentence.

Gellan chose to duck his head and take another bite. "Why do you think that happened?" he asked after he'd swallowed.

Roger shrugged, staring around. "I dunno. I guess because you fit best in a particular spot and it shifted everybody this way or that way to put you there."

"Oh." Gellan looked over at a girl whose eyes were still red, her face streaked with tears. "Is that a bad thing?"

"Some people might be upset about it for a while," Roger said, glancing around. "But that's just how it is. If you get moved, you get moved. And there's nothing you can do about it. Of course, usually it's at the beginning of the year, but—well, everyone knows that's how it works."

Several students were wandering around the hall now—some talking to friends and others meandering aimlessly, waiting until they were sent off to their new dormitories. Gellan found it harder to ignore the pointed glances and open whispering from other students now that he was less focused on eating.

It was another twenty minutes before a pipkin—female, Gellan guessed, and much older than Worley—came in through the side door and gave an "all clear" signal to Professor Fisk. He nodded and stood up.

"Back to your seats, please," he said. He waited several seconds while the wanderers found their seats again, some spinning on their heels for a moment before they remembered where their new spots were.

"Now then," Professor Fisk said, "the staff have worked their magic as usual and all of your things have been moved to your new dormitories. In an orderly manner, please, each person will find their name on the Mag Map, then out through the side door to bed."

He seemed content to let the students decide for themselves what "orderly" meant. Some raced forward, some stayed seated to wait for the milieu to die down, and many took their chance at in-between gaps. There was much pointing and discussion as each person found their name.

After another fifteen minutes, Gellan, who was following Roger and feeling utterly exhausted, finally got close enough to the Mag Map to help look for their names. All he could think of now was finding something reasonably comfortable to sleep on—anything was better than a hard bench in a sky pod that was careening through the air.

"I wonder if we'll be in the same dormitory," Roger said, scanning the map. "You're not always with the people you sit by at dinner. I used to be with Archer Galloway"—he pointed across the hall at a brown-haired boy who was just leaving—"Martin Kirkpatrick"—a very freckly, plump boy who was still eating—"and Castor Fabian." He pointed at a black-haired boy looking rather peevish at a far table.

When he got up to the map, Gellan searched for his name. Further and further over he went, until Roger, pointing, said, "Yes, here we are. And we're with Jack and Andy—they're twins, so no surprise that they're together. I think they're a couple of grades above us. And Corben Timmel. He's in our year."

"Do you know them?" Gellan asked, glad to be able to follow Roger rather than have to find the way himself.

"A bit," said Roger. "They're all decent. But I think Corben is gone, visiting his grandmother. Otherwise he would've been sitting across from you at our table. I saw his candle there."

They ascended the main staircase, which took them up seven stories. Gellan tried to stick landmarks and other details in his memory at each level, hoping to avoid getting horribly lost the minute he had to traverse the maze of corridors and staircases on his own, but the fog of exhaustion made the statues seem extraordinarily alike, and some of the paintings seemed to change like mirages as he walked by.

Through a set of large doors on the second floor, Gellan could see what looked like brightly lit kitchens with dozens of busy pipkins. He considered asking Roger more about them—where they came from, and how they came to be at Gilsthorne—but decided his questions could wait for another day. The third and fourth floors looked similar, with large, open spaces filled with chairs ringed by smaller class-rooms around two sides. The other two sides appeared to be solid rock, which slowly began arching toward them, squeezing the stair-case as the boys ascended to the fifth and sixth floors. On the seventh floor, the large staircase ended and they walked to a wooden staircase.

"How far does this go?" asked Gellan.

"Four more floors," said Roger. "No one talked about the best way to make a convenient building when they built Gilsthorne, that's for sure."

"So Gilsthorne is eleven floors altogether?"

"No, that's just how tall it is inside the hill. Then we have another staircase that takes us up into the towers, and another one to the turret where our dorm is."

Gellan found the interface between the building inside the hill and the building on top of it very curious. He had expected to pop up through a hole in a thick rock foundation and find himself in the middle of a castle.

Instead, the solid rock of the walls seemed to slowly break up into the many hundreds of large stones that formed the human-made structure, embedding the towers directly in the solid rock of Gilsthorne Hill. The steps of the staircase they were on grew shal-lower and wider, curving ever so slightly until it gently conveyed them onto the smooth stone floor of a long hall. Gellan could see students emerging from a similar staircase all the way at the other end of the hall.

The two streams of students broke up into four as they moved toward one of the spiral staircases in each of the four corners of the building. Above them there were occasional shafts that went right up to the skylights in the roof, through which he could see starlight. Along these shafts were balconies on every floor.

"This way," said Roger. "We're in Cupcake Tower."

Gellan did a double-take. "Um... what? Cupcake Tower?"

Roger shrugged. "The pipkins like food words, so I'm guessing they were the ones that named everything. Like Tart Tower, or Ambrosia Atrium, or Gingerbread Gym. They're a bit bonkers, really. Every tower and room has a number too, but I think the names are easier to remember."

Gellan nodded. Considering what other words they could've used, Cupcake Tower didn't seem so bad.

As they stepped onto the landing of the second floor, Roger paused for a moment, watching a boy at the far end of the corridor who was on his hands and knees, patting the stone wall around the door. Roger paused for a moment, before shrugging and moving on up the staircase.

"What's he doing?" Gellan asked.

"That's Declan Bray," Roger said. "He's trying to get the key for his dorm. He's supposed to be on the next floor up. I saw his name on the Mag Map. I wonder if I should..." He shrugged again.

Up and up, five more floors, until at last Roger stopped in front of a large wooden door in the shape of a keyhole.

"Here we are," said Roger. "This is the Cupcake Tower. Now we just have to find..." He ran his hand along the sides of the door, and when nothing happened, he started patting the stones next to the door. At his touch, one of them suddenly disappeared. "Ah, here it is."

Roger reached in, grabbed a key, and unlocked the door in front of them. The door swung open, slightly off-kilter, and a large, round room spread out before them. As they shut it behind them, the key disappeared and the lock clicked in the heavy door.

"Looks like that's the boys' bathroom over there," Roger said, pointing to a widely-arched doorway edged by gray stone. "And that must be the girls' bathroom." It was edged in white stone. "Don't get them mixed up, or... everyone will know. And this is our turret," he said as he walked toward a smaller doorway to the right of a fireplace.

When Roger ducked right through a flimsy, sheer curtain that was hanging across the doorway before disappearing up the steep spiral steps, Gellan had just enough energy to feel briefly surprised. He stopped and reached out his hand, sticking it through the misty, swirling curtain. It felt soothing and warm, like dipping your hand into a basin of warm water.

Shaking his head, he followed his hand through the curtain and climbed the steps up to their dorm room, where five beds were arranged at odd angles. They were surrounded by thick curtains that gave each student a section of personal space.

Gellan looked around and saw his trunk and other possessions next to a bed on the far side. He had just dropped to his knees in front of it, ready to push it open, when he heard a chime float up from the bottom of the stairs.

"What's that?" Gellan asked.

"It's just the dormbell," Roger replied, getting up. "The callicurtain prevents people who aren't in our dorm from coming up. Hang on, I'll go see who it is."

Gellan pulled off his shoulder bag and was just looking through the assortment of clothes and bathroom necessities that Uncle Ivan had packed for him when Roger called from the doorway.

"It's someone for you," he said to Gellan. "I don't know her name. And anyway, I think I'll go see if Declan is still stuck."

Knowing his visitor could only be Drina, Gellan got up with a sigh and followed Roger down the steps.

"Hi," she said when he appeared. She edged off to the side a bit, like she wanted him to follow her. Other students occasionally entered the large room and looked over at them curiously before disappearing through one of the turret doorways, but she ignored them.

"You still have that thing on, right?" she asked quietly.

"Yeah," said Gellan.

"Good. Just so you know, only people who belong in your dorm can get in there, so by and large, it's a pretty safe place," she said, looking around the common room again. "Also, if *your* trunk is under *your* bed, no one is supposed to be able to touch it. There are spells that prevent students from meddling with each other's stuff. So I think the best thing you can do for now is put that thing in your trunk, shut it tight, and shove it under your bed."

"Oh good," Gellan said. He'd been worried about it, but at this point he was nearly too tired to care.

"Make *sure* you close your trunk and put it under your bed *every* time," she said. "And keep it in that bag. And wrap it up tight in a jacket or something to try to keep the light from being seen by anyone else. I hope it works, but I can't think of anything else to do at the moment."

"Right," said Gellan.

"All right, then," she said. "I'm going to go to bed. I'm tired and I expect you are too."

He nodded. "Where are you at?"

"I've been moved up to one of these turrets too," she said. "I'm over there, in turret number seventeen."

"Oh," said Gellan. "What number am I in?"

"Number nineteen."

"Oh," he said again. "Well, good night."

He went back up to his dorm room and, before anyone else managed to get there, quickly pulled off the hidden pocket, wrapped it in a thick sweater, and stuffed it in his trunk. He pulled out his pajamas, then slammed the trunk shut and shoved it under his bed.

After shutting the curtains around his bed, he glanced out of the window to where he could just see moonlight glinting on the ocean through the gap in the outer mountains where the river ran through. He climbed into bed, and within a few short moments he was sound asleep, oblivious to the chatter and laughter of the others as they prepared for bed.

He didn't even wake up when a little black shadow pecked at his window for several minutes before ruffling its feathers irritably and flying off.

CHAPTER TEN

EVALUATION

G ellan woke early the next morning feeling much better. After dressing, he poked around the common room for a while, discovering what he had been too tired to see the night before. It was filled with the same overstuffed chairs he'd seen throughout Gilsthorne, long couches, and variously sized tables under a low, arched ceiling. There were desks or seats in front of every window, tapestries and paintings on the walls, a couple of narrow bookcases full of books, and a bust of a man in one corner and a woman in another.

He was just about to head out of the common room when Worley popped up in the doorway.

"Good morning, Master Gellan," Worley said, patting his right hand over his heart and moving it forward.

"Hi, Worley!" Gellan said, not quite sure if he was supposed to perform the same gesture.

Before he could, however, Worley said, "I've been asked to bring you these." He held up a stack of clothing. "They're your uniforms, sent over from The Cob."

"Thanks," said Gellan, taking them.

"Also, I've been asked to tell you that you're to be in the assembly room on the third floor by eight o'clock this morning. Professor Dinsmore will be evaluating you there."

"Okay," said Gellan. "Uh, can you tell me where—?"

"Oh yes," said Worley. He pulled a thick pamphlet out of a pocket of his uniform. "This is your map of Gilsthorne Building. Every student gets one when they first come, and you'll probably need it for your first couple of years, so don't lose it. But first I need to link it to you, so if you'll just put your hand on it for me..."

Worley placed his hand over Gellan's for a brief moment, and Gellan felt a tingle in his palm.

"Now, let's find where we are to make sure it worked," Worley said as he turned the map upside down, opened a flap, rotated it, opened one more flap, and found Cupcake Tower. Sure enough, there was now a small decorative box with "Gellan Parker" written in his own handwriting in miniscule letters on a tiny, floating candle.

"Good," said Worley with satisfaction, refolding the pamphlet and handing it to Gellan.

"Thanks," said Gellan. "Is breakfast in the Great Hall?"

"Yes. All your meals will be served there."

Seventeen floors both ways, every time, Gellan thought gloomily, but he didn't let Worley see his disappointment. Instead he thanked him once more, waving good-bye as he turned to head back up to turret nineteen to change.

Roger was just getting up. "Hey, mate," he said to Gellan quietly, so as not to wake the others. "Been out and about already?"

"No, not really," said Gellan. "Worley brought me my uniform before I got very far."

"Give me a minute and we can head down to breakfast together."

Gellan pulled on his new uniform and sighed out loud at his appearance in the mirror—though secretly he thought he looked rather nice. Only, it might be nice to get a haircut, because it was sticking out a bit at the sides.

He rummaged through his trunk, found the bag with the cap and cuffs in it, and stuck the cap on to try to hide his hair, but it didn't look much better. As he threw it back into the trunk and shoved his hair back off his forehead, he saw Uncle Ivan's green candle. He scribbled a quick note and sent it off before shutting his trunk and taking care that it was fully underneath his bed.

When Roger was ready, Gellan followed him on a new route down to the Great Hall that involved only nine flights of stairs and two slides formed by enormous indoor drainpipes—though, thankfully, they were *almost* entirely clean.

"Well," said Gellan, "at least the going down is easier than I thought it would be."

"Yeah," Roger replied, "you'd think they would have come up with something to take us up too. Then again, maybe they haven't done anything about it on purpose." He shrugged.

They walked through the enormous doors of the Great Hall and found a handful of students already eating. Gellan sat down at his spot and saw a small quantity of toast and scrambled eggs on trays in front of them, as well as a small assortment of bowls with jams, honey, and butter. He loaded up his plate, looking up and down and back and forth as he ate.

"Where does the food come from?" he asked Roger eventually.

"The kitchens," Roger answered in a why-are-you-asking sort of voice.

"No, I mean how does it get onto the table? Like last night, when it just came and went."

"Oh!" said Roger, comprehending Gellan's question. "They use the transport charm."

Gellan was still none the wiser, but he shrugged. "And who cooks the food?"

"Lots of people. The pipkins—they're brilliant at cooking, and they're in charge. Some students too—if you take cooking classes, you get to help. Madame Neppie is the head chef. And there's some other staff too. It takes a lot of people to run a school like this, even with magic."

Roger took a large bite of toast topped with eggs. Between chewing, he continued talking. "Sometimes kids take the class because they think they'll be able to lounge about in the kitchens and eat leftovers and stuff. But I've heard that Madame Neppie is quite a slave driver and she doesn't let them get away with that for a moment. Earlier this year, I actually saw Brogan Beardsley wiping away tears after his cooking class one day." He grinned and stuffed the remainder of the toast into his mouth, then reached for a newspaper that was sitting in the middle of the table. It had been turned inside out by another student.

"They think it's important for us to know what's going on," Roger said. "That's why they put newspapers on the table every morning. Sometimes teachers will give you extra points if you're able to tell them what was in the newspaper that day."

"Like national politics and stuff?"

"Not so much—I mean, occasionally they'll ask about that," said Roger. "But usually they ask questions about Cremstoll and what's going on here. Or in Washington State, since that's the state we're in. Or for the few students whose families aren't here in Cremstoll, they'll ask them questions about their hometowns—it helps them stay connected to where they're from."

He rearranged the newspaper with one hand while continuing to eat toast with his other hand until he managed to get the front back to where it was supposed to be.

Gellan scanned the headlines over Roger's shoulder as he added some jam to another piece of toast. He left the dripping jam knife hovering in mid-air when he saw one headline:

Magical Flare Likely Related to Poseidon's Quake

Roger was obviously reading the same article, and Gellan pointed to the last two words of the headline. "They reported on that here?"

"Of course," said Roger. "It's kind of big news everywhere. They say it's never happened before." He held up the paper so they could read the article together.

A flare that was spotted four days ago along the northern California coast has been determined to be of magical origin.

"We know that normal flares set off by non-magical means have a very predictable pattern," said magical pyrotechnics expert Jimson Hughes of the magical hazards department at MajMinster, "and this particular flare didn't fit any of the patterns we've documented."

Others in the same office, however, still had their doubts.

"Perhaps it was just very windy that day," said Roy Collins, a low-ranking researcher. "Also, our information on its location and trajectory is not entirely accurate since it is based solely on eyewitness accounts."

However, most agree that the fact that it occurred along the same stretch of coast where Poseidon's Quake is presumed to have originated is interesting and not likely a coincidence.

After interviewing locals who had observed the event, it was determined that not only...

cont. on pg. 4

"People at MajMinster think they know everything," Roger said, rolling his eyes.

"What's that?" Gellan asked.

"You know," said Roger, "the government of magic peoples of the United States."

"Uh, no," said Gellan. "I didn't know. Why do you call it MajMinster?"

"Er, because it's... let's see, the government here in Cremstoll was... well, I think there's an Eastminster government thing, somewhere," Roger said, thinking hard, "so the magical government got nicknamed MagicMinster." He rubbed his head. "There's an official title for it, but no one uses it and... I can't remember it. Anyway, we all just call it MajMinster."

"So, that's different than Faulkner and Madame Guillèn and everything over on Providence Island?" Gellan asked.

"They're just the governors of Cremstoll," Roger said. "MajMinster is President Humphrey, the Congress, and the judges. It governs all the magic people in the country."

"Is it in Washington, DC?" Gellan asked.

"No," said Roger. "It's in Philadelphia. That's why my family lived there for a while—my dad did diplomatic work for them."

"Why isn't it in Washington, DC?" Gellan asked.

"Dunno," said Roger. He turned the newspaper over and scanned the headlines on the lower half of the page as Gellan sandwiched scrambled eggs between the folded halves of another piece of toast. Roger suddenly sat up straighter, holding the newspaper taut. "What in the world...?!"

"Whath?" Gellan asked with his mouth full as he looked back at the newspaper. He managed a hard swallow. "What? Which one?" he asked again, leaning over.

Roger pointed to a small article in the bottom right-hand corner.

Wizard Turned to Wynkler

Medi-wizards have concluded their examination of George Samwick, well-known inventor and clock tinkerer, who disappeared during the second dark day, which occurred shortly before Christmas. He was found sitting on the steps of the Capitol Building the following morning with no memory of what had happened to him.

"We are sad to report that Mr. Samwick has lost all magical abilities and has, in effect, become a wynkler," Medi-Wizard Arthur Gourley reported. "We have not yet determined what could have caused this condition, nor why it is, so far, irreversible."

A spokesperson from the office of Lieutenant Governor Ben Sedargren assured us that they are doing all they can to ensure the safety and protection of the citizens of Cremstoll.

"For obvious reasons, I can't give details about what we're doing to prevent this from happening again," said Ivor Knoll, a former senior scout who has recently qualified as a low-level Vanquor. "All I can say is that we feel confident it will not."

"Has that ever happened before?" Gellan asked.

"Not that I've ever heard of," said Roger. He folded the newspaper and set it aside. "Weird, though. D'you think he'll eventually be—you know—a wizard again?"

"You're more likely to know that than me," said Gellan. "I had no ideas witches or wizards even existed until a few days ago."

"Really?" Roger asked. "No idea at all?"

Gellan shook his head.

"Huh," said Roger. "Seems obvious to me." He shrugged, then pointed at the nearly empty toast basket. "D'you want that one?"

Gellan nodded and reached for the last piece of toast, then stopped.

"What's the matter?" asked Roger.

"Aren't there other kids who haven't eaten yet?" Gellan asked.

"Well, sure," Roger said. "But the empty basket will go back to the kitchens, and they'll fill it up and send them back. They don't like to waste food around here, so they only send a bit at a time."

Gellan took the last piece of toast, and the basket disappeared. Within a couple of minutes another batch was sitting in front of them. Roger grinned and took a fresh piece.

"Nice," said Gellan with a wry smile. "You let me take the last, cold slice so you could have a nice warm one."

"Every new kid has to learn the ropes somehow," said Roger. He checked his watch. "I'd better get going. I have to finish up something before class starts." He slopped some jam on the toast and took it with him.

Gellan finished eating a few minutes later. Even though it was only seven-thirty, he was worried he would have a difficult time finding the assembly hall, so he headed off in search of it. He tried to unfold his map as he walked, but soon realized that wasn't going to work. He found a large, isolated corner, where he began to carefully unfold the map and spread it across the floor. After several minutes the map had extended out much further than he had thought was possible, with no end in sight.

Not only that, but there seemed to be hundreds of pop-up flaps with instructions. Some were tiny and written with miniscule lettering ("It is advised that you avoid this ladder; otherwise you may find yourself going down instead of up, or up instead of down"). Some were large ("Do not be alarmed if this classroom begins rocking about like a ship—it has never yet caused any harm or death; the cause is unknown"). One warned about a sink's mysterious habit of pouring water out of the drain, and draining through the tap. Still another indicated that a particular door sometimes did not lead into the room beyond it and instead transported a person to the very spot in Gilsthorne Building he was trying to avoid going at that moment.

Trying to find the path of least resistance, Gellan memorized a befuddling route to the assembly room, spent several minutes folding up his map, and then bolted off. All was going well until he found an uncooperative suit of armor standing in his way. Not wanting to challenge something that was wielding a heavy-looking ax, he backed away and paused just around the corner, unfolding the map and trying desperately to find another route.

His second attempt took him out onto some crumbling battlements and down a very narrow stairway that led to an undersized door... which miraculously opened into the back of the assembly room. He poked his head in and found, to his relief, that nobody was there yet.

It was a moderately-sized square room with steps at each corner and lots of wooden benches. It was lit by large, bright windows on two sides. Down at the bottom, in the center of the room, was a square platform.

He began walking around and around the room on each level, poking into corners and peering under benches. He didn't really expect to find anything unusual, but a building this old surely had secrets long forgotten, and he was determined to find as many of them as he could.

He was near the bottom of the room when he heard someone clear their throat high behind him. He spun around and was surprised to see that it was Faulkner. He had his hands deep in his pockets and was staring at Gellan as though he'd been there for quite some time. He removed a fedora and a thick, deep brown cloak and tossed them both onto one of the top benches.

"Well, now, what might you be up to?" he asked as he walked slowly down the steps. His voice reverberated around the room.

"I was told to be here to be evaluated, sir," Gellan replied. "Did I get the wrong room?"

"No, this is the right room," Faulkner said. "That's why I'm here too. I wanted to observe your evaluation."

"Why?" asked Gellan. He wasn't sure he wanted Faulkner there.

"Because of... the unusual circumstances surrounding your coming here," said Faulkner.

Gellan knew he wasn't getting the whole truth, and it annoyed him.

"I meant to ask about your curious habit of tapping the sides of the wall as you were walking along," Faulkner added.

"I was just testing, to see if it was all... real," Gellan said.

Faulkner paused near the bottom, giving Gellan a bemused look.

"And did you find anything out of the ordinary?" he asked with a smile.

Gellan turned away. He did not like being laughed at. "No," he said, and he sat down on one of the stone steps, his back to Faulkner.

"Well, you just might come across something if you keep look-ing," said Faulkner. "A building this old, having been built in fits and starts over so many centuries, can't help but have many secrets, and I doubt all of them have been found yet. Especially since it wasn't humans who first hollowed out the hill, and we rarely have the mind to understand other beings."

"Really? Who did hollow it out, then?"

"American Mountain Dwarves," said Faulkner. "At least that's what we think based on some of the carvings in the rocks you'll see in some classrooms. And they had plenty of reason to hide things."

It was quiet for a minute or two.

"Have you written to your uncle yet?" Faulkner asked.

"Yes," said Gellan. "I sent him a note this morning." He wished Professor Dinsmore would hurry and join them.

Faulkner nodded his approval. "Good," he said. "You'd better make sure you keep doing that, or I'm quite sure he'll make good on his promise to hunt us down."

"Ah, good, you're already here," a feminine voice said above them.

Gellan jumped and spun around. The speaker was a middle-aged woman with rich brown hair cut in a perfect bob, and surprisingly deep blue eyes. Her face was strong, but still very feminine, with high cheekbones, a pointed chin, defined eyebrows, and a slightly pinched nose. She was wearing a sky-blue tweed outfit, with odd boots of the same color.

"Thank you for being punctual, Mr. Parker," she said as she descended the last few stairs. "I'm Professor Dinsmore."

She set the things she was carrying onto the bottom bench and held out her hand to Gellan. He shook it briefly and then shoved his hair back.

She nodded at Faulkner. "Hello, Abe."

He gave a small nod back. "Hello, Annie. How are you?"

"I didn't know you were going to be here," she said without answering his question as she arranged the things she'd brought with her.

"I just thought it'd be interesting to pop in and watch." His voice sounded intentionally casual.

She eyed him for a moment, then turned to Gellan.

"So," she said, "you want to go to school here?"

"I wasn't really given much choice in the matter."

"Oh?" She looked around at Faulkner for an explanation, but he seemed to be so busy looking at his fingernails that he hadn't heard. She sniffed and turned back to Gellan.

"Well, then, do you *wish* to go to school here now?" she asked.

Gellan thought for a moment. "Yes."

"Very good, then," she said. "We just need to evaluate you to be sure you can keep up with the other students. So—if you'll step up there on that center platform for me, we'll start with a few basic things."

She rummaged in a bag and pulled out an egg-shaped stone.

Gellan recognized it at once—it was a signall like the one Drina had used.

Professor Dinsmore picked up the wand and tapped the signall. "What color is the light?" she asked Gellan, holding it up.

Gellan looked at it and his heart sank.

"I can't see a light, Professor," he said.

She blinked at him for a moment. "Nothing at all?" she asked.

"No." He shook his head. "I asked Drina why that was, but she didn't know."

"Why what was?"

"Why I can feel things with my hands—magical things—but a lot of times I can't see them."

"I see. That *is* a bit of a riddle," said Professor Dinsmore. "So you can feel magical objects more easily than you can see them?"

"Well, I can see *that*," he said, pointing to the signall, "just not the light it gives off. So I guess it depends—I'm not sure."

Professor Dinsmore paused for a moment, thinking. Then she touched her wand to the signall again and said, "Duwn." She held the wand out to Gellan.

"Take this," she said. "It's our testing wand and it's quite old, so be careful with it."

Gellan took it gingerly.

"Now," she said, holding out the signall to him, "light the signall yourself."

Gellan did, and immediately saw the rock glowing a deep orange color.

"Well done. Do you see a light now?" Professor Dinsmore asked.

"Yeah," Gellan said, feeling ecstatic. "It's orange!"

"Interesting," she said. She pulled another wand out of her sleeve, tapped her clipboard a couple of times, then stuck the wand back up her sleeve.

"All right," she said. "Go ahead and turn it off."

Gellan touched the wand to the signall and said, "Duwn," then watched as the light faded away. He held both objects out. She took the signall, but motioned for him to keep the wand.

"So we know you can likely do all the basic spells," she said. "Let's have you try another one. How about the wind charm? The spell is 'ventus.'" She enunciated the last word.

"What does this one do?" he asked.

"It creates a light breeze. People use it to fan themselves when they're hot, or blow dust off furniture or floors, that sort of thing."

"Oh, okay," he said. "Uh—hang on—"

"Ventus," she repeated.

He cleared his throat, then said, "Ventus!" holding the wand out in front of him.

A strong rush of air issued from the wand and Professor Dinsmore's clipboard, which was lying on the bench, nearly had the papers ripped right out of it. The intensity surprised Gellan and he swung the wand up, as though to turn it off, but the air continued to blow. Dust and cobwebs from the high stone walls began raining down on all three of them.

"Turn it off, Mr. Parker!" said Professor Dinsmore, covering her head with her clipboard.

"How?!" he asked, shielding himself from a spray of rock dust.

"Finitum!" she shouted over the wind.

He repeated the word, and the rushing sound ceased. Dust continued to settle on them for several seconds. Professor Dinsmore pulled a cobweb off her shoulder and let it fall to the floor, then tapped the clipboard with her wand.

"I think we'll need to work with you on controlling your outflow," she said.

"Sorry," he muttered.

She dismissed his apology with a wave of her hand. "Do you know any other spells, or have you seen any others performed?"

"Leuf, the obstructos one, um—the firestone spell but I don't remember it—uh, hang on—adhero, and I guess that's all I remember right now."

"Have you tried any of them yourself?" she asked him.

"Um, yes—" said Gellan, looking over at Faulkner out of the corner of his eye. "I've done the flare spell."

Professor Dinsmore looked at Gellan for a moment, and he noticed that her eyes twitched sideways briefly to look at Faulkner, who was again determined to *not* meet her glance.

"Well, I don't think it would be a good idea for you to do that one in here," she said to Gellan. "I think we've seen enough of wandwork anyway."

Gellan handed her the wand and she set it aside before reaching into the bag again, this time pulling out a small potted plant.

"This is a hoblot plant," she told Gellan. "It grows in dark areas like caves. We use it in our testing of new students because it can detect the light, or the spark, that gives you the ability to do magic."

She set the plant on the bench and pulled out an old stopwatch that looked like the ones Gellan used to take apart to watch the working gears.

"If you would come over here, Mr. Parker," she said, motioning him to the bench. "Now, just hold your hand over it for me—quite close to the leaves, please."

He did as she asked, and the stopwatch started ticking. A split second later, he gasped and pulled his hand back as though he'd been burned. The top two or three leaves of the plant had turned a glowing red color, and the lower leaves were beginning to flush. Gellan glanced up and saw that both Faulkner and Professor Dinsmore looked surprised. The stopwatch ticked on, forgotten by them all.

Professor Dinsmore cleared her throat again and stopped the metronome. "Once more please, Mr. Parker. And don't worry, the red leaves won't hurt you. They're just reacting to... you."

Gellan reached out his hand again and placed it directly over the plant. This time he tilted his head to look curiously at it as the leaves changed to the same red, glowing color.

"That will do," said Professor Dinsmore after a moment, and Gellan withdrew his hand. The plant became deep green once more.

It was quiet for several minutes as Professor Dinsmore tapped the clipboard with her wand. Gellan passed the time by holding a finger over one leaf and then another, watching the bursts of red appear and then fade.

At last, Professor Dinsmore addressed him again as she pulled out a small, leather-bound booklet.

"I see you've already been signed up for five classes," she said, looking at another paper on her clipboard. "The most you can take is nine classes on our rotating schedule, but that ends up being a really full day and a very full week. Most of our younger students take a maximum of seven."

"What options do I have for other classes?" Gellan asked.

"You'd have to take the Magic Introductions class, which is combined with basic Latin and Welsh..."

"Latin and Welsh?!"

"A lot of old references and spells are either in Latin or Welsh, so it's crucial you get a basic understanding of them," she said firmly. "So, what else would you like to take?"

"What would you recommend I start with?"

"Let's see... you could take Basic Biology of Magical and Non-Magical Plants. That's a very popular one, of course. And it goes really well with Magical Mixtures, which would be a double period for you on Tuesdays, Wednesdays, and Thursdays, leaving you one study hour on Monday and Fridays. A lot of times you'll use plants you grow and harvest during your biology class in your Magical Mixtures class, so it's best if you take them together."

"Okay. I'll try those ones. How many more can I take?"

"Let's just do one more, if you'd like. Or you can just leave it open as a free period. Which might be a good idea so you don't get over-whelmed—"

"No, I'd like to take something. What's available?"

Professor Dinsmore scanned the schedule. "Looks like there's a spot open in Spells and Charms, Level I."

"I'll try that one too."

Professor Dinsmore shook her head a little as she tapped her clipboard. "If you start thinking it's too much after a few days, let me know and you can drop one or two of them." After a moment, she handed him some papers. "Here's your class schedule. And this is your book list. If you give it to Governor Faulkner, I'm sure he'll see to it that you get the rest of your schoolbooks somehow. You'll also need a handful of potion vials and finishing salt for your Magical Mixtures class."

Gellan turned reluctantly to Faulkner and handed him the book list.

"Of course," said Faulkner, taking the list from Gellan and addressing Professor Dinsmore, "I'll take care of it."

"And this is for you," said Professor Dinsmore, handing Gellan the hoblot plant. "It's tradition that during testing time at the beginning of the year, one of the new students gets to keep the hoblot plant. Since you're the only one tested today, I guess it's yours. Water it about once a month, and other than that, you can just keep it in your trunk."

Gellan took the little plant and stuck it in his shoulder bag.

"Well, Gellan," said Faulkner as he stood up, "looks like we need to get you back up to The Cob to get a wand and some books. I'll take him now—if you're done with him, Professor Dinsmore?"

She nodded as she gathered up her things, and Faulkner set off up the stairs at once. As they wound their way around corridors (the suit of armor was standing dutifully against the wall again, though the helmet turned as he went by) and down stairways, Gellan tried to stick more landmarks in his mind. He began to wonder if this was a fruitless exercise when he saw a painting of a big brown desk with no one sitting at it, though he was quite certain someone had been there when he had passed it before.

As they were making their way back through the hills on the edge of Gilsthorne Island, the land pod picking up speed on their descent from the mountains to the ocean, Gellan couldn't help asking a few questions.

"Governor, sir, what do I have to do to pick a wand?" he asked. "I've never seen anyone do it."

"It's not hard," Faulkner said. "A lot of people have superstitions about getting the exactly correct wand. And for some people, perhaps it is essential that they get a very specific wand; but in most cases, three or four wands would do very well for each person. It usually doesn't take long to find at least one or two that suit you."

"Who makes the wands?"

"There are a handful of wandmakers in America," Faulkner said. "Here in Cremstoll, we have Albury Wands."

"What are they made out of?"

"Typically they're made out of wood, with a conductive core. Think of it like the wires that carry electricity in the wynkler world. That's... at least somewhat similar."

"Oh. Right. What's in the—the conducted—"

"The conductive core? There are a lot of different options. Something powerfully magical. Sometimes it's a strand of quartz, or water from a magical fountain, or something from a magical animal. And very occasionally, a wand doesn't have a separate core, but those wands are rare because they can only be made out of very specific parts of very specific trees that have imbibed magical conductive properties."

"Oh," said Gellan.

They'd reached the shore, and he immediately hopped out of the land pod. As he was stepping into the sea pod, he saw an orca breaking the surface of the water some distance away.

"Do orcas come around here often?" he asked, pointing, then sat down quickly as the pod set off at Faulkner's command.

"They live here year-round," said Faulkner. "So don't go swimming in areas you're not supposed to."

He didn't say anything more, and Gellan turned back to the window. A moment later, far off, Gellan saw the orca jump again. With an almighty belly flop, it splashed back into the water.

After what felt like a very long time, they were finally walking under the arch toward The Cob. Having made a quick stop at The Quigrapher (Gellan could hardly wait to have a chance to peruse his splendid new books), Faulkner led Gellan down a curious little side street.

Straight in front of them, at the dead end, was a gray stone three-story building. It had three large gables facing the street, set into the cross-gabled roof. Like most buildings in The Cob, it had plants set out to decorate the front of the shop. However, it was notable for several reasons, not least of which was that there was a tree growing out of its roof between the center and right gables, and also that it looked rather older than the buildings squished around it, which was saying something. A barely legible sign that said *Albury Wands* sat at a slight angle over a narrow portico.

Faulkner pushed the door open and ushered Gellan in.

CHAPTER ELEVEN
WHAT'S IN A WAND

Gellan's gaze was immediately drawn to the tree, which was growing up through the floor off to the right of the shop. The branches leaned toward light that was coming through what Gellan now realized must be an obstructos. Its trunk was thick and bent, and the twisting, winding shape of its branches as they climbed high up into the light created an enchanting effect.

The whole right side of the shop was empty, except for the tree, but shelves filled the rest of the shop from floor to ceiling, and all were crammed with boxes and cylinders of all shapes and colors. In the front left corner was a spiral staircase that led up to balconies running along the second and third-floor levels all around the shop.

A youngish man came toward them through a door on the left, wiping his hands on a towel. He looked surprised.

"Faulkner, what a pleasure to see you," he said, holding his hand out.

"Good to see you too, Edmond," said Faulkner, shaking hands with him. "It's been a while. Is your father here?"

"No," said Edmond. "I'm afraid he's not doing well at the moment.

He just got back from a trip last night, and he must have caught something while he was abroad. I took him to Imple's Infirmary earlier this morning; they think it's Mirage Measles, but they said he should recover soon enough."

"I'm very sorry to hear that," said Faulkner. He looked disappointed. "Well, I'm sure you'll be able to help us. This is Gellan. He's starting school and he's had his evaluation. Now all he needs is a wand."

"Excellent," said Edmond, sticking the towel into his belt and rolling up his sleeves. "Well, we're glad to have you, Gellan. We have a few wands from different makers here, and several made by my father too, of course. Are there any in particular that interest you?"

Gellan looked at him blankly. "I'm sorry, sir," he said. "I'm afraid I wouldn't know one wand from another, so I really couldn't tell you."

"No problem, no problem," said Edmond. He walked over to a counter and pulled out a thick wooden clipboard. It was so old it had turned black around the edges. Edmond tapped it with his wand, and a sheet of black paper unfurled itself onto it. Then, without warning, he flicked his wand at Gellan.

Within a split second, Gellan was enveloped in a blue light similar to the one Drina had used to take a picture of the black-uniformed soldier. It made his eyebrows prickle, and the inside of his nose felt like he'd just taken a deep breath of frosted air. The hair on his arms stood on end and his toes curled in his socks.

Gellan coughed and fell backward a couple of steps as the swirling blue light left him and reentered Edmond's wand. Unconcerned by Gellan's reaction, Edmond sent the blue light toward the clipboard and watched its effect on the black paper. His expression changed and he looked around, perplexed.

"What's the matter?" Faulkner asked.

"Nothing," said Edmond. "It's just—I mean—there's nothing." He held up the clipboard, and Gellan saw that the black sheet of paper was entirely blank.

"What should have happened?" Gellan asked.

"Well, usually it gives some magical measurements, and a

diagram of a person's—hang on, do you mind if I try it again?" Edmond asked him. "I've done this dozens of times. I'm quite skilled at it... usually."

Gellan shook his head, and a moment later, with a flick of his wand, Edmond repeated the process.

"Nothing," he said, examining the black paper. "What in the blanders...?" He straightened up and shook his head. "Never mind. We'll just have to do it manually, I guess."

He removed the black sheet of paper and replaced it with a plain white one. Then, with a wave of his wand, a pen zoomed out of a nearby desk drawer and poised itself above the clipboard; together, they followed Edmond as he headed off around the corner and ascended a ladder.

"Now, I'm going to ask you a bunch of questions, so answer them as best you can, all right?" he called down to Gellan as he began looking through the boxes and cylinders crammed on the shelves.

"Right," said Gellan.

"How old are you?"

"Thirteen."

Edmond glanced over at the pen, which had started scrawling across the paper. He looked up, chose a box and, using his wand, sent it flying through the air to land on the counter at the front of the shop.

"And where were you born?"

"California. I think."

"You think?" Edmond looked over at him. "Don't you know?"

"Not for sure."

Edmond blinked for a moment, then looked over at Faulkner, who didn't appear to notice. Edmond looked down at the clipboard, the pen tentatively scratching out something. He seemed undecided what to do for a moment, then chose a cylinder and sent it over to the counter.

"What do you like to do in your spare time?"

Gellan wasn't sure he wanted to answer truthfully in front of

Faulkner, but he also didn't want to get a dud of a wand. "Exploring—hunting and searching for... things, I guess."

The pen once again began scribbling furiously.

Edmond paused and looked over at him again. "What is it you go searching for, exactly?"

"Answers."

"To what questions?"

Gellan thought for a long moment. "The ones I don't know about yet."

There was a loud screeching noise, and the pen skidded off the side of the clipboard and clattered to the floor. Edmond waved his wand at it, and it fluttered back into position.

Edmond looked over at Faulkner again. This time Faulkner shrugged his shoulders and shook his head, but his disappointment was clearly turning to amusement. A pause, a scratching sound; another box flew through the air.

"What's your favorite subject in school?"

Gellan had to think about that one. The truth was that he loved learning, but he hated doing it on other people's terms. He'd read more books on his own during his summers than he ever had at school. But he knew one thing he liked: "Finding out how all the subjects go together."

Edmond squinted at him, then looked at Faulkner to see if he thought Gellan was being impudent. When Faulkner didn't respond, he took a deep breath and turned back to the shelves once more.

"Are you a first child, second child—?"

"Only child."

"And each of your parents?"

"I don't know."

This time Edmond didn't bother looking around at Gellan. He just shook his head. By now there was quite a stack of boxes and cylinders on the counter. Edmond paused his perusing and motioned Gellan over to the counter as he proceeded to open all of the containers. Wands in the boxes were lying on velvety pillows, and the cylinders held their cargo upright in the center surrounded by cotton stuffing.

With all the wands in a neat row, Edmond stood back. "Now, run your hand over the wands," he instructed Gellan.

Gellan felt a bit silly, but he did as he was told. Both Faulkner and Edmond watched closely. Gellan didn't see anything happen, but he just assumed that it was business as usual for him. He looked at the other two. "Well?"

"Nothing at all," said Edmond. "Hmm..." The pen started scribbling like mad, spitting ink off the clipboard. Gellan stepped back to avoid the spray.

This time, Edmond climbed up to the second story of shelves, still sending questions down to Gellan, who wandered around as he answered—first examining a couple of portraits hanging on the side of one stack of shelves and then getting a closer look at the tree.

"I don't suppose you know if either of your parents were magically trained?"

"No, sorry."

Edmond sighed. "If you like exploring, I expect you prefer to be outdoors?"

"Most of the time. But buildings can hide fascinating secrets too. Especially old buildings where a lot of living has been done."

Edmond paused and looked toward the roof, apparently thinking for a moment (or collecting his patience), before sending two boxes to the counter and continuing to sort through the shelves.

"Do you like spiced food?"

"Spiced, as in cinnamon and cloves? Or spicy, as in hot peppers?"

"Either."

"Both."

A few minutes later, Edmond came back down and repeated the process of laying out all the wands collected on the counter. He had a smile on his face, as though he felt quite sure they would have at least one successful wand in this batch. But his smile quickly faded, and Gellan knew there hadn't been a single reaction.

"What do you find repeating in your brain over and over when you're not thinking about anything else?"

"Oh, gee whiz, um..." Gellan scratched his head. "Can I come back to that one?"

"Okay, let's do... favorite animal?"

"Um... gosh, I've never thought about it. Maybe a bird? Or an otter?"

"Why?"

"I'd get a new view of things if I was a bird, but they don't have hands. But otters have hands, and they're nimble in the water *and* on land. So, I think—wait, that's a macrodon! Yeah, definitely the best."

Another wave across a third batch of wands and—nothing. Soon Gellan had lost count; was that the tenth? The sixteenth? Then the twentieth?

Faulkner and Gellan were now repacking all the tried-and-rejected wands, and moving them off to one corner of the shop as quickly as Edmond was sending new ones over to be tried. Gellan was beginning to feel defeated and dejected. Maybe he wasn't good enough to take magic classes after all; maybe there was a reason he hadn't been on The List.

After yet another round of wands and still no glimmer of success, Edmond began pulling everything off a single shelf and bringing them to the counter, systematically going through all the wands in the entire shop.

Two and a half hours later, with dismay on both Edmond and Faulkner's faces, Gellan ran his hand over the last batch of wands. Not a single one in the entire shop had responded.

Edmond poked under the counter, looked in every last nook on every last shelf, but no more were to be found. He looked wearily at the enormous pile of boxes stacked across the front of the shop, entirely occluding all of the light from the windows.

Gellan slumped in a corner of the shop, his head in his hands. He watched through his fingers as Faulkner and Edmond directed their wands at the enormous pile and, as one might imagine butterflies rising from a tree, the boxes lifted off the floor, flying over and up and sideways and down, before coming to rest in their original locations.

"I've never seen a case like this in my life," Edmond said after a moment. "And I doubt my father has either. Not when someone has already passed evaluation. Did the evaluation wand work for him?"

"Yes, incredibly well," said Faulkner.

"Oh, well—I thought maybe he'd just squeaked by or something," Edmond said.

"No, not at all," Faulkner said. "I'm absolutely stunned."

It was silent for several seconds, and then Faulkner said, "Is there anything at all in wand lore that could explain this? Any stories you've heard of?"

"None that come to mind. I'm sure you understand the basic wand lore just as well as I do."

"There are a lot of wands in the vicinity—not just the ones in this shop—and there are many people with the magical ability to attract them," Faulkner said. "But what if... perhaps a particular wand that is already in someone else's possession happens to be nearby and it negates... any connection he may have to a wand in here?"

"I don't think that's a possibility," Edmond said. "Not for wands that have already been claimed." He paused, both of them thinking. "What'll you do now?" he asked.

"I don't know. Maybe take him to Portland to Garrange's Wand Shop or something."

Edmond looked insulted. "Maybe in this case, any wand in the shop would do. Maybe the point is that it doesn't matter which one he uses. Perhaps we should just let him pick his favorite and see if it would be claimed."

"That's a possibility," said Faulkner. "Though, to be honest, I was hoping for more information about who he is, based on the type of wands fit for his use."

Edmond looked over at him sharply. "Maybe that's why none of them responded. I think you may have jinxed it." He looked sullen.

"You think it's my fault?" Faulkner asked. "I highly doubt that—"

"Very possibly," Edmond interrupted. "That's not what wands are for. Something like that probably interfered with the whole process." He turned his back to Faulkner, tidying and straightening boxes and containers on the shelf in front of him. "Well, I think you have two options if you'd like to avoid a trip to Portland. You can either have him pick out the materials himself from one of the outer islands, and I'll make a wand for him. Or you can have him just pick any wand in the shop that he likes and we can see..."

Gellan got up and wandered through the door that Edmond had appeared through when they'd first arrived, leaving the two men to their heated discussion. He found a workshop filled with all sorts of interesting things: lengths of wood of many colors and sizes, polishing varnishes, and jar after jar filled with all sorts of things. On the walls were pictures of fantastical animals and a variety of crystals, as well as an enormous map of the world peppered with dozens of pins. He examined the labels on the pins and saw some familiar words ("fairy rings" and "dragons") and some less-familiar words ("windrague," "indrik," and "firebirds"). He also found a few labeled "magical fountains." He searched through all the pins and found only nine magical fountain pins in total; three of them were in America. One of these was on the farthest north island of the Cremstoll archipelago.

When he got tired of the map, he looked through the shelves and their contents. As he made his way around the workshop, he saw a narrow box on the workbench. On top of it, an unfinished wand lay askew. Gellan picked it up and examined it. It was slightly longer than average and unlike any of the other wands he'd seen that day. The wood was black and swirly, there were three bands of mother-of-pearl encircling the handle, and he could see a tiny purple rock showing at the tip.

"Gellan, would you come here please?" Faulkner called.

Gellan jumped and dropped the wand back on the box. He rejoined Edmond and Faulkner out in the front area.

"I think we're just going to have you pick a wand," Faulkner said. "If it doesn't work for you over the next few weeks, we'll have to see about getting you matched with a wand in Portland."

"Just... any wand?"

"Almost any wand should work for you well enough," said Edmond. "Some might be better for you than others, but since we have no idea what ones those might be, you'll just have to guess. Do you remember any that you liked in particular?"

Gellan turned and looked up and down the two stories' worth of shelves. "Could I maybe just have the wand that's back there?" he asked, pointing to the workshop door.

To his surprise, Edmond's cheeks turned red. "Well, it's not finished yet," he said. "And anyway, it's an experimental wand."

Faulkner looked at him. "What do you mean?"

"I was just trying something new, and... while my dad was traveling I thought I'd see if I could..." He trailed off at the look on Faulkner's face. "Come and see what I mean," he sighed, and led them into the workshop.

Edmond picked up the wand and handed it to Faulkner, who briefly examined it. "What's it made out of?" he asked, handing the wand back.

"The wood is from the San Juan ebony tree," said Edmond. "I just thought it would look nicest with mother of pearl inlaid into it."

"We don't use wood from that tree," Faulkner said. "It's entirely too unstable."

"I know," said Edmond. "I told you I—"

"Does it have a core?" asked Faulkner.

"Sort of..." said Edmond slowly.

"Sort of?"

"Well, its core is—it doesn't have a continuous one," said Edmond. "It's kind of an amethyst chain—and I was just kind of experimenting—" His cheeks turned a deeper shade of red.

"What's an amethyst?" asked Gellan.

"It's just a type of quartz crystal that happens to be purple," said Edmond. "They're very common. Same with the wood. It grows wild around here. I was just using some inexpensive materials to experiment with, since I didn't even know what it would do."

"I think it's really neat," said Gellan. "Can I try it?"

Edmond looked at Faulkner, who shrugged and looked annoyed. Edmond set the wand back on the desk and gestured toward it. Gellan ran his hand over the wand, hoping for some response.

All of them were surprised when a single, tiny spark shot out of its end.

"Whether that's a good sign or a bad sign, I don't know," said Faulkner. "It may be safer to just pick one of the normal wands—otherwise you may be liable to blow up the whole of Gilsthorne Hill."

"I doubt anything that severe would happen, Faulkner," Edmond said.

Gellan picked up the wand and ran his fingers up and down the smooth, dark wood. In his experience, wood from dead trees dried out quickly, even in the wet weather of Ferndale. But this wand felt strong and alive and slightly bendy, not at all like he would have expected.

"Well, we'd better test it first," said Faulkner.

"How?" Gellan asked.

"First try leuf and duwn," said Faulkner.

Edmond took a step back and cringed just a little as Gellan raised the tip of the wand to eye level, but when Gellan had successfully completed both spells without causing an explosion, he let out a long breath.

"Good," said Faulkner. "Now, just out of curiosity, do the light spell again, and then, without any words, tell the wand to make it brighter or dimmer."

"But I thought he—" Edmond began, but Faulkner threw out an arm to silence him.

"Leuf," Gellan said, holding the wand upright, and the tip lit up. He looked at it and imagined it glowing brighter; the wand responded. He watched it dim down in his mind, and the wand correspondingly obeyed. "Duwn," he said, and the light went out.

He looked at Faulkner, who was watching him intently.

"Well, that clinches it," Faulkner said after a minute. "A wand is really just a conduit for your will and intentions. This one obviously works well enough for you, and as you haven't caused a catastrophe, it seems safe enough. So, let's have you solidify your connection with it."

"How?" asked Gellan.

"It's called 'claiming the wand,'" said Edmond. "It writes your name, indicating that it knows who you are and that you are its master, essentially."

"Like this," said Faulkner. He pulled a wand out of a long side pocket on his pants. "Nomine iungo." He gave a sweeping movement and momentarily left behind wisps of smoke that spelled out his name: *Abelard Caspian Leonardo Faulkner.*

"That's quite a name, sir," said Gellan.

"Never mind that," said Faulkner. "A single word would've sufficed for me, I'm sure, but you can't control what foolish names your parents give you. Now, repeat the spell yourself, and the wand will indicate that it recognizes you through your name."

Gellan cleared his throat and said, "Nomine iungo," imitating the wand movement Faulkner had performed. His wand left behind a stream of light smoke, but nothing formed into distinct letters.

He looked at Faulkner. "Did I do it wrong?"

"No," said Faulkner. "What a puzzle. It should either write your name or not do anything—am I right?"

"Yes," said Edmond. "I've never observed any wand do anything different. Until now, of course."

"Well," said Faulkner, "I'll consider that success enough. Maybe someday we'll figure you out, Mr. Parker."

Gellan had never been more delighted to purchase something in his life. He carefully counted out the coins and handed them to Edmond.

"You'll have to come back when you get a chance," said Edmond as he hastily wrote out an official certificate for the wand. "It's supposed to have one more layer of lacquer on the outside so it's properly finished." He handed the certificate to Gellan, who stuck it carefully into his shoulder bag.

"Now, if you'll just step out for a moment, Mr. Parker," said

Faulkner, "and wait for me in the front area, please. You'll find a pocket along the thigh of your trousers for your wand."

Gellan meandered out of the workshop, distracted by his attempts to find the pocket for his wand. He finally tried sticking his wand straight down by his left thigh and found it made its way into a narrow pocket he hadn't noticed before. He wandered around the shop until Faulkner and Edmond appeared. Faulkner was stuffing a thick roll of papers into an inside pocket of his cloak. Gellan waved good-bye as he followed him out of the shop, leaving a still-flustered and flummoxed Edmond behind them.

Their last stop, at the *Elixir Emporium*, was far too short for Gellan to have a chance to look at all the fascinating objects on the shelves. He soon had about two dozen vials and a tiny container of finishing salt carefully stowed in his shoulder bag.

They walked back to The Corner in silence, and as they approached the hill, Faulkner looked at his watch.

"Well, Mr. Parker, I have other things to tend to. And since you are now equipped with a wand, I trust you can get yourself back to the school without a problem?"

"Yes, sir," said Gellan.

"Off you go, then. You should be in time for lunch. And straight up to the school, mind," said Faulkner sternly as he turned and began walking off. "I'll know if you take any detours."

Gellan stood there for a moment, then said, "How, sir?"

Faulkner didn't even turn around as he continued walking away, but Gellan heard him chuckle. Then he threw out a hand and said, "Off with you!"

CHAPTER TWELVE

MASTER ECKHART

Gellan did make it back in time to grab a quick lunch. Then, not wanting to be late to his first class, he bolted out of the Great Hall with his map held out in front of him and his shoulder bag banging him from behind. He looked at his watch now and then, the minutes ticking down as he tried to find the right classroom.

After going up one staircase, halfway down another, through an odd archway and down a corridor, he finally spotted the door to his Spells and Charms class. He stepped through, only a couple of seconds before the bell, then found an empty desk at the back of the class and sat down, listening to the chatter of his fellow students.

"It's only Tuesday?" one boy asked, sighing. "It's going to be a long week."

"Have you seen Tristen?" another girl asked her friend, who responded with a shake of her head.

Gellan noticed Roger sitting near the front on the opposite side of the room. Roger, who had apparently been watching him, gave him a goofy grin before turning back to the front, just as a man entered the classroom through a side door.

He had old-fashioned glasses, a thin, straight mouth, and an unusually thick mop of dark blond hair, considering the years that showed in his face. Gellan checked his class schedule—Professor Atticus Newbury.

"Has everybody checked in?" he asked.

There was a murmur of assent.

Professor Newbury spotted Gellan, who was looking around, confused. "Ah, Mr. Parker," he said. "Are you joining this class?"

"Yes, sir," said Gellan.

"May I see your class schedule, please?"

"Yes, sir," said Gellan.

He was halfway out of his seat when the paper was whisked out of his hand. Professor Newbury caught it deftly and looked at it.

"Indeed, you are," he said. "Have you had a chance to get your books?"

"Yes, sir."

"And you have a wand?"

"Yes, sir."

"Well done," said Professor Newbury. "If you'll just check in, please, by tapping the top left corner of your desk with your wand."

Gellan did so, and saw his name appear on a chalkboard high on the wall behind Professor Newbury in the same scrawl that had appeared on the candle the night before. He was beginning to wish he'd taken a little more care—his name was barely legible.

"And you'll need this," Professor Newbury said, grabbing a little booklet from his desk. With a flick of his wand, he sent it flying over to Gellan, along with his class schedule. "Now, if you'll all turn to page three hundred eighteen in your books, we're going to be attempting a detangling spell today."

Gellan pulled the book titled *Household Spells and Charms* by Carlotta Teasdell out of his bag and found the correct page. But before they could do anything else, Professor Newbury went over what appeared to be much-rehearsed wand basics, given the bored looks some of the students were exhibiting. One boy with spiky black hair looked over his shoulder at Gellan with a surly look on his face, and Gellan wondered if Professor Newbury was repeating the lesson purely for his sake, to the annoyance of the rest of the class. Then he realized he recognized the boy—it was Castor, one of Roger's former roommates.

Next, they spent quite a bit of time copying down notes about the philosophical and scientific theories behind untangling spells, discussing situations in which they might be useful and noting what could go wrong, as well as practicing the appropriate incantation. As Gellan raced to keep up with his note-taking, not wanting to miss anything, he realized there must be a lot more to properly doing magic than he'd first thought.

They were finally instructed to pick up their wands, and Gellan was quite sure he was about to make a fool of himself in front of his classmates who had months (and perhaps years) of more practice than him. He decided he'd better try not to care.

"I found these in the groundskeepers' shed," Professor Newbury said as he sent a different tangled mass of strands to each of them— from thick rough rope to thin white strands, reddish ribbons like seaweed to stiff leather straps. "I'm sure they'll be pleased if we help them out." Then, just loud enough for them to hear, he added, "At any rate, you can't tangle them up worse." He looked around. "I would advise you girls with long hair to find a large, empty space to practice in, just to be on the safe side. If anyone's spell backfires—"

A couple of girls with particularly long hair looked around at the boys sitting behind them and, appearing slightly alarmed, picked up their tangled balls, moving off to isolated areas of the classroom.

"Oh, and Tina," said Professor Newbury, "I think we'll have you head to that big open spot back there." He pointed rather nonchalantly to a large, empty space behind all the desks. Tina obeyed, looking somewhat chagrined. Gellan noticed that her chin-length brown hair was uneven as she scooted down the row past him.

"All ready?" said Professor Newbury. "Remember to speak clearly and precisely. We don't want any accidents from sloppy wordage. Off you go, then."

Gellan picked up his wand but, curious to see his classmates' work first, paused... and gaped at the utter chaos that erupted around him.

Professor Newbury leaned back on his desk and folded his arms in front of him, an unconcerned look on his face. This must have been a common scene, and Gellan began to feel much better about being a beginner. He couldn't possibly do worse than the girl next to him, whose ball of yarn started racing around her desk as she desperately tried to hit it with a spell. Or the boy in front of him, whose mass of twine started winding itself tighter and tighter, despite his shouts.

A minute later, a girl with long black hair who hadn't heeded Professor Newbury's warning suddenly had her chin thrust down as her hair was pulled straight up into the air by a poorly aimed spell. She whimpered and grabbed at her hair. With a flick of his wand, Professor Newbury released her and she immediately moved off to another corner of the classroom, tears starting in her eyes.

Gellan finally looked down at the mass of very thin threads sitting on the desk in front of him. He picked it up and looked it over for several seconds, following the maze of it here and there with his eyes. He could see several ends poking out, and he realized that it wasn't one long thread tangled up on itself—it was several. As he turned it over, he noticed that the threads, though mostly white in color, seemed to shimmer with other colors, depending on how they caught the light.

He set it down, pulled out his wand and, mimicking the simple wand movements diagrammed in the booklet, set to work.

After several attempts during which absolutely nothing happened, he paused and looked his wand over. Most of the other kids were failing spectacularly, but at least *something* was happening with their wands. He had the brief thought that maybe his wand was dull or less capable after all, but he shook that thought away—he could feel the strength in it. The weak link could only be himself.

He sighed, picked up the white mass, and moved off to a back corner. He set it on the ground and knelt over it, placing the tip of his wand just over the end of one string, and again muttered, "Renèo."

After several more tries, the thread finally began to move. It felt as if the end of it was attached to his wand. He carefully pulled his wand back, and the thread followed in fits and starts.

A loud noise behind him caused him to jump, and he snapped the thread. Tina's ball of rope had just exploded. She looked up at Professor Newbury with hairless eyebrows and an innocent shrug as several students laughed. Professor Newbury grimaced and simply sent another tangled rope over to her without a word.

Gellan turned back, trying to make his movements smoother. After some time, he succeeded in freeing one string. His confidence boosted, he set to work on another one. This one was more stubborn, and it took him several tries to coax it out. As the ball of string decreased, it became easier and easier. After a few more minutes, he was holding several strings in a neat group in his hand—some long, some short, but all as straight as though they had been ironed, and surprisingly heavy.

He admired the way the threads sparkled with different colors as he made his way back to his seat. Professor Newbury was busy untangling the short, curly hair of a girl who was glaring daggers at another student, so Gellan sat down at his desk and just watched everyone else.

"Parker!" Professor Newbury called as the girl with curly hair stomped off to a vacant corner. "This is work time. No daydreaming, please."

"I've finished, sir," Gellan said.

Professor Newbury looked surprised. "Have you?" He walked over and took the heavy, glistening strings from Gellan.

"Excellent work, Mr. Parker!" he said enthusiastically. "Indrik hair can be tricky."

"Indrik hair?" Gellan asked. "What's an indrik?"

"They're one of the wild unicorn species that live on Athos Island. Would you like to work on something else?"

Gellan accepted an enormous ball of thick rope. He heaved it on top of his head and retreated back to his corner. He soon discovered that the rope needed a little more persuasion—the rough fibers prevented the thick strands from slipping past each other as easily as the indrik hair. At one point he was heaving his wand over his shoulder as though he was hauling up an anchor, the rope following with great reluctance.

He nearly had it completed when Professor Newbury called out, "All right, gang. We've got three minutes to the bell. Please come and show me your progress, or lack thereof, so I can note it down before you go."

After Gellan returned the ball of rope, he pulled out his class schedule and map. Roger came and peered over his shoulder.

"Oh good, you've got the magical and non-magical plants class next, same as me," he said, pointing. "We'll have to get going as soon as the bell rings, because it's four stories down and on the other side of the building."

Gellan felt relieved to be able to follow him... until they found themselves staring at a dead end. Roger turned around, looking back the way they'd come and scratching his head, obviously confused. A handful of other first-year students piled up behind them, looking equally baffled.

Gellan shook his head and pulled out the map, finding that they were indeed in the right corridor, but a tiny note mentioned its tendency to block itself up on rainy days. He found a different route, and they all made it to class with a few seconds to spare.

It was a very large room, split into two sections. Half was a classroom filled with desks, and the other half was a brightly lit greenhouse crowded with plants around several round, barely accessible worktables.

A woman with shoulder-length, straight gray hair had her back to them while she worked at the far end of the greenhouse. Gellan pulled out his class schedule and looked at it: Professor Demetria Bramwell. A moment later, she turned and looked at them all, clapping her gloves together and brushing herself off.

"We'll be working in here today," she said, shoving her glasses back up on her nose and leaving a smudge of dirt on her cheek. "We need to fulfill some requests from Master Eckhart for your next class. He gave me a list of ingredients you'll need for Magical Mixtures today. So make sure you've checked in, stow your things in the lockers, then gather around in here."

Gellan looked at his class schedule again. Sure enough, his next class was Magical Mixtures with Master Thorin Eckhart. Having shoved his things into a locker and put on an apron with the rest of the students, he rolled up his sleeves and joined the others thronging the worktable, trying not to trip over plants.

"All here?" asked Professor Bramwell, looking around at them as she shoved her glasses back up her nose again. "Very good. Before we collect what you'll need for your next class, we'll be doing some repotting. Who can tell me what these are?" She pointed to some plants with thick, deeply lobed, ruffled leaves. Most of the class raised their hands, including Gellan.

"Mr. Parker, let's give you a shot at it," she said, looking surprised.

"They look like geraniums, Professor," he said.

"Very close," she said, "and often confused. But not quite. Anyone else?"

A pretty girl with long, dark hair and stunning green eyes raised her hand. "They're pelargoniums. The flowers are different in structure from geraniums, and they can't handle the cold as well." Her eyes flickered toward Gellan briefly and she gave him a small smile, as though she was sorry to correct him, especially on his first day.

"Excellent, Cressida. Pelargoniums also have scented leaves, and they can smell like lemons or roses or nutmeg or chocolate—really quite a wide variety of things. These scents give us some indication of their different uses in magical mixtures, and there are many. They're extremely useful. Now, I started this group"—she picked up a tray of small bushy seedlings—"as cuttings a few weeks ago, and now they're nearly too big for their containers, so we need to pot them on."

She grabbed a bigger pot from a large stack and demonstrated the technique, then set them to work in groups at the round worktables.

Gellan was just beginning to thoroughly enjoy himself when he felt a clod of dirt hit him in the back of the neck, some of it making its way down into his shirt.

He turned around quickly and saw Castor looking innocently at Professor Bramwell as others at his table hid laughter behind their hands.

"My hand slipped," he was explaining. "Honest."

"Let's be a little more careful then," she said, "or my hand might do the same over a detention slip." She strode away.

Castor smirked at Gellan and turned back to his table.

"Want me to hex him for you?" Roger asked, reaching for his wand pocket.

"No," said Gellan. "I don't think that would start me off on very good footing. The last thing I need is someone complaining to the headmaster about me on my first day."

"Tomorrow it is, then," said Roger as he tamped soil down around another plant. "He really is the worst. He's like that to pretty much everybody, and you're easy pickings, being the new kid and all."

"How in the world did you stand being his roommate this whole year?"

"I went home pretty much every night," said Roger. "A lot of kids do, especially those of us that live over in Gilsthorne Village."

"Why do they provide dorms for everyone if most kids' families are here in Cremstoll?" Gellan asked as he tapped a plant out of its pot and put it into a bigger one.

"Just in case they're needed," replied Roger. "Sometimes there's a big event—like the feast days or other special occasions—and they end much later than the classes. Most of us sleep here for things like that. And it's just nice, if you're really busy with schoolwork, for example, to be able to stick around and study instead of traveling back and forth." He picked up another pot and started filling it with soil.

"What are the other dorms like?" asked Gellan, setting a finished plant on the tray. "Are they all as nice as the towers?"

"I don't know," said Roger. "I've only ever been in the towers so far.

My older sister was in the lower dorms last year, though, and I never heard her complain about them."

"Might be nice to be in one of the lower ones then." Gellan tapped out another plant.

"Why?" asked Roger. "Everyone wants to be in the turrets, you know, or at least *somewhere* in the towers. That's probably why Castor's mad at you—we used to be in turret fifteen, but he's been moved down."

"They're the furthest from classes, the Great Hall, from pretty much everything," said Gellan. "It takes *forever* going up and down like that. If you forget something—" He shook his head as he worked soil around the roots of another plant.

"Yeah, but you get an incredible view," said Roger, absentmindedly rubbing one of the leaves and smelling it. "Only about a fifth of us fit in the towers, so it feels kind of, you know, special, I guess. Gosh, these plants *do* smell good, don't they?" He worked another one out of its pot.

"Why do you think you got placed with him as your roommate?" Gellan asked. "I thought you were supposed to be placed with others that you're compatible with."

"Yeah, well, they also say you sometimes get put with kids who might—uh, teach you lessons you need to learn." He shook his head. "So I guess you never know. Maybe it's just totally random but they like us to *think* the Mag Map knows what it's doing." He shrugged.

After another half hour, Professor Bramwell directed them to clean up their work areas as she pulled out a stack of small metal pails. She began handing them out along with a short list of plants for each of them to collect.

"You'll each need one periwinkle flower," she said. "They're just beginning to bloom in patches along the outside edges of the courtyard. They're the small, purplish-blue flowers. Be careful along the path—I don't want any horsing around too close to the ridge." She looked over her glasses sternly at the class. When she felt her warning had sunk in, she continued. "You'll also need a handful of the tulsi basil—it's labeled over there." She pointed to a tray sitting in full sunlight filled with bushy green plants. "And you'll also need one long leaf of lemongrass, just there." She pointed to a large potted plant in one corner. "Off you go, and be back here in exactly ten minutes."

After collecting some leaves from the basil and clipping one from the lemongrass, Gellan headed for the courtyard. He wandered out of the lower east gardens by the greenhouse and along the narrow path above the switchbacks, which led around to the courtyard at the south end of Gilsthorne, where other students were already looking for the small flowers. Gellan found a small patch, chose a flower, and dropped it into his pail. He was making his way back to the greenhouse when he was bumped hard from behind, and he pitched to the ground.

"What's the matter, Parker?" asked a familiar voice. "Your legs don't want to stay underneath you?"

A chorus of derisive laughter sounded in his ears, and several students pushed past him.

"Watch it, Castor," Gellan heard a female voice say as he pushed himself back to his feet and gathered up his bucket.

"What are *you* going to do about it, Burman?" Castor said.

"Oh, nothing," the girl said in a sweet, airy voice. "I just noticed your shoelaces were loose and I didn't want you to trip."

Gellan looked up just in time to see Castor plunging spectacularly into the mud, grabbing two of his buddies on his way down and creating a jumbled mess of students and buckets. Cressida Burman rolled her eyes as she carefully stepped around them, slipping past Gellan just as Professor Bramwell thundered down the path toward them all.

"I said no horsing around close to the ridge!" she shouted, pointing her wand at the group.

Gellan hastened back toward the greenhouse, picking bits of dirt off the periwinkle flower as he went, hoping it would still be usable for the next class.

Back at the greenhouse, Castor and his muddy buddies were looking mutinous as they had their faces scrubbed by wet, dirty rags, directed by Professor Bramwell's wand. Gellan moved to the opposite side of the classroom, where Roger was enjoying the spectacle.

"How'd you manage that?" Roger asked, motioning toward Castor and the other two.

"I didn't do it, that Cressida girl did," Gellan said. "At least, I *think* she did. Or maybe Castor's shoelaces really were untied."

"Brilliant," said Roger.

"It is *not* brilliant," said Gellan. "You just wait. He'll think up something really nasty—"

"Nah, don't worry about that," said Roger. "He's not smart enough for that. He pretends he is, but he's mostly bluster. He's probably part Gilding or something; he's practically a wynkler."

"Wait, the Gildings are wynklers? I thought they were supposed to be the most important magic people or something because they made Gilsthorne, or... something like that."

"That was a long time ago. But the magic has died out in the line now, mostly."

"Does that happen a lot? Magic dying out, I mean."

"No, I don't think so."

"Then why'd it happen with the Gildings?"

Roger shrugged, and led the way out of the classroom at the sound of the bell. As they walked the short distance to their next class, Gellan realized that Castor was headed in the exact same direction. He sighed and trudged into the classroom, following Roger to seats in the corner. A moment later, he forgot about Castor as he ran his hand over the smooth, hard surface of the table in front of him. Then, with a sudden realization, he dipped his head under the table.

An odd, raspy voice rang out. "Are you in need of some Right-Side-Up Restoration, Mr. Parker?"

Gellan sat up fast, bumping his head on the unusual table. "Uh, no, sir," he said, rubbing his head. And then he did a double-take, staring at the man standing in front of him.

He was not quite as tall as the average man, but he was very broad with a thick chest and sturdy shoulders. He had the same pale, blueish skin as the pipkins, with slightly pointed ears, a long, narrow face, and thick white hair. There was something odd about his teeth, and his eyes were the same color as his skin.

"You were obviously not informed that one of your teachers was of the elfin race, Mr. Parker?"

"Uh, no—I didn't know that—I mean I never knew—"

"That there are such things as elves?"

Gellan felt his cheeks go red and he looked down. Then he heard a peculiar chortling, and he looked up to see that it was coming from Master Eckhart. He was not smiling, but his eyes gleamed with amusement.

"You're not the first, Mr. Parker, nor will you be the last," he said. "And yes, the tables in this room are carved out of the solid rock. Since most of our ingredients are plants, it is best that we don't contaminate them by chopping or bruising them on wooden boards which are, of course, plants themselves. Otherwise we might experience unexpected, and occasionally disastrous, results in our magical mixtures. Thus, it is far better that we prepare our concoctions on solid rock. You understand?"

"Yes, Professor," said Gellan.

"Ah, and one more thing. Elves do not go by the title of professor. As teachers, we do not *profess* to be experts. We *are* experts. We are masters of our craft. Therefore, you may call me Master Eckhart."

Gellan swallowed and nodded.

Master Eckhart turned to the rest of the class. "Now, if you'll all please turn to two hundred eighty-nine in your books. We will be working on a mixture called the Politèsseris, otherwise known as... the Etiquette Elixir."

There was a groan throughout the classroom.

"I knew you'd all be pleased." Master Eckhart grinned rather maliciously. "And whether or not you manage to brew yours properly, at the end of class you'll each get to take some that *I* have prepared for you. You will note the effects it has on you, including behaviors you are—shall we say *influenced*—to change, and you will write a two-page essay about your experience."

There was a louder groan from the class. Gellan realized Master

Eckhart was serious when he turned to the correct page in his book and found a detailed description and analysis of the Etiquette Elixir, along with a recipe for its preparation.

For the first few minutes, the class took notes as Master Eckhart lectured them about the various ingredients and their properties and reactions.

"This elixir, though reasonably basic, is still far too complicated to complete in a single class, even a double period," said Master Eckhart, "which is why I have had the fourth-year students do the majority of it for you. Your job is to take a sample of the nearly completed potion and finish it using the ingredients you have brought with you, beginning with step thirty-nine. You will also need half a gram of powdered lion's-mane mushroom, which I have for you over there. Everyone understand? All right then, off you go."

Gellan followed his classmates as they each grabbed a vial of partially completed potion and dumped the contents into a small black pot, of which there were several on each table. Then, reading carefully, he found he was supposed to gently reheat the potion by means of a firestone. He looked around and saw some of his classmates grabbing flat stones off a shelf at the side of the classroom. After watching some of the others, he prodded his firestone until it glowed the same color as everyone else's.

Gellan had hoped his years of cooking would have prepared him for a class like this, but as he read the instructions in his textbook, he realized that making potions would require much more precision than he'd ever had in the kitchen. He began to carefully measure out the necessary weights for the ingredients, trying not to look nervous as Master Eckhart wandered past. Then he proceeded with the chopping, bruising, and crumbling of the ingredients, before adding them to the simmering mixture. As he stirred it, he watched the mixture slowly turn a dark yellow color. The last step was to roll three of the periwinkle flower petals before pressing them tightly between his fingers and dropping them one at a time, stirring left and right, left and right. Master Eckhart paused nearby and watched as Gellan rolled, pressed, and added the third periwinkle petal. The mixture turned a dull, grayish color.

"Hmm," said Master Eckhart. "Not nearly as blue as it should be. Next time, roll the petal more tightly and press it more deliberately in order to release all of its essential compounds. Like this—" Master Eckhart took one of the extra petals, rolled it impossibly tightly, and pressed it firmly. A moment later, a thick drop of purple liquid rolled off his forefinger and dropped onto the stone table.

Gellan gaped. Master Eckhart hadn't just pressed the moisture out of the petal—he had *liquefied* the petal entirely! Was that part of the magic required to make a proper mixture?

"Your mixtures should be nearly complete now," Master Eckhart called out to the class as he moved to the front. "When you're quite sure you're done, don't forget to add one grain of finishing salt to your mixture, *after* removing your firestone, and stir it *one* time. Then fill one of your vials and label it with your name, to be turned in for grading."

With the last stir, Gellan's mixture immediately stopped simmering and steam no longer rose from it. He took out one of his vials and filled it, knowing his hadn't turned out nearly as good as some of the others. Still, neither was it the absolute worst—it was at least gray, instead of an incomprehensible pink like the sample Martin, one of Roger's previous roommates, was handing in.

When Gellan handed his sample to Master Eckhart, he received a small glass cup in return. It contained a single swallow of a thick, perfectly periwinkle-colored liquid. He paused and sniffed it, then drank it down in one go.

It made his stomach feel a bit tingly, but he didn't think it was too bad. When he returned to the table to clean up, however, he found Roger holding his stomach and looking more than a little queasy.

"That stuff tasted delicious, but it makes my stomach feel horrible," Roger said. "I think I'm going to vomit."

"You can't," said Gellan. "That wouldn't be polite."

Roger punched him lightly in the shoulder, trying to smile, but he looked extremely uncomfortable. Gellan couldn't help sending one glance over at Castor and tried not to feel just a little bit satisfied to see he was looking downright ill.

Gellan was putting his things back into his shoulder bag when he noticed that the hoblot plant Professor Dinsmore had given him had one blackened branch. He stared at it for a moment, then looked around for Roger.

"Roger, *Roger*." Gellan motioned him over, then pointed to the plant.

"What's wrong with it?" Roger asked.

"I don't know," Gellan said.

"Maybe you should ask Master Eckhart," said Roger. "He's an expert with plants."

The bell rang and the rest of the class scrummed at the door. Gellan hesitated, then pulled the plant out. "Come on, let's go ask him."

"You go," said Roger, looking gray and sick. "I've got to go get something to eat so that potion isn't the only thing in my stomach." He followed the rest of the students out of the door, leaving Gellan in the large, echoing room by himself.

Gellan took a deep breath, walked up to the wooden door that was slightly ajar behind Master Eckhart's desk, and knocked.

"Yes, come in."

Gellan carefully pushed the door open. "Master Eckhart, sir?"

"Yes, what is it? Oh, Mr. Parker. How can I help you?"

"It's just..." Gellan held out the hoblot plant. "It's this." He pointed to the blackened branch. "Do you know what caused that to happen? I only got this just today, at my evaluation."

Master Eckhart raised one eyebrow and reached out for the plant. He flicked one finger at the blackening branch, and it fell into his hand.

"As far as I am aware, there is only one thing—you say you got this plant just today?"

"Yes, sir."

"And it was just fine when you got it?"

"Yes, sir."

"And you've only been in Gilsthorne Building today?"

"Well, no, sir. I went to The Cob to get a wand and the rest of my books."

"Where *exactly* did you go in The Cob?"

Gellan described his route, and Master Eckhart paid close attention to which shops he mentioned.

"I see. Well, Mr. Parker, yes, I am quite certain what might have caused it, though I didn't think it... possible. Not in Cremstoll." He handed the plant back to Gellan. "I'll keep this branch, if that's okay with you?" Gellan nodded and Master Eckhart dropped the branch into a small jar. He examined it for a moment, his face creased and thoughtful. "Well, I doubt there's anything for you to worry about here at Gilsthorne. And the rest of the plant should be okay."

"But what do you think caused it?"

Master Eckhart didn't reply as he examined the blackened branch; then he suddenly turned and stared straight at Gellan for several moments, a strange expression on his face. Gellan backed away a couple of steps. He was about to turn and run when Master Eckhart stepped back and his face relaxed.

"I don't think it's anything you need to worry about after all," Master Eckhart said.

"Uh, right. Thanks." Gellan swallowed hard, then turned to go.

"One more thing—" Master Eckhart called out as Gellan reached the classroom door.

"Yes, sir?"

"Keep that plant in your bag, would you? And just keep an eye on it over the next few days. Bring it to me again if you notice anything else unusual, all right?"

A shiver ran down his spine as he managed a "Yes, sir," and then Gellan bolted out of the classroom.

CHAPTER THIRTEEN

THE OCKERNOOT COULI

Days, and then weeks, went by. Gellan still carried the hoblot plant everywhere, though it never again had a branch turn black. As things began to feel more normal—or at least, a new kind of normal—with a routine of classes, study, and (mis)adventure, Gellan would have a sudden realization that he hadn't sent a note to his uncle for three or four days. He often opened his trunk to find the candle had spouted half a dozen notes before he managed to send one in return.

His uncle, as always, was a man of few words. He would mention something about the chickens or tell Gellan he'd left something behind. Occasionally he would send a single-sentence news item about someone in Ferndale. But most often, only two words would appear: "Update please." Gellan sometimes wondered if Uncle Ivan sent off a note just to experience the novelty of how the candle worked over and over again.

After sitting through a lot of very long days, Gellan began to wonder if he should've taken fewer classes. Then he would think about becoming a scout like Drina, and he knew he would have a better chance of being accepted if he stuck with his classes.

Sometimes, though, he managed to find enough hours of free time on Saturdays to join Roger in broomstick games with other students in the gardens surrounding the towers. He had relished the opportunity of learning to fly on a broomstick and enjoyed playing the normal games of childhood—like freeze tag, duck duck goose, and capture the flag—in a considerably more fast-paced and exhilarating way. The school brooms weren't great, according to other students who had experience with better and faster ones. Having nothing else to compare them to, though, Gellan thought they were wonderful, even when he occasionally got bucked off. He had so far managed to land in peony bushes and carrot patches, avoiding the many shrub roses that were dotted throughout the garden borders.

He also managed to find a little time for exploring the building and its grounds. He had a growing mental list of places he wanted to see—like the rocky crags below on the west side of Gilsthorne Building and the steep switchbacks spanning the southeast corner.

Or the full extent of the cobbled path that ran down and around Gilsthorne Hill, splitting off as it continued to the east side, through the tunnel under the spring that gushed from beneath Gilsthorne Building...

Not to mention the expansive forest that began near that cobbled path and spilled down to the lake and up the sides of the distant ring of mountains. And not forgetting the multitude of mines in that outer ring of mountains...

There was also the island in the middle of the lake with old stone ruins that he could see from his turret window.

And that was only *outside* Gilsthorne Building!

Inside Gilsthorne, he had spent quite a lot of time already in the multi-storied library, its shelves filled with everything from giant tomes to tiny pipkin-sized books.

Mr. Quip, the head librarian, had helped him to find a book on owls, and he had identified his black owl at last. There was a two-page section in *Wildlife of Cremstoll* devoted to the species. One part had been particularly informative:

> *It is believed that the first pair of Tilly Owls were brought to the*
> *islands some time around 1580. Written accounts are inconclusive,*
> *but historians generally give credit to the history of a woman*
> *named Juliana, who claims to have stowed away on* The Golden
> Hind *during one of Sir Francis Drake's raids on Spanish forts along*
> *the west coast of South America. She claimed to have brought the*
> *owls on board as her pets, and if so, she would likely have had them*
> *when she departed the ship with the Gilding three.*
> *What is known for certain is that the Gilding group left* The
> Golden Hind *when it was anchored along the western coast of*
> *America, possibly somewhere along what is now the state of*
> *California.*
> *Modern study has established that the original breeding pair were*
> *probably from the species now known as the Black-Banded Owl*
> *from Peru (which also gives credence to Juliana's claim), but time*
> *and adaptations have changed their physical appearance enough*
> *that Tilly Owls are now considered an entirely different species.*
> *The main difference between the Tilly Owl and the Black-Banded*
> *Owl is the lack of white edging on the feathers of the Tilly Owl,*
> *except for on the lowest feathers of the abdomen and occasionally*
> *on tail or wing feathers. Both owls typically exhibit white speckling*
> *around the eyes, and some Tilly females have small bands of white*
> *just above their feet. Tilly Owls can occasionally be entirely black*
> *with no white marks at all, though these individuals are rare, and*
> *only one purely white individual has ever been seen.*

Gellan had named the little owl Artemas when *he* was quite sure the *owl* was sure it belonged to him. It had seemed a decent name for an owl. But once he learned it was actually a female, he changed her name to Artemisia.

For her part, Artemisia had learned that Gellan was often grumpy when she woke him up in the middle of the night, so she'd taken to tapping on the narrow, arched window next to his bed just as the sky was lightening—his wake time, her bed time.

Though she visited nearly every day, she never stayed very long. Gellan was always glad to see her and he had begun keeping a little container in his bag which he used to hold live crickets, beetles, and other bugs to give her. Sometimes she brought him a leaf or a flower as a gift, or occasionally a shell fragment or a small gray stone, smoothed by wind and waves. She seemed to enjoy trading her little treasures in exchange for the beetles.

Gellan's other female friend, however, seemed much more elusive, and many days would pass when he wouldn't see Drina at all. She seemed very busy, and he assumed it must be a combination of school, scouting, and shyness. The only time he ever had a chance to speak to her was while she was working on homework in their tower common room.

It was almost the last day of March before he finally saw the boy who was placed across the table from him in the Great Hall. The boy was reading intently, and didn't seem to notice Gellan at all until he looked up to take a bite.

"You must be the new kid," he said.

Gellan nodded. The boy looked back at his book.

"You must be Corben," Gellan said.

Corben nodded, but didn't look up again.

Gellan didn't see him again until several days later. By that time, March had turned into April, and the fields to the west were changing from grayish green to deep green and vibrant yellow as the daffodils began to bloom.

A huge banner was hung in Gilsthorne Village, visible from the towers. There was a palpable excitement about the upcoming Merry Fairy Festival, which was to take place the first weekend of April—not least because the students were to have that Friday off from school.

"We *have* to go to Providence Island," Roger emphasized again one evening. "That's where the fair food will be. There's all kinds of cheeses and desserts—I can't *wait* to try ALL of the scones. I'm sure there'll be butternut fudge and pumpkin doughnuts..."

"And funnel cakes and diddy dumplings..." Gellan finished Roger's well-rehearsed list for him.

Roger grinned and took another bite of potatoes. It all sounded luscious, and Gellan had been trying to work out how many coins he could spare for it all.

"And then there's the final Ockernoot match!" Roger said after swallowing hard. "Did you hear? It's being held on Gilsthorne Island this year, so we can all go!"

"Yeah, I heard about it," Gellan said. "I've never been much interested in watching sports and stuff. So, I dunno. I don't think I'll—"

"You have to go!" said Roger, looking shocked. "My dad got us tickets and everything!"

"He did? Why?"

Roger just shook his head. "Because it's *Ockernoot,*" he said. "Anyway, you have to go."

"Where is it at?" Gellan asked. "There's nowhere big enough here or in Gilsthorne Village."

"There's a stadium in the north mountains. I think it might've been carved out by the American Mountain Dwarves too."

"It was." Corben's book obscured his face as he ate his dinner across from them, but he had apparently been listening to their conversation.

"How d'you know?" asked Roger, as Corben lowered his book to look at them.

"I'm reading about it," said Corben, pointing to the book he had in his hand (*Wondrous Ways to Watch an Ockernoot Match*).

"Course you are," said Roger, rolling his eyes. When Corben had disappeared behind his book once more, Roger turned to Gellan and whispered, "I wonder if he'll put down his book about Ockernoot long enough to actually *go* to an Ockernoot match."

"I heard that," said Corben. "And yes, of course I will."

"Yeah, right," said Roger. "You can't even put it down long enough to *eat.*"

"It happens to be a very interesting book."

"You're *always* reading an interesting book," said Roger.

"And you never are," said Corben.

"Yes, I do," Roger retorted. "I just prefer not to read when I'm doing something more important." He held up a buttered turnip with his fork and wagged it.

"Like what?" asked Corben, without looking up.

Roger didn't bother to answer. He rolled his eyes and stuffed the turnip in his mouth.

Friday morning was bright and clear, and Gellan and Roger joined the other students streaming out of Gilsthorne Building. Some went fishing or to the abandoned mines, but most of them headed straight for Providence Island and the festival.

They were not disappointed. The Corner had been filled with a variety of carnival rides, some of which Gellan had never seen before, and which he suspected could only operate with magic. Surrounding the rides were dozens of white canvas tents and stands filled with an abundance of food and flowers and other goods for sale.

Gellan tried not to feel guilty as he was persuaded by Roger to use a few of the halfpennies from his uncle so he could join Roger on a couple of the rides, and two copper pennies to try some of the food on offer, which he ate while they watched a small parade.

In the late afternoon they found a broomstick obstacle course, with a grand prize of fifteen silver jacks, and spent an hour attempting the fastest time—though with only public brooms to use and minimal experience, Gellan knew he had no chance of actually winning. Especially when some older teens showed up with shiny new brooms made of a sleek, dark wood.

When Gellan was nearly knocked off his broom by several wobbly riders speeding past him, he turned his broom skyward and came to a halt high above the course, watching the speed and skill of the teenagers below as they raced around the obstacle course—spinning, diving, and whirling.

Roger was still attempting to beetle his way up toward him when

Gellan suddenly noticed a small sailing vessel docking at the ancient, crumbling docks on the north side of the island.

"Roger, d'you see that?" Gellan asked, pointing, just as Roger puttered up.

"What? Where?" Roger squinted in the direction Gellan was pointing.

"It doesn't have its sails up," said Gellan. He reached around, carefully fishing in his bag, and pulled out his binoculars.

"Yeah, you're right," said Roger, still squinting. He turned and looked below.

"Why would it be docking there?" asked Gellan as he looked through the binoculars. "D'you think—"

Two figures jumped off the boat and looked around. They slunk over to a shadowy area at the base of some buildings and then, a moment later, they disappeared from sight.

"C'mon, let's go see what they're up to," Gellan said.

"It's probably nothing—" Roger began, but Gellan had soared away, high above the square. Roger groaned as he turned his broom to chase after his friend.

A minute later, both boys landed in one of the rooftop gardens of *Potter's Plants*. The slanted roof made Gellan's legs feel wobbly, and it took him several seconds to make it over to the edge of the building. They both grabbed the ledge, trying to steady themselves as they peered over.

They watched the men below them for several minutes, snatches of conversation floating up to them as the two went back and forth several times from the boat to the buildings, carrying large, heavy crates.

"—can't miss a single one. You 'eard what 'e—"

"—coulda waited till tomorrow—"

"—tha's the las' thing we need—"

Suddenly, a deep, rumbly voice spoke and a man came striding out of the alleyway between the two buildings. His shoulders were broad, and he towered over the other two men.

"Crippen! Cox! Hurry up!" the man said in a loud whisper. "We need to get this finished!"

Both men turned and grumbled a reply, then hastened off for their last loads. A few minutes later, they reappeared, dusting themselves off and standing warily in front of the larger man, who looked up and down the meandering cobbled road along the coast. Gellan caught a glimpse of his face and his eyes grew large. He turned to Roger and mouthed, "Wilkes!" Roger nodded and turned back to watch.

"Good," Wilkes said, apparently satisfied. "Looks like we managed it in time." He held out two small bags to the two men. They each took their share, then dumped the contents in their hands, counting and comparing. "Now get yourselves out of here, before—"

"When d'you want the next load?" one of the men asked as he retied the bag and stuck it into one of his pockets.

"Soon," said Wilkes. "I'll let you know."

"Don' send it like ya did las' time," said the other. "Yer gettin' careless, and las' thing we need's Sedargren finding out."

"Watch it, Crippen," said Wilkes. "I'm not paying you for your input. Even if Sedargren found out about it, what could he do?" He scoffed.

"But 'e might," said Crippen. "You jes' watch yerself. And you mind wha' I said, or I won' be haulin' any more loads for you."

"You'll do it," said Wilkes, and his voice dropped to a low growl. "If I need you to, you'll do it." He turned around and disappeared back down the alley between the two buildings.

Cox and Crippen grumbled as they got back into their boat and began maneuvering it the way they'd come.

Roger turned to Gellan. "He's threatening them? And he doesn't want Sedargren to know? Maybe you were right, mate. Sounds like Wilkes is up to something. What d'you think it is?"

"Dunno," said Gellan. "I wish I'd gotten a look at what was in those crates. Should we try to sneak down into the basement?"

"How about *no*," said Roger. "I don't feel like getting arrested today, if you don't mind. And anyway, we'd better get these brooms back, or *we'll* get reported to Sedargren."

They returned to Gilsthorne just before sunset, where they found the Cupcake Tower common room filled with frivolity and pandemonium.

Some of the older students were practicing spellwork for amusement. Levitation spells sent erasers and wads of paper at various targets in an impromptu fashion. Balloons burst high above them, showering them with confetti, only to be reformed, blown up, and burst again. Some boys were making wooden pencils duel each other in mid-air, trying to force their opponent's pencil into the roaring fire. Gellan's roommates, Jack and Andy, had somehow managed to get hold of some tiny fireworks, which they were exploding inside large glass bubbles.

One person, however, seemed determined to concentrate on homework despite the din. Drina was sitting at a desk in front of one of the windows, her papers and books spread before her. She looked around occasionally before turning back to her work. Gellan wandered over after a while, and pulled a chair up next to her.

"Hi," she said, with a quick glance at him.

"Hi. Behind on homework?"

"Just a bit. I've been really busy." She scribbled away for a moment, then looked up at him when she reached the end of a sentence. "By the way, you are planning on trying to become a scout, aren't you?"

"Definitely," said Gellan. "I've been working hard in my classes. I hope it'll help—"

"Just don't miss the deadline to turn in your scout application."

"I didn't even know there was a deadline."

"I figured." She gave him a side smile. "I'd really like you to be a scout. I might be able to pick up an application for you. I need to go to Providence Island in a few days."

"Thanks," said Gellan, distracted as he batted away a paper airplane Andy had aimed at the back of his head. "Can you even concentrate?" he asked Drina.

She shrugged. "Not as much as I could if I were somewhere quiet. But it's nice to be around everyone sometimes, even if I don't have the time to join in."

"What's kept you so busy?" Gellan asked.

Drina waited a moment before answering, watching Gellan chuck a balled-up piece of paper at Jack after a firework exploded in a bubble right next to them. "I went on a short scouting mission last weekend as part of my continued training. And I've had to... be somewhere most evenings, the last few weeks."

"Where've you had to be? For what?"

"Never mind about it. You'll see tomorrow."

"What're you doing tomorrow?"

She shook her head firmly. "You'll *see*."

At breakfast the next morning, Professor Fisk gave a little speech advising them to take warm cloaks with them to the match and not to forget that many of them had midterm exams in the coming week.

Gellan and Roger tried to keep that in mind for a little while, but found it very hard with so much commotion no matter where they went in Gilsthorne Building that day. Nearly all the students had stayed over for the weekend rather than going home, and with the classrooms empty, the corridors and common areas felt very full.

Dinnertime came at last. The bustle and noise lasted for a few minutes, but no one lingered very long. Pretty soon everyone was flooding out of the doors, through the courtyard, and down the wide cobbled path that wound west, down and around behind Gilsthorne Hill. Gellan and Roger dragged Corben away from his book, though he protested that the match didn't start for another couple of hours and he had plenty of time to get there. But once he realized they weren't going to take no for an answer, the three of them were soon slipping and sliding down the algae-covered cobbles.

The left fork led them to a road where dozens of large, and very old, wooden wagons were sitting flat on the ground, their wheels apparently misplaced. Students began piling into the wagons, shifting around until everyone was comfortable. Not a single person other than Gellan seemed concerned that the wagons had no way of conveying them anywhere.

Suddenly, the moment the first wagon had reached its capacity, it lifted straight up into the air and shot off toward the north mountains. The mystery was solved at once when Gellan saw two very large broomsticks lifting it from underneath, the bristles sticking out the back like rocket propellers.

"C'mon, Gellan!" Roger shouted. "Or you're going to get left behin—"

One last student jumped into the wagon that Roger and Corben had seated themselves in, and the wagon took off without waiting another moment.

"I guess we'll see you there!" Roger called out as they were whisked away.

"You can join us, if you want," Gellan heard someone say. He looked to his right and saw a wagon almost completely full of girls. The speaker was a girl with dark auburn hair, neatly combed and braided. She had turquoise glasses perched on a tiny button nose.

"Oh, thanks anyway, but—" he started to say, but someone shoved him hard and he stumbled toward the wagon.

"That's right, Parker," said a snide voice. "Go hang out with the *girls*. I bet you'll fit right in."

"Leave him alone, Castor," said another girl. "You're just jealous because we would never invite *you* to ride with us." It was Cressida who had spoken this time. Though Gellan hadn't interacted with her much, she was in several of his classes.

Several of the girls snickered.

Castor scoffed and was about to retort when Gellan squared his shoulders, strode straight to the wagon, and jumped in. Castor and his buddies hooted with laughter as they watched the wagon take off.

If Gellan had known it would take them a full half-hour to get to the stadium, he might have thought twice, but he had to admit that the ride wasn't too bad. Most of the girls ignored him, including Cressida, who hardly said anything to anyone the whole ride as she stared around at everyone and everything.

The only one who spoke to him at all was the auburn-haired girl, who introduced herself as Eleanor Sheffield. She told him much more than he needed to know about her father's orchards, and she promised to give him some apples to try when harvest time came around in the fall.

Gellan tried to pay attention to all the various names she mentioned, but the road soon entered a canyon, carved straight out of the vertical rock walls. The road narrowed and became just wide enough that two wagons could pass each other, and he could see dozens of words and other symbols carved into the rock. He became distracted as he watched for words he recognized. The most he got was an occasional "n," "t," or other letter. Everything else looked like gobbledygook.

It seemed as thought the narrow, winding road would never end, but they suddenly came to a large, flat valley. Some distance away was an arena, open down the middle with two curved seating areas carved straight into the sides of the very steep cliffs. People in wagons and land pods or on brooms were pouring in from two other roads as well. A rough building was carved into the mountainside, some distance nearer, and streams of people were heading for it before going through two enormous gates and into the stadium. Gellan could see Corben and Roger among them. They waved at him as the wagon slowed, and as soon as it had stopped and settled itself on the ground, Gellan said a quick "thank you" and rushed off to join his friends.

"Why in the world did you choose *that* wagon?" Roger asked.

Gellan told them what had happened. Roger shook his head. "I have a good nickname for Castor," he said. "Wanna hear it?"

"I still don't get why he hates me," Gellan said.

Roger shrugged. "He's just the kind that needs *someone* to pick on."

Once they reached the stadium, Corben and Roger had a brief disagreement about which part of the student section they wanted to sit in. Corben's book insisted that sitting level with the roule was the best spot. Roger wanted to watch it from as high up as they could go, assuming it would give them the best vantage point for the whole game.

Gellan didn't give any input, since he had no idea what the roule was. Even though he'd picked up bits and pieces of the rules of Ockernoot, as students had discussed it endlessly over the last few days, he hadn't been able to fully picture it.

In the end, Roger and Corben compromised and they ended up sitting about halfway up, just off to one side and slightly above the roule. With the field spread before him, Gellan felt he could finally ask intelligent questions about the game and its rules.

The roule turned out to be something similar to a giant water-wheel, only it was turned on its side and hoisted high up in the air on a tall pillar. The center of the roule was flat and solid, except for a small hole in the very center and six other openings spaced evenly around the edge. Three of them were painted green and the other three white, with the line between the two colors running cleanly down the middle of the roule.

At each end of the field was a matching half-mill-wheel, sitting at a slight angle atop an equally tall post, a flag waving from the top. The white flag had a picture of a seabird and the words "Gilsthorne Gannets" in gold. The green flag had a picture of a scythe and the words "Thrace Threshers" in silver.

As the noise in the stadium grew, and with the trappings of the game in front of him, Gellan couldn't help but feel some of the excitement of everyone around him. He settled in with his back against the stone bench behind him. The benches were so deep that he was able to comfortably sit cross-legged, and he wondered vaguely if giants had once sat here.

The time passed both quickly and slowly, but finally, a few minutes before seven o'clock, a loud voice boomed across the stadium.

"Welcome, one and all, to the opening Ockernoot match of Cremstoll! Please welcome to the field our opposing teams—the Thrace Threshers and the Gilsthorne Gannets!"

Five people entered the field from each side of the stadium. On each team there were three people that were carrying brooms and two that weren't. At their appearance, the crowd whooped and cheered.

"You see the two players that aren't carrying brooms?" Roger asked Gellan, pointing. Gellan nodded. "Those are the coulis."

"Coo-lees?" Gellan repeated. It was an odd word to him.

"Yeah. The coulis are the wings—the fliers that don't use brooms," said Roger very loudly, as the noise in the stadium thundered around them. "They're the most exciting ones to watch because they're able to do more stuff. But it's also a bit more dangerous to be a couli. You'll see what I mean in a minute."

"Nothing can be *that* dangerous, can it?" Gellan shouted back. "Not with so many people that can do magic!"

Each team stopped about a quarter of the way down the field and formed themselves into a perfect line. Then, as if on cue, the coulis on each team stepped forward and spread their arms sideways—a strange material unfurling from their outstretched arms to their ankles—before giving a mighty jump and rocketing upwards in synchronization, their arms pushed high above their heads.

The crowd cheered as each put on a small display of loops and turns before landing deftly on the top of the roule. As they removed their helmets and waved at the crowd, Gellan recognized the girl on the white half—her long hair was tied back in a low bun.

"Drina?!" he said in astonishment.

"What?" Roger asked, over the roar.

"That's Drina!" Gellan said, pointing.

"Is that the girl you were talking to yesterday in the common room?"

"Yeah!" said Gellan. "I had no idea—"

Just then, two people in referee shirts walked onto the field, both carrying brooms. One went and stood directly beneath the roule, and the other mounted her broom and flew to the top of it, where she dismounted and stood off to one side. Under her direction, the four coulis shook hands, then all ten players and the two referees put their helmets on. The coulis turned their backs to each other and walked to the edge of the roule as their teammates, still on the ground, mounted their brooms.

The same voice boomed out. "Let the match begin!"

But rather than going ballistic like Gellan thought it would, the crowd suddenly became very quiet—watching, waiting. The stillness felt odd.

"What're they waiting for?" Gellan asked.

"The clock," Roger said, pointing to one of the four giant clocks at each corner of the field. "The balls will be released right at seven o'clock, and then the blots will start coming sometime later."

The crowd counted down the last ten seconds, their collective voices growing louder and louder.

And then the hour struck.

Four balls shot straight up out of the opening in the roule and began falling in a slow-motion arc. Two were half gray and half white, and the other two were half gray and half green.

As the balls were released, the six players on brooms kicked off from the ground. Drina's teammate did a frontflip off the roule, and Drina followed suit with a jump and a side roll in midair before spreading her arms and swooping off to retrieve a ball that was headed for the ground.

As the game proceeded, Roger pointed out various elements of the game with far more coherency than he ever had before. He hardly took a breath as he explained everything he could as it was happening, with interjections from Corben.

"See how that Thresher rider has one of the balls for his team? Now there he goes—he's dropped it through the roule to his teammate, so now it's solid green, see? That's how they turn it into a live ball—"

"And don't forget, it doesn't matter if it's put through up or down!" shouted Corben. "It just has to go through your side before it can be used to score a goal."

"Right—and now they're headed for the Gannets' goal—oh good, the keeper blocked it. If it falls—but look! A Gannet rider got it! If he gets it through the roule on *his* team's side, it's a dead ball for the Threshers and they can't use it to score a goal until it's sent back through their side—and he... got it through, so now it's a dead ball—"

"Dang it!" Corben put his hands on his head, nervously watching the game's progress. Gellan had never seen him this animated. "Now the Gannets have lost one of *their* live balls! But look, now the Threshers' balls are both on the ground!"

"What happens if it's on the ground?" asked Gellan.

"Only their couli can fetch it," answered Roger. "Yes, look, there he goes—and dang, there goes another one of the Gannets' balls, but their couli can't get it because look—the blots are starting to be released—they'd better focus on those first or the blots could block their spaces on the roule—"

The blots turned out to be golden leaf-looking things that were shot up at random intervals from the center of the roule. As they floated down, the players intermittently sped back to the roule to bat them away from their side, sending them down to the ground.

Sometimes several blots gushed out of the roule at one time, and other times it was only one or two. Every time they appeared, both teams became a little more erratic as various players tried to reach them as quickly as they could, sometimes hitting them away, and sometimes collecting them as they sped by and throwing them away from the roule.

A loud gong sound rang out, indicating that the Gannets had scored the first goal. The crowd clapped and cheered, but none of the players paused to acknowledge their appreciation. A moment later, another gong rang out. The Threshers had also scored.

The relentless pace continued for another twenty-four minutes. It was all the coulis could do to keep up with the blots and the balls as the riders desperately blocked each other and tried to score their own goals.

"Oh no, look!" yelled Roger, and Gellan saw that an unusually large blot had been released. One of the Threshers' coulis reached it first and hit it hard toward the Gannets' side of the roule. "That was dirty! I mean, obviously you can do that, but usually they don't because then it starts to become more about blocking each other than scoring—dang it all! There's no way any—" Roger began.

But he had underestimated Drina. She was running along the ground to pick up one of the Gannets' fallen balls. Without missing a step, she scooped up the ball, hurtled upward into the air, and sent *herself* through the roule with the ball under her arm, just in time to force the blot to ricochet off her. It cemented itself against the side of the roule like a gleaming shield—but it wasn't blocking the opening.

"YEAH!" all three of them shouted at the same time, jumping to their feet and cheering with the rest of the crowd.

"I guess that's one of the advantages of having a smaller player for a couli!" Roger whooped, pumping the air with his fist.

At 7:27pm, a stream of sparks shot straight up from the posts on which the four giant clocks were mounted, and both referees blew their whistles. The players immediately swooped off the field via the doors through which they'd entered, as the referees collected the balls and returned them to the roule.

"Halftime," said Corben. "I'm gonna go find my dad. He should be here soon." He edged past a few people and made his way out to the stairs behind them.

Gellan watched the halftime show with mild interest. He didn't know the singers or the songs, but he was entertained by seeing pieces of the stage gliding over them and grouping themselves in the center of the field, each with a singer or musician on it, forming an obvious map of the islands of Cremstoll.

It took Corben a long time to return. The halftime show was nearly over when he appeared, followed by a tall man who looked just like him. They were both carrying two large bags of popcorn. As they sat down, the man held one of them out to Roger.

"Here," he said, "I got these for all of us."

"Uh, thanks, Mr. Timmel," Roger said as he accepted the popcorn. Corben handed the other one to Gellan.

Mr. Timmel turned to Gellan. "Corben says you're the new kid that shook things up pretty good at the school."

Gellan shrugged, not knowing what to say.

"Pretty unusual circumstances, I hear?" said Mr. Timmel. When Gellan still didn't say anything, he changed subjects. "How are you getting on in your classes?"

Gellan shrugged again. "Fine," he said.

Mr. Timmel was about to ask another question when Corben elbowed him and pointed to the players, who were returning to the field as the pieces of the stage left the same way they'd come.

A minute later, with the coulis positioned back on top of the roule, the last few seconds ticked down to eight o'clock and they were off as before, just as the sun was setting.

The second half was just as exciting and fast-paced as the first half had been. One of the Threshers' coulis miscalculated a turn and nearly collided with the roule as he attempted to snatch away a blot. One of the Gannets' riders *did* collide with a goal post and was left stranded, struggling to hang on until one of her teammates was able to fetch her fallen broom.

With a minute and a half to go, the score was tied. The crowd was in a frenzy, shouting encouragement, suggestions, and pleas as the two teams battled it out to the end.

The Threshers were in a compromised position, with two of their three openings on the roule so covered with blots that they couldn't get the ball through them at all, and the third opening barely large enough to squish a ball through—which the Gannets were making sure they never had time to do.

Both Thresher riders hovered near the Gannets' side, determined to prevent them from gaining any live balls with which to score, which would force the game into overtime. Several attempts by the Gannet riders to break the siege were unsuccessful, and both balls fell to the ground. Drina, who looked absolutely exhausted, nevertheless swooped to the ground, snagged both balls, and then lunged upwards. Expecting her to attempt to go through the roule from

220

below, the riders converged underneath it, but she hurled past them in a wide arc and continued upward.

A moment later, the crowd gasped as she furled herself tightly and began a freefall. Just before she reached the roule, she straightened out like an arrow, holding the balls above her head as she shot through it, scattering the riders. One didn't make it out of her way in time and was sent toward the ground, his broom spinning out of control. With a great turn, Drina threw the balls to her two rider teammates and— with barely a second to go—one of the balls made it past the keeper.

The loud gong sounded and a split second later, sparks exploded upwards out of the clock posts. A great stamping and cheering threatened Gellan's eardrums as both teams returned to the ground.

The players all removed their helmets and shook hands, then turned and waved at the crowd, before the Gannet riders and keeper mounted their brooms and joined the coulis in a victory lap around the field.

As they made their way out of the stadium, orange, yellow, and green fireworks lit up the sky above them in the shapes of the Cremstoll islands, and the crowd burst into what Roger told Gellan was the Cremstoll anthem while the stars twinkled overhead.

That night, tired of the noisy common room but knowing he wouldn't be able to get to sleep for another hour at least, Gellan wandered down the stairs and along a corridor, losing himself in his thoughts. Now that the Merry Fairy Festival was over, July looked a lot closer, and he wanted to find a way to make sure he was accepted for scout training.

He wandered around a corner and found a small open study area. Other than the moonlight coming in through the window, there was only one other light on, and it was illuminating the desk in front of a solitary person with long blonde hair. Gellan was surprised to see that Drina's hair had changed—it was curly, and some sections of the curls were tightly scrunched against her head. Her back was to Gellan, but she didn't seem to be doing any work at the moment.

Gellan wasn't sure whether to let her know he was there, or to walk away. Then he heard her sniff, and he froze. The only female he had ever seen cry (frequently) was Aunt Misera, and he was always quite certain she wasn't actually sad but just wanted something. He had no idea what to do for a girl who was actually sad.

He cleared his throat, and Drina turned around and saw him.

"Oh, thank goodness it's just you," she said, before turning back to the desk and trying to act as though she was working on her homework.

"I—uh—just wanted to see if you were all right?" he asked.

"I'm fine," she said.

He walked slowly around to stand by the fireplace against the wall, then looked back at her.

She shook her head at him. "No, really, I'm fine," she said. "I'm just very tired. And sometimes when a girl is really tired, she just needs to cry a little." She blew her nose and hiccupped. "Then I find my nerve again and I can keep going for a while longer and everything is... okay."

Gellan nodded, but he didn't say anything for a long time. He watched the flames of the flickering fire dancing to the sound of her pen scratching against the paper. She seemed to be working as quickly as she possibly could, desperately attempting to decrease the list of assignments still uncompleted.

"You were amazing today, you know," Gellan said at last, breaking the long silence.

She paused for just the slightest moment. "Thanks," she said, her pen returning to paper. "But really, you know, I don't have the luxury to do otherwise."

"What's that supposed to mean?"

"It means that I simply can't afford *not* to do well. So I just make sure that I do."

"Because—?"

She obviously didn't want to answer, but she seemed to think he'd bug off sooner if she did. "I kind of don't have anyone else but myself, anymore," she said, pulling on one of the tight curls before letting it go with a sad smile. "So when I play as a couli, or when I do scouting work, I really can't afford to do badly, otherwise I'll be let go from the team or from scouting, which is already kind of on the edge because of the inquiry. And I'm not even an official part of the Gilsthorne Gannets yet, I'm just a fill-in for Jordi Fray. But... I need the work. So I just try to focus on the job I've got to do, and hope everything works out. Anyway, I'm sorry to be brief, but I need to focus."

Gellan couldn't help feeling a little bit cross with her. The world wouldn't end if she turned in an uncompleted assignment or two, but he knew she couldn't see that right now. He turned to leave, then stopped at the corridor. "You know, just because you did those things because you feel you *have* to doesn't make them any less extraordinary."

She didn't even pause to acknowledge she'd heard what he said, but he saw her eyes flicker to the side as her hand continued to scrawl words across the page in front of her. He left, leaving her to her work and her thoughts.

CHAPTER FOURTEEN

TWO BECOME FOUR

A few days later, when Gellan woke to Artemisia's methodical tapping at his window, he could see her fluttering her feathers in a peeved and disgruntled manner through the wavy diamond glass panes. He unlatched the window and pulled it open.

"What's the matter with you?" he asked as she hopped through the window.

In reply, she dropped something onto the floor, then clicked her beak at him.

In the split second he realized it was a snake, Gellan jumped back and stifled a shout, but after a moment, he realized the snake wasn't moving. He bent to look at it... and chuckled. This didn't seem to help matters much—Artemisia clearly did not like being laughed at, and she turned her back to him.

Gellan picked up the rubber snake and tried to explain the matter to Artemisia, but no matter what he did, she kept turning this way and that, refusing to look at him. After a few minutes, Gellan gave up, took out the little container of beetles he'd collected the day before, opened it, and set it in front of her. Grudgingly, she ate the beetles, ruffled her feathers once more, and took off through the open window.

Gellan dropped the rubber snake under his pillow and shook his head. He dressed quickly and grabbed his bag, shoving some unfinished homework inside. He'd found that the amount of homework he had at Gilsthorne was a little more demanding than he was typically used to, though the assignments were anything but typical. Instead of writing an essay on "Farming Practices and the History of Ferndale," he usually wrote on something like "Differences Between Magical and Non-Magical Mushrooms."

But he wasn't intending to do any homework at the moment; he would save that for evening. The early morning hours had become his favorite time for exploring, since nearly everyone else was still in bed. Except for the pipkins. No matter how early he was up, some of the pipkins would already be bustling about. He had begun learning their names, and tried to find ways to tell them apart.

He could now recognize Sprout and Cricket, Willow and Hugo, Myrtle, Silvius, and a few others, though he knew he had about a hundred to go. Their frightened little squeaks when they happened upon him unexpectedly had startled him at first. But they soon became used to finding him wandering about the building, and he was getting used to their funny little ways.

He found they were quite strict about the cleanliness of doorknobs, and they all carried little fuzzy cloths just for wiping them down every time they encountered one. At first he thought it must be to get rid of germs, but one day, Sprout begrudgingly paused in her work to tell him that since doorknobs were a good height for pipkins to see their reflections in, they must be sure to clean any smudges on the doorknobs in case it turned out to be a smudge on their clothing.

Sometimes when he was near enough to the kitchens, he heard them singing their twinkling little songs together. On other occasions, he found groups of pipkins climbing up the walls with their little hands and feet to wipe dust off portraits. He had learned to look up for them when he entered any new area, after having one land smartly on the floor right in front of him when she'd finished a dusting job. Gellan had nearly fallen down a staircase, and the pipkin had nearly ended up in the fire as they both had lunged backwards in fright.

"You should have made your presence known, Master Gellan," Willow had scolded him as she jumped to her feet, her hands on her hips. "*We* go about our business like we always have, but *you* aren't being a normal student."

"I'm sorry," said Gellan, feeling properly told off. "I had no idea you could be... up there."

So he took to whistling a few notes as he entered and exited each doorway, just in case.

He also found that not all of the portraits could move, and even fewer of them could (or would) talk. One early morning he was trying to talk to four little elves who were laughing and singing the same song over and over as they sat on a garden bench when a pipkin walked by.

"*They* can't talk to you," he said. "Can't you tell?"

"Uh, right—yeah, I was just—" Gellan said lamely at the pipkin's back as it walked away, its squeaky laughter echoing down the corridor.

After that, he would usually watch a painting intently, waiting for some sign of intentional movement or noise, before he tried talking to it. Only, this tactic occasionally backfired too, such as when an old monk turned his back to Gellan, saying in a disgruntled tone, "I don't like to be stared at, if you don't mind."

Still, regardless of all the awkward encounters in his pre-dawn jaunts, he had begun to find more little secrets of the building as he poked about. He soon realized that the map he'd been given must have been created by someone who either didn't know the full layout of Gilsthorne Building, or by someone who had decided students shouldn't be told everything. He guessed it was some of both.

Today, after having an incomprehensible, early-morning conversation with one of the portraits in the Cupcake Tower common room—

"It could be that if you search long enough and find enough of the
secrets of Gilsthorne Building, you may discover it is not the
building that makes the map, but the map *that makes the*
building."
Gellan stared blankly. "That doesn't sound at all possible. What is
the map for, if it's not a depiction of Gilsthorne Building as it
already is?"
Sniffing... "Possible. Not possible. Is. Isn't. Neither exists without the
other... I take it you have not been schooled in the field of
philosophy?"

—he made his way to a wooden back staircase he'd discovered
that was just off the marked areas on the map. He followed it down
through several floors until he was sure he must be in the main part
of the building. Continuing downward until he reached the bottom,
he walked slowly until he saw his name reappear on the map. He
made a few notes and drew in the missing area as best he could, then
kept poking around until he found his way into an unused office. A
door at the back of it led him into another corridor that didn't appear
on the map—neither did it appear to go anywhere else, as though the
dwarves had advanced this far, then turned around without explanation and set off in another direction.

It was a small hallway, entirely surfaced by smooth stone. He
poked up and down it, finding nothing at all except for two symbols
carved into the rock near the ceiling that, from this angle, looked
something like a D and a G.

After scouring every inch of the corridor, he finally concluded
that other than the odd carving, there was nothing else to find there,
and he made his way to the Great Hall to get some breakfast.

When he returned to his room to grab a missed assignment, he
sent off a quick note to Uncle Ivan. With less and less time amidst
classes, homework, broomstick games, and exploring, Gellan had
gotten so lax about writing to his uncle that Uncle Ivan had been
threatening to come and get him. To solve the problem, Gellan had
made a whole stack of identical notes that said—

I'm alive. Good day today.
—Gellan Parker

—so he could send one off, lickety-split, anytime he needed to.

But now Uncle Ivan had begun asking for news about when the school year would be ending and how "those people" were planning on getting Gellan back to Ferndale. Gellan could answer the first question (middle of June), but he realized he had no idea how to answer the second one. He doubted that every student had a Macrodon carry them to and from school every year.

He had a chance to ask Roger about it as they walked to lunch after a particularly entertaining Spells and Charms class where they had been attempting to fill empty pails with water.

"You'll take the *Olympic Steamer*," said Roger, his shoes squelching as they descended the staircase.

"What is that?" asked Gellan, who was trying to dry an assignment for his next class as they walked. "Some kind of ship?"

"Yes, exactly."

"Where does it go to?"

"To the mainland, near Seattle. That's where your uncle can come pick you up."

Gellan groaned. "It's a ten-hour drive from Ferndale to Seattle," he said. "It'll take my uncle two whole days to come get me."

"I'm sure your uncle knows one of the jump portals he can take."

"What's a jump portal?"

"You know," said Roger. "The spots where you can drive through and come out miles away, closer to where you want to go?"

"Uh... no. I've never heard of them before. And neither has my uncle," said Gellan. "He's a wynkler."

Roger raised an eyebrow. "Wow, that's... that really stinks. Then yeah, I guess it'll be a long couple of days for him."

Gellan sighed, then thought of something else. "What in the world do all the wynklers think when we all start pouring out of the ship with our, uh—*unusual* school stuff?!"

"They don't know we're there, mate," said Roger.

"They don't?"

"Course not."

"What, are we invisible?" Gellan asked as they entered the Great Hall. "That might make it a bit hard for my uncle to come pick me up."

"Wish I was invisible sometimes," Roger said, grinning. "Then I wouldn't get told off so much... But anyway, a couple of weeks before the end of term, they always send out letters to the parents, giving instructions on exactly where to go and what to look for to get to the Hidden Inlet where the ship comes in."

"Oh." Gellan had something else on his mind. "Do you know how I can get back here if I get accepted to scout training?"

"Same way," said Roger. "You'll come back by ship. I'm sure they'll give you instructions."

While they were eating, Drina came up the row toward them.

"Hi, Gellan," she said, reaching her hand into her bag. "I got these for you while I was at Providence Island." She pulled out some papers and handed them to him.

He looked at them and saw it was the application to become a scout. "Thanks!" he said.

Roger nodded. "Yeah, my dad sent me one yesterday. It's time to get those filled out and turned in, isn't it?"

"I didn't know you wanted to be a scout," Gellan said.

"It's not about wanting to or not wanting to," said Roger. "It's about the experience I'll get—my dad thinks it'll be good for me."

"What does your mom think?"

Roger shrugged. "She's not thrilled. But when my parents got married, they agreed that my dad got final say with the boys and my mom got final say with the girls. Since I have so many sisters, she gets final say a lot. So this is one of the few times my dad gets it."

Drina was standing there awkwardly. She finally said, "Well, that's... interesting," and scurried away.

"She's a bit odd, isn't she?" said Roger, watching her, his mouth full of potato salad.

"No, she's not," said Gellan. "She's a couli *and* a scout."

"That doesn't mean she's not a bit odd," said Roger. "And I don't mean that's necessarily a bad thing."

"Well, yeah, okay. Maybe," Gellan conceded. He looked back at the application. "It says here that we need to turn our applications in to the office of the Vice Governor by next Friday. Isn't that Faulkner?"

"Yeah, he's over all the underage scouts," said Roger. "I'm just glad there's someone between us and Madame Guillèn. She's pretty stern." He shook his head. "And I'm kind of glad it's not Sedargren either."

"Yeah... I've been wondering," said Gellan. "Why do we have *three* governors?"

"We *don't* have three governors," Roger corrected him. "Madame Guillèn is *the* governor, which means she oversees everything here in Cremstoll. Faulkner is just a Vice Governor, which puts him in charge of all the day-to-day stuff—like..." He paused, thinking. "Transportation and the school... including the students. That's why the underage scouts are under his charge. And then Sedargren is Lieutenant Governor, so he's specifically in charge of security and protection, and keeping an eye on the borders. All the other scouts and the vanquors and stuff are under him."

"Oh," said Gellan. "Maybe that's why his hand was injured."

"What d'you mean?" asked Roger.

"When I first got here, I saw that a couple of Sedargren's fingers looked purple and bruised pretty bad. He must've been in a skirmish or something."

"Yeah, probably," said Roger. "It happens."

"What is a vanquor, exactly?" asked Gellan.

"They're the highest-level security people," said Roger. "They have to do a lot of training to get to that point."

"Then why aren't the scouts under Sedargren?" asked Gellan. "Wouldn't the vanquors be the best at teaching us scout stuff?"

"Well, maybe," said Roger. "But they're just... I mean, I know Governor Sedargren is responsible for keeping tabs on the goings-on in Cremstoll. But he can just—I don't know—make you feel like you're doing something wrong even when you're not. And all the while he's got a big smile on his face and he's acting like he's your best friend. I know pretty much everybody else likes him, and he does his job well. I dunno." He shrugged.

"When should we go to Providence Island to turn these in?" Gellan asked, waving the papers. "Do we have to get permission to do that?"

"Yeah—usually we ask Professor Fisk or Professor Dinsmore," said Roger. "And let's go tomorrow. It's the last Saturday we have before the application is due."

Gellan continued to peruse the papers while Roger ate, and then suddenly saw something that made his heart sink. He double-checked his math on a napkin, and then shook his head.

"I can't apply," he said.

"What?!" asked Roger, looking over.

"It says you have to be thirteen-and-a-half by July 1st, the start date of scout training," Gellan said. "I won't be that old until July 20th."

"Oh come on," Roger said. "I'm sure it's relative."

Gellan shook his head and pointed. "No, look." He sighed.

"Well, it doesn't hurt to try," said Roger, giving the form a dismissive glance as he scooped a large portion of sweet potato fries onto his plate.

"You think so?"

Roger knew Cremstoll better than Gellan did. He shoved the papers into his bag and decided he would try for it anyway.

The next morning, Gellan was woken early by wind whistling around the tower. The sky was dark and surly, but the rain hadn't begun to fall as yet. He didn't see any sign of Artemisia; he assumed she was taking shelter somewhere. As he examined the sky, he thought about what Uncle Ivan often said on days like this:

"Somethin' interesting is definitely going to happen today. You always feel like somethin' interesting is about to happen on days like this."

To which Gellan would usually say, "Yeah. It's going to rain." And then Uncle Ivan would turn away in a grumpy sort of way.

Thinking about Uncle Ivan gave him an unexpected pang of homesickness. He knew he'd be glad to see home again. But he also knew that the moment he left here, he would miss Gilsthorne.

After a couple of hours of exploring and making notes on his much-used map, he wandered into the Great Hall shortly after the doors were opened. Food was just appearing on the tables, and he paused at his table to dish up a bowl of steaming oatmeal. He dropped a dollop of butter, a large spoonful of brown sugar, and a pinch of salt into it. Then, using a napkin to protect his hand from the hot bowl, he ate as he ambled around the Great Hall. He studied the stones on the floor and ran a hand along the rock walls.

Some time later, he happened to be studying half of the Mag Map, partially hidden behind one of the doors, when he heard someone call his name. He turned around and saw Drina running up to him.

"*There* you are! I've been looking everywhere for you," she said. "I got permission from Professor Dinsmore to go to Providence Island today, and she told me you were going as well. Do you want to go together?"

"Sure," said Gellan. "Roger is coming too. After we turn in our applications, we were going to go to the Elixir Emporium and then to Albury Wands. I still need Edmond to finish my wand."

Her face fell a little. "Oh," she said.

"What's wrong?" Gellan asked.

"It's just—well, I think Roger thinks I'm a bit... strange," she confessed.

Gellan shrugged his shoulders. "So is he, in his own way," he said. "So am I, really—*you* know I am. Anyway, you don't need to go feeling all oddball by yourself."

She smiled unexpectedly. "Really? Okay, then. You don't mind?"

Gellan shook his head. "Besides, who would want to go by them-selves on a day like this? I think we were planning on heading out just after lunch. We'll meet you in the entrance hall around one o'clock, okay?"

She nodded and left him standing there, still studying the Mag Map. A few minutes later, he heard his name again. He turned and looked behind him. It was Cressida.

"Hi again," she said as she walked up.

"Hi," said Gellan, shoving his hands in his pockets.

"I need to go to Providence Island today," Cressida said, "and Professor Dinsmore said you're going too, with some others. Do you mind if I go with you all? I don't really feel like going by myself."

"Yes—I mean no, I don't mind. You can come with us. We're meeting in the entrance hall at one o'clock."

"Thanks!" she said, and she swished away.

A minute later, he realized his shoulders were protesting his slightly hunched-over posture and he straightened up, clearing his throat as he turned his focus back to the Mag Map.

Half an hour later, when Roger finally entered the Great Hall, Gellan joined him at the table and tried to mention casually that Drina and Cressida would be coming with them.

Roger groaned. "I always say the dumbest things around girls," he said. "I don't even know why. It just happens. They're going to be with us the *whole day!*"

"Just until we get there, mate," said Gellan, trying to cheer him up. "Then they'll be off doing their own thing." But he felt a squirming discomfort himself.

"You just watch," said Roger, shaking his head, "they'll think that they'll offend us or something if they take off. We'll be stuck with them from the moment we leave until the moment we get back. Great. Just great." He comforted himself with another bowl of oatmeal.

"Well, at least we've got the whole morning to do other things," Gellan said.

"Yeah, except there's no chance of any broomstick games," said Roger. "Not in weather like this. We'd be blown straight out over the lake and get swallowed up by the Lake Lion or something."

"Well, how about we do some homework?" Gellan asked.

Roger rolled his eyes. "Got any other bright ideas?"

"You could come with me," Gellan said. "I want to check behind all the portraits in the back corridor of the fourth floor. Some of them are positioned strangely."

"Sure," said Roger with a resigned sigh. "Why not? Sounds interesting enough. I'd be curious to see what you've been up to every morning."

———

"Don't you two have anything *better* to do?" a woman in a portrait asked them as they tried to poke their wands around the edges of her frame. She was wearing a highly ruffled collar and was sitting in a regal-looking chair next to a large wooden desk.

"Not really," said Gellan. "It's pouring rain outside."

"I know," she said, pointing to the window in her portrait, and Gellan was surprised to see rain cascading past the panes.

"Is there anything interesting behind your portrait?" asked Roger.

"I don't know," she said with a sniff. "I never thought to check."

"*Can* you see behind your portrait?" asked Gellan.

"Of course I could, if I wanted to," she said, "though I prefer to stay in here."

"Well, how about it then?" said Roger, gesturing.

"If it means you'll leave me alone sooner..." she said. The next moment, she stepped out of the portrait, stretched her transparent arms, then turned and stuck her head through the painting.

Gellan gasped and threw himself backward, landing hard on the stone floor. Roger looked over at him.

"What?" he asked. "Haven't you ever seen a ghost?"

"I beg your pardon?" said the woman indignantly as she pulled her head back out of the portrait. "I prefer to be called a *presence,* if you don't mind. And no, there isn't anything behind there. Just the Gilsthorne symbol carved into the stone wall."

"The Gilsthorne symbol?" Gellan asked, his voice squeaking as his heart continued to pound in his chest. He cleared his throat. "What's that?"

She pointed to the wooden armrest of her painted chair. "It looks like that," she said.

Gellan got to his feet and moved closer to the portrait. Painted into the wooden chair were the same D and G symbols he'd seen in the dead-end corridor.

"I've seen those before!" he said, pointing. "Does it mean anything?"

"No," said the woman, shrugging. "It's just the symbol of Gilsthorne. Entirely common. It's what connects this painting to my office."

"Wait... office?"

She gestured at the painting. "Yes, my *office*."

"A real office? Do you actually—"

"How about some lunch, mate?" Roger interrupted, and he grabbed Gellan's arm and started pulling him along the corridor.

The woman sniffed and turned away.

"Oh... sorry!" Roger called back over his shoulder.

"What's wrong?" Gellan asked.

"It's rude to imply that they may not be real," Roger said. "And then I mentioned food. Double whoops. They can't eat, you know... not like we do, anyway. Oh well."

"No, I didn't know," said Gellan. "And I didn't know the moving portraits were actually ghosts. Nice of you to mention that."

"No, not *all* of the moving ones are ghosts," said Roger. "Just the alive ones. I mean the dead ones." He stopped and scratched his head. "I mean the ones that are an actual person... ghost... presence. Never mind." He sighed.

Shortly before one o'clock, they left the Great Hall as they pulled their thick tweed cloaks around them and shoved their caps on tightly.

Drina arrived a minute later and stood off to one side, shifting from one foot to the other. When no one moved, she looked at Gellan with a questioning look.

"We're waiting for one more person," he said.

"Who?" she asked.

"Cressida," Gellan said.

"That's me," said Cressida, walking up behind them and shoving some papers in her bag. "Sorry if I've kept you waiting."

The boys shrugged and looked down. Drina shook her head. "No, you're fine. We just got here."

"Well, is that everyone?" Cressida asked. They all nodded. "Then we might as well go," she said. "I don't think the weather is going to get any better."

They pulled open one of the large doors with difficulty, because of the wind that was rushing past, and trudged across the courtyard. There they climbed into a land pod and were soon speeding across the bridge. They watched the wind gusting through the fields and whipping up the water on the lake far below them. None of them said a word, but Cressida's large, green eyes so intently watched them all that Gellan felt she could have been trying to read their thoughts.

As the land pod rolled to a stop near the docks, they jumped out and moved quickly into a sea pod, scooting as far into the interior as they could to get out of the wind. Roger sighed as it began to pull away. "I always get seasick in these things in the best of weather," he said.

"You should ask Madame Eckhart for some Queasy-Quelling Potion," said Cressida. "I'm quite sure she'd give you some, and it doesn't take much to do the trick. A small vial of it would last you quite a long time."

"Wait, *Madame* Eckhart?" Gellan asked. "Is she related to Master Eckhart?"

"Yes." It was Drina who spoke. "She's his wife. She's the school healer. She's brilliant at it."

The sea pod picked up speed and began to bump alarmingly over the whipped-up waves, and they all grabbed at handholds. Drina pulled out her wand, touched it to the glass, and dragged it downward. The pod slowed considerably.

"The elfin race has an innate affinity to working with plants and herbs, particularly for using them in healing," Drina continued, keeping an eye on the waves in front of them. "We're really lucky to have them both at Gilsthorne."

When they were finally back on land, Gellan made a mental note to be sure to visit Madame Eckhart to get his own vial of Queasy-Quelling Potion. It took him a moment to realize the two girls were standing off to one side, waiting for him and Roger to join them.

"So, uh—we have to go drop off some applications at Governor Faulkner's office," Gellan said, pointing with his thumb over his shoulder. "I guess you girls probably have other errands to do—"

"I'm dropping an application off at Governor Faulkner's office too!" said Cressida with a bright smile.

"I don't mind coming along," said Drina.

"Told you so," said Roger quietly to Gellan as they made their way up the hill to The Corner.

After the three would-be scouts had handed their applications to Cline, Cressida said, "Well, the only things I was planning on doing were visiting the bookshop and the Elixir Emporium for a couple of things for class."

"Oh—well—I don't think we need to—" Roger began, motioning to himself and Gellan, but Drina spoke over him.

"Gellan needed to go to the Elixir Emporium too!" she said. "Should we go there first?"

"Let's go there last," said Cressida. "We should probably start with The Quigrapher and then work our way along the road."

Apparently considering it settled, the two girls turned around together and led the way back down the corridor. Roger groaned and whacked Gellan, who shook his head helplessly. Both boys sighed, then turned to follow the girls.

Three hours later, after their combined list of errands had taken them far longer than Gellan would ever have thought possible, they finally left the Elixir Emporium just as the sun broke through the clouds for the first time that day, on its descent toward the horizon. The two girls suggested they go and see the view from the rooftop garden, and without waiting for a word from either of the boys, they took off up the stairs on the side of the building.

"C'mon," said Gellan as he pulled Roger up the stairs.

While Roger shuffled away and found a bench to sulk on, Gellan wandered through the garden with interest, reading the plant labels and comparing them with ones he was familiar with. The gardens that he'd seen throughout Cremstoll had all been impressive, regardless of their size, but he thought the Elixir Emporium's gardens were the best of them all.

There was a small stream running diagonally across the roof, dividing it into two halves. On the side where they had entered was a double row of trees with oversized, deep green leaves. Gellan leaned over to look at the sign at the base of one of the trees.

Fair Ficus Trees

Fair Ficus trees are known particularly for the magical blue leaves that they occasionally produce. These leaves always grow in the middle of the winter and take several weeks to fully develop. They're prized by potion masters for use in potions such as the Fairness Concoction and the Weal Elixir.

He wandered down the stone path between the trees, admiring the spring flowers and meadow grasses that were growing all around them. The path led him up to a red wooden bridge and over the stream to the other half of the garden, which was filled with handwoven planters stuffed with herbs and flowers of all kinds.

The south and west walls were formed of brick, laid in steps climbing upwards until they peaked at the corner. They were mostly covered by different kinds of vines, which cascaded partway down the face of the building, except for a large porthole opening.

Gellan was looking through the porthole in the wall, down to the street, when a small black shape whizzed overhead. Artemisia landed on a nearby brick ledge, hopping a little as the wind gusted over the wall. Gellan's smile at her appearance dissipated when she turned around and he saw she was holding a small black snake in her beak that was clearly real... though also clearly dead. She dropped the snake into the planter below, and clicked her beak at him.

"I am *not* going to pick that one up for you," he said, crossing his arms over his chest. "What is it with the snakes? What about leaves and flowers and some of the other *nice* things that you used to—"

He stopped as the day grew suddenly dark. Gellan looked up and saw a thick, dark cloud moving in front of the sun. He was turning back to finish scolding Artemisia when he suddenly heard the girls shriek and Roger calling out. All three of them sounded terrified. His heart jumped to his throat and he sprinted around the maze of planter boxes, trying to see where they all were, hardly noticing the cries coming from down below in the street.

"Drina! Cressida!" he called out. "Roger! Where are you?!"

"Gellan?" He heard Cressida's voice. "Gellan, where are you? What's happening?"

He followed her voice and coming around the row of Fair Ficus trees, he found the two girls sitting on a park bench, clutching each other.

"There you are," he said, skidding to a halt. He looked around, but he couldn't see any reason for the petrified looks on their faces. He felt slightly annoyed. "What in the world is the matter?"

"Gellan? Can't you—?" Cressida asked, the words coming out in a wail. She had her wand out and the tip was lit, but she was holding it down in an awkward position.

"Can't I what?" He whirled around, but saw nothing. "What are you talking about?" he asked again.

"Gellan, where are you?" Drina asked, releasing her hand from its white-knuckled grip on the bench and reaching toward Gellan's voice.

Gellan watched her, dumbfounded. She looked like a blind person groping in darkness. He stretched out his arm for her to grasp.

"Drina," he said quietly, with growing worry, "what exactly is wrong?"

"We can't see anything," Drina said. "It's totally dark!"

"No, it's not," he protested, but his mouth went dry and he knew she wasn't lying.

"Then it's—it *must* be—" She paused, thinking hard. "It must be some kind of magical darkness. I wonder if they know—they thought it was the weather—but we can't—Gellan, *you* can see?"

"Yes," he said. "It got a little dimmer when that big cloud went in front of the sun, but that was all."

"But *you* can *see*?" she repeated again. "It's not all dark to you?"

"No, I can see just fine," he said.

Drina took a deep breath. "Okay. First, go find Roger. Bring him here so at least the three of us are together. And try to be quiet, okay?"

Gellan didn't pause to ask any questions. He knew something must be wrong, though he wasn't sure how yet. He took off around the garden until he found Roger sitting with his back against the wall, the tip of his wand lit but apparently doing him no good either.

"Roger," he said quietly. "Is it all dark to you too?"

Roger turned his head toward Gellan's voice. "Yes," he said, and his voice shook a little. "Can *you* see?"

"Yes."

"How?" asked Roger. "It's pitch black."

"Not to my eyes," said Gellan. "Drina says it's a magical darkness, and for some reason, it's not affecting me. She wants me to bring you to where she and Cressida are so the three of you can at least stay together. Here, take my hand and I'll lead you over to them."

Roger waved his hand around and Gellan caught it, Roger grasping him like a lifeline. Gellan led him carefully to Drina and Cressida and helped him sit on the bench so he didn't end up sprawled on the ground.

"All right," said Drina, "I've been thinking about what to do. I want you to go to the edge of the building and see if there's anything odd going on below. I heard a lot of noise coming from down in the street, so I'm guessing everyone else has been affected, just like before."

"Before?"

"I don't have time to explain. If it *is* a magical darkness, and not just some weird weather phenomenon like they've been telling us, that probably means someone is using it to do something undercover. But be careful, okay? Don't let anyone see you—just in case there's someone that *could* see you."

"Okay," said Gellan. "You all stay here."

"Go now, quickly!" said Drina.

Gellan ran to the wall of the building and carefully looked over the edge to the street below. He saw several people sitting with their backs to shop walls or holding tight to tree trunks or posts. A couple of babies were crying, their mothers attempting to rock and soothe them, unable to see themselves.

And then... along a narrow side street, he saw a group of men. They were moving quietly, and apparently without any hindrance to their own vision. Gellan watched as one after another stepped away from the group and entered a shop, holding something in their hands.

The group continued along the side street, then turned onto the main road heading in the other direction. Again and again, a person would leave the group and slip into one shop after another, before leaving the shop empty-handed and returning to the group.

Gellan reached into his shoulder bag and pulled out his binoculars, trying to focus on the object each person was carrying. It was difficult in the dim light, and they were quite some distance away, but he managed to get a good glimpse of one of the objects when the tallest man held it out to a younger man. It appeared to be nothing more than a small, gray stone.

As they headed further away, Gellan stuffed his binoculars into his bag and ran back to the others.

"There's a group of men moving down the streets," he told them. "I don't know who they are, but there's something off about them. I'm going follow them and see what they're up to. Here." He took off his shoulder bag and shoved it into Drina's lap. "I'm going to leave this here with you so it doesn't make a racket if I have to run. You three just stay here, okay? I don't want to be worried about you."

"How many are there?" Cressida asked.

"Maybe eight or nine," Gellan answered.

"Be careful, won't you?" said Drina, a worried look on her face. "If they're not blinded by the darkness, I would hazard a guess that they're probably wynklers, so at least you'll have that advantage over them. But it's also possible that they're wizards, so—"

"Yeah, but the only spells I know aren't attacking ones, really."

"Well, you can always use the flare spell. We know you can do that one, and it ought to scare them pretty good, if they are wynklers. And don't forget about the shielding spell. You've learned that one, right?"

"Yes," said Gellan, standing up. "But I'm not very good at it yet."

"And you could try restringos," Drina said. "It's a binding spell."

"Restringos," Gellan repeated. "Got it. All right. I'll see you all in a few minutes."

CHAPTER FIFTEEN
CLOSE CALL

G ellan ran back to the wall overlooking the street and found the location of the group of men; they were quite a distance away now. He hurried down the steps as quickly and quietly as he could, pulling out his wand. He had to be careful not to bump anyone, and he nearly tripped over a cat that went pelting across the road in front of him, chasing a pair of mice that scurried beneath a potted plant.

A mother was singing lullabies to her baby, sounding close to tears herself.

"It always ends," an old woman next to her was saying, over and over. "It never lasts too long."

"Yes, but who will disappear this time?" asked the mother, pausing in her song. Gellan could hear the fear in her voice; she was clutching her baby tightly.

"They always come back, dearie," said the old woman. "They've always come back—"

Gellan didn't understand what they were talking about, but he felt a sudden pang of fear. Throwing caution to the wind, he began to run down the street as fast as he could. His footsteps startled a young boy, who asked shrilly, "What's that? Mommy, what's that sound?" and gripped his mother's leg even more tightly.

"Probably just a dog," his mother said. But her face betrayed her calm voice, and she pulled him closer, her other hand clenched in a fist around her wand.

Gellan still couldn't see anyone from the group of men, and the feeling of dread was growing the further he went. Then he heard commotion ahead and skidded to a stop next to a cheese shop, listening carefully. He realized that the noise was coming from *The Wabbit Hole*, which was just ahead.

Turning, he headed down the narrow alleyway between the curved form of *The Wabbit Hole* and the shop next to it. He found that the side door was hanging from its hinges, and he slipped in.

The scene in front of him was surreal. People were sitting frozen against the wall or in corners, gripping each other and holding tight to anything they could—some crying quietly, others looking grim and determined. There were overturned chairs and tables, broken glass and food spread across the ground.

The commotion he'd heard was coming from the back: there were clatters and clangs, screams and yells, and a hissing sound. Goose-bumps stood out on Gellan's skin, and he tried to move as quietly as he could so he wouldn't frighten the people in the restaurant more than they already were. He stooped down and ran around the counter, then edged his way over to the door leading to the back where all the shouting was coming from.

Through the crack between the door and the wall, he saw the group of men overpowering a wizard who was swinging his body, trying desperately to free his arms, his eyes blank and staring. Two waiters and a waitress were cowering in the corner, and the girl was screaming and pleading for them to stop. Gellan felt a surge of anger, and suddenly, he didn't care what happened next—he was ready to do whatever he needed to.

He threw open the door and pulled out his wand. "Illuminare!" he shouted, and a flare hit the ceiling, showering them all in sparks.

One of the men immediately rushed toward him. "Restringos!" he shouted, just before the man reached him. The man's arms snapped to his sides, and he crashed into Gellan as he fell.

Gellan shoved him off and jumped up.

"Illuminare!" he shouted again and again. Flares shot out of his wand, this time hitting two of the men with force, leaving holes singed in their clothing. Several of them fell as they ducked. One of Gellan's spells went slightly awry and hit the wizard, who yelled as his shoulder was hit, leaving a red, angry burn.

Two of the attackers managed to scramble back to their feet, but instead of running toward Gellan, they turned and burst through the back door. Gellan had a momentary thought that this likely meant they really were wynklers, as Drina had supposed.

The tall man released the wizard at last. He fell to the ground, gasping, as the tall man made a dive for Gellan.

"Restringos!" Gellan shouted, stumbling backwards. "Restringos!" The man's body went stiff, and he crashed to the floor next to his companion.

The five remaining men finally managed to get to their feet and ran out the back door, leaving their two immobile companions behind. Gellan ran after them, aiming more flares at their backs for good measure.

"Get out!" he shouted at them, his blood thundering in his ears. "Get out of Cremstoll! And don't come back!" He suddenly skidded to a stop as he watched them run away along the sand, two courses of action battling it out in his head. He knew he had to go back and leave the possibility of following them until later.

With a loud grunt of frustration, he flipped around and ran back into the kitchens.

"Who are you?" he demanded angrily of the two men still there, his wand pointing at them. "What are you doing here? Where did the darkness come from?" They glowered at him, though neither of them answered—Gellan didn't know if the spell allowed them to or not.

"Are you...?" came a hoarse voice across the room. "Who are you, boy?"

Gellan ran over to the wizard. He looked terrible. Blood was coming from his nose and his right arm was at an odd angle. His breath came out in a wheeze.

"My name is Gellan Parker," he said. "I'm a student from Gilsthorne. Are you all right?"

"I'm…" The wizard coughed. He was holding his ribs with his left arm, and he tried to shove himself into a better position. Gellan helped him. "Aren't you the boy who started up at the school recently?"

"Yeah."

"My daughter, Cressida, told me about you," the man told him.

"Cressida?" asked Gellan. "Cressida Burman?"

"Yes," said the man. "I hope she's all right. She told us she was going to come to The Cob today."

"Yes, she came with me and my friends," said Gellan. "She's fine. She's in the gardens on top of the Elixir Emporium."

"Oh, thank goodness." Mr. Burman heaved out a sigh. "Who are the people that attacked me?"

"I don't know," said Gellan, "but as soon as you all can see again, we can ask them. I've got two of them stuck here."

He glanced over at the two men again, and at that moment, there was a cry from the waitress in the corner. She blinked and rubbed her eyes as the two waiters moved forward.

"Has it lifted?" asked Gellan. "Can you all see?"

"Yes—yes," said the girl. "It's gone. Finally." She covered her face with her hands and let out a sob.

"Good!" Gellan ran to the door, calling over his shoulder, "I'll be back soon! Get Mr. Burman to the healers!"

Their shouted questions dissolved in the wind rushing past his ears as he pounded down the beach, desperately following the trail of footprints in the sand before they disappeared with the coming in of the tide.

Twenty minutes later, Gellan found himself crossing Penep Lane, the causeway connecting Providence Island with Cromllech Island. The waves lapped at his heels from both sides and, with the tide coming in, he didn't know how he'd get back. But that didn't matter to him at the moment—he was determined to find those men.

Cromllech Island was very sparsely populated, especially compared to Providence Island. The only buildings were large, old houses made of gray stone that sat heavily on the rocky and grassy knolls, often accompanied by barns or stables. Nearly the whole island was on a plateau that sat up to ten feet above the beach along which Gellan was running. Ancient-looking stone fences that ringed the escarpment raised the height another few feet, making it impossible for him to see much else, except when he came to an occasional gate.

The footprints were fading now, their shapes becoming indistinguishable from other natural dents and bumps in the sand. Gellan slowed down, letting his eyes unfocus just a little—the way he used to do with Magic Eye pictures—which brought the trail of footprints into focus by the consistent direction of their shadows.

He ran on, an uncomfortable feeling of vulnerability washing over him as he focused on the footprints instead of his surroundings. The bleating of a sheep just on the other side of the fence startled him, and he jumped backward against the rock escarpment, his wand at the ready. After looking around carefully, he shook his head and looked back at the trail of footprints. Only a short distance further on, they curved away from the beach and ended at the solid rock of the escarpment.

Gellan stooped and slowed, carefully moving closer, now hugging the base of the escarpment. In a little hollow in the rock, a short distance away from the abrupt end of the footprint trail, he paused. Then he backtracked several yards and blew away his footprints before returning to the rock hollow. With a circular wand movement, he had soon secreted himself behind an obstructos, prepared to watch what he assumed must be another obstructos until something, or someone, emerged.

Several hours later, Gellan was feeling cramped and tired. Ever since nightfall, he had been debating with himself about whether or not this was a pointless exercise. Perhaps what was behind the obstructos wasn't a cave, but a tunnel. If so, the men would be long gone. And what if there was something behind the obstructos that would give him a clue to the actions of the wynkler men? He knew it was there, so he ought to be able to walk through it—he should definitely go take a look around. But then, what if the men *were* still in there and he walked right into an ambush? This series of questions ran around and around in his head, but every time he came to the same conclusion and decided to stay put—for a little longer.

When he got cold, he searched in the sand for a small stone, which he turned into a firestone. It gave off just enough heat to keep him decently comfortable as he sat in the damp sand.

He checked his watch again—10:41 pm. He knew his friends and perhaps others would be worried and wondering about him, but he hoped Drina would be able to make excuses for him, knowing him as she did. Though if something didn't happen soon, even she wouldn't be able to explain his long absence.

He twiddled his wand in his hands. If nobody appeared in the next ten minutes, he was going to go into the cave and see what was there.

Nine minutes... The slim light of the moon was the only thing making the movement of the waves visible as they lapped inches away from his hiding spot.

Eight minutes... A little black shape flew by—she must know he was there.

Seven minutes... What if someone did come out? Could he send spells through the obstructos?

Six minutes... A hoot and a bleat, as the wind whipped some of the saltwater toward his obstructos.

Five minutes... What if they had a wizard with them now? Only a wizard could have made that obstructos. Then again, what if it wasn't an obstructos and Gellan was just wasting his time?

Four minutes... But where else would they have gone? Wynklers couldn't just disappear. And the escarpment would be impossible for anyone but himself to climb.

Three minutes... He shifted, anticipating the moment, as the time continued to tick down.

Two minutes... Firestone extinguished. Heels dug in. Wand out and ready to remove the obstructos.

One minute to go—and then suddenly, there was movement right next to him. He threw himself back and hit his head on the rock as a pair of legs sloshed by, leaving sinking footprints in the sand directly in front of his hiding place. He chided himself for having been too interested in watching the numbers on his watch at just the wrong moment. New plan, new action... what to do now?

First, how many were there? It took some effort to count them in the dark: eight. Only seven had run away from *The Wabbit Hole*.

Their voices weren't fully discernible over the sound of the waves and the wind, but three of them were obviously arguing, standing on the beach as their boots were sloshed halfway up by the movement of the waves. Gellan listened as carefully as he could but with little success.

Very carefully, he removed the obstructos, not sure what he intended to do yet, but grateful for the deep shadow around him. Their voices became a bit clearer.

"—left them behind!"

"I told you it's not my fault!" said a short, stubby man, pointing his finger at a tall man. "Ben said no one would be able to see us!"

"You have to get him back!" said a lanky teenager, leaning up into the face of the tall man in front of him. "You have to do whatever it takes to get him back!"

"You know what, Alex? I've had more than enough of your whinging," said the other. "You all knew what you were doing was risky, regardless of my help. And *you* left your father behind."

"Get him out!" bellowed Alex. "Get him out! Or I'll go straight to them and tell them what you've done!"

There was a quick movement, and Gellan saw a narrow object being shoved into Alex's chest.

"I have a better solution," said the one called Ben. "How about I make it so you can't?"

A third man made a lunge for Ben, but he had barely moved before he was sent flying back toward the rock with a flash of orange light from Ben's wand. With another orange flash, Alex fell into the waves with a gurgled yell. Again and again there was a flash of light, and within seconds, seven men were either on the ground or crumpled against the rocks, groaning and struggling to get up. Gellan's heart raced, trying to figure out what to do. He knew he was no match for the wizard.

Ben walked over to Alex, his wand pointing down at him. "You knew the penalty for disobeying my orders," he said. "I think the only solution is to make sure you can't possibly tell anyone about this—don't you?"

Gellan didn't fully understand what was about to happen, but he had enough of an idea, and it horrified him. Without a word, the anger and fear pulsing through him discharged through his wand as he jumped forward.

His flare missed, but in the light it created, Gellan saw that Ben was masked. The wizard reacted quickly; Gellan barely managed a sufficient shield charm, which caused the red curse Ben sent at him to glance away. He was still thrown to the ground with its force, and he had to cover his head as the spell shattered against the rock behind him.

In the next moment, several things happened almost simultaneously.

There was a thud next to Gellan and he rolled away and shoved himself to his feet, realizing that a person had materialized at his side. At first he was afraid it was the wizard Ben, but he could see the newcomer's face clearly unmasked in a glowing ball of light issuing from his outstretched wand—it was Faulkner. At the same moment, with a swirl of his cloak, the wizard called Ben vanished as several other witches and wizards materialized out of nowhere. Gellan recognized some of them, including Governor Sedargren and Roman.

"The wynklers!" Gellan called to the newcomers. "Get them out of the surf before they drown!"

All of the witches and wizards obeyed at once, rescuing the three men who were face-down on the ground. All seven of the wynkler men were quickly checked over to make sure they were all right, before being pulled to their feet and magically bound. The moment Gellan was sure everyone was okay, he ducked into the cave he'd been feet away from for hours.

"Leuf!" The cave walls were thrown into high relief and about ten yards in, something twinkled in the darkness. Gellan ran toward it and found a massive mound of small, round gray stones.

"Gellan, get away from those!" a voice thundered, and Faulkner came running in behind him.

Gellan flipped around and held his wand out, facing Faulkner.

Faulkner stopped. "I mean it for your own good, Mr. Parker," he said, more quietly.

"And how do I know that?" asked Gellan, the adrenaline still pulsing through him.

"Because I think I know what those are," Faulkner said.

"Yeah? What are they?" asked Gellan. "And how do you know what they are if you just barely got here? Or were you here before?" Despite being in the cave, there was a rushing sound in his ears.

Faulkner stared at him for a moment, the other witches and wizards gathering behind him. "I think those are atrophius stones," he said. "I could feel their effect the moment I got here. If I'm right, it means they contain an evil magic. They're like a black hole that sucks the spark out of witches and wizards."

"Darn right, they do!" shouted one of the wynklers with glee, and another one began kicking him. One of the witches sent a spell toward them, and the wynkler was frozen in place with one leg bent.

"If you had enough atrophii pulling on you," Faulkner continued, "you'd lose all ability to do magic. Sometimes the damage is even permanent."

"I don't feel anything," said Gellan, refusing to take his eyes off Faulkner, still not sure what he wanted to do.

"Who the heck do you—" Governor Sedargren started forward, but Faulkner threw out his arm and Sedargren fell silent.

The vice governer turned and stared at Gellan once more, then said, "Well, we always knew you were a little different somehow, Mr. Parker. Now, if you would, please, come and take this bag from me"— he conjured a leather bag in midair—"go fill it with seawater, and we will take a small number of these stones back with us. We'll need them for evidence."

It took Gellan another moment, looking from face to face as he stood there, to move forward to obey Faulkner. He took the leather bag and edged nervously around everyone else to the lapping tide.

"Now, *without touching the stones*, can you quickly get three or four of them into the bag?" Faulkner asked him when he returned.

Gellan held onto the sides of the leather bag and gently scooped it toward the pile of stones, letting four fall into the water inside the bag before tightening the drawstrings, feeling very aware of all the eyes watching him.

"You can keep it for us, if you would, Mr. Parker," Faulkner said. "Roman and Meda, I'd like you to stay here with me, please. Governor Sedargren, I'm sure you'll want to get those men back to The Corner."

Governor Sedargren nodded. "Will we see you back at The Corner soon? Madame Guillèn will have plenty of questions, I'm sure."

"As soon as we can. I'm just going to dispose of all of these atrophii."

"Where?" asked one of the wynklers as he was pulled to his feet. A moment later his question was left hanging behind him as he was whisked forward, gliding along in the air with his comrades, surrounded by the group of witches and wizards, who were sitting comfortably in breezy armchairs.

"At the bottom of the ocean," said Faulkner under his breath as he turned back to the pile of stones. He motioned to Gellan. "I need everyone to move to the front of the cave before I do anything."

Gellan trudged forward. Cold and tiredness were starting to seep deep inside him now. He shoved his wand into the pocket on his trousers, then rubbed his arms, trying to get warm, one hand still clutching the leather bag.

"It won't be long, and we'll be back on Providence Island drinking a good cup of nilla nog," said the woman called Meda. She passed a hand across her face. "What a night it's been already."

"What d'you mean?" asked Gellan, but their conversation ceased as they watched Faulkner direct his wand toward the stones.

"Back!" Faulkner shouted at them as the stones began hurling out of the cave in a thick, steady stream. "Get back!"

They all scooted further away from the entrance. In the glow of the spell, they watched the stones hurl themselves far out into the ocean. An odd, shrill pinging sound made Gellan cover his ears as the stones dove beneath the surface of the water.

When the last one disappeared, Gellan let out a breath, unaware that he'd been holding it.

"Why did you dump them in the ocean like that?" he asked Faulkner.

"Most magic that humans perform is dampened or sometimes entirely undone with water," Roman answered for Faulkner. "So they won't affect us anymore, down there."

"Especially saltwater," Faulkner added breathlessly, and to Gellan's surprise, the wizard sank to his knees. His breath continued in great gasps, and Roman ran over to him, a concerned expression on his face. Faulkner waved him away. "It's the same reason that Heklah Island has been sunk underwater," he continued after several moments. "It prevents those that are imprisoned on there from being able to use magic to effect an escape."

"Oh," said Gellan. He had many more questions, but he kept them to himself at the moment, more worried about the way Faulkner was looking.

It was another few minutes before Faulkner was able to push himself to his feet. They all watched him carefully move further into the cave. He performed several spells, before finally nodding in grim satisfaction and joining the other three back at the entrance.

"It's all clear," he told them. "But I think this place will be affected forever."

A minute later, Gellan was being instantaneously pulled through an expanse of blackness before landing clumsily on the granite setts of The Corner square. If he'd had anything left in his stomach, he probably would've vomited. Roman pulled him to his feet.

"Yeah... it'll do that to you at first," he said, sympathetically. "You'll get used to it if you do it enough."

"I think you're probably in need of a good meal, Mr. Parker," said Faulkner. "So you might as well come and give us your story while you eat. I'm sure the pipkins can pull something together for you."

"I think we ALL could use something to eat," said Meda, folding her arms. "Some of us have been standing on guard duty for *hours*."

"I want to see the wynklers first," Gellan said.

"I'm not sure that's a—" Faulkner began.

Gellan folded his arms. "I'm pretty sure I've earned that right." He paused, then added, "I just want to see if Alex is okay."

Faulkner hesitated, and then nodded. "Yes; very well," he said. "I'll take you to them. They're in the Brislan Building. I'd like to check on the situation, anyway."

He led Gellan, Meda, and Roman into the thick, gray-stoned building. To Gellan's surprise, the men were in a comfortable-looking room filled with couches, chairs, and enough beds for them all, with only a single guard standing on duty. Not only that, but the broad doorway had been left entirely open except for a shimmering silvery-blue curtain, similar to the callicurtain in the doorway leading to his dorm. But before Gellan could walk through it, the guard threw out his arm.

"Don't walk through there—that's a mortibius."

"A what?"

"A mortibius, in the doorway," explained Faulkner from behind

Gellan. "It paralyzes anyone who touches it—at least for a while. It keeps the prisoners secure."

"Oh," said Gellan. "Can they hear me through it?"

"Yes, we can," said one young man who was sitting in an easy chair. "Who're you?"

"I'm—Gellan," Gellan replied.

"Oh."

Gellan looked around. "Could you tell me which one of you is Alex?"

The men looked at each other. "Who's Alex?" one of them asked.

Gellan counted quickly—there were nine, as he had expected. A cold feeling started creeping across his chest. He turned to the young man who had first spoken.

"What's *your* name?"

The young man stared at him blankly, then shrugged. "I'm not sure." He shook his head and scratched his chin.

Faulkner stepped forward. "What?!" He pointed at another man. "What about you?" The man shrugged. Then another, and another.

Faulkner exchanged a look with Roman.

"No, surely not," Roman said, but he balled up one of his hands.

Faulkner rounded on the guard. "Terrence, what happened? Who has had access to them since they got here?"

"No one!" Terrence said in alarm. "I was here when they were brought in, and no one else has come!"

Faulkner swore under his breath. "Let's get up to the council room," he said. "We need to find out—I just can't believe—who could've possibly—?" He turned on his heel and stalked out of the building.

Gellan swallowed hard, looking back at all the mild faces one last time before he turned to go. "Have they... is it possible to... have they had their memories *removed*?" he asked Roman as they hurried across the square to the Capitol Building.

"Yes, it *is* possible, and someone must have done it," said Roman. "I have no idea how they managed it. Or who in the world would have done something like this..."

Gellan felt sick. What kind of magic could remove a person's memories? He wasn't sure he wanted to know.

———————

Gellan soon found himself seated in the conference room he'd first come to when he'd arrived in Cremstoll. Once again, he tried to ignore the melee of voices around him and avoid catching anyone's attention.

He watched a tiny pipkin, the youngest he'd ever seen, shove silverware up onto the table next to him. She could barely reach it, and gave a squeaky little grunt with the effort. He was tempted to help her, but he knew by now that they didn't like to be helped. So he watched her until she'd completed her task and skipped off, clearly very pleased with herself.

A few minutes later, she brought him a tray with steaming soup and hot buttered toast, balanced on top of her head. He took it from her and thanked her, and she beamed as she scampered from the room.

"Where could they have gotten them?" Madame Guillèn was asking as Gellan bit into his toast. "They don't occur naturally anywhere in the islands. They must have been brought here intentionally."

Gellan listened to them talk, watching the pen poised perfectly above a ream of paper right next to Roman as it scratched away of its own accord, setting the discussion down in ink.

"Yes, we are all aware of that," said Governor Sedargren, talking over the end of her sentence. "The minerals in the stones should be analyzed to see if they have the same patterns of known deposits. That might help us identify—"

"I'll see to that first thing in the morning," said Faulkner. His voice was back to its measured tone and he was drinking a hot, sweet-smelling, dark brown vanilla drink that the pipkins had brought him. "Midas Wymes should be able to do an analysis for us."

"How do we know for sure if they were atrophii?" asked a wizard whose nameplate read 'Maxwell Morris.'

A rising chorus of voices began clamoring around the table. Gellan dipped his toast in his soup and took a bite, wondering if he could somehow sneak out of the room, down the stairs, and onto a sea pod headed for Gilsthorne. A rapping noise on the table made him cover his ears for a moment, his head already aching.

"That's *enough*," said Madame Guillèn. "Now, I'm going to sit here until dawn if I have to, to get all the details I need. You're each welcome to stay or go, but you are only allowed to speak if you have something to say that will contribute. Otherwise, I expect silence."

"We can ascertain whether they are atrophii for certain right now, if you'd like," Faulkner said.

"Go ahead," said Madame Guillèn.

"Mr. Parker, the leather bag, please," said the vice governer, holding out his hand.

Gellan handed the bag over to him, noticing that those around him leaned away when he pulled it out of his pocket. Faulkner waved his wand, and a hoblot plant appeared in front of him. Holding the leather bag carefully, he used a spoon next to his plate to fish out one of the stones inside. The moment the stone hit the air, the water shrank away from it and the top immediately appeared dry.

Faulkner moved the stone close to the hoblot plant, and there was a general gasp as the entire plant instantly began to wilt. Within a few seconds, the branch closest to the stone had turned black and fallen off.

Faulkner nodded gravely, then dropped the stone back into the leather bag, pulling the drawstrings tight. The hoblot plant perked back up, though the shriveled, blackened stem remained.

"I'd call that conclusive," Madame Guillèn said after a moment. There was a murmur of assent around the room. "But are these what is causing the darkness?" she asked the room at large, before looking back at Faulkner.

"No, I don't think so," said Faulkner.

"Then do you have any ideas what *is* causing it?"

Faulkner shook his head. "I have some ideas, but I really don't know anything for certain."

"Very well; I'll expect a report *soon*," Madame Guillèn said. "At least a preliminary one on what you're looking into." She turned. "Ben, what report do you have from questioning the wynklers? Was there anything they could tell you?"

Gellan started at the name and looked up, his eyes widening as he followed Madame Guillén's gaze to Governor Sedargren. Only Faulkner seemed to observe Gellan's reaction, and a strange flicker of emotion crossed his face.

"Nothing," Governor Sedargren said. "They either won't or can't tell me anything at all."

"That's what we found as well," Faulkner said. "Their memories have been removed."

"What?!" This time Madame Guillèn jumped up, knocking her chair backward; it slammed against the wall. "Who would've—who could've—Ben! You were responsible for them!"

Sedargren looked startled. "We brought them back and they were immediately questioned," he said. "By then their memories were gone. There's no way any of us could have... I assumed it had happened at the beach!"

"*I* didn't think so," Meda interjected. "We were all there, and they seemed normal then."

"Perhaps you just thought so because you weren't with the group of us that took them back to The Corner!" said Morris.

"Perhaps it happened on the way?"

"Impossible," said Sedargren. "I would've noticed—it must have been at the beach, before we arrived."

"The only one who can tell us that is Mr. Parker," said Faulkner. "And I believe we should ask *him* about his experience tonight." He flicked his wand and righted Madame Guillèn's seat. She sat and, after a moment, nodded her approval.

"I believe you have something to say at the moment, Mr. Parker," Faulkner continued. "What is it?"

Gellan looked briefly at Faulkner before looking back at Governor Sedargren, trying to determine if he could place anything in his memory—the clothes, the hair, the profile he'd seen in the shadow of the moon. But then... Sedargren had arrived with the others, at the moment when the wizard called Ben had disappeared. Hadn't he?

"It's just—they, the wynklers—they called him Ben. The wizard that came. The one they were working for."

Silence filled the room. It was Governor Sedargren who spoke first.

"I can assure you, Mr. Parker," he said, his expression composed and unperturbed, "if they were working for a man named Ben, it was not me. However, I'm curious"—he leaned forward—"how is it that you ended up so far out on Cromllech Island? Your friends were adamant you'd been with them on the top of the Elixir Emporium when the darkness descended. Surely you didn't just wander out there, blinded as we all were?"

"Yes, let's get the full details of your experience, if you would," Madame Guillèn said. "Start at the beginning."

"Well, I—" Gellan began, then stopped. It was the briefest of moments; he found himself momentarily sidetracked as he followed Sedargren's gaze—he was watching Faulkner, who was looking at Wilkes, who was staring intently at Gellan. Gellan felt his heart pound with a rush of irritation, not knowing what to think about any of them.

Madame Guillèn cleared her throat impatiently.

"I *was* on top of the *Elixir Emporium*," Gellan finally managed. "We'd done some errands and then we went up to the gardens. And that's when the darkness came. But for some reason, it didn't affect me."

"Indeed?" asked Faulkner, turning his gaze back to Gellan. "You weren't affected at all?" He looked interested, not disbelieving.

"Well, it all looked a little bit darker to me," said Gellan. "But I could see just fine. And then Drina told me that it must mean it was a magical darkness."

A man down on the other end of the table thumped it with his hand. "I knew it!" he said. "I was *sure* it wasn't the weather!"

"Yes, well, that is nice to know for certain, finally," said Madame Guillèn. "At least now I can stop sending the weather-science team out."

"Perhaps we should've taken Mr. Estik's assertions more seriously," said Faulkner.

"I agree," said Sedargren to Madame Guillèn, ignoring Faulkner. "But now that we know it's likely a magical darkness, and all those men are wynklers, that would point to a collaboration between them and a wizard somewhere on Providence Island. So the next question, really, is who is the *wizard* behind these attacks?"

"Yes, precisely," said Madame Guillèn. "If this continues, I believe we'll know who is behind it all fairly soon—they won't be able to conceal it for much longer, I would think."

"Unless the shield is cracking," said Sedargren.

"That's simply not possible," Madame Guillèn retorted. "And anyway, even if it is, we couldn't do anything about it anyway... unless... Faulkner? Have you—"

"No, not yet," Faulkner said, and he looked dejected. "I've spent all the spare time I can devote to it to tracing it. But so far, I've been unsuccessful."

Madame Guillèn pursed her lips, nodded, then continued. "Well, back to the main point. We now know that *someone* is causing this darkness, and because it is allowing threats to proceed unnoticed—" She glanced over at Gellan. "Or at least mostly unnoticed—"

"Except for Mr. Estik," Faulkner interjected. "His account of—"

"—I *would* consider that your responsibility, Ben."

"Yes, indeed," Sedargren said. "And we *are* working on it—we can't work miracles, you know."

"No, I wouldn't expect that," said Madame Guillèn curtly. She shifted in her seat and turned to Faulkner. "Abe, I'd like to just clarify something; you have not been present during any of these—these dark occurrences, have you?"

"No," said Faulkner in a calm, unconcerned voice. "They have, mysteriously, always occurred when I've been away."

"Very unusual," said Sedargren.

Faulkner stared at Sedargren for a moment, though he said nothing in reply.

"And what's that supposed to mean, Ben?" Madame Guillèn asked for him.

"Only that I find it—interesting," said Sedargren. "My job is to note and observe things. I'm merely noting and observing."

"Well, then, put that to good use and come up with something that can be done!" Madame Guillèn thundered, pounding the table. "It's no use pointing fingers... find the *real* culprit!"

There was a knock at the door.

"Come in!" Madame Guillèn snapped.

A young woman entered and handed Madame Guillèn an envelope. "President Humphrey has replied, ma'am," she said. She stood waiting as Madame Guillèn pulled out a long note and read it. Her face turned pale, then red.

"Will there be a reply, ma'am?" the young woman asked.

"Yes, tell him I'll respond to him myself as soon as I can," Madame Guillèn said, folding up the letter.

The young woman nodded and left.

No one said anything for several seconds.

"So where were we?" Madame Guillèn asked after a moment, looking at the paper next to Roman where the pen was still scribbling away. "Yes, Mr. Parker was on top of the Elixir Emporium and he could still see. All right, Mr. Parker, carry on."

Gellan sighed and picked up the story. "When I told my friends I could still see, it was Drina who told me to go to the edge of the building and watch for anything unusual. So I did. And that's when I saw that group of men moving down the street."

"They were just walking down the street?" asked Madame Guillèn.

"No, not exactly," said Gellan. "The big man had a bag of something, and he was handing them out one at a time to the others, and they were entering shops and stuff. I'm pretty sure they were those—those atrophii. They would go in the shops with one, and then they would come out without it."

"What?!" a woman named Blanche Darby who was sitting across the table shouted in alarm. "Is that what's been going on with the darkness? They could have been putting them anywhere! How are we going to—"

Faulkner threw out a hand to silence her. "We'll deal with that in a moment," he said. "And then?" he asked, turning back to Gellan.

"And then I went back and told Drina what they were doing, and I told my friends I was going to go follow them. I lost track of the men for a bit, but I knew the direction they were headed. Then I heard a lot of noise when I got close to *The Wabbit Hole*. And that's when I found them attacking Mr. Burman there."

"Yes, he told us about that," Madame Guillèn said. "Go on."

"Most of them ran off, but I managed to bind two of them there. Then when the darkness lifted, I asked the waiters to help Mr. Burman and to manage the two wynklers, and I ran after the others. And their footprints led to that place where I was," Gellan said.

"The cave?" Roman asked.

"Well, yes, but it looked like solid rock when I got there. But the footprints led right up to it, so I figured it was an obstructos. I didn't know if it was a cave or a tunnel, but I thought I might as well wait and see if anyone came out. At least for a while."

"Without anyone knowing where you were?" Faulkner asked.

Gellan shrugged. "No one ever really knew where I was in Ferndale," he said.

"So you stayed there and waited?" Faulkner asked. "Stayed *where,* exactly?"

"Oh, in a small hollow nearby, in the rock. I just did an obstructos in front of myself too, and I sat there and waited."

"For hours?" Governor Sedargren scoffed.

Gellan didn't answer.

"And then?" Faulkner prodded.

"Then all of a sudden, the obstructos in front of the cave was gone," said Gellan, "and the men were coming out. I knew there should only have been seven, but there were eight. So... I just sat and watched for a bit. Three of them were arguing. One called Alex said it was Ben's fault and that he had to get his dad out. That's probably one of the ones that I bound in *The Wabbit Hole*. And then the wizard— Ben—said that they had known that what he was doing was dangerous so it wasn't his fault. Alex threatened to tell other people what the... what Ben had done. The other wynklers tried to attack Ben and then he stunned all of them, or something. And he said that the best way to solve the problem was to... to make it so they didn't remember any of it."

There were gasps around the room.

"Are you quite sure?" Faulkner asked Gellan.

Gellan nodded. "I couldn't tell if that meant he would kill Alex or —or something else. But either way it just sounded so awful, and I... that's when I jumped up and I sent a spell at him—I think it was illuminare—it hit Ben on the shoulder. And then he sent a red spell at me and it hit the rocks behind me. And that's when you and the others started showing up and Ben disappeared."

There was silence in the room for several moments.

"Well, that's... that's quite a story," said Madame Guillèn at last, staring at him.

Gellan couldn't tell if she believed him or not.

"Could the Ben wizard have removed their memories at that point? Before he disappeared?" asked Morris.

"Unlikely," said Faulkner. "Not all of them at least. It would've been—"

Gellan turned back to his soup, disregarding the voices around him again. When he'd finished, he shoved the tray away, stood up and began to walk out of the room.

"Where do you think you're going, Mr. Parker?" Faulkner called out behind him.

"Madame Guillèn said we're each welcome to stay or go. I'm going."

And without another word, he shoved the door open and left. He was tired, angry, and, deep down, apprehensive, though he wasn't sure exactly why.

Before he managed to make it out of the building, several footsteps came pattering down the hallway behind him. He turned and saw five pipkins racing forward, each pulling on a fluffy coat, their little black boots spotlessly clean.

"Master Faulkner asked us to come with you, Master Gellan!" one of them said. "We'll take you up to Gilsthorne!"

"No need," Gellan said irritably. But it was very hard to be rude to a pipkin, and when he saw their faces fall, he added with a sigh, "Although I'd be very happy if you did."

They were as good as their word, not letting him out of their sight until they'd gotten him through the doors of Gilsthorne Building and deposited into the care of the pipkins there. Then, accompanied by Daisy and Alfie, he made it up to his dorm room.

As he stumbled toward his bed, he heard movement behind him, and then Roger's voice spoke through the darkness.

"Gellan? Is that you?"

"Yeah," said Gellan.

"Where the *heck* have you *been*?!" Roger said, a clattering sound indicating that he had fumbled his wand.

"Quiet, or you'll wake the other three," Gellan whispered.

"They're not here," said Roger as he lit his wand. "They must be with their families for the weekend. Where in the world did you go?" He took in Gellan's disheveled appearance and the sand clinging to the bottom of his pants.

"Long story," said Gellan. "I'm too tired to—"

"Cressida's dad said you were the one who stopped him from being taken by the wynklers," interrupted Roger.

"Yeah, I did, but—"

"And Governor Sedargren said that was ridiculous, and Madame Guillèn acted like he was lying or something—"

"Wait, what? Like *who* was lying?"

"Cressida's dad," said Roger.

"Oh. Well, he wasn't. Listen, I'll tell you all about it tomorrow morning. I'm sure the girls—wait, are they okay?"

"Yeah, we're all fine. We saw the waiters from *The Wabbit Hole* headed to the infirmary with Mr. Burman. Cressida almost fell down the stairs, she was crying so much. When we got to the infirmary, he told us everything that had happened while they were fixing him up. Did you see who was responsible for the darkness?"

"No." Gellan shook his head. "I'm still not sure about that. But I do have a lot to tell you—only not tonight. I'm tired. And the girls will just ask me all the same questions, so let's wait until we're all together tomorrow morning."

Gellan went off for a quick shower. He had a funny feeling in his stomach that he hadn't quite been able to identify—there had been too much going on. But mulling it all over in the shower, he knew what it was. As he pulled the covers up to his chin in the dormitory that night, he was finally able to put that feeling into words.

Cremstoll had somehow changed for him, and he was quite sure it would never feel the same again. Before, it had been a place full of witches and wizards who surely could fix any problem or win any battle—people who were extraordinary. And he had felt special to be one of them.

But he had seen today that, just like any group of people, they could be vulnerable too.

CHAPTER SIXTEEN

THE OLYMPIC STEAMER

G ellan woke suddenly the next morning and realized that he'd been dreaming of wandering in circles, repeating unformed questions to himself all night. He lay there for a moment, thinking, and the questions slowly solidified into words.

Why hadn't he been blinded by the magical darkness? Was he less of a wizard than he had thought? He had never even considered that such magic as he'd seen last night was possible—was he sure he wanted to continue to train as a wizard? What was the "shield" Madame Guillén had mentioned?

Knowing he wouldn't be able to go back to sleep even though it wasn't quite five o'clock, he got up and dressed as quietly as he could. When he opened his trunk to put away his pajamas, he saw the green candle and was suddenly plunged into a small moral dilemma. He knew his uncle would want to know what had happened yesterday. But if he was completely honest with Uncle Ivan, he was pretty sure he would soon find himself back in Ferndale, never again to return to Gilsthorne.

He picked up the candle and took out a piece of paper, then sat back and ruminated for a few minutes. Decision made, he wrote out a short note and sent it to Uncle Ivan before throwing the candle back and quietly closing his trunk. He shoved it under his bed and left his dorm room before he could change his mind.

After wandering for a very long time, lost in his thoughts, he made his way to the Great Hall. Though it was still early, Drina and Cressida were there with Roger, eager for news of what had happened the night before. What Gellan *hadn't* expected was that both girls would be scrunched into his chair, so he made his way around to the other side to sit in Corben's empty chair.

After a great deal of talking and the exchange of information from both sides, Gellan learned that after Mr. Burman had been fixed up by the medi-wizards, they'd made their way up to The Corner to see what had happened to the two wynklers and tell their stories to the three governors. Though Madame Guillèn and Sedargren had clearly doubted them, Faulkner hadn't.

"Since we weren't sure where you'd gone, Faulkner wanted a whole bunch of the Vanquors to keep watch across Providence and Cromllech Islands," said Roger. "Sedargren wasn't happy about it— he's over all of them, you know, and he thought it was a waste of time. But in the end, he agreed. So when you sent that flare at the Ben wizard, I bet Faulkner and some of the others saw it and that's when they appeared there."

"Do you think that the wizard named Ben was Governor Sedargren?" Gellan asked.

Roger looked surprised, then thoughtful. "Did you get a good look at him?"

Gellan shook his head. "No. It was really dark last night and he was masked. Then when Faulkner and the others showed up, he disappeared."

The other three looked at each other, then all shook their heads at the same time.

"No, I just don't think so," said Drina.

"He's not the kind you could ever be friends with," said Roger, "but I don't think he'd do anything to harm Cremstoll. He's in charge of *protecting* Cremstoll. And even though I personally don't like him, he *is* good at his job."

"I think it must be a different Ben," Drina said.

"Or maybe that's just what that wizard *told* the wynklers his name was," interjected Roger. "What if it was someone named—I don't know—James or Omar or something."

"True," said Drina. "We have no way of knowing."

"Maybe whoever it was told them that his name was Ben so that *if* anyone caught them like this, then people would *think* it was Governor Sedargren," Cressida suggested.

"That's possible too," said Drina.

They were all quiet for a minute, and then Cressida looked around at them all with her bright eyes. "Well, there's no sense in wasting the day," she said. "It's gorgeous outside. What do we want to do?"

Roger raised his eyebrows and mouthed *"We?"* at Gellan. Gellan shrugged, and Drina, missing the interaction, seemed to think that was an opening for suggestions.

In the end, though, they all had a wonderful day in the gardens by the towers, playing broomstick games. Even Roger had to admit that he'd enjoyed himself.

"They're not super-girly girls, like my sisters," he said to Gellan as they made their way down to dinner at the end of the day. "I mean, in a way it might be nice to have friends that are girls. Maybe they can give us advice, you know, when we get older. And did you see Drina's stunt dive?" He whistled. "I've got to see if she can teach *me* to do that!"

Two weeks later, Gellan was halfway down the southeast switchbacks when he looked at his watch and realized (as he often did) that he only had twenty minutes before class started.

He raced to the Great Hall and, without bothering to check if his spot was open first, headed to the other side of the table to Corben's place. Sure enough, Drina and Cressida greeted him from his spot the moment he sat down. He didn't mind, really. He couldn't help thinking that one good thing had come from the dark day: Drina had found a fast friend. And anyway, the end of term was only a few days away now—a realization that had hit them all with a sudden jolt as they faced their last weekend to study before final exams began.

Having to exercise a great deal of self-control, Gellan stuck himself to a chair for the whole of Saturday, trying to make sure he managed to pass his classes. The common room had become quieter and quieter at the end of each day, as everyone began cramming more of the year's material into their heads. Even those who pretended they weren't even a little bit worried were found stuck on poufs shoved into corners, or holding notebooks up to one of the assistant ghost portraits as they pointed to a problem.

Gellan was assured by Drina that, as a first-year student, he would be quite able to perform whatever spells or tasks he was asked to do.

"They really don't give first-year students much credit," she said. "As long as sparks come out of the end of your wand and you don't set anything on fire, they'll give you at least a passing grade. And if they ask you to do wandwork you've never done before, I expect since you came late in the year, they'll at least give you the spell and just see how well you can do it, whereas everyone else will have to have it memorized."

This reassured Gellan somewhat, but it was the theories and science he was worried about. Knowing the pathways of spell effects, instances of rebounds or interferences, possible mishaps and their causes, and other such trivia for each spell seemed the more difficult task. The only comfort he had was that as he completed his exams one or two per day, he would have more and more free periods to study for the exams later in the week... or to spend poking about before he left Gilsthorne (possibly for good).

Monday morning came all too quickly. Gellan's history exam didn't go too badly—he'd been able to fit the dates concerning the history of American magical settlements fairly neatly in his head alongside what he already knew about Columbus and Sir Francis Drake and the Pilgrims. English and science were about the same.

But he did struggle with the Spells and Charms written exam. Professor Newbury had assured him he would take Gellan's late start into consideration, but Gellan had wanted to measure up well despite that, and he left the classroom feeling disappointed that he'd missed so many months of school.

Tuesday brought the practical exam for Spells and Charms, as well as the written exams for his math, Latin and Welsh, Intro to Magic, and Magical and Non-Magical Plants classes.

By Thursday he had only one left—the practical exam for his Magical Mixtures class. For this, they had to brew a randomly chosen potion from start to finish in an extra-long class period. As he approached the classroom, he momentarily wished he had acquired some Brilliance Brew, even though they'd been warned that it was banned during exam-taking. Perhaps a Breathe-Easy Elixir would've been more helpful.

Master Eckhart was standing at the door. He handed a sealed envelope to each student as they approached.

"Open this," Master Eckhart repeated to them each in turn, "and follow the instructions carefully for whichever potion you are given to do. You may be required to go outside or to the greenhouse to harvest one or two of your needed ingredients. Good luck."

Gellan felt a nervous sweat break out on his forehead as he took the envelope Master Eckhart held out to him. He chose a seat next to Roger and Cressida, tore open the top of the envelope, pulled out the papers, and read:

Sweet Dreams Draught

The goal of this potion is to ensure that a person's mind seeks only good and lovely things to dwell on while they're asleep. If properly brewed, this potion resembles a cup of tea in texture, with a rich lavender color.

One key element with this potion is that it must be very gently heated and cooled—do not allow any sudden increases or drops in temperature. This means that you must finish your potion with enough time before the end of class to allow it to cool before adding the single grain of finishing salt, otherwise it will cool too rapidly and the final product will most likely be ruined.

Gellan scanned the ingredient list. He recognized most of them, including valerian and the California poppy, but a few of them were still unfamiliar to him. He pulled out his textbook to quickly look those ones up, very aware of the ticking clock and the quiet bustle of students around him who were already chopping ingredients and brewing their own mixtures.

Half an hour later, after collecting all the ingredients, he was finally able to start making the potion. He set his cauldron on a stand over a firestone rather than directly on the firestone itself, to keep it from heating too quickly, and set to work.

Roger and Cressida were both much further along in their work, though he noticed that Cressida was double- and triple-checking something as though she wasn't sure what to do next. A few moments later, Roger had to grab a metal ladle and use it to shove the firestone out from underneath his cauldron as the contents bubbled over.

Two hours later, it was all over. Whether they liked it or not, they were done with their exams, though this fact was apparently taking some time to set in, because they all trudged up the stairs, discussing their success (or lack thereof).

"I think it said that the Hiccup Halting Potion is *supposed* to be that thick," said Roger. "And just because some of it boiled over doesn't mean it was all totally ruined. I think the sample I turned in was quite good, actually."

"Mine was the right texture," said Cressida, "but the color was off. The potion was supposed to be red, but it was barely pink."

Gellan had waited until the last possible second before Master

Eckhart called "Time" before he dropped the grain of finishing salt into his mixture... but he wasn't sure it had had time to cool enough first. As they climbed back up to the towers, he shrugged away the test re-run that was playing itself over and over in his mind.

At about that same moment, it finally began to dawn on all three of them that they had the rest of the day *and* the whole of Friday ahead of them, with no responsibilities and worries. The last flight of stairs was filled with happy chatter and lots of ideas of how to fill their time together.

Gellan was handing a book over to Mr. Quip the next morning when he saw Faulkner sitting cross-legged on the floor in a far corner of the library. Faulkner had piles of books around him and he seemed oblivious to everything, except for the book he was holding close to his nose. Gellan's curiosity got the better of him, and he edged down a row of shelves, trying to get close enough to see the titles on the spines of some of the books tossed haphazardly on the floor.

Faulkner shut the book he was holding with a sudden snap and flung it onto the floor in front of him. He caught sight of Gellan through one of the gaps in the shelves.

"Oh, hello, Mr. Parker," he said. He looked around at the books in piles around him, and his gaze landed on the book he'd just tossed aside. "Goodness, I'm not setting a very good example in how we treat books, am I?" He pulled off his glasses, folded them, and stuck them into the pocket of his vest. He took out his wand, and with a great sweep of his arm, the books all rose up and hurtled themselves in all directions to find their original spots—one of them just missing Mr. Quip as he walked across an aisle. Mr. Quip grimaced at Faulkner, who didn't seem to notice as he snagged one book in mid-air and pulled it back.

"Doing research for something, sir?" Gellan asked.

"No... yes... sort of," Faulkner replied, still distracted.

"Sort of?"

"I mean, it's... well, to be honest, I don't know *what* I'm researching, which is my main problem. I've been trying to find someone—I don't know who it is, I'm not sure of anything about them, and I can't be certain such a person even exists."

"Then how do you know where to start?" Gellan asked.

"Well, that's just it," said Faulkner. "I don't. But... I was just trying to see if I could find anything more to help me narrow down my search... or at least to rule out some of my theories. But I've found nothing. Nothing at all!" He sighed. "I was just looking at this old yearbook, from when I used to be a teacher here."

"I didn't know you used to teach at Gilsthorne, sir," said Gellan.

"Yes, I was the Magical Mixtures teacher before Master Eckhart," said Faulkner, turning pages in the book. "I've always enjoyed concocting things. I used to make very good mud pies as a kid. Of course, Master Eckhart is a vastly superior teacher to myself. But... I think I did well enough." He grew silent, staring at a picture. "It's just... this girl..."

"Who?"

"I've tracked down a lot of my guesses," Faulkner said with a sigh, "but they've all led to unsatisfactory conclusions. Except one, which has led to nowhere at all. It's this girl—she seems to have just... disappeared. She was actually a student of mine, a long time ago."

"Oh, well, then I don't think I'd be of any help," Gellan said.

"Yes, right," Faulkner said, distracted once more as he put his glasses back on, looking closely at the text in the book.

"Well, good luck, sir," Gellan said, taking a step away. "My mom always said that the moment you've started something, you're nearly finished with it, so I'm sure it won't be too long until you find—"

He stopped. Faulkner had ripped off his glasses and was staring straight at him.

"What?" Gellan asked. "I'm sorry, did I—?"

"No, no, it's just that... that's exactly what she always used to say—the girl I've been searching for."

"Who? Said what?"

"Jane Young. She used to say that very thing—that once you

started something, you were nearly finished. She was very optimistic —at least most of the time."

Gellan's heart started beating very fast. He felt his mouth go dry, and for the first time in his life, he was entirely speechless.

"Jane Young?" he repeated. He cleared his throat. "Is she in there? Is there a picture?"

Faulkner held the book out and pointed. Gellan took it from him, staring at the picture. He was just able to trace the worn features from his memory of his mother on the young face of the girl. She was laughing, looking slightly off to one side, as though someone had made a joke just as the picture was taken. Gellan reached up and touched the picture.

"Do you know her, Mr. Parker?" Faulkner asked.

"She was... is... I think that's my mom," Gellan said, and he choked a little. He only had one picture of his mother, which his uncle had found amongst her possessions after she had died. To see her here, suddenly, in a way he'd never seen her—or imagined her— before, was difficult to take in.

"Your *mother*?!" Faulkner said. "Mr. Parker, are you quite sure? I found some newspaper articles detailing that she had married a Gilding, not a Parker. I knew the Gilding boy a little bit, as a matter of fact, though he only came here for one year."

"I don't know her history," Gellan said, "but I'm sure that's my mother. I had no idea she was a... a witch."

"If she was your mother, she wasn't just any witch," Faulkner said. "She was an incredibly talented one. But how... how did she become a Parker, instead of a Gilding? Why are *you* a Parker, instead of a Gilding?"

"I have no idea," Gellan said, and he felt his stomach fall away a bit. He realized he knew so little about his mother. His memories of her laughing at his antics or grimacing at his muddy footprints across her clean floors—none of that told him who she was, what she had done; nothing of her past.

"There might be another picture of her," Faulkner said, reaching over and flipping some pages as Gellan continued to hold the book. "I think she was on the sailing team that year."

Sailing? His mother had liked to sail?

And then there she was, perched on the edge of a dock in front of a fleet of small sailboats with about a dozen other students. This time she had one eyebrow cocked, a side smile flickering across her face. Gellan recognized that look—it was what he saw every time he looked in the mirror when he had a new place in mind that he wanted to explore.

"Who was the man that she married?" Gellan asked. "The Gilding man?"

"Well, he... his name was Henry. Henry Gilding. He was a red-headed boy, same as his twin brother. He was the older one. Ivan was the younger one."

"Ivan?!" exclaimed Gellan.

"Do you know an Ivan Gilding?"

"My uncle's name is Ivan," Gellan said. "The uncle that I live with, now that—"

"Your uncle is Ivan Gilding?"

"He's Ivan Parker to me," Gellan said.

"Well, there's one way to check if we're talking about the same person," Faulkner said, stepping over to the shelves and scanning them for another yearbook. "Here—this was the year they were here, Henry and Ivan. They only came that one year."

He flipped through the book until he found their pictures. The two boys were obviously not identical twins, though they both had the same thick, curly red hair that Gellan had. One boy had a handsome, laughing face, his hair shoved back from his forehead. The other, though his mouth naturally downturned, had kind, twinkling eyes.

"Well?" asked Faulkner.

"Yes, that's Uncle Ivan," Gellan said. "So why is he a Parker now?"

"I don't know," said Faulkner. He stared at the pictures for several minutes, then replaced the book on the shelf. "Why don't you ask him when you go home for the summer? I'd be very curious to know that myself."

He suddenly set off down the aisle, and Gellan trailed after him, wondering where he was going. Faulkner abruptly turned to say something, and noticed that Gellan was still holding the other book. "Oh, let's put that one back, shall we?"

He flicked his wand. The book pulled itself out of Gellan's hand and rushed away, back down the shelves. Gellan felt a pang as he watched it go.

"Well," said Faulkner as they reached the large double doors at the entrance of the library, "I have a lot more questions I'd like to ask you, Mr. Parker, but I think I've done enough damage for today. And though you might like to ask *me* questions, I don't think I'm the best one to tell you anything more at the moment. Anyway, you'll see your uncle tomorrow, and I suddenly have a great many things to do. So, I'll say good-bye here."

Gellan nodded and watched Faulkner walk away, then made a beeline back to the yearbooks. It was hours later, with only ten minutes left until the end of lunchtime, when he finally tore himself away for long enough to get some food.

The Great Hall was surprisingly full for this time of day, and he found the other three waiting for him.

"Where on *earth* have you been?" asked Roger. "We haven't seen you all day!"

"Just... busy, as usual," said Gellan.

Drina looked at him, one eyebrow raised. Cressida looked at Drina, then at Gellan, her eyes filled with curiosity, but she didn't say anything.

"Well, I'm glad you're finally here," said Roger, missing the nonverbal exchange, "because we wanted to open our letters together."

"What letters?" asked Gellan.

"The letters about our scouting applications," said Cressida, pointing to the envelope on the table next to his plate. "They arrived this morning."

Gellan reached over and picked up the letter. He saw that his name was handwritten on the front of the envelope. He would've preferred to open it alone, but they were all beaming and looking expectantly at him, so he worked his open as Cressida and Roger tore into theirs.

Cressida was the first to get there. "Accepted!" she shouted, and she hugged Drina excitedly.

Roger looked up from his paper. "Me too!" he said, and his face broke into a smile. "My dad'll be pleased."

"What about you, Gellan?" Drina asked.

Gellan was reading to himself—he hadn't wanted to jump ahead.

"Come on," Roger said, giving him a slight kick under the table. "What does it say?"

Gellan ignored him, reading carefully on, until he came to: "... *Pleased to inform you that you have been accepted to begin training as an underage scout for Cremstoll.*"

He looked up with a grin on his face. "Unbelievable," he said. "I've actually been accepted."

As the others whooped and hollered around him, part of him felt a huge sense of relief, hoping that this made it certain he would be allowed to return to Gilsthorne.

The final feast was an extremely entertaining occasion, with everyone in a joyous mood and performances provided by the school orchestra, choirs, and other groups. Gellan had never fully appreciated how much *fun* magic could be. Couples from the ballroom dance team conjured circles of glass floors that slid along with their movements, raising them up and down as they whirled around. The percussion section of the orchestra let off colorful bubbles and sparks, smoke and ribbons with almost every sound they made, adding visual effect to their songs.

Gellan wondered if the pipkins might've added a bit of Merry-Makers Mixture to each of their drinks, such was the mood that night. It was all very grand and wonderful, and everyone went to bed feeling happy and contented.

By seven-thirty the next morning, the courtyard and the entrance hall were filled with hundreds of students, teachers, trunks and other luggage, a few personal broomsticks, a smattering of pets, and dozens of pipkins—some of them handing out lunch bags to all the students and some helping students load their luggage onto carts. Just before eight o'clock, someone shouted out the time, and to Gellan's surprise, everyone stopped what they were doing and ran to the west side of the courtyard.

"C'mon, mate!" Roger shouted. "Don't you want to see it?"

"See what?" Gellan asked as he jogged over. But he didn't have to wait long.

A minute later, the ground shook slightly, and Gellan grabbed onto one of the pillars at the edge of the courtyard. Sudddenly, he saw water rushing through the canyon he had seen when he'd flown over Cremstoll on his arrival. He realized the canyon was widening and a fjord was forming. The land on the other side of the canyon was lifting up and pushing back, and he could see people watching from the edge of Gilsthorne Village.

The water gushed through for several minutes, and when it finally began to slow, they heard a sound like a foghorn, reverberating from deep within the mountains. A minute later, the horn sounded again just as a steamship appeared, sailing straight toward Gilsthorne Hill.

It had three levels of decks, a giant red paddlewheel, and two gold and black smokestacks. Across the front of the pilot house at the top of the ship was the name *Olympic Steamer*. They watched as it docked, and then there was a rush as students grabbed packs and trunks, lunch sacks and cloaks, and headed down the cobble path to the steamship. They took the right fork this time, which led them through the small tunnel under the gushing spring and down to the wide dock, where the ramp of the *Olympic Steamer* had been secured.

Mr. Burman was there to see them all off (which, according to Cressida, was his way of trying to say thank you to Gellan). Even though the other three lived in Cremstoll, they would be coming along for the voyage.

"It's tradition," Drina had told him, "for the students who live in Cremstoll to take the ship to Seattle, and then we just stay on board for the voyage back. Since the majority of us live in Cremstoll, it'd be a pretty lonely trip if we didn't come along."

Mr. Burman insisted on taking some pictures before they boarded the ship. He waved them together on the far side of the dock, the steamship in the background. "All right, gang, together now," he called to them, trying to get their attention for a picture. "Roger— Roger! Turn around. All right, squeeze together—One... two..." He took several quick pictures before they had a chance to move. "... Three!" He put the camera down and grinned.

They were nearly the last to board, and the four of them found an empty compartment on the top deck. They stowed Gellan's trunk under the bench, then stepped out onto the deck to wave good-bye.

The ramp was drawn up and as the ship slowly began to back away and turn its course, Mr. Burman waved them off. "Have a good trip! We'll see you soon!"

"It feels a bit weird to be going home," said Gellan, settling into a seat in the cabin. "I'm surprised at how long *and* how short it's felt since I came."

"You were here for most of the year, though," said Roger.

"No I wasn't," said Gellan. "I came in March. That's only a little over three months ago."

"Really?" asked Roger. "It feels like you've been here for ages."

"Is he that difficult to get along with as a dormmate?" asked Cressida, her big eyes filled with amusement.

"No, I didn't mean *that*," said Roger, his cheeks going red. "I just mean... no, really, he's a good dormmate..." Roger's cheeks flushed darker, and the girls laughed.

"Cremstoll always feels really quiet during the summer," Cressida said a few minutes later, with a sigh. "I'm glad we'll all be starting scout training soon, or I think this summer would be so dead boring after the school year we've just had."

Gellan looked out of the window as they entered the canyon, the sheer cliff walls casting dark shade over the entire ship. They slowly made their way through the islands of Cremstoll and toward the Juan de Fuca Strait, and then into the Puget Sound. The view from their cabin gave them plenty to see of the scenery, from islands edged with thick conifer forest to the low-lying mountains topped with snow behind them.

After three hours, with the city of Seattle not far off, Gellan could see they were headed straight for a canyon as deeply cut as the one they'd left behind, though the cliff walls were not quite as high. It extended about a mile inland, heading straight toward the heart of the city.

Once they were properly docked, Roger helped Gellan haul his luggage down, and they loaded it onto a cart. Gellan looked around as they crossed the ramp to the docks, but he didn't see Uncle Ivan yet. Drina tugged on Gellan's arm, and when he turned she was holding out two gray candles.

"Do you mind?" she asked. "I was hoping to have a way for us to keep in touch with you."

"No," said Gellan, "that'd probably be good."

They positioned their hands as Gellan had done before with Uncle Ivan, and Cressida performed the spell for them. The candle in Gellan's right hand once again stayed gray, but the one in his left hand turned a deep blue. Drina pocketed the gray one, and Gellan shoved the blue one into his back pocket.

Gellan heard someone call his name, and he turned around in time to see Uncle Ivan coming toward him from a parking area. Without a word, his uncle raised his hand in a stiff greeting. Gellan began moving off toward him, but he was stopped by another tug on his sleeve.

It was Drina. "Keep that—that *thing* safe," she said to him quietly so the others couldn't hear. "And bring it back with you to Gilsthorne. I think it's safer there than in Ferndale."

He nodded. "And I'll get a hidden pocket of my own, soon," he said. "Then I can give this one back to you."

She shook her head. "Don't worry about it. You can keep it. I'll get another one. Anyway, I'll see you in a month."

She stepped back and waved good-bye to him with the others as he followed Uncle Ivan to the car. Gellan loaded his luggage into the trunk of Uncle Ivan's car and watched Drina, Cressida, and Roger cross the ramp back onto the ship. Then he climbed into the car, where he found Uncle Ivan trying to orient himself on a small map that was clearly from Cremstoll.

"GPS doesn't work here—I've already tried." Uncle Ivan sighed. "I hate all that fast traffic and I don't want to risk going the wrong way. Durn thing—here, see if you can figure it out," he said, thrusting the map toward Gellan.

Gellan watched some of the other cars pull away, watching to see where they exited, shaking his head when they appeared to drive straight into the rocky cliff face. After a minute, he found the exit point they wanted and directed Uncle Ivan toward it, then he kept his mouth shut while his uncle navigated the spaghetti bowl of highways.

An hour later, Uncle Ivan was much more relaxed with the city behind them, and fields or forest on either side of the highway.

"Are you hungry?" he asked after a while, jabbing his thumb toward the back seat. "I brought us lunch. We won't get back home until late tonight."

Gellan wrangled the heavy lunchbox onto his lap. He looked through it and found a couple of egg-salad sandwiches, some apples, and a couple of pastries from Uncle Ivan's shop. He unwrapped one of the sandwiches and handed it to Uncle Ivan, who took it gladly, munching on it as he drove.

"I've already eaten," Gellan said. "They gave us lunches to take on the boat."

"Who's they?"

"The pipkins. They run the kitchens."

"What's a pipkin?"

"Don't you remember what a pipkin is?" Gellan asked slyly, looking at his uncle.

Uncle Ivan stopped in mid-air as he was about to take another bite. He glanced at Gellan. "And what's that supposed to mean?"

"I'm sure you saw plenty of them, when you were at Gilsthorne."

Uncle Ivan finished taking the bite, then chewed for a long time. After he finally swallowed, he said, "Well, yes, I guess so. Now that you mention it."

It was quiet for several minutes.

"So you're Ivan Gilding."

"Was."

"And my dad was Henry Gilding?"

"Is."

"So... he's definitely still alive?"

"Yeah."

"And... my mom?"

"No, I'm sorry, son," Uncle Ivan said, setting the sandwich down. "She really is gone."

"You're sure?"

"I'm sure."

It was silent for a very long time.

"So she was a witch," Gellan finally said.

Uncle Ivan nodded.

"And you're a wizard."

"Guess so."

"And my dad?"

Uncle Ivan shook his head. "Somewhere in between. The magic runs in our blood, but it's pretty weak, most of the time. I was lucky enough to pass the evaluation. Your father only managed to pass because I was standing close to him, making it look like he could do things."

"Oh."

"You passed your evaluation, then?"

"Yeah."

Another long silence.

"Erm, if you don't mind," said Uncle Ivan, "now that you know about me bein' part of it all, maybe we'll take a shortcut home."

"Shortcut?" Gellan asked.

"Yeah. Should put us home in the next hour or so. Change the GPS to Mount Rainier, would you? There's a jump spot there. I'll know where I'm going once we get closer."

"You could've mentioned some of these things sooner," Gellan said as he typed in the new directions. "I wish you'd told me." He couldn't keep the resentment out of his voice.

"I know. I think I probably should've. It's not for wanting to keep secrets or anything like that. Well, not from you, anyway. I just didn't know at what point, exactly, would be the right time."

"Who do we we have to keep it secret from?"

"The whole village of Ferndale," said Uncle Ivan. "Including your aunt."

"She doesn't know about any of this?"

"No."

"Why?"

"It's a long story..."

"What about my dad?" asked Gellan. "Why hasn't he... is there a reason you never...?" He felt so confused he wasn't even sure how to start asking questions. And he couldn't deny that something inside him was giving him a sharp pang.

Uncle Ivan sighed deeply. "Do you mind if we wait a bit on that?" he asked. "I need to figure out how to talk about some of it. Partially because I'm not even sure about some things."

"Like what?" asked Gellan.

"Like why things changed," said Uncle Ivan. "Or even if they changed."

"Changed from what?"

"Your dad," said Uncle Ivan. "He was... I mean, we were..." He sighed again and rubbed his forehead. "Let me figure things out in my head. Then I'll tell you what I can."

It was silent for several minutes, and then Uncle Ivan glanced at his unfinished sandwich. "Did you get enough to eat while you were there?" he asked.

"Oh yeah, the food is good," said Gellan.

"What's it like?"

"The food?"

"No, the school. And the area. I haven't been there in years." Uncle Ivan picked up his sandwich and munched through it while Gellan told him more about his time in Cremstoll. He tried to feel the same openness he'd always had with Uncle Ivan, but it was restrained by his resentment at realizing just how little Uncle Ivan had told him of all that he must know.

"Sounds kind of like what you do here," said Uncle Ivan, when Gellan paused. "Going wherever you like, no one knowing where you are. Just as long as you keep an eye on yourself, I guess that's what matters."

"Will I be able to go back there for school in the fall?" Gellan asked.

Uncle Ivan didn't say anything for a few minutes. "If that's what you'd like to do, I won't stop you," he said at last.

"And—I've been accepted to do training as a scout," Gellan added.

"As a what?"

"A scout. For Cremstoll."

"Why?"

"Because scouts get to do cool things, and we get more training and—and *education*," he added, stressing the last word.

"I don't want you doing anything that'll compromise your schoolwork."

"Underage scouts don't usually do much, especially not during the school year, so it doesn't usually take away from schoolwork."

"Usually? Hmmph. What does it require?"

"Well, I'd have to go back to Cremstoll a bit earlier to start training."

"What kind of training?"

Gellan hesitated. "I'm not entirely sure. I know they do some survival skills stuff—they have to learn a lot more spells and..."

"What do they use the scouts for?"

"Mostly the underage scouts just gather plants and mushrooms for the Magical Mixtures classes, or check on wild animals that live on the other islands. That sort of thing."

"What kinds of wild animals?"

"Like the macrodons."

"Hmph. I bet they send you to work with the dragons then too. That'd be just like those—" He stopped short and glanced over at Gellan, who was watching him with his mouth open.

"Dragons?! There are dragons too?! Nobody mentioned... Which island—?"

"Never you mind. Maybe there are dragons and maybe there aren't. I was just saying that if there were..." Uncle Ivan cleared his throat. "Erm, when do you have to go back, then?"

"The boat leaves in the middle of July."

"That's barely a month away."

Another long pause.

"You just... make sure you do all your laundry before you go. I won't have you looking or smelling like a vagabond. And this time, you pack your own stuff. I don't like worrying that I've forgotten something."

Gellan grinned, leaned back in the seat, and enjoyed the picturesque scenery as they neared Mount Rainier. He stuck his arms behind his head and thought with happy anticipation of seeing Ferndale again, content to know that he would most definitely be going back to Gilsthorne!

Thank You!

To each reader who picked up this book and read it all the way through, thank you! That is the biggest compliment an author can receive.

If you loved it, there's one more thing that you can do that would mean a LOT to me. **Please take a moment to go rate and review this book** on whichever retailer you originally purchased it from. **Even a short review helps a lot** (but the wordy ones are super fun for me to read)!

If you don't know where else to leave a review, you could always just go to Goodreads or Book Bub.

If you'd like to stay up to date on the Gellan Parker series and be the first to get all the news about release dates and special events, you can sign up for the newsletter through my publisher here:
(https://www.ploppletop.com/newsletter/).

All my best,

A. L. Wicks

A. L. WICKS grew up in eastern Idaho in the United States, surrounded by potato farms, and working potato harvest as a teenager. She earned a degree in nutrition at BYU, and became a wife and mother... and then a homeschooling mom.

Throughout her life, she has been a voracious reader and a prolific writer. Besides maintaining a daily journal for years, she wrote lots of short stories in her younger years and did garden writing in her twenties, before turning to writing fantasy and real-to-life stories in the children's and YA categories in her thirties.

[f] facebook.com/thealwicks

[o] instagram.com/a.l.wicks

[BB] bookbub.com/authors/alwicks

[twitter] twitter.com/thealwicks

[g] goodreads.com/alwicks

[a] amazon.com/author/alwicks

Also by A. L. Wicks

THANKSGIVING ON A SUGARBUSH (November 2020) *8-11 yrs.*
Two Thanksgivings, a dog named Maple, and a disagreement that could affect three generations of the Swenson family. Sadie and Albert need to find a way to make their second Thanksgiving as happy as their first was.

SILAS AND THE PAPER AIRPLANE (Spring 2022) *8-11 years*
School is out, and Silas Milligan can't figure out what in the world he'll do for a whole, looooong summer. Until his mother helps him make a paper airplane.

WYN AND THE WELSH MOUNTAIN SHEEP (December 2020) *8-11 years*
Christmas isn't always a happy season . . . unless we take the time to make it special.

KIDS IN THE GARDEN (Summer 2021) *6-9 years*
What happens when kids venture out into the garden? See what Lorna and David discover with their friends.

GELLAN PARKER SERIES, BOOK 2 *(2022)* 10-17 YEARS
Planned for release in the first half of 2022. If you would like to sign up to the newsletter for updates on the series, go to:
https://www.ploppletop.com/newsletter/

CPSIA information can be obtained
at www.ICGtesting.com
Printed in the USA
LVHW111629111021
700155LV00007B/192/J